Advance Praise for *Deity*

"My TOP BOOK OF 2012. This is the best Covenant book so far."
— The Book Goddess

"5 stars: a must read. I've never had a book I felt more like giving more than 5 stars to than this book!... The ending will absolutely shake you to your core!"
— Valerie, Stuck in Books

"*Deity* will leave you breathless, aching for a clue about what is next for Alex, for Aiden, for Seth—and for the fragile world that rests upon their shoulders."
— YA Sisterhood

"A great blend of action, drama, and romance... *Deity* was just simply amazing from beginning to end."
— The Reading Geek

"Deity ramps up the action, suspense, and romance without ever losing a step, and it makes me crave the sequel like I need it to breathe."
—Sydnee Thompson, Dreams in Tandem

"5 out of 5 stars: This book was all sorts of amazing and I am still in shock... *Deity* is a perfect addition to this series that had me on the edge of my seat from the first to the very last page."
— Sharon, Obsession with Books

"It's no secret that Jennifer L. Armentrout is one of my very favorite authors but seriously, if you haven't picked up this series yet, go out and get it! You will be caught up in the story and you will not regret it!"
— Book Loving Mommy

"I just can't express how much I love this book... addictive prose, lovable characters, and jaw-dropping twists in the insane plot. I am positively dying for *Apollyon*."
— Sophia, The Book Basement

"I want more! Need more! CRAVE MORE! The series demands it! I thought *Pure* was the epitome of AWESOME! Yes that indeed it was, but this book! This book goes right up there with it!"
— BookLove101

"Oh. My. Gods. There are no words to explain just how phenomenal this book is."   — Kayleigh, K-Books

"Without a doubt the best book I have read in 2012. That is saying something since *Pure* was released earlier this year."
— Cassandra's Reviews

"*Deity*... has all the romance anyone could ask for, plus a whole lot of action and suspenseful drama as well."
— Laura, The Revolving Bookcase

"5 of 5 stars: I've never read a book that screwed with my emotions as much... *Deity* made me want to throw my book across the room numerous times, and to me, that just shows how great Armentrout is at her craft. Because when a reader is that invested in characters from a book, the author has clearly done something right."
— Nicole Sobon

"Aiden has stepped up his GAME this time around! I LOVE HIM! I WANT TO MARRY HIM! HAVE SENTINEL BABIES WITH HIM!"
— Alice Belikov

"Overall Awesomeness? Freaking 10/10! *Deity* has got to be Jennifer's best book so far and that's saying a lot, since pretty much everything written by Jen is amazing."
— Kindle and Me

"Every time I read a Jennifer L. Armentrout novel, I always become so absorbed and invested in the story. I feel like with each new book her stories keep getting more and more awesome and exciting! *Deity* is no exception, and it is by far my favorite out of all the books and novellas I've read by JLA."
— Collections

"*Deity* is action-packed and full of romance. This emotional roller coaster will have fans begging for the next installment!"
— Amber, Fall Into Books

"If you're a crier you will cry! I bawled in a few places but the crying is so worth it! This story absolutely rocks and the ending?!?!? ...you will be dying to get your hands on *Elixir* like I am!"
— Jaime, Two Chicks On Books

"*Deity* is an AMAZING book. It has a lot of twists in it that you will love. I read in one day and still can't get over it. I loved it from the beginning to the end."   — Savanna, Sucked into Books

"I read this book in one sitting. I wanted to take it slow and enjoy it like a fine wine, but Jennifer just dragged me in and I ended up slamming this book back like a lush!"
— AwesomeSauce Book Club

"The Covenant series just keeps getting better and better! Deity is my favorite so far!   — The Readers Den

"*Deity* ramps up the action, suspense, and romance without ever losing a step, and it makes me crave the sequel like I need it to breathe."
— Quill Café

"5/5: *Deity* was an A-M-A-Z-I-N-G read from beginning to start."
— Amanda, Stuck In YA Books

"*Deity*...Oh my god....It's officially my favourite read of 2012!"
— Book Passion for Life

"*Deity* was insanely thrilling right to the core. The twists hit me like a hurricane when I wasn't expecting it."
— Coffee, Books, and Me

"5/5: *Deity* was one of the most intense books I've read! A real rollercoaster of emotions... I gave 5 stars to books 1 and 2 but if I could I would give *Deity* a 10 + stars!"
— Steffy, Book Reader Addicts

"Every page leaves me feeling the WOW factor!... This is one of my most favorite series!"
— Mindy, Books Complete Me

"*Deity* took me on one exhilarating roller-coaster of a ride, leaving me in emotional turmoil by the end. In short, I cherished every minute of it."
— Sam, Realm of Fiction

"Undeniably Epic! Pure Awesomesauce!"
— Tina Gagnier

"HOLY FREAKING COW! That's what I said upon finishing Jennifer Armentrout's *Deity*! It was one heck of a thrill ride! Jennifer never ceases to amaze me with what she can do with this series!"
— Jessica, A Great Read

"Perfect for fans of both Greek mythology and romance, *Deity* will enrapture the reader with its world building, romance, and to-die-for characters. This series is utterly captivating, and I cannot wait for more!"
— Tiffany, About To Read

"WOW, JUST WOW! ...I just can't get enough of this series, the storyline, the characters and the dialogue just has me in stitches from constantly laughing... I cannot praise this book, series or author enough! I give this a huge 5/5."
— Head Stuck in a Book

"The book leaves you on the edge of your seat and crying because the book is over. I CAN'T WAIT FOR THE NEXT BOOK!"
— Cora, Stuck in Books

Praise for *Half-Blood*
USA Book News BEST BOOKS 2011 Finalist
National Indie Excellence Awards 2012 Finalist

"I've found my new favourite series."
— Safari Poet

"If I could describe this book in one word it would be: AMAZING!"
— Catching Books

"Amazing doesn't even do this book justice."
— The Magic Attic

"This is one debut that will rock you off your toes!"
— Books Over Boys

"Jennifer Armentrout has delivered an action packed book full of twists, romance, and paranormal powers and a great unique Greek Mythology."
— Mundie Moms

"I was completely blown away and left utterly speechless."
— Amy G., The YA Sisterhood

"*Half-Blood* is a book that will sink its teeth into you and won't let go."
— [Fict]shun

"Intense, dramatic, and downright un-put-down-able."
— 365 Days of Reading

"This book is perfect! A total MUST READ!!"
— Darkest Sins

"A wonderful new YA series that no one should miss reading."
— Books to Brighten Your Mood

"This is a book you will finish, and weeks later still be mind blown about, just trying to think of the words to use for how much you loved it."
— Ya-Aholic

"Completely entertaining and utterly compelling, *Half-Blood* has definitely earned its place high up on my favourites list!"
— Mimi Valentine

"Paced with precision, the story unfolds gradually to the perfect end, filled with unanswered questions and a desperate longing."
— Writing Jewels

"It's literally impossible to put *Half-Blood* down until totally devoured....and then you are licking your lips for more."
— Novels on the Run

Spencer Hill Press

Contact: Spencer Hill Press, PO Box 247, Contoocook, NH 03229, USA

Please visit our website at www.spencerhillpress.com

First Edition: November 2012.
Second Printing: December 2012.

Armentrout, Jennifer L. 1980
Deity : a novel / by Jennifer L. Armentrout – 1st ed.
p. cm.

Summary:
As her Awakening draws nearer, Alex faces new threats from those who fear what she will become.

The author acknowledges the copyrighted or trademarked status and trademark owners of the following wordmarks mentioned in this fiction:
BMW R1200 C Motorcycle, Buffy the Vampire Slayer, Charlie Brown Christmas, Cheetos, Dial, Dr. Evil, 5-Hour Energy, Godzilla, Google, Hallmark, Hostess CupCakes, Hummer, James Bond/007, Kleenex, Mario Go Cart, Mortal Holiday Tree, My Little Pony, National Lampoon's Christmas Vacation, Pepsi, Popsicle, Ritalin, Royal Rumble, Scrabble, Spider-man, Super Mario Brothers, Supernatural, Taco Bell, Terminator, Tomorrow Never Dies, Twinkies, Valium, Wal-Mart, Wii

Cover design by K. Kaynak with artwork by Misha and Eduardo Fuentes Guevara.

ISBN 978-1-937053-14-7 (paperback)
ISBN 978-1-937053-15-4 (e-book)

Printed in the United States of America

Deity

The Third Covenant Novel by

Jennifer L. Armentrout

SPENCER HILL PRESS

The *Covenant* Series

Daimon (novella)
Half-Blood
Pure
Deity
Elixir (novella)
Apollyon (April 2013)
Sentinel (Fall 2013)
Covenant novellas are available as free downloads in several formats
at www.SpencerHillPress.com.

Also by Jennifer L. Armentrout

From Spencer Hill Press:
Cursed

Coming from Disney-Hyperion:
Don't Look Back

From Entangled Publishing:
Obsidian (Book 1 in the Lux Series)
Onyx (Book 2 in the Lux Series)
Opal (Book 3 in the Lux Series) (December 2012)

Writing as J. Lynn:
Tempting the Best Man
Unchained

To Kayleigh-Marie Gore, Momo Xiong, Valerie Fink, Vi Nguyen,
and Angela Messer for being über Covenant Series fans...
and the first to respond on Twitter.
And to Brittany Howard and Amy Green of YA Sisterhood,
for just being, well, awesome.
And to the Greer family,
for being the official first family of the Covenant Series.

Pronunciation Guide for *Deity*

Aether:	EE-ther
Agapi:	ah-GAH-pee
Akasha:	ah-KAH-sha
Apollyon:	a-POL-ee-on
Daimon:	DEE-mun
Hematoi:	HEM-a-toy
Zoi mou:	ZOY moo

CHAPTER 1

RED SILK CLUNG TO MY HIPS, TWISTING INTO A TIGHT bodice that accentuated my curves. My hair was down, silky around my shoulders like the petals of an exotic flower. The lights in the ballroom caught each ripple in the fabric so that, with every step, I looked like I was blooming from fire.

He stopped, lips parting as if the mere sight of me had rendered him incapable of doing anything else. A warm blush stole over my skin. This wouldn't end well—not when we were surrounded by people and he was looking at me like that, but I couldn't make myself leave. I belonged here, with him. That had been the right choice.

The choice I… hadn't made.

Dancers slowed around me, their faces hidden behind dazzling bejeweled masks. The haunting melody the orchestra played slipped under my skin and sunk into my bones as the dancers parted.

Nothing separated us.

I tried to breathe, but he had stolen not just my heart, but the very air I needed.

He stood there, dressed in a black tux cut to fit the hard lines of his body. A lopsided smile, full of mischief and playfulness, curved his lips as he bowed at the waist, extending his arm toward me.

My legs felt weak as I took the first step. The twinkling lights from above lit the way to him, but I would've found him in the dark if necessary. The beat of his heart sounded just like mine.

His smile spread.

That was all the reinforcement I needed. I took off toward him, the dress streaming behind me in a river of crimson silk. He straightened, catching me by the waist as I looped my arms around his neck. I burrowed my face against his chest, soaking in the scent of ocean and burning leaves.

Everyone was watching, but it didn't matter. We were in our own world, where only what we wanted—what we'd desired for so long—mattered.

He chuckled deeply as he spun me around. My feet didn't even touch the ballroom floor. "So reckless," he murmured.

I smiled in response, knowing he secretly loved that part of me.

Placing me on my feet, he clasped my hand and placed the other on the small of my back. When he spoke again, his voice was a low, sultry whisper. "You look so beautiful, Alex."

My heart swelled. "I love you, Aiden."

He kissed the top of my head, and then we spun in dizzying circles. Couples slowly joined us, and I caught glimpses of wide smiles and strange eyes behind the masks—eyes completely white, no irises. Unease spread. Those eyes… I knew what they meant. We drifted toward a corner where I heard soft cries coming from the darkness.

I peered into the shadowy corner of the ballroom. "Aiden…?"

"Shh." His hand slipped up my spine and cupped the nape of my neck. "Do you love me?"

Our eyes met and held. "Yes. *Yes.* I love you more than anything."

Aiden's smile faded. "Do you love me more than him?"

I stilled in his suddenly lax embrace. "More than who?"

"Him," Aiden repeated. "Do you love me more than him?"

My gaze fell past him again, to the darkness. A man had his back to us. He was pressed against a woman, his lips on her throat.

"Do you love me more than him?"

"Who?" I tried to press closer, but he held me back. Uncertainty blossomed in my belly when I saw the disappointment in his silvery eyes. "Aiden, what's wrong?"

"You don't love me." He dropped his hands, stepping back. "Not when you're with him, when you chose him."

The man twisted at the waist, facing us. Seth smiled, his gaze offering a world of dark promises. Promises that I'd agreed to, that I'd chosen.

"You don't love me," Aiden said again, fading into the shadows. "You can't. You never could."

I reached for him. "But—"

It was too late. The dancers converged and I was lost in a sea of dresses and whispered words. I pushed at them, but I couldn't break through, couldn't find Aiden or Seth. Someone pushed me and I fell to my knees, the red silk ripping. I cried out for Aiden and then Seth, but neither heeded my pleas. I was lost, staring up at faces hidden behind masks, staring at strange eyes. *I knew those eyes.*

They were the eyes of the gods.

I jerked straight up in bed, a fine sheen of sweat covering my body as my heart continued to try to come out of my chest. Several moments passed before my eyes adjusted to the darkness and I recognized the bare walls of my dorm room.

"What the hell?" I ran the back of my hand over my damp and warm forehead. I squeezed my watery eyes shut.

"Hmm?" murmured a half-awake Seth.

I sneezed in response, once, and then twice.

"That's hot." He blindly reached for the box of tissues. "I can't believe you're still sick. Here."

Sighing, I took the tissues from him and cradled the box to my chest as I pulled a few free. "It's your fault—*achoo!* It was your stupid idea to go swimming in—*achoo!*—forty-degree weather, jerk-face."

"I'm not sick."

I wiped my nose, waiting a few more seconds to make sure I was done sneezing my brains out, and then dropped the box on the floor. Colds sucked daimon butt. In my seventeen years of life, I'd never gotten a cold until now. I hadn't even known I *could* get one. "Aren't you just so damn special?"

"You know it," was his muffled response.

Twisting at the waist, I glared at the back of Seth's head. He almost looked normal with his face planted into a pillow—*my* pillow. Not like someone who'd become a God Killer in less than four months. To our world, Seth was sort of like any mythical creature: beautiful, but usually downright deadly. "I had a weird dream."

Seth rolled onto his side. "Come on. Go back to sleep."

Since we'd returned from the Catskills a week ago, he'd been up my butt like never before. It wasn't like I didn't understand why, with the whole furie business and me killing a pure. He probably was never going to let me out of his sight again. "You really need to start sleeping in your own bed."

He turned his head slightly. A sleepy smile spread across his face. "I prefer your bed."

"I prefer that we actually celebrate Christmas around here, and then I'd get some Christmas presents and get to sing Christmas songs, but I don't get what I want."

Seth tugged me down, his arm a heavy weight that pinned me on my back. "Alex, I always get what I want."

A fine shiver coursed over my skin. "Seth?"

"Yeah?"

"You were in my dream."

One amber-colored eye opened. "Please tell me we were naked."

I rolled my eyes. "You're such a perv."

He sighed mournfully as he wiggled closer. "I'll take that as a no."

"You'd be correct." Unable to fall back to sleep, I started chewing on my lip. So many worries surfaced at once that my brain spun. "Seth?"

"Mmm?"

I watched him snuggle further down into the pillow before I continued. There was something charming about Seth when he was like this, a vulnerability and boyishness missing when he was fully awake. "What happened when I was fighting the furies?"

His eyes opened into thin slits. This was a question I'd asked several times since we'd returned to North Carolina. The kind of strength and power I'd displayed as I'd faced the gods was something only Seth, as a full-blown Apollyon, should've been able to accomplish.

As an un-Awakened half-blood? Yeah, not so much. I should've gotten my rosy rear handed to me when I fought the furies.

Seth's mouth tightened. "Go back to sleep, Alex."

He refused to answer. Again. Anger and frustration rushed to the surface. I flung his arm off me. "What aren't you telling me?"

"You're being paranoid." His arm landed on my stomach again.

I tried wiggling out of his grasp, but his grip tightened. Grinding my teeth, I rolled onto my side and settled next to him. "I'm not being paranoid, you asshat. Something happened. I've told you that. Everything... everything looked amber. Like the color of your eyes."

He blew out a long breath. "I've heard that people in high stress situations have increased strength and senses."

"That wasn't it."

"And that people can hallucinate while under pressure."

I swung my arm back, narrowly missing his head. "I didn't hallucinate."

"I don't know what to tell you." Seth lifted his arm and rolled onto his back. "Anyway, are you going to go back to class in the morning?"

Instantly, a new worry surfaced. Classes meant facing everyone— Olivia—without my best friend. Pressure built in my chest. I squeezed my eyes shut, but Caleb's pale face appeared, eyes wide and unseeing, a Covenant dagger shoved deep in his chest. It seemed I could only remember what he'd really looked like in my dreams.

Seth sat up, and I felt his eyes boring holes in my back. "Alex...?"

I hated our super-special bond—absolutely loathed that whatever I was feeling fed into him. There was no such thing as privacy anymore. I sighed. "I'm fine."

He didn't respond.

"Yeah, I'm going to class in the morning. Marcus will have a fit when he gets back and realizes I haven't been to class." I flopped onto my back. "Seth?"

He inclined his heard toward me. Shadows cloaked his features, but his eyes cut through the darkness. "Yeah?"

"When do you think they're coming back?" By *they* I meant Marcus and Lucian... and Aiden. My breath caught. It happened whenever I thought about Aiden and what he'd done for me—what he'd risked.

Easing down on his side, Seth reached across me and grabbed my right hand. His fingers threaded through mine, palm to palm. My skin tingled in response. The mark of the Apollyon—the one that shouldn't be on my hand—warmed. I stared at our joined hands, not at all surprised when I saw the faint lines—also the marks of the Apollyon—making their way up Seth's arm. I turned my head, watching as the marks spread across Seth's face. His eyes seemed to brighten. They'd been doing that a lot more lately—both the runes and his eyes.

"Lucian said they'd be back soon, possibly later today." Very slowly, he moved the pad of his thumb down the line of the rune. My toes curled as my free hand dug into the blankets. Seth smiled. "No one's mentioned the pure-blood Guard. And Dawn Samos has already returned. It appears Aiden's compulsion worked."

I wanted to pull my hand free. It was hard to concentrate when Seth messed with the rune on my palm. Of course, he knew that. And being the tool that he was, he liked it.

"No one knows what really happened." His thumb now traced the horizontal line. "And it'll remain that way."

My eyes drifted shut. The truth of how the pure-blood Guard had died would have to remain a secret, or both Aiden and I would be in deep trouble. Not only had we almost hooked up over the summer—and then I'd had to go and tell him that I loved him, which was *totally* forbidden—I'd killed a pure-blood out of self-defense. And Aiden had used compulsion on two pures to cover it up. Killing a pure meant death for a half-blood, no matter the situation, and a pure was forbidden to use compulsion on another pure. If *any* of it came out, we'd both be totally screwed.

"You think so?" I whispered.

"Yes." Seth's breath was warm against my temple. "Go to sleep, Alex."

Letting the soothing sensation of his thumb against the rune lull me away, I drifted back to sleep, momentarily forgetting all the mistakes and decisions I'd made in the past seven months. My last conscious thought was of my biggest mistake—not the boy beside me, but the one I could never have.

Deity

On a good, normal day I hated trig class. The whole subject seemed pointless to me. Who cared about Pythagorean Identities when I was attending the Covenant to learn how to kill things? But today my hatred of the class had hit an all-time high.

Almost everyone had their eyes on me, even Mrs. Kateris. I sank low in my seat, shoving my nose into the book I wouldn't read if Apollo came down and demanded that I do so. Only one set of eyes really affected me. The rest could suck it.

Olivia's stare was heavy, condemning.

Why, oh why, couldn't we change seats? After everything that'd happened, sitting next to her was the worst kind of torture.

My cheeks burned. She hated me, blamed me for Caleb's death. But I hadn't killed Caleb—a half-blood daimon had. I'd just been the one who'd gotten him to sneak out on a campus that'd been under curfew for what'd turned out to be a really good reason.

So in a way, it was my fault. I knew that, and gods, I'd do anything to change that night.

Olivia's outburst at Caleb's funeral was probably why everyone else kept sneaking peeks at me. If I remembered correctly, I think she'd yelled something like, "You're the Apollyon" as I stared at her.

Back at the New York Covenant in the Catskills, the half-blood kids had thought I was pretty damn cool, but here… not so much. When I met their gazes, they didn't look away fast enough to hide their unease.

At the end of class, I shoved my book in my backpack and hurried out the door, wondering if Deacon would talk to me next period. Deacon and Aiden were poles apart on almost everything, but both Aiden and his younger brother seemed to view halfs as their equals—a rare thing among the pure-blood race.

Whispers followed me down the hall. Ignoring them was harder than I'd imagined. Every cell in my body demanded that I confront them. And do what? Jump on them like a crazy spider monkey and take them all out? Yeah, not going to win me any fans.

"Alex! Wait up!"

My heart sank at the sound of Olivia's voice. I picked up my pace, practically barreling through a few younger half-bloods who stared at me with wide, frightened eyes. Why were they afraid of me? I wasn't the one who was going to go all God Killer soon. But oh no, they stared at Seth like he *was* a god. Just a few more doors and I could hide in Technical Truths and Legends.

"Alex!"

I recognized Olivia's tone. It was the same one she used to get whenever she and Caleb were about to have one of their quarrels—determined and stubborn as hell.

Crap.

She was right behind me now and I was only a step away from my classroom. I wasn't going to make it. "Alex," she said. "We need to talk."

"I'm not doing this right now." Because really, being told that it was my fault Caleb was dead was not on the top of my list of things to hear today.

Olivia grabbed my arm. "Alex, I need to talk to you. I know you're upset, but you're not the only one who's allowed to miss Caleb. I was his girlfriend—"

I stopped thinking. Whirling around, I dropped my bag in the middle of hall and caught her by the throat. In a second, I had her against the wall and on the tips of her toes. Eyes wide, she grabbed my arm and tried to push me off.

I squeezed just a little bit.

Out of the corner of my eyes I saw Lea, her arm no longer in a brace. The daimon half that'd broken her arm had also killed Caleb. Lea stepped forward like she wanted to intervene.

"Look, I get it," I whispered hoarsely. "You loved Caleb. Guess what? So did I. And I miss him, too. If I could go back in time and change that night, I would. But I can't. So please just leave me—"

An arm the size of my waist shot out from nowhere and tossed me back a good five feet. Olivia slumped against the wall, rubbing her throat.

I whirled around and groaned.

Leon, the King of Impeccable Timing, glared at me. "You are in need of a professional babysitter."

I opened my mouth, but then I closed it. Considering some of the things Leon had interrupted in the past, he had no idea how true his statement was. But then I realized something more important. If Leon was back, then my uncle and Aiden were also back.

"You," Leon gestured at Olivia, "get to class." He turned his attention back to me. "You are coming with me."

Biting my tongue, I grabbed my bag off the floor and commenced my walk of shame down the now-crowded hallway. I caught a glimpse of Luke, but looked away before I could gauge his expression.

Leon took the stairs—gods know how I loved them—and we didn't speak until we stood in the lobby. The furie statues were gone, but the empty space left a cold hole in my stomach. They'd be back. I was sure of it. It was just a matter of when.

He towered over me when he stopped, nearly seven feet of pure muscle. "Why is it every time I see you, you are about to do something you shouldn't?"

I shrugged. "It's a talent."

Reluctant amusement flickered across his face as he pulled something out of his back pocket. It looked like a piece of parchment. "Aiden asked me to give this to you."

My stomach dropped as I reached out and took the letter, hands shaking. "Is… is he okay?"

His brows furrowed. "Yes. Aiden is fine."

I didn't even try to hide my sigh of relief as I turned the letter over. It was sealed with an official-looking red stamp. When I looked up, Leon was gone. Shaking my head, I went over to one of the marble benches and sat. I had no idea how Leon could move such a massive body around so stealthily. The ground should tremble in his wake.

Curious, I slid my finger under the crease and broke the seal. Unfolding the letter, I saw Laadan's elegant signature at the bottom. I quickly scanned the parchment once, and then I went back and read it again.

And I read it a third time.

I felt unbearably hot and cold all at once. My mouth dried, throat seized. Fine tremors racked my fingers, causing the paper to flutter. I stood and then sat back down. The four words replayed before my eyes. It was all I could see. All I cared to know.

Your father is alive.

CHAPTER 2

HEART RACING, I TOOK THE STEPS TWO AT A TIME. SPY-ing Leon near my uncle's office, I broke into a sprint. He looked mildly alarmed when he saw me.

"What is it, Alexandria?"

I skidded to a halt. "Aiden gave this to you?"

Leon frowned. "Yes."

"Did you read it?"

"No. It wasn't addressed to me."

I clutched the letter to my chest. "Do you know where Aiden is?"

"Yes." Leon's frown turned severe. "He's been back since last night."

"Where is he *right now*, Leon? I need to know."

"I don't see how there could be any reason you'd need Aiden badly enough to interrupt his training." He folded thick arms across his chest. "And shouldn't you be heading to class?"

I stared a moment before I spun around and took off again. Leon wasn't stupid, so he hadn't accidentally told me where Aiden was, but I didn't care enough to look into the reason behind that.

If Aiden was training then I knew where to find him. A cold, damp breeze sprayed my cheeks as I burst through the lobby doors and headed toward the training arena. The milky gray sky was typical for late November, making summer seem so long ago.

Classes for lower level students were being held in the larger training rooms. Instructor Romvi's impatient barking from behind one of the closed doors followed my quick footsteps down the empty hall. Toward the end of the building, across from the med room where Aiden had brought me after Kain had handed my ass to me in training, was a smaller room equipped with the bare necessities and a sensory deprivation chamber.

I had yet to train in that thing.

Peeking through the crack in the door, I saw Aiden. He was in the middle of the mat, squaring off with a punching bag. A fine sheen of sweat coated his ropey muscles as he swung, knocking the bag back several feet.

Any other time I would have admired him rather obsessively, but my fingers spasmed, crunching the letter. I slid through the gap and crossed the room.

"Aiden."

He whipped around, eyes flaring from a cool gray to a thunderous shade. He took a step back, wiping his arm across his forehead. "Alex, what... what are you doing here? Shouldn't you be in class?"

I held the letter up. "Did you read what was in this letter?"

He had the same look as Leon. "No. Laadan asked me to make sure you got it."

Why had she trusted Aiden with such news? I couldn't even begin to figure that out unless... "Did you *know* what was in this letter?"

"No. She just asked me to give it to you." He bent, swiping a towel off the mat. "What's in the letter that has you chasing me down?"

A stupid, totally unimportant question rose to the surface. "Why did you give it to Leon?"

He averted his eyes, growing still. "I thought it would be best."

My gaze dropped from his face to his neck. There was that thin, silver chain again. I itched to know what he wore, since he wasn't a jewelry type of guy. I dragged my eyes back to his face. "My father is alive."

Aiden tilted his head toward me. "What?"

A bitter feeling settled in my stomach "He's *alive*, Aiden. And he's been at the New York Covenant for years. He was there when I was there." The swirling emotions I felt when I first read the letter picked up again. "I saw him, Aiden! I know I did. The servant with the brown eyes. And he knew—he knew I was his daughter. That must be why he always looked at me strangely. It's probably why I was so drawn to him whenever I saw him. I just didn't know."

Aiden looked pale under his natural tan. "Can I?"

I handed him the letter and then dragged shaking hands through my hair. "You know, there was something different about him. He never looked doped-up like other servants. And when Seth and I were leaving, I saw him fighting the daimons." I paused, drawing in a deep breath. "I just didn't know, Aiden."

His brows furrowed as he scanned the letter. "Gods," he murmured.

Turning away from him, I hugged my elbows. The sickening feeling I'd been staving off flowed through my stomach. Anger boiled the blood in my veins. "He's a servant—a freaking *servant*."

"Do you know what this means, Alex?"

I faced him, shocked to find him so close. At once I caught the scent of aftershave and saltwater. "Yes. I have to do something! I have to get him out of there. I know I don't know him, but he's my father. I have to do something!"

Aiden's eyes widened. "No."

"No what?"

He folded up the letter in one hand and grabbed my arm with the other. I dug in my heels. "What are you—?"

"Not here," he ordered quietly.

Confused and a bit startled by the fact that Aiden was actually touching me, I let him lead me to the med office across the hall. He shut the door behind him, turning the lock. An uncomfortable heat flooded my system as I realized we were alone in a room with no windows, and Aiden had just locked the door. Seriously, I needed to get a grip because this was *so* not the time for my ridiculous hormones. Okay, there really *wasn't* a time for them.

Aiden faced me. His jaw flexed. "What are you thinking?"

"Uh…" I took a step back. No way was I admitting that. Then I realized he was angry—furious with me. "What did I do now?"

He placed the letter on the table I'd once sat upon. "You will not do something crazy."

My eyes narrowed as I snatched up the letter, finally catching onto why he was so angry. "You expect me to do nothing? And to just let my father rot in servitude?"

"You need to calm down."

"Calm down? That servant in New York is my father. The father I'd been told was dead!" Suddenly, I remembered Laadan in the library and how she talked about my father as if he was still alive. Rage socked me in the stomach. Why hadn't she told me? I could've spoken to him. "How can I calm down?"

"I… I can't imagine what you're going through, or what you're thinking." He frowned. "Well, yes, I can imagine what you're thinking. You want to storm the Catskills and free him. I know that's what you're thinking."

Of course I was.

He started toward me, his eyes turning a brilliant silver. "No."

I backed up, clutching Laadan's letter to my chest. "I have to do something."

"I know you feel like you need to, but Alex, you cannot return to the Catskills."

"I wouldn't storm it." I edged around the table as he grew closer. "I'll think of something. Maybe I'll get in trouble. Telly said all I needed to do was make one more mistake and I was being sent to the Catskills."

Aiden stared.

The table was now between us. "If I could get back there, then I can talk to him. I have to talk to him."

"Absolutely not," Aiden growled.

My muscles locked. "You can't stop me."

"You want to bet?" He started around the table.

Not really. The fierceness in his expression told me he'd do everything to stop me, which meant I needed to convince him. "He's my father, Aiden. What would you do if it was Deacon?"

Low blow, I know.

"Don't you even dare bring him into this, Alex. I won't allow you to get yourself killed. I don't care who it's for. I won't."

Tears burned the back of my throat. "I can't leave him in that kind of life. I can't."

Pain flickered in his steely gaze. "I know, but he's not worth your life."

My arms fell to my sides and I stopped trying to outmaneuver him. "How can you make that decision?" And then the tears I'd been fighting broke free. "How can I not do something?"

Aiden didn't say anything as he placed his hands on my upper arms and guided me to him. Instead of pulling me straight into his embrace, he backed up against the wall and slid down, bringing me along with him. I was nestled in his arms. My legs curled against him, one of my hands fisting his shirt.

The breath I took was shallow, filled with a kind of hurt I couldn't let go. "I'm tired of people lying to me. Everyone lied about my mom, and now this? I thought he was *dead*. And gods, I wish he were, because death is better than what he has to live through." My voice broke and more tears spilled over my cheeks.

Aiden's arms tightened around me, and his hand smoothed a comforting circle over my back. I wanted to stop crying because it was weak and humiliating, but I couldn't stop. Discovering my father's true fate was horrifying. When the worst of the tears subsided, I pulled back a little and lifted my teary gaze.

Damp silky waves of dark hair clung to his forehead and temples. The dim light of the room still highlighted those high cheekbones and lips I'd memorized so long ago. Aiden rarely ever fully smiled, but when he did, it was breathtaking. There'd been a few times I'd gotten to bask in that rare smile; the last time had been at the zoo.

Seeing him now, truly seeing him, the first time after he'd risked everything to protect me—I wanted to start crying again. Over the last week, I'd replayed what had happened over and over again. Could I've done something differently? Disarmed the Guard instead of shoving my blade deep into his chest? And why had Aiden used compulsion to cover up what I'd done? Why would he risk so much?

And none of that seemed important right now, not after learning about my father. I wiped under my eyes with my palms. "Sorry for… crying all over you."

"Never apologize for that," he said. I expected him to let go of me at that point, but his arms were still around me. I knew I shouldn't, because it would just bring a world of hurt later, but I let myself relax against him. "You have this knee-jerk reaction to everything."

"What?"

He lowered an arm and tapped my knee. "It's the first initial response. The immediate thought when you hear something. You act on that instead of thinking things through."

I burrowed my cheek against his chest. "That's not a compliment."

His hand moved to the back of my neck, fingers tangling deep in the mess of hair at the nape of my neck. Wondering if he was aware of what he was doing, I held my breath. His hand tightened, holding me so I couldn't pull back too far. Not that I would—no matter how wrong it was, how dangerous or stupid.

"It's not an insult," he said softly. "It's just who you are. You don't stop to think of the danger, only what is right. But sometimes it's not… right."

I mulled that over. "Was using compulsion on Dawn and the other pure a knee-jerk reaction?"

He took what seemed like forever to answer. "It was, and it wasn't the smartest thing to do, but I couldn't do anything else."

"Why?"

Aiden didn't answer.

I didn't push it. There was a comfort in his arms, in the way his hand traced a soothing circle along my back, that I couldn't find anyplace else. I didn't want to ruin it. In his arms, I was calmer—strangely. I could breathe. I felt safe, grounded. No one else offered that. His was like my very own prescription of Ritalin.

"Becoming a Sentinel was a knee-jerk reaction," I whispered.

Aiden's chest rose and fell under my cheek. "Yeah, it was."

"Do… do you regret it?"

"Never."

I wished I had his kind of resolve. "I don't know what to do, Aiden."

His chin tipped down, brushing over my cheek. His skin was smooth, warm, thrilling, and calming all in one. "We'll figure out a way to get in touch with him. You said he never seemed like he was under the elixir? We could get a letter to Laadan; she could pass it to him. That would be the safest step."

My heart did a stupid, happy dance. Hope was spreading out of control inside me. "We?"

"Yes. I can easily get a letter to Laadan—a message. It's the safest way for right now."

I wanted to squeeze him, but refrained. "No. If you get caught… I can't have that happening."

Aiden laughed softly. "Alex, we've probably broken every rule there is. I'm not worried about getting busted over passing on a message."

No, we hadn't broken *every* rule.

He pulled back slightly, and I could feel his intense stare on my face. "Did you think I wouldn't help you with something as important as this?"

I kept my eyes closed, because looking at him was a weakness. *He* was my weakness. "Things are… different."

"I know things are different, Alex, but I will always be here for you. I will always help you." He paused. "How can you ever doubt that?"

Like a fool, I opened my eyes. I was sucked right in. It was like everything that'd been said, everything I knew, didn't matter anymore. "I don't doubt that," I whispered.

His lips tipped up on one side. "Sometimes I just don't get you."

"I don't get myself half of the time." I lowered my eyes. "You've already done… too much. What you did in the Catskills?" I swallowed the lump in my throat. "Gods, I never thanked you for it."

"Don't—"

"Don't say it's not worth thanking you for." My gaze flicked up, locking with his. "You saved my life, Aiden, at the risk of your own. So, thank you."

He looked away, his eyes focusing on a spot over my head. "I told you I'd never let anything happen to you." His gaze came back to me and amusement sparkled in those silver pools. "It seems more like a full-time job, though."

My lips quirked. "I've really been trying, you know. Today was the first day I even did anything remotely stupid." I left out the part where I'd been sequestered in my room with a nasty head cold.

"What did you do?"

"You really don't want to know."

He laughed again. "I figured Seth would be keeping you out of trouble."

Realizing I hadn't even thought about Seth since the moment I'd read the letter, I stiffened. I hadn't even thought about the bond. Dammit.

Aiden drew in a deep breath and dropped his arms. "You do know what this means, Alex?"

I struggled to pull myself together. There were important things to deal with. My father, the Council, Telly, the furies, a dozen or so pissed off gods, and Seth. But my brain felt like mush. "What?"

Aiden glanced at the door, as if he was afraid to say it out loud. "Your father wasn't a mortal. He's a half-blood."

CHAPTER 3

I DIDN'T GO BACK TO MY CLASSES. INSTEAD, I WENT TO my dorm room and sat on my bed, the letter resting in front of me like a snake ready to spread its venom. I was reeling from learning that my dad was still alive and.... I felt so stupid for not figuring it out right away. Laadan's letter didn't come out and say it. Obviously, I understood why she skirted the true bomb she was dropping in the brief letter. How else would the Council have been able to get my father under control? And I'd seen him fight. He was like a ninja with those candleholders.

My father was a freaking half-blood—a *trained* half-blood. Hell, he'd probably been a damn Sentinel, which totally explained how my mom had known him before she met Lucian.

A half-blood.

So what in the holy Hades did that make me?

The answer seemed too simple. I flopped on my back, staring blindly at the ceiling. Gods, I wanted Caleb to talk this through with, because this couldn't be what it was.

A pure-blood who had children with other pures made happy, little pure babies. A pure-blood who got it on with a mortal created the ever-useful half-blood. But a pure-blood and a half-blood getting together—which was so forbidden, so taboo that I couldn't think of one situation where a child was actually produced—made... what?

I jerked straight up, heart thundering. The first time Aiden had been in my dorm room and I'd looked at him—well, I'd been ogling him, but whatever—and wondered why relationships between halfs and pures had been forbidden for eons. It wasn't the fear of a one-eyed Cyclops, but it kind of was.

A pure-blood and a half-blood made an Apollyon.

"Shit," I said, staring at the letter.

But it had to be more than just that. There was typically only one Apollyon born every generation, with the exception of Solaris and the First, and Seth and I. Which would mean a half and a pure only produced a child a handful of times since the time the gods had walked this earth. There had to be more times when it happened. Or were those babies killed? I wouldn't put it past the pures or the gods to do such a thing if they knew what could come from the joining of a pure and a half. But why had Seth and I been spared? Obviously they knew what my father was since they've kept him around for whatever reason. My heart clenched, as did my fists. I pushed the anger down to revisit later. I'd promised Aiden I wouldn't do anything reckless, and my anger always led to something idiotic.

A shiver inched its way down my spine. A sound came from my door, much like a lock being turned. I glanced at the letter, chewing my bottom lip. Then I looked at the clock beside the bed. I was way late for training with Seth.

The door opened and shut. I grabbed the letter, quickly folding it. I knew the moment he stood in the doorway without looking up. A level of awareness danced over my skin and the air filled with electricity.

"What happened today?" he asked simply.

There was very little I could hide from Seth. He would've sensed my emotions from the moment I read the letter and everything that I had been feeling while I'd been with Aiden. He wouldn't know exactly what was causing my feelings to be all over the place—thank the gods—but Seth wasn't stupid. I was a little surprised that he'd waited this long to come find me.

I lifted my gaze. He looked like one of those marble statues that adorned the front of every building here, except his skin was a unique golden color—otherworldly perfection. Sometimes he looked cold, impassive. Especially when his shoulder-length blond hair was pulled back, but it hung loose now, softening the lines of his face. His full lips were usually curved in a smug smile, but now they were pressed together in a hard, tight line.

Aiden had suggested that I keep the letter and its contents to myself. Laadan had broken gods know how many rules by telling me about my father, but I trusted Seth. We were, after all, fated to be together. A couple of months ago I would've laughed if someone had said that we would be doing whatever it was that we were doing. It'd been a case of mutual dislike when we first met, and we still had some epic moments. It wasn't too long ago that I'd threatened to stab him in the eye. And I'd seriously meant it.

Silently, I held out the letter.

Seth took it, quickly unfolding it with long, agile fingers. I tucked my legs underneath me, watching him. There was nothing in his expression that gave away what he was thinking. After what seemed like forever, he glanced up. "Oh, gods."

Not exactly the response I was shooting for.

"You're going to do something incredibly stupid in response to this."

I threw up my hands. "Jeez, does everyone think I'm going to Sparta-charge the Catskills?"

Seth's brows rose.

"Whatever," I grumbled. "I'm not going to attack the Covenant. I have to do something, but it won't be… reckless. Happy? Anyway, do you remember the half-blood we passed when we were watching the Council the first day there?"

"Yes. You were staring at him."

"That's him. I know it. That's why he looked so familiar to me. His eyes." I bit my lip, looking away. "My mom always talked about his eyes."

He sat beside me. "What are you going to do?"

"I'm going to send a letter back to Laadan, a letter for my dad. From there, I don't know." I looked at him. Thick strands of hair shielded his face. "You know what this means, right? That he's a half-blood. And this—" I gestured at us. "We're the reason why relations of the fun kind are forbidden between halfs and pures. The gods know what'll happen if a pure and half hook up."

"It's probably more than that. The gods like the idea of subjugating the halfs. What do you think they did to the mortals during their heyday? The gods subjugated the mortals until it went too far. They still treat the half-bloods like dirt worthy of only being walked upon."

Man, was Seth on a god-hating kick or what? I stared down at my right palm, at the faint rune that only Seth and I could see. "It was him—my father—in the stairwell. I can't explain it, but I know it was."

Seth looked up then, his eyes a strange shade of yellow. "Who knows about this?"

I shook my head. "The Council has to know. Laadan knew because she was friends with my... my mom and dad. It wouldn't surprise me if Lucian and Marcus knew, too." I frowned. "Do you remember when we overheard Marcus and Telly talking?"

"I remember dropping you on your butt."

"Yeah, you did because you were staring at Boobs."

His eyes widened and he let out a shocked laugh. "Boobs? What?"

"You know—that girl who was all over you in the Catskills." When his brows rose, I rolled my eyes. So like Seth that he'd have trouble remembering *which* girl. "I'm talking about the one who had, well, huge boobs."

He stared off into the distance for a moment and then laughed again. "Oh. Yeah, that one—wait a second. You named her Boobs?"

"Yeah, and I bet you don't even remember her name."

"Ah..."

"Glad we're on the same page now. Anyway, Remember how Telly said that they already had one there? That they could keep them together? Do you think he was talking about my father and me?" If Marcus and Lucian knew, I wanted to bash their heads together, but confronting them would place Laadan in danger.

Seth glanced down at the letter. "That would make sense. Especially considering how badly Telly wanted you to be placed into servitude."

Minister Telly was the Head Minister of all the Councils and he'd had it out for me from the get-go. My testimony about the events in Gatlinburg had been a complete ruse to get me in front of the entire Council so they could vote me into servitude. And I truly believed that

Telly was behind the compulsion that'd been used on me the night I almost turned into a human popsicle. If Leon hadn't found me, I'd have frozen to death. Then there was the night the equivalent of an Olympian roofie had been given to me in a coarse attempt to catch me in a compromising position with a pure. It would've worked if it hadn't been for Seth and Aiden spotting me with the drink.

My cheeks burned as I remembered that night. I'd pretty much molested Seth—not that he'd complained. Seth had known I was under the influence of the brew and he'd tried to control himself, but the bond between us had spewed my revved-up lust all through him. I would've lost my virginity if I hadn't ended the night by puking up my guts. I know the whole situation bothered Seth. He felt guilty for giving in. And Aiden's fist had done a number on Seth's eye after discovering me on the bathroom floor... in Seth's clothing. Aiden couldn't understand how I'd forgiven Seth... and sometimes I couldn't, either. Maybe it was the bond, because what linked us together was strong. Maybe it was something more.

Then there was the pure-blood Guard who'd tried to kill me, saying he needed to "protect his kind." I suspected Minister Telly had been behind that, also.

"Who else knows about this?" Seth dragged me from my musings.

"Laadan asked Aiden to give me this letter, but Leon did instead. Leon claims he didn't look at the letter, and I believe him. It was sealed. See." I pointed out the broken stamp. "Aiden didn't know what was in it, either."

Seth's jaw flexed. "You went to Aiden?"

I knew I needed to proceed with caution. Seth and I weren't together or anything, but I also knew he wasn't messing around with anyone else now. The hot flashes I'd picked up on since returning from the Catskills had only been when he was around me, mostly during our hands-on training sessions. Seth was foremost a guy. It happened... a lot.

"I thought maybe he knew, since Laadan entrusted him with the letter, but he didn't," I said finally.

"But you told him?"

There was really no point in lying. "Yes. He knew I was upset. Obviously, he's trustworthy. He's not going to say anything."

Seth was silent for a heartbeat. "Why didn't you come to me?"

Oh, no. I focused on the floor, then my hands, and finally the wall. "I didn't know where you were. And Leon told me where Aiden was."

"Did you even attempt to find me? It's an island. It wouldn't have been hard to do." He placed the letter on the bed, and out of the corner of my eye, I saw his feet point to me.

I bit my lip. I didn't owe him anything, or did I? Either way, I didn't want to hurt his feelings. Seth might act like he had none, but I knew differently. "I just wasn't thinking. It's not a big deal."

"Okay." He leaned over and his breath warmed my cheek. "I felt your emotions this afternoon."

I swallowed. "Then why didn't you come looking for me?"

"I was busy."

"Then what's the big deal about me not looking for you? You were busy."

Seth brushed the thick hair off my neck, tossing it over my shoulder. My muscles locked up. "Why were you so upset?"

I turned my head. Our gazes locked. "I just found out that my dad's alive, and that he's a servant. That's kind of emotional."

His eyes deepened to a warm amber. "That's a good point."

There wasn't much space between our mouths. A sudden nervousness took over. Seth and I hadn't kissed since the day in the labyrinth. I think my cold had grossed him out, and it wasn't like I'd been pushing it, but I hadn't sneezed or sniffled since early this morning. "You know what?"

He smiled slightly. "What?"

"You don't seem very surprised about my father. You didn't know, did you?" I held my breath, because if he did, I didn't even know what I'd do. But it wouldn't be pretty.

"Why would you even think that?" His eyes narrowed. "You don't trust me?"

"No. I do." And I really did... most of the time. "But you just weren't surprised at all."

Seth sighed. "Nothing surprises me anymore."

I thought of something else. "Do you know which of your parents was a half-blood?"

"I guess it had to be my father. Mother was a pure through and through."

I didn't know that. Then again, there was very little I knew about Seth. Sure, he liked to talk about himself, but it was all on a superficial level. Then there was the greatest mystery of all. "What's your last name?"

"Alex, Alex, Alex," he chided softly, rising to his knees.

I squeezed my hands together, recognizing the calculated edge to his gaze. He was *so* up to something. "What?"

"I want to try something."

Since we were on my bed and Seth was a pervert most of the time, my suspicion level was pretty high. It showed in my voice. "Like what?"

Seth pressed me back until I was lying flat. He hovered above, a slight tilt to his lips. "Give me your left hand."

"Why?"

"Why are you so damn inquisitive?"

I arched a brow. "Why do you always have to invade my personal space?"

"Because I like to." He patted my stomach. "And deep down you like it when I do."

My lips pressed together. I was pretty sure the bond between us liked it when he did. I could feel it right now. It practically purred. Whether I liked it was something I was still trying to figure out.

"Give me your left hand," he ordered again. "We're going to work on your blocking technique."

"And we have to be holding hands to do this?" *In my bed*, I wanted to add.

"Alex."

Sighing loudly, I gave him my hand. "Are we going to sing songs now?"

"You wish." He straddled my thighs, placing a knee on either side. "I have a lovely singing voice."

"Do we have to do this right now? I'm not really feeling it after everything." Practicing blocking techniques of the mental kind required concentration and determination—two things I was lacking right now. Well, to be honest, concentration was something I usually lacked on most days.

"Now is the best time. Your emotions are all over the place. You need to learn how to push through that." Seth grabbed my other hand, threading his fingers through mine. He bent so far that the edges of his hair brushed my cheeks. "Close your eyes. Picture the walls."

Closing my eyes was something I did not want to do with Seth sitting on me. The bond between us had been growing stronger every day. I could feel it moving low in my tummy, thrumming to the surface. My toes curled inside my fuzzy socks. The same feeling I had the day I blew up the boulder swamped me. I wanted to touch him. Or the bond wanted me to touch him.

Seth tipped his head to the side. "I know what you're feeling right now. I totally approve of it."

My cheeks burned. "Gods, I hate you."

He chuckled. "Picture the walls. They're solid, cannot be breached."

I pictured the brick walls. In my mind, they were neon pink. With sparkles. I gave the walls sparkles because they gave me something to focus on. Seth had said the technique could work against compulsions if done correctly, but when dealing with emotions, the walls weren't built around the mind, they were built through the stomach and over the heart. The walls formed in my mind first and then I shifted them down, giving myself a body of armor.

"I can still feel it," Seth said, shifting restlessly above me.

This really must suck for him, I realized. He could tell I was still obsessed with Aiden, upset over my dad, and conflicted over him. And the only thing I got to pick up from him was when he was feeling randy.

The damn cord inside me—my connection to Seth— started to hum, demanding that I pay attention. It was like an annoying pet… or like Seth. I wondered if I could use the cord to block my emotions. Opening my eyes, I started to ask but then shut my mouth.

Seth had his eyes closed and he looked like he was really concentrating on something. His lids fluttered every so often, lips drawn into a tight, tense line. Then the marks flowed over his skin, moving so fast that the glyphs were nothing more than a blur as they raced down his neck, under the collar of his shirt.

My heart jumped. So did the cord inside me. I tried to pull my hand free before those marks reached my skin. "Seth."

His eyes snapped open, glazed over. The marks glided over his skin. A burst of crackling amber light radiated from his forearm. Struggling to get out from underneath him and away from that damn cord, I only succeeded in having my hands pinned down.

Panic unfurled, ripping through me. "Seth!"

"It's okay," he said.

But it wasn't okay. I didn't want that cord to do what I knew it was going to do. And then it was doing it. The amber cord wrapped around our hands, snapping and sparking, spreading down my arm. I jerked back, trying to scoot sway, but Seth held on, his eyes locked with mine.

"The cord—it's the purest power. Akasha," he said. Akasha was the fifth and final element, and it could only be harnessed by the gods and the Apollyon. The hue of Seth's eyes turned luminous. They almost looked crazy. "Hold on."

He wasn't giving me much of a choice. My gaze fell to our hands. Pulsating, the cord tightened and flared a brilliant amber. A blue cord wiggled out from underneath the amber cord, spilling drops of incandescent light onto the bedspread. Vaguely, I hoped we didn't catch the bed on fire. That would be hard to explain.

The blue cord flickered in and out, fluttering. Vaguely, I realized it was mine and weaker than the amber one. Then the blue jumped and pulsed. My left hand started to burn as the skin pricked. Recognizing the feeling, I freaked.

I squirmed, trying to scoot back. I didn't want another rune, and we hadn't held on this long last time. Something was very different about this. "Seth, this doesn't feel—" My body jerked, cutting off my own words.

Seth's body tensed. "Good gods…"

And then I felt it—akasha—shifting through the cords, leaving me and entering Seth. It was kind of like a daimon tag, but not painful. No… this was nice, heady. I stopped struggling, letting the glorious tug and pull lift me away. I didn't think about anything. There were no concerns or fears. The pain in my hand melted away, leaving only a dull ache that was spreading elsewhere. There was just this… and Seth. My eyes drifted shut and a sigh leaked out. Why had I been so afraid of this?

There was a flash of light that I could still see even though my eyes were closed. Seth dropped my hand and it fell limply to my side. The bed dipped beside my head from where he placed his hands. I felt his breath on my cheek, and it felt like warm, salty air rolling off the ocean.

"Alex?"

"Hmm…?"

"You okay?" He placed his lips to my cheek.

I smiled.

Seth chuckled, and then his mouth was making its way to mine, and I opened for him. The edges of his hair tickled my cheeks as the kiss deepened. His fingers drifted down the front of my blouse and then they were sliding over the bare skin of my stomach. I wrapped my leg around his, and we were moving together on the bed. His lips were dancing all over my flushed skin as his hands slid down, fingers finding the button on my jeans.

A second later, there was a knock on my door and a booming voice. "Alexandria?"

Seth stilled above me, panting. "You have got to be freaking kidding me."

Leon knocked again. "Alexandria, I know you're in there."

Dazed, I blinked several times. The room slowly came back into focus, as did Seth's disgruntled expression. I almost laughed, except I felt… off.

"You better answer him, angel, before he barges in here."

I tried, but failed. I took a deep breath. "Yeah." I cleared my throat. "Yeah, I'm in here."

There was a pause. "Lucian is requesting your presence immediately." Another gap of silence followed. "He is also requesting to see you, Seth."

Seth frowned as the gleam in his eyes faded. "How in the world does he know I'm in here?"

"Leon… just knows." I pushed at him weakly. "Get off."

"I was trying to." Seth rolled over, running his hands down his face.

I scowled at him and sat up. A wave of dizziness swept over me. My gaze moved from Seth to my curled hand. Slowly, I opened it. Glowing in iridescent blue was a glyph that was shaped like a staple. Both of my hands were marked.

He leaned over my shoulder. "Hey, you got another one."

I swung at him and missed by a mile. "You did that on purpose."

Seth shrugged as he straightened his shirt. "You didn't mind, now did you?"

"That's not the point, you douchenozzle. I shouldn't have these."

He glanced up, brows arched. "Look, I didn't do it on purpose. I have no idea how or why it happens. Maybe it's happening because it's supposed to."

"People are waiting," Leon called from the hallway. "Time is of the essence."

Seth rolled his eyes. "They couldn't have waited another thirty or sixty minutes?"

"I don't know what you think you were going to get accomplished in that extra time."

Still feeling a little dizzy, I swayed when I stood and looked down at my unbuttoned shirt and bra. *Now how did that happen?*

Seth grinned at me.

I fumbled with the buttons, turning a thousand shades of red. My anger with Seth smoldered inside me, but I was too tired to get into a verbal smackdown. And then there was Lucian. What the hell could he want?

"You missed one." Seth sprung to his feet and clasped the button above my navel. "And stop blushing. Everyone is going to think we weren't training."

"We were?"

His grin spread, and I wanted to smack him upside the head. But I took the time to smooth my hair and tug out the wrinkles in my shirt. By the time we met Leon in the hall, I felt like I looked pretty decent.

Leon eyed me like he knew exactly what had been going on in the dorm. "Nice of you two to finally join me."

Seth shoved his hands into his pockets. "We take training really seriously. Sometimes we get so caught up in it, it takes a few minutes for us to come down."

My mouth dropped open. Now I really wanted to hit him.

Leon's eyes narrowed on Seth then he turned stiffly, gesturing for us to follow him. I trailed behind the two, wondering why Leon would care what I was doing in the room. Everyone wanted us to embrace our Apollyon goodness. Then I thought of Aiden and my heart seized.

Well, probably not *everyone*.

A weird, twisty feeling took over my stomach. What'd just happened in there? We'd gone from talking to full-on making out when nothing like that had occurred since the Catskills. I glanced down at my hands.

The super-special cord had happened.

I felt sort of sick when I looked up and watched Seth swagger down the hall. Cheeks glowing, he looked like he could barely contain the energy rushing through him. Confusion swept through me. The whole energy transfer thing had actually felt good, and so had the stuff afterward, but Aiden's face haunted me.

Seth glanced over his shoulder at me as Leon opened the door. Darkness had already started to fall, but the shadow that crept over Seth's face was no product of the night.

I tried to build up the wall around me.

And I failed.

CHAPTER 4

I WAS EXHAUSTED BY THE TIME I DROPPED INTO THE seat furthest from Marcus' desk. Those stairs had been a bitch, but I was grateful that I hadn't been expected to walk to the adjoining island where Lucian lived. I didn't believe I'd have made it. All I wanted to do was curl up and go to bed—go anywhere other than this brightly-lit room.

"Where is everyone?" Seth asked, standing behind me. His hands rested on the back of the chair, but his fingers, shielded by my hair, were pressed into my back. "I thought time was of the essence."

Leon looked smug. "I must have mistaken the time."

A tired smile tugged at my lips as I pulled my legs up, tucking them under me. Like I said, Leon was the King of Impeccable Timing. Maybe I'd get a nap before everyone showed up. I closed my eyes, scarcely paying attention to Leon and Seth trying to outsnark one another.

"Most training doesn't occur in a dorm room," Leon said. "Or have they drastically changed methods?"

Snark point two to Leon.

"The kind of training that we have to do is unconventional." Seth paused and I knew he had that horrible smile on his face. The one I'd wanted to drop-kick off so many times. "Not that a Sentinel would fully understand the amount of effort that goes into preparing an Apollyon."

Snark point three to Seth.

I yawned as I scooted down in the chair, resting my cheek on the back of the chair.

"Is something wrong, Alexandria?" Leon asked. "You look awfully pale."

"She's fine," Seth answered. "Our training was rather… exhausting. You know, there's a lot of moving around. Sweating, thrus—"

"Seth," I snapped, reluctantly handing over snark points four, five, and six to him.

Thankfully, the doors to Marcus' office opened and an entourage of people entered. First was my pure-blood uncle, the Dean of the Covenant in North Carolina. Behind him was my pure-blood stepfather Lucian, the Minister of the North Carolina Covenant. He was in his ridiculous white robes, his stark black hair hanging down his back, secured in a leather thong. He was a handsome man, but there was always a level of coldness and fakeness to him no matter how warm his words might be. He was flanked by four of his Guards, as if he expected a fleet of daimons to jump on him and suck out all his aether. I suppose, given the recent events, he couldn't be too careful. And behind them were Guard Linard and Aiden.

I averted my eyes and prayed Seth actually kept his mouth shut.

Marcus glanced at me as he sat behind his desk, brows rising curiously. "Are we keeping you from a nap, Alexandria?"

No, *how are you?* or *good to see you alive*. Yeah, he loved me lots.

Leon retreated to the corner, folding his arms. "They were *training,*" he paused, "in her room."

I wanted to die.

Marcus frowned, but Lucian—oh, dear Lucian—had a typical response. Sitting down in one of the chairs across from Marcus, he spread out his robes and laughed. "It is expected. They are young and drawn to one another. You cannot fault them for seeking privacy."

I couldn't help it. My eyes found Aiden. He stood beside Leon and Linard, his gaze flitting over the room, stopping and lingering on me before passing on. I let go of the breath I'd been holding and focused on my uncle.

Marcus' eyes were like emerald jewels, just like my mother's, but harder. "Fated or not, the rules of the Covenant still apply to them,

Minister. And from what I've heard, Seth has a hard time remaining in his own room at your house during the night."

This seriously couldn't get any more embarrassing.

Seth leaned over the back of my chair and lowering his head. He whispered in my ear. "I think we've been found out."

There was no way Aiden could've heard Seth, but anger rolled off him in waves, so much so that Seth tipped his head up, met Aiden's stare, and smiled.

I'd had it. Sitting up straight, I knocked Seth's arm off the back of my chair. "Is this why we're having a meeting? Because, seriously, I could really use a nap instead."

Marcus eyed me coolly. "Actually, we are here to discuss the events at the Council."

Ice drenched my stomach. I tried to keep my face blank, but my eyes darted to Aiden. He didn't look too concerned. In fact, he was still eyeballing Seth.

"There are several things that we have discovered regarding our trip," Lucian said.

Marcus nodded, his fingers forming a steeple under his chin. "The daimon attack is one of them. I know that some have been able to plan attacks."

My mother had been one of them. She'd been behind the attack on Lake Lure during the summer, the very first proof some daimons could form cohesive plans.

"But that type of large-scale attack is... it's unheard of," Marcus continued, glancing at me. "I know... I know your mother had insinuated that such was coming, but to pull something off of that kind of nature seems improbable."

Aiden cocked his head to the side. "What are you saying?"

"I think they had help."

My heart tripped up. "From the inside—from a half or a pure?"

Lucian huffed. "That is absurd."

"I do not think that is entirely out of the question," Leon said, eyes narrowing upon the Minister.

"No half or pure would willingly assist a daimon." Lucian folded his hands.

"It may not be willingly, Minister. The pure or half may've been coerced," Marcus continued, and where I should've felt relief, something ugly still sat inside me. What if someone had actually let them in past the gates?

No. No way could that have happened. If Marcus' suspicions were right, it had to be under duress.

Marcus glanced at me. "It's something we need to keep in mind for Alexandria's safety. The daimons were there for her. They could try it again. Capture a half or pure Guard or Sentinel, have them lead the daimons right to her. It is something to be aware of."

I grew very still and I imagined so did Seth and Aiden. The daimons hadn't been after me. It'd been a lie that we told so that I could leave the Catskills immediately after… after I'd killed the pure-blood Guard.

"I agree." Aiden's voice was remarkably even. "They could make another attempt."

"Speaking of her safety," Lucian twisted in his seat toward me. "Minister Telly's intentions were painfully clear, and if I'd been aware of what he'd planned, I never would have agreed to the Council session. My utmost priority is to see that you remain safe, Alexandria."

I shifted uncomfortably. Growing up, Lucian hadn't even pretended to care about me. But since I'd returned to the Covenant at the end of May, he'd acted like I was his long-lost daughter. He didn't fool me. If I weren't the second coming of the Apollyon, he wouldn't be sitting here right now. Who was I kidding? I'd probably have been eaten by daimons in Atlanta.

His eyes met mine. I'd never liked his eyes. They were an unnatural black—the color of obsidian and cold. Up close, there didn't seem to be any pupils. "I'm afraid that Minister Telly may have been behind the compulsion and the unsavory act of giving you that drink."

I suspected as much, but to hear him say it left me queasy. As the Head of all the Ministers, Telly exerted a lot of control. If it hadn't been for Minister Diana Elders' vote, I would've been cast into slavery.

"Do you think he will attempt something else?" Aiden's deep, melodic voice was hard not to respond to.

Lucian shook his head. "I would like to say no, but I fear that he will attempt something again. The best we can do at this point is to ensure that Alexandria stays out of trouble and does not give the Head Minister any excuse to place her into servitude."

Several pairs of eyes landed on me. I smothered another yawn and tipped my chin up. "I'll *try* not to do anything crazy."

Marcus arched a brow. "That would be a nice change."

I glared at him, rubbing my left palm over my bent knee. The skin still felt weird and tingly.

"Isn't there a more proactive method?" Seth asked, leaning on my chair. "I think we all can agree that Telly will try something again. He doesn't want Alex to Awaken. He's afraid of us."

"Afraid of you," I muttered, then yawned again.

Seth tipped my chair back in response, causing me to grasp the arms. He grinned at me, which was so at odds with his next words. "He almost had Alex. He was one vote shy of servitude. Who says he won't build some trumped-up charge against her and sway their votes in his favor?"

"Diana will never compromise her position to serve Telly's wishes," Marcus said.

"Whoa. On a first name basis?" I said.

Marcus ignored my comment. "What do you suggest, Seth?"

Seth pushed off the back of my chair and moved to stand beside me. "How about removing him from his position? Then he has no power."

Lucian watched Seth with an approving look in his eyes and I'd swear Seth beamed. Almost like he'd brought home his report card with all A's on it and was about to get a pat on the head. *Weird.* Weird and extraordinarily creepy.

"Are you suggesting a political coup? That we rebel against the Head Minister?" Marcus turned his disbelief on Lucian. "And you have no response to this?"

"I would never want to stoop to something so distasteful, but Head Minister Telly is rooted in the old ways. You know that he wants nothing more than to see us regress as a society," Lucian replied smoothly. "He will go to great extremes to protect his beliefs."

"What are his beliefs, exactly?" I asked. The leather made unattractive squishing noises as I sank back in the seat.

"Telly would love to see us no longer intermingling with mortals. If he had his way, we'd do nothing but dedicate ourselves to worshipping the gods." Lucian smoothed a pale hand over his robes. "He feels it is the Council's duty to protect Olympus instead of leading our kind into the future and stepping into our rightful place."

"And he sees us as a threat to the gods," Seth said, crossing his arms. "He knows he can't come after me, but Alex is vulnerable until she Awakens. Something has to be done about him."

I made a face. "I'm not vulnerable."

"But you are," Aiden's eyes were gunmetal gray when they settled on me. "If Head Minister Telly truly fears that Seth will be a threat down the road, then he will seek to take you out of the equation. He has the power to do so."

"I understand that, but Seth isn't going to go crazy on the Council. He's not going to try to take over the world once I Awaken." I glanced at him. "Right?"

Seth smiled. "You'd be by my side."

Ignoring him, I wrapped my arms around my legs. "Telly can't want to take me out just on some idea of a threat." I thought of my father. I knew beyond a doubt he was behind that, too. "There has to be more to it than that."

"Telly lives to serve the gods," Lucian said. "If he feels they may be threatened, that is all the reason he needs."

"Do you not live to serve the gods?" Leon asked.

Lucian barely looked in the direction of the pure-blood Sentinel. "I do, but I also live to serve the best interests of my people."

Marcus rubbed his brow wearily. "Telly is not our only concern. There are also the gods themselves."

"Yes." Lucian nodded. "There is also the issue of the furies."

I ran my hand over my forehead, forcing myself to concentrate on this conversation. It was a big deal that they were even including me in this. So I guessed I should pay attention and keep the snark to a minimum.

"The furies attack only when they perceive a threat to the pure-bloods and to the gods," Marcus explained. "Their appearance at the Covenants before the daimon attack was solely a precautionary act from the gods. It was a warning that if we could not keep the daimon population under control, or if our existence was exposed to the mortals through the daimons' actions, they'd respond. And when the daimons launched their attack on the Covenant, the furies were released. But they went after *you*, Alex. Even though there were daimons they could've fought, they perceived you as the biggest threat."

The furies had ripped through daimon and innocent alike in those bloody moments after the daimon siege and had come after me. Not going to lie—I'd never been more terrified in my life.

"They will be back," Leon added. "It is their nature. Maybe not immediately, but they will."

My head was spinning. "I figured as much, but I haven't done anything wrong."

"You exist, my dear. That is all they need," said Lucian. "And you are the weaker of the two."

I was also the sleepier of the two.

Seth rocked back on his heels. "If they come back, I'll destroy them."

"Good luck with that." I closed my eyes, giving them a break from the harsh light. "They'll just burn up and come right back."

"Not if I kill them."

"With what?" asked Aiden. "They are gods. No weapon made by man or demigod will kill them."

When I opened my eyes, Seth was smiling. "Akasha," he said. "That would put them down permanently."

"You don't have that kind of power now," Leon stated, jaw tensed.

Seth just continued to smile until Lucian cleared his throat and spoke. "I never did get to see the furies. It would have been… something to witness."

"They were beautiful," I said. Everyone turned to me. "At first, they were. Then they changed. I'd never seen anything like that. Anyway, one said that Thanatos wouldn't be pleased with their return after… I got rid of them. She said something about the road the Powers had chosen and that I would be their tool. The oracle had said something like that too, before she poofed."

"Who are 'the Powers'?" Leon asked.

Aiden nodded. "That's a good question."

"That is not a concern. The furies are," Lucian responded, dismissing the concept with a flick of his slender wrist. "Like Telly, they are operating on old fears. The furies are loyal to Thanatos. If the furies come again, I fear that Thanatos will not be far behind."

Marcus dropped his hand to the top of the glossy mahogany desk. "I cannot have the gods attacking the school. I have hundreds of students I must keep safe. The furies show no discrimination in their kills."

Not once had he mentioned keeping me safe. That kind of stung. We might be related, but it didn't make us a real family. Marcus hadn't even smiled at me—not once. I really didn't have anyone left. That made getting to my father all the more important.

"I suggest we move Alex to a safe place," Lucian offered.

"What?" My voice squeaked.

Lucian glanced at me. "The furies know to look for you here. We could move you some place safe."

Seth sat on the arm of my chair, crossing his long legs at the ankle. He didn't seem surprised by any of this.

I tapped his back, gaining his attention. "Did you know about this?" I whispered.

He didn't answer.

The look I gave him promised trouble later and not the fun kind. Seth could've at least given me a heads-up about this.

Aiden frowned. "Where would you take her?"

My eyes went to him again. The muscles in my chest clenched when our gazes locked momentarily. At the moment, if I concentrated hard enough, I could still feel his arms around me. Not the best tactic when everyone was discussing my future like I wasn't even sitting here.

"The fewer people who know, the better," Lucian replied. "She would be well protected by my best Guards and Seth."

Marcus appeared to consider this. "We wouldn't have to worry about the furies attacking here." He looked in my direction, his expression guarded. "But if she leaves the Covenant now, she will not graduate and become a Sentinel."

My stomach turned over. "Then I can't leave. I have to graduate."

Lucian smiled, and I wanted to punch him. "Dear, you do not have to worry about becoming a Sentinel now. You will become an Apollyon."

"I don't care! Being an Apollyon isn't my whole life! I need to become a Sentinel. That's what I've always wanted." Those last words sat oddly on my chest. What I always wanted was to have choices. Becoming a Sentinel was the lesser of two evils in reality.

"Your safety is more important than what you desire." Lucian's voice was hard, throwing me back to when I'd been the little girl who'd ventured into a room I wasn't supposed to be in or dared to speak out of turn. That was the real Lucian and it snuck through his facade.

No one else noticed.

I squeezed my thighs until they ached. "No. I need to become a Sentinel." I looked at Seth for help, but he was suddenly interested in the tips of his boots. "None of you understand. Daimons took my mom from me and turned her into a monster. Look at what they did to me! No." I struggled for breath, knowing I was two seconds from losing it. "Besides, no matter where you take me, the furies will find me. They're gods! It's not like I can hide forever."

Lucian faced me fully. "It would give us time."

Anger rushed through me. I almost came out of the chair. "Time for me to Awaken? Then what? You don't care what happens to me?"

"Nonsense," Lucian said. "Not only will you have power, Seth will be able to protect both of you."

"I don't need Seth to protect me!"

Seth glanced over his shoulder at me. "You know how to make a guy feel useful."

"Shut up," I hissed. "You know what I mean. I can fight. I've killed daimons and I fought the furies and lived. I don't need Seth to be my babysitter."

Leon snorted. "You do need a babysitter, but I doubt he's qualified for the job."

Aiden coughed, but it sounded an awful lot like a choked laugh.

"Do you think you can do a better job?" Seth's voice was casual, but I felt him tense. I also knew he wasn't talking to Leon. "Because you're more than welcome to try," he added.

Aiden's eyes went from gray to silver. His full lips tilted into a smirk as he met Seth's stare. "I think we both know the answer to that."

My jaw hit the floor.

Straightening, Seth squared his shoulders. Before he could say something, which I felt sure would be very bad, I jumped from the seat. "I can't leave the—" Bright dots danced before my eyes, making everything a blur as my stomach tilted dangerously. "Whoa…"

Seth was at my side in an instant, an arm around my waist. "Are you okay?" He lowered me back into the chair. "Alex?"

"Yeah," I breathed, slowly lifting my head. Everyone was staring at me. Aiden had stepped forward, eyes wide. My cheeks burst with heat. "I'm fine. Seriously. I'm just a little tired."

Seth knelt beside me, taking my hand. He squeezed gently as he glanced over his shoulder. "She's had a cold all week."

"She's had a *cold*?" Lucian curled his lip. "How… very mortal."

I shot him a hateful look.

"But we… halfs do not get sick," Marcus said, eyes narrowing on me.

"Well, you can tell that to the box of Kleenex I've been living with." I dragged my fingers through my hair. "Seriously, I'm fine now."

Marcus suddenly stood. "I think we are done for the evening. We all can agree that nothing needs to be decided at this moment."

Lucian, who had grown quiet and docile, nodded.

The discussion ended and I got a momentary reprieve. I wouldn't be leaving the Covenant now, but I couldn't shake the dread gnawing at my stomach that, eventually, the decision wouldn't be mine to make.

CHAPTER 5

I OVERSLEPT THE FOLLOWING MORNING AND MISSED my first two classes. It kind of worked out, since I didn't have to face Olivia after trying to choke her the day before, but the exhaustion from the previous night continued to drag at me. I spent the break before my afternoon classes arguing with Seth.

"What is your deal?" He pushed his chair back.

"I've already told you." I glanced around the sparsely populated common room. It was better than eating in the cafeteria where everyone stared at us. "I know you knew about Lucian's plan to put me in the Apollyon Relocation Program."

Seth groaned. "Okay. Fine. He may have mentioned it. So what? It's a smart idea."

"It's not a smart idea, Seth. I need to graduate, not go into hiding." I looked down at my barely touched cold-cut sub. My stomach turned over. "I'm not going to run."

He leaned back in the chair, lacing his hands behind his head. "Lucian does have your best interests in mind."

"Oh, gods. Do not start with the Lucian crap. You don't know him like I do."

"People change, Alex. He may have been a giant douche before, but he's changed."

I leveled a look at him, and suddenly, I didn't even know why I was arguing. My shoulders slumped. "What is the point, anyway?"

Seth frowned. "What do you mean?"

"Nothing." I toyed with my straw.

He leaned forward, nudging my plate. "You should eat more."

"Thanks, Dad," I snapped.

He held up his hands, sitting back. "Simmer down, cuddle-bunny."

"All of this is your fault, anyway."

Seth snorted. "How is this my fault?"

I scowled. "No one wants to kill you, but you're the one who'll have the potential to wipe out the entire Olympian Court. But everyone is like, 'Let's kill the one who isn't doing anything!' And you can just skip off into the sunset while I'm dead."

His lips twitched again. "I wouldn't skip off if you were dead. I'd be sad."

"You'd be sad because you wouldn't be the God Killer." I picked up my sub, turning it over slowly. "Olivia hates me."

"Alex…"

"What?" I looked up. "She does, because I let Caleb die."

His eyes narrowed. "You didn't let Caleb die, Alex."

I sighed, suddenly wanting to cry. It was official: I was certifiably whacked out today. "I know. I miss her."

"Have you tried talking to her?" His eyes widened at my look. He motioned at the sub. "Eat."

Grudgingly, I took a huge, sloppy bite.

Seth arched a brow as he watched me. "Hungry?"

I swallowed. The food formed a heavy lump in my stomach. "No."

We didn't talk for a few minutes. Without wanting to, I turned over my left hand and looked at where the staple-shaped rune glowed softly. "Did… did you do this on purpose?"

"What? The rune?" He took my hand, holding it so my palm faced up. "No, I didn't do it on purpose. I've already told you that."

"I don't know. You looked like you were concentrating really hard when it happened."

"I was concentrating on your emotions." Seth ran his thumb around the glyph, coming close to touching it. "You don't like this, do you?"

"No," I whispered. Another mark meant one more step toward becoming someone—something else.

"It's natural, Alex."

"It doesn't feel natural." My eyes flicked to his. "What does this one mean?"

"Strength of the gods," he answered, surprising me. "The other one means courage of the soul."

"Courage of the soul?" I laughed. "That doesn't make sense."

His hand slid to my wrist, resting his thumb over my pulse. "They are the first marks the Apollyons receive."

My wrist seemed so small in his hand, fragile even. "Did yours come early?"

"No."

I sighed. "What happened... between us last night?"

A wicked grin played over his lips. "Well, most kids call it making out."

"That's not what I meant." I pulled my hand free and rubbed my palm over the edge of the table. "I felt it—the energy or whatever you want to call it—leaving me and going into you."

"Did it hurt you?"

I shook my head. "It kind of felt good."

His nostrils flared as if he smelled something he liked. Then, without any warning, he leaned over the table between us, clasped my cheeks and brought his mouth to mine. The kiss was soft, teasing, and felt really weird. Kissing last night really hadn't counted—or at least I'd convinced myself of that. So this was the first real kiss since the Catskills, and it was a totally public display. And I was still holding the sub in my right hand. So yeah, it felt bizarre.

Seth pulled back, smiling. "I think we should do that more often, then."

My cheeks were burning, because I knew people were staring. "Kissing?"

He laughed. "I'm all about kissing more, but I meant what happened last night."

Out of nowhere, anger crept over me. "Why? Did you feel anything?"

One brow arched. "Oh, I felt something."

I took a deep breath and let it out slowly. "I meant when you were holding my hand and the mark appeared. Did you feel anything?"

"Nothing you apparently want me to talk about."

"Gods." I squeezed the sub. Globs of mayo splattered off the plastic plate. "I don't even know why I'm talking to you."

Seth slowly exhaled. "Are you PMSing or something? Because your mood swings are killing me."

I stared a moment, thinking *wow, did he really just go there*? And then I cocked back my arm and launched the sub across the table. It hit his chest with a somewhat satisfying plop, but it was the look on his face as he jumped out of his seat that almost had me smiling. A cross between disbelief and horror marked his features as he knocked pieces of lettuce and ham off his shirt and pants.

There were only a handful of people in the common room, mostly younger pure-bloods. All of them stared, eyes wide.

Throwing a sub at the Apollyon probably wasn't something that should be done in public. But I couldn't help it; I laughed.

Seth's head jerked up. His eyes were a heated, angry ocher. "Did that make you feel better?"

My eyes watered from laughing so hard. "Yeah, it kind of did."

"You know, let's cancel training after class for today." His jaw flexed, cheeks flushed. "Get some rest."

I rolled my eyes. "Whatever."

Seth opened his mouth to say something else, but stopped. Brushing off the last of the ham and cheese, he pivoted around and left. I couldn't believe I'd just thrown my lunch at Seth. That seemed a little extreme even for me.

But it was funny.

I giggled to myself.

"Are you going to clean that up?"

Jumping a little in my seat, I looked up. Linard stepped out from behind one of the columns, eyeing the mess on the floor. "Are you, like, watching me?"

He smiled tightly. "I'm here to make sure you are safe."

"And *that* is kind of creepy." I pushed out of my seat, grabbing a napkin off my plate. I picked up what I could, but the mayo was stuck to the carpet. "Is this Lucian's idea?"

"No." He folded his hands behind his back. "It was Dean Andros' request."

I stilled. "For real?"

"For real," he replied. "You should get going. Your next class will begin soon."

I nodded absently, tossed my trash, and grabbed my bag. Marcus' order surprised me. I expected Lucian to sic his Guards on me. He wouldn't want anything to happen to his precious Apollyon. Maybe Marcus didn't find me as distasteful as I thought he did.

Linard followed me out of the common room, keeping a discreet distance. It reminded me of the day I'd bought the spirit boats that Caleb and I had released into the sea. The memory tugged at my heart and worsened my foul mood. I was like a zombie in the rest of my classes. After a quick change into my training clothes, I walked into Gutter Fighting. Instructor Romvi looked absurdly pleased with my appearance.

I dropped my bag and leaned against the wall, pretending that I wasn't bothered by the fact that I had no one to talk to. The last time I'd even been in this class, Caleb had still been alive.

Pressing my lips together, I let my gaze roam over the wall where the weapons were kept. I'd grown so used to this room during my practices with Aiden that it was like home to me. Standing near the wall of things meant to kill daimons with, Jackson grinned at something another half-blood said. Then he looked straight at me and smirked.

Once upon a time I'd found him hot, but somewhere between my daimon mom murdering his girlfriend's parents—if he was actually still with Lea—and the last time I squared off with him, I'd stopped thinking so highly of him.

I held his stare until he looked away. Then I continued my perusal. Olivia stood next to Luke, tying her curly hair into a ponytail. Bruises marked the caramel-colored skin of her neck. I glanced down at my hands. I'd done that.

Gods, what had I been thinking? Guilt and shame tore through me. When I looked up, Luke was watching me. His stare wasn't hostile or anything, just… sad.

I looked away, chewing on my lip. I did miss my friends. And I really missed Caleb.

Class quickly began, and even though I was tired, I threw myself into it. I got paired with Elena for a series of cinch work and holds. Going through the various techniques, my brain was finally able to shut down. Here, in training, I didn't think of anything. There was no sorrow or loss, no fate to deal with or father to save. I imagined this was what being a Sentinel would be like. When I'd eventually go out hunting, I wouldn't have to think about anything other than locating daimons and killing them. Maybe that was the real reason behind wanting to be a Sentinel, because then I could go through life… and do what? Kill. Kill. And kill some more.

That wasn't what I really wanted, deep down inside. I was just realizing that now?

Even slow on my feet, I was a bit faster than Elena. When we moved into take-downs and reversals, which consisted of getting thrown down and trying to get out of it, I was able to keep her pinned, but I was slowing down, growing weary.

She broke my hold and tipped her hips, rolling me onto my back. Staring down at me, she frowned. "Are… are you feeling okay? You look really pale."

I really needed to Google how long the lingering effects of a cold lasted, because this was seriously getting annoying. All I wanted was a bed. Before I could respond to Elena's question, Instructor Romvi appeared behind us. I bit back a groan.

"If you're able to talk, perhaps you are not training hard enough." Romvi's pale eyes were like glaciers. He loved to terrorize me in class; I'm sure he'd missed me. "Elena, off the mats."

She stood and slinked off, leaving me with the Instructor. Around us, students were sparring. I rolled to my feet and shifted my weight restlessly, preparing myself mentally for whatever he was going to throw at me. I turned away, placing my hands on my hips.

His hand smacked down on my shoulder. "One should never turn their back in war."

Shrugging his grip off, I faced him. "I didn't realize we were at war."

Something gleamed in his eyes. "We are always at war, especially in my class." He looked down his hawkish nose at me, which was a common practice since he was a pure-blood who'd once been a Sentinel. "Speaking of which, it is nice of you to finally join us, Alexandria. I was beginning to believe you thought training was no longer necessary."

Several responses rolled to the tip of my tongue, but I knew better than to let them out.

He looked disappointed. "I heard that you fought during the daimon siege."

Knowing fewer words usually ended with less of my butt being kicked, I nodded while I pictured a pegasus landing on his head and biting him in the neck.

"You also fought the furies and survived. Only warriors could claim such a feat."

My gaze slid past him to where Olivia and Luke now stood watching me from the edge of the mats. How many times had we been in this position? But this was different, because Caleb used to be among them.

"Alexandria?"

I focused on him, mentally cringing. I should never take my eyes off Romvi when he was talking. "I did fight the furies."

Interest sparked in his eyes. "Show me what you did."

Caught off-guard, I took a step back. "What do you mean?"

A small smile tugged up one side of his lips. "Show me how you fought the furies."

I dampened my lips nervously. I had no idea how I'd fought the furies and survived—only that everything had turned amber, like someone had splashed the tawny color over my eyes. "I don't know. Everything was happening so fast."

"You don't know." He raised his hand and the sleeve of his tunic-style shirt slipped up his arm, revealing the downward-turned torch tattoo. "I find that hard to believe."

I experienced a momentary lapse of sanity. "What's up with the tattoo?"

His jaw clenched, and I expected him to attack. But he didn't. "Jackson!"

Loping onto the mats, Jackson came to stop and rested his hands on his narrow hips. "Sir?"

Romvi's eyes held mine. "I want you to spar."

I glanced at Jackson's smiling face. What Romvi wanted me to do was show him how I'd fought the furies and survived, using Jackson to do so. It didn't matter who I was fighting; I couldn't show what I didn't know.

As Romvi headed off the mats, he stopped and whispered to Jackson. Whatever he was saying brought an easy grin to Jackson's face right before he nodded.

Wiping my hand over my clammy forehead, I slowed down my breathing and tried to ignore the fine tremors running through my legs. Even tired I could take Jackson. He was a good fighter, but I was better. I had to be better.

"You're going to be hurting by the end of class," Jackson taunted, cracking his knuckles.

I raised a brow and motioned him forward with one hand. I may've have a serious hankering for a pillow, but I could take him.

I waited until he was only a foot away before I launched a brutal offensive. I was fast and light on my feet. He would feint in one direction to avoid a sharp thrust and end up with a sideways kick in his back. Before long, he ended up on his back, panting and swearing from a fierce spin kick.

"I'm going to be hurting?" I said, standing above him. "Nah, I don't think so."

Breathing harshly, he jumped onto the balls of his feet. "Wait and see, baby."

"Baby?" I repeated. "I'm not your baby."

Jackson didn't respond to that. He flew into a butterfly kick, which I dodged. Those kicks were brutal. Blow after blow, we went after each other—each hit more vicious then the last. Admittedly, I was taking this a little too seriously myself. I wasn't going easy on the douchebag. A weird kind of darkness rose in me as I blocked a series of kicks and jabs that would have brought even Aiden down. I grinned in spite of the sweat pouring off me and the way my forearms ached. I channeled all of my earlier anger into fighting Jackson.

Our sparring eventually drew the attention of the other students. I was only slightly surprised when Jackson's fist glanced off my jaw and Instructor Romvi didn't call the fight off. If anything, he looked like he was getting his jollies off by watching the brutal fight.

So Jackson didn't want to play by the rules and Romvi didn't care? Whatever. He swung his fist around again, but this time I caught his hand and twisted it backward.

Jackson broke the hold too easily, which showed that I was reaching my own limits. I turned on my heel, saw that the overhead lights flickered—or was it my eyes? — and with one powerful roundhouse kick, I took Jackson's legs right out from under him. There wasn't a moment to celebrate his obvious defeat. I saw Jackson move for my legs. I tried to jump like we'd been taught, but worn down, I was too slow. His leg caught mine, and I landed on my side, immediately rolling out of range.

"I'm sure that's not how you defeated the furies." Instructor Romvi sounded smug.

I didn't have a second to think about how much I wished I could drop-kick Romvi. Jackson whipped around. I scooted to the side, but his kick caught me in the ribs. Pain exploded, so unexpected and so intense, that I froze.

Sensing that Jackson wasn't done yet, I brought my hands up, but that teeny, tiny second cost me. Jackson's heel slipped past my hands, hitting my chin and cutting my lip right open. Something warm gushed into my mouth, and I saw flashes of light. Blood—I tasted blood. And beyond the flashing lights, I saw Jackson's boot come up one more time.

CHAPTER 6

JACKSON WAS GOING TO STOMP MY HEAD IN.

That was so not a part of training.

At that last possible second, someone caught Jackson by the waist and tossed him to the mat. My hands flew to my mouth. Something sticky and warm covered them immediately.

All I tasted was blood. Hesitantly, I ran my tongue along the inside of my mouth, checking to make sure I hadn't lost any teeth. When I figured that I still had a full set, I pushed to my feet, spitting out blood. Then I lunged at Jackson.

I came up short. Shock nearly brought me to my knees.

Jackson was already preoccupied with fending off someone else, and that someone was Aiden. Pain was momentarily forgotten as I vaguely wondered where *he* had come from. Aiden didn't watch my classes anymore. He didn't even train me, so it wasn't like he had a reason to be hanging around these rooms.

But he was here now.

Entranced by the odd blend of grace and brutality, I watched Aiden pull Jackson off the mat by the scruff of his shirt. Their faces were inches apart. The last time I had seen Aiden *that* angry was when he'd gone after Seth the night I'd been slipped the brew.

"That is not how you spar with your partner," Aiden said in a cold, low voice. "I'm sure Instructor Romvi has taught you better than that."

Jackson's eyes grew impossibly large. He was on the tips of his toes, arms dangling at his sides. It was then that I realized Jackson's nose was bleeding—bleeding worse than my mouth was. Someone had hit him—that someone most likely being Aiden. Because only a pure would be able to do that and have no one intervene.

He let go of Jackson. The half fell to his knees, cradling his face. Aiden spun around, his eyes quickly assessing the damage. Then he turned to Instructor Romvi, speaking too low and quick for me or the class to understand.

Before I knew what was happening, Aiden crossed the mats and caught hold of my arm. We didn't speak as he walked me from the training room. "My bag," I protested.

"I'll have someone retrieve it for you."

In the hall, he grasped my shoulders and turned me around. His eyes went from dark gray to silver when his gaze fell to my lip. "Instructor Romvi never should've allowed it to go that far."

"Yeah, I don't think he cared."

He swore.

I wanted to say something. Like "these things happen"… or at least, about how it could be expected since I didn't have a lot of friends here. Or maybe I should thank Aiden, but by the warring emotions playing out across his striking face I could tell he wouldn't appreciate it. Aiden was furious—furious for all the wrong reasons. He'd reacted as if a common *guy* had hit me, and not a half-blood. As a pure-blood, there had been no reason for him to intervene. That was the Instructor's job. Aiden had forgotten that in a moment of complete, unbridled rage.

"I shouldn't have done that—lost my temper," he said quietly, sounding and looking terribly young and vulnerable for someone I believed to be so powerful. "I shouldn't have hit him."

My eyes flicked across his face. Even though my face throbbed, I wanted to touch him. I wanted him to touch *me*. And then he did, but not in the way I wanted. Placing his hand on my lower back, he steered me toward the med office. I wanted to touch my mouth to see how bad it was. Actually, I wanted a mirror.

The pure-blood doctor took one look at my face and shook her head. "On the table."

I hoisted myself up. "Is it going to scar?"

The doc grabbed a cloudy-looking white bottle and several wads of cotton. "Not sure yet, but try not to talk right now. At least until I make sure there is no damage inside the lip, okay?"

"If it scars, I'm gonna be so pissed."

"Stop talking," Aiden said, leaning against the wall.

The doc shot him a smile, apparently not curious as to why I had been escorted by a pure. She turned back to me. "This may sting a bit." She dabbed the cotton over my lip. *Sting?*—it burned like crazy. I nearly jumped off the table.

"Antiseptic," she said, offering a sympathetic look. "We want to make sure you don't get any infections. Then you would scar."

Burning? I could deal with that. It took the doc a couple of minutes to clean up my lip. I waited, somewhat impatiently, for the verdict.

"I don't think you're going to need stitches on the lip itself. It's going to swell and be a bit tender for a while." She tipped my head back and gently poked at my mouth. "But I think we're going to need a stitch right... under your lip here."

I winced as she started poking there too and focused on her shoulder. *Show no pain. Show no pain. Show no pain.* The doc dipped her fingers in the brown jar and pressed the torn skin together. I yelped as a scalding pain radiated from the skin under my lip and spread across my face.

Aiden started forward, stopping when he seemed to realize there was nothing he could—or should—do. His hands fell to his sides, and his gaze met mine, eyes an endless thundering gray.

"Just a little bit more," she said soothingly. "Then it will all be over. You're lucky you didn't lose any teeth."

Then she squeezed the skin once more. This time I didn't make a sound, but I squeezed my eyes shut until lights danced behind my closed lids. I wanted to jump off the table and find Jackson. Hitting him would make me feel better. I believed in that.

The doc stepped back to the cabinets. Returning with a damp wipe, she started to clean the blood away, mindful of the stitch. "Next time you train her, be a little more careful. She's only this young and pretty once. Don't ruin it for her."

My eyes snapped to Aiden. "But—"

"Yes ma'am," Aiden interrupted, cutting me a stern look.

I stared back at him.

The doc sighed, shaking her head again. "Why do you halfs choose this? Surely, the alternative is better. Anyway, do you have any other injuries?"

"Uh, no," I mumbled. The doc's words surprised me.

"Yes," Aiden said. "Check the left side of her ribs."

"Oh come on," I said. "It's not that bad—" My words were cut off when the doc tugged up the hem of my shirt.

The doc pressed on my ribs, running her hands along the side. Her fingers were cool and quick. "None are broken, but this…" She frowned, leaning closer. Inhaling roughly, she dropped my shirt and faced Aiden. It seemed to take her a moment to collect herself. "Her ribs aren't broken, but they are bruised. She should take it easy for a few days. Also, she should limit talking so the stitching is not pulled."

Aiden looked like he wanted to laugh at the last suggestion. When he agreed with the doctor, she left the room pretty quickly.

"Why did you let her believe you did this?" I asked. "You're not even training me anymore."

"Aren't you supposed to be limiting your speaking?"

I rolled my eyes. "Now she thinks you're some great and terrible half-blood beater or something."

He pointed to the door. "It wouldn't be a far stretch of the imagination. Your Instructor allowed it to happen. The doc sees more cases like this than she probably cares to."

And she probably saw very few pure-bloods who even cared enough to make sure the half was okay. I sighed. "What were you doing over here, anyway?"

There was a ghost of a smile. "Didn't I tell you that making sure you stay safe is a full-time job?"

I started to smile, but quickly remembered not to. "Ow." I ignored his amused look. "So why were you here, for real?"

"I just happened to be over here and looked in the room." He shrugged, staring over my shoulder. "I saw you sparring and watched. The rest is history."

I didn't really believe him, but I let it go. "I would've had Jackson, you know? But this damn cold has kicked my butt."

Aiden's gaze settled on me again. "You shouldn't be sick." He stepped forward, reaching out and carefully placing his hand around my chin. He frowned. "How did you get sick?"

"I can't be the first half to get sick."

His thumb moved over my chin, careful to avoid the tender spot. That was Aiden, always so careful with me even though he knew I was tough. My heart jumped. "I don't know," he said, dropping his hand.

Unsure of how to respond, I shrugged. "Anyway, thanks for, um… getting Jackson to stop."

A hard, lethal look flickered across his face. "I will make sure Jackson is punished for what he has done. The Covenant has enough on its shoulders without halfs trying to kill one another."

I lightly touched my chin and winced. "I don't know if it was his idea."

Aiden grabbed my hand and pulled it away from my face. "What do you mean?"

Before I could answer, a fine shiver went down my spine. Seconds later, the door to the room flew up. Seth came through, eyes wide and lips thinned. His gaze went from my lip to where Aiden held my hand. "What the hell happened?"

Confusion and then understanding dawned on Aiden's face. He released my hand and stepped back. "She was sparring."

Seth shot Aiden a scathing look as he made his way to where I sat on the table. He clasped my chin with two slender fingers, just like Aiden had. My heart didn't flutter, but the cord did. "Who were you sparring with?"

"It's no big deal." I felt my cheeks start to burn.

"It doesn't look that way." Seth's eyes narrowed. "And you hurt elsewhere. I can feel it."

Gods, I really needed to work on that shield.

"Thank you for keeping an eye on her, Aiden." Seth didn't take his eyes off me. "I have it taken care of."

Aiden opened his mouth to say something, but then he closed it. He turned around and left the room quietly. The urge to jump off the table and run after him was hard to ignore.

"So what happened to your face?" he prompted again.

"I broke it," I muttered, straining away from him.

Seth tilted my chin to the side, frowning. "I can tell. This was really done while sparring?"

"Yeah, well, it was done to my face in class."

His frown deepened. "What is that supposed to mean?"

I knocked his hand away and slid off the table. "It's nothing. Just a busted lip."

"Busted lip?" He caught me around the waist, pulling me back. "I swear I see a boot print on your chin."

"Really—is it that bad?" I gingerly touched my chin, wondering what he'd think if he saw the boot print on my ribs.

"So vain." Seth grasped my hand. "Who were you sparring with?"

I sighed and tried to wiggle free, but it was no use. Seth—and the cord—wanted me to be here with him. I placed my cheek against his chest. "It doesn't matter. And aren't you still mad at me for throwing food at you, anyway?"

"Oh, I'm not too happy about that. I think mayo stains." His embrace loosened a little. "Does it hurt?"

Lying was pointless, but that's what I did. "No. Not at all."

"Yeah," he murmured against the top of my head. "So who did you spar with?"

I closed my eyes. Being this close to him, with the bond and everything, it was easy to stop thinking. Just like it had been while fighting. "I always get paired with Jackson."

After class the following day, I piddled around the training center. I found myself walking into the smaller room Aiden had been in when I'd found out about my father. Of course, he wasn't in there now. No one was. Dropping my bag just inside the door, I approached the punching bag hanging in the middle of the mats. It was an old, raggedy thing that had seen better days. Sections of the black leather had been knocked off. Someone had taken duct tape and patched it up. I ran my fingers over the edges of the tape.

Restlessness inched over my skin. The idea of going back to my dorm and spending time alone wasn't appealing. I hadn't seen Seth since he'd dropped me off yesterday. I guessed he was still pissed about the sub issue.

I pushed the bag with my palms. Then I flipped my hands over. Two softly glowing glyphs stared back at me.

My gaze went back to the punching bag. Had my father trained at this Covenant? Stood in this very room? It would explain how he'd known my mother so well. Again, melancholy crept over me.

The door to the room opened. I turned, expecting Guard Linard. But it wasn't him. My heart did a brief, stupid happy dance.

Aiden stepped inside the training room, the door sliding shut behind him. He wore the garb of a Sentinel: a black long-sleeved shirt and black cargos. I just stared at him like an idiot.

The way my body responded to him—to a pure-blood—was entirely unforgiveable. I knew this, but it didn't stop the way my breath caught or the warmth that stole over my skin. It wasn't just how he looked. Don't get me wrong—Aiden had the whole rare masculine beauty thing going for him. But it was more than that. He got me in a way very few people did. He didn't need a bond to do so, like Seth. Aiden figured me out through his unwavering patience… and not putting up with any of my crap. During the summer we'd spent hours together training and getting to know one another. I liked to think something beautiful had grown out of it. After what he'd done to protect me in New York… and then with Jackson, I could no longer really be angry with him about the day he'd told me he couldn't love me.

Aiden watched me curiously. "I saw Seth entering the main part of Deity Island and you weren't with him. I figured you'd be here."

"Why?"

He shrugged. "I just knew you'd be in one of the training rooms even though you were told to take it easy."

Whenever he was dealing with something, he hit the mats. I was the same way, which reminded me of the night I'd accosted him after learning my mom's true fate. I turned away, running my fingers down the center of the bag.

"How are you feeling—your ribs and lip?"

Both were sore, but I'd felt worse. "Good."

"Have you written the letter for me to give to Laadan?" he asked after a few moments.

My shoulders slumped. "No. I don't know what to say." It's not like I hadn't thought about it, but what do you say to a man you'd believed dead—a father you'd never met?

"Just tell him how you feel, Alex."

I laughed. "I don't know if he wants to know all of that."

"He would." Aiden paused, and the silence stretched out between us. "You've seemed... out of it lately."

I still felt out of it. "It's the cold."

"You looked like you were going to faint in Marcus' office and, let's face it, there is no reason why you couldn't have taken Jackson down yesterday... or at least moved out of the way. You've been looking exhausted, Alex."

Sighing, I faced him. He was slouched against the wall, hands shoved deep in his pockets. "So what are you doing here?" I asked, seeking to take the focus off me.

Aiden's expression was knowing. "Watching you."

Warmth fluttered in my chest. "Really? That's not creepy or anything."

A teeny tiny smile appeared. "Well, I'm on duty."

I glanced around the room. "Do you think there're daimons in here?"

"I'm not hunting right now." A lock of wavy, dark brown hair fell into his gray eyes as he tipped his head to the side. "I've been given a new assignment."

"Do tell."

"Along with my hunting, I'm guarding you."

I blinked and then I laughed so hard my ribs hurt. "Gods, it must suck to be you."

His brows furrowed. "Why would you think that?"

"You just can't get rid of me, can you?" I turned back to the bag, eyeing it for a weak spot. "I mean, not that you want to, but you keep getting saddled with me."

"I don't consider it being *saddled* with you. Why would you think that?"

I closed my eyes, wondering why I'd even said that. "So, Linard also has a new assignment?"

"Yes. You didn't answer my question."

And I wasn't going to. "Did Marcus ask you to do this?"

"Yes, he did. When you're not with Seth, it will either be Linard, Leon, or myself keeping watch. There's a good chance that whoever meant you harm—"

"Minister Telly," I added, balling up my fist.

"*Whoever* meant you harm in the Catskills will try something here. Then there are the furies."

I punched the bag, immediately wincing as it pulled the sore muscles over my ribs. Should've wrapped them first. Stupid. "You guys can't fight the furies."

"If they show up, we will try."

Shaking my hand, I took a step back. "You'll die trying. Those things—well, you saw what they are capable of. If they come, just step out of the way."

"What?" Disbelief colored his tone.

"I don't want to see people die for no reason."

"Die for no reason?"

"You know they'll just keep coming back, and I don't want someone to die when it all seems… inevitable."

The breath that he sucked in was sharp, audible in the small room. "Are you saying you believe your death is inevitable, Alex?"

I pushed the punching bag again. "I don't know what I'm saying. Just forget it."

"Something… something is different about you."

A desire to flee the room filled me, but I faced him instead. I glanced down at my palms. The marks were still there. Why did I keep checking on them like they'd go away or something? "So much has happened, Aiden. I'm not the same person."

"You were the same person the day you found out about your father," he said, eyes turning the color of a thundercloud.

Anger began low in my stomach, humming through my veins. "That has nothing to do with this."

Aiden pushed off the wall, hands coming out of his pockets. "What is *this*?"

"Everything!" My fingers dug into my palms. "What's the point in all of this? Let's just think hypothetically here for a second, okay? Say Telly or whoever doesn't manage to send me into servitude or kill me and the furies don't end up tearing me apart, I'm still going to turn eighteen. I'm still going to Awaken. So what's the point? Maybe I should leave." I stalked to where I'd dropped my bag. "Maybe Lucian will let me go to Ireland or something. I'd like to visit there before I be—"

Aiden grabbed my upper arm, turning me so that I faced him. "You said you had to stay at the Covenant so you could graduate, because you needed to be a Sentinel more than anyone else in the room." His voice dropped low as his eyes searched mine intently. "You were passionate about this. Has that changed?"

I yanked on my arm, but he held on. "Maybe."

The tips of Aiden's cheekbones flushed. "So you're giving up?"

"I don't think it's giving up. Call it… accepting reality." I smiled, but it felt icky.

"That is such bull, Alex."

I opened my mouth, but nothing came out. I'd argued to stay at the Covenant so I could become a Sentinel. And I knew, deep down, I still wanted to become one for my mom, for me, but I wasn't sure it was what I needed anymore. Or what I could agree with if I was honest with myself. After seeing those servants slaughtered on the floor and no one cared… no one came to help them.

I wasn't sure I could be a part of any of this.

"You've never been one to wallow in self-pity when the odds are stacked against you."

My jaw snapped. "I'm not wallowing in self-pity, Aiden."

"Really?" he said so softly. "Just like you aren't settling for Seth?"

Oh, good gods, not what I wanted to hear. "I'm not settling." *Liar,* whispered an evil voice in my head. "I don't want to talk about Seth."

He looked away for a second and then settled on me again. "I cannot believe you've forgiven him for what... for what he did to you."

"That wasn't his fault, Aiden. Seth didn't give me the brew. He didn't force—"

"He still knew better!"

"I'm not talking to you about this." I started to back away.

The hand beside him clenched. "So you are still... with him?"

Part of me wondered what had happened to the Aiden who held me in his arms when I'd told him about my father. That version had been easier to deal with. Then again, obviously I wasn't behaving like the person I was before either. And a part of me liked the way he said "him"—as if the very name made him want to punch something. "Define 'with,' Aiden."

He stared.

I tipped my head up. "Do you mean am I hanging out with him or are we just friends? Or did you mean to ask if we're sleeping together?"

His eyes narrowed into thin slits that shone a fierce silver.

"And why are you asking, Aiden?" I pulled back, and he let go. "Whatever the answer is doesn't even matter."

"But it does."

I thought about the marks and what they meant. "You have no idea. It doesn't. It's fate, remember?" I grabbed for my bag again, but he caught my arm again. I looked up, exhaling slowly. "What do you want from me?"

Realization crept over his expression, softening the hue of his eyes. "You're afraid."

"What?" I laughed, but it came out sounding like a nervous croak. "I'm not afraid."

Aiden's eyes drifted over my head and determination settled into his eyes. "Yes. You are." Without saying anything else, he turned me around and pulled me toward the sensory deprivation chamber.

My eyes shot wide. "What are you doing?"

He kept pulling until we stopped in front of the door. "Do you know what they use this for?"

"Um, to train?"

Aiden glanced down at me, smiling tightly. "Do you know how ancient warriors trained? They used to fight Deimos and Phobos, who used the warriors' worst fears against them during battle."

"Thanks for the daily weird god history lesson, but—"

"But since the gods of Fear and Terror have been off the circuit for awhile, they created this chamber. They believe that fighting using only your other senses to guide you is the best way to hone your skills and face your fears."

"Fears of what?"

He opened the door and a black hole greeted us. "Whatever fears are holding you back."

I dug in my heels. "I'm not afraid."

"You're terrified."

"Aiden, I am two seconds from—" My own surprised shriek cut me off as he hauled me into the chamber, shutting the door behind him, casting the room in utter darkness. My breath froze in my throat. "Aiden... I can't see anything."

"That's the point."

"Well, thanks, Captain Obvious." I reached out blindly, but only felt air. "What do you expect me to do in here?" As soon as the question left my mouth, I was assaulted with totally inappropriate images of all the things we could do in here.

"We fight."

Well, that blew. I inhaled, catching the scent of spice and ocean. Slowly, I lifted my hand. My fingers brushed against something hard and warm—his chest? Then there was nothing but empty space. Oh gods, this wasn't going to be good at all.

Suddenly, he grasped my arm and spun me around. "Get into stance."

"Aiden, I really don't want to do this right now. I am tired and I got kicked in the—"

"Excuses," he said, his breath dangerously close to my lips.

I locked up.

His hand was gone. "Get into stance."

"I am."

Aiden sighed. "No you're not."

"How do you know?"

"I can tell. You haven't moved," he said. "Now get into stance."

"Jeez, are you like a cat that can see in the dark or something?" When he didn't respond, I groaned and moved into the stance: arms halfway up, legs spread, and feet rooted in place. "All right."

"You need to face your fears, Alex."

I squinted, but saw nothing. "I thought you said I was fearless."

"You usually are." Suddenly, he was in front of me and his scent was driving me to distraction. "Which is why being scared now is so hard for you. Being afraid isn't a weakness, Alex. It's only a sign of something you must overcome."

"Fear is a weakness." Expecting him to still be in front of me, I decided to go along with him. I threw an elbow out, but he wasn't there. And then he was at my back, his breath dancing along the back of my neck. I swung around, grasping air. "What are you afraid of?"

A whoosh of air and he was behind me again. "This isn't about me, Alex. You're afraid of losing yourself."

"Of course not. What was I thinking?" I whipped around, cursing when he was gone. This was making me dizzy. "So why don't you tell me what I'm afraid of, oh-fearless-one?"

"You're scared of becoming something you have no control over." He caught my arm as I swung toward the sound of his voice. "That scares you to death." He let go, backing off.

He was right, and because of that, anger and embarrassment flooded me. Out of the darkness surrounding me, there was patch thicker than the rest. I threw myself at him. Anticipating the move, he caught me by the shoulders. I swung out, catching him in the stomach and chest.

Aiden pushed me back. "You're angry because I'm right."

A hoarse sound moved up my throat. I clamped my mouth shut and swung again. My elbow connected with something. "A Sentinel is never afraid. They'd never tuck tail and run."

"Are you tucking tail and running, Alex?"

The air stirred around me, and I jumped, narrowly missing what was probably a perfect leg sweep. "No!"

"That's not what it sounded like earlier," he said. "You wanted to take Lucian up on his offer. Visit Ireland?"

"I… I was…" Dammit, I hated it when he was right.

Aiden laughed from somewhere in the darkness.

I followed the sound. Going too far, too caught up in my anger, I lost my sense of balance when I attacked. Aiden caught my arm, but neither of us could gain our footing in the darkness. When I fell, he came with me. I landed on my back, with Aiden right on top of me.

Aiden caught my wrists before I could hit him again, pinning them above my head and down on the mats. "You always let your emotions get the best of you, Alex."

I tried to push him off, not trusting myself to speak. A sob was rising in my throat as I wiggled under him, managing to get one leg free.

"Alex," he warned softly. He pressed down, and when he breathed in, his chest rose against mine. In the utter darkness of the sensory deprivation room, his breath was warm against my lips. I didn't dare move. Not even a fraction of an inch.

His grip around my wrists slackened and his hand slipped over my shoulder, cupping my cheek. My heart was trying to come out of my chest in those seconds and every muscle locked up, tensed with anticipation. Was he going to kiss me? No. My lip was busted, but if he did, I wouldn't stop him and I knew that was so wrong. Chills went down my spine, and I relaxed under him.

"It's okay to be afraid, Alex."

I threw my head back then, wanting to be far away from him as much as I wanted to be right where I was.

"But you have nothing to fear." He guided my chin down with gentle fingers. "When will you learn?" His voice was heavy, gruff. "You're the only person who has control over who you become. You're too strong to ever lose yourself. I believe that. Why can't you?"

My breath came out shaky. His faith in me was nearly my undoing. The swelling in my chest would've lifted me off the mats. Several moments passed before I could speak. "What are you afraid of?" I asked again.

"I thought *you* said I was afraid of nothing once," he threw back.

"I did."

Aiden shifted slightly and his thumb caressed the curve of my cheek. "I'm afraid of something."

"What?" I whispered.

He drew in a deep, shuddering breath. "I'm afraid of never being allowed to feel what I do."

CHAPTER 7

THE AIR HITCHED AS I TRIED TO BREATHE. I WISHED I could see his face, his eyes. I wanted to know what he was thinking right at this moment, to touch him. But I lay there, my heart the only part of me that was moving.

His thumb brushed my cheek once more. "That's what scares me." Then he lifted himself off me. He backed up, the mats rolling under his unsteady step. "I'll be in the other training room when you're ready... to walk back to your dorm."

There was a brief flash of light from the outside training rooms when he slipped out the door and then darkness covered me again.

I didn't move but my brain raced on. He was afraid of never being allowed to feel what he did. Gods, I wasn't stupid, but I wished I was. I knew what he meant and also knew it didn't mean a damn thing. Part of me was angry, because he dared to say it when all it did was make my chest heavy with an aching want—a want so intense that it felt like it could crush me under its weight. And why admit it now, when I'd begged him before to just tell me he felt the same and he'd denied it? What was so different now?

And he was right about the other thing. I was terrified of becoming something I couldn't control, of losing myself to the bond, to Seth. It seemed like, even if I got past all the other obstacles in my way, there was *that* one—the one I couldn't hurdle over with good ole Alex recklessness.

The door opened again and the soft murmur of two male voices floated through the room. There was a deep, husky chuckle as the mats dipped under their feet. I could've said something, but I was too lost in my own thoughts to even utter a single word.

A second later, feet tangled with my legs and a surprised yelp sounded. The mats gave way as a body crashed down, half-sprawled atop me. I let out an *"oomph"* and pushed the hands off my chest.

"Gods, Alex!" exclaimed Luke, rolling off me and sitting up. "Holy Hades, what are you doing in here?"

"How'd you know it was me by just feeling up my boobs?" I grumbled, throwing an arm over my face.

"It's a superpower."

"Wow."

Luke snorted. I felt the mats roll as he faced his silent, mystery partner. "Hey," Luke said. "Can you give us a few minutes?"

"Sure. Whatever," the guy responded, dipping back out the door. The voice was super familiar, but as best as I tried, I couldn't place it.

"Pervert," I said. "What have you been using these rooms for, Luke? Naughty."

He laughed. "I'll go with something a hell of a lot more entertaining and normal than what you've been using them for. You're the one lying in a dark sensory room like a little freak. What are you doing in here? Plotting to take out the Covenant? Meditating? Self-pleasuring?"

I made a face. "Don't you have something better to do?"

"Yeah, I do."

"Then go. This room is already occupied."

Luke sighed. "You're being ridiculous."

I thought that was funny considering he had no idea why I was being a "little freak" in the sensory room. Luke had no idea what had just gone on in here. He probably thought I was hiding from everybody or having some sort of mental breakdown. That last part was still up in the air and could be a strong possibility. If it'd been Caleb who'd stumbled upon me, he would've known. I sucked in a sharp breath.

Missing him wasn't getting any easier, I realized suddenly.

"It sucks not having any friends, doesn't it?" Luke asked after a few moments.

I frowned. "You know, it's a good thing you can't become a therapist, because you really suck at the whole 'making people feel better about themselves' thing."

"But you do have friends," he continued as if I hadn't said a damn thing. "You just seem to have forgotten us."

"Like who?"

"Like me." Luke stretched out beside me. "And there's Deacon. And Olivia."

I snorted. "Olivia hates my guts."

"She does not."

"Bullshit." I dropped my arm, facing him in the darkness. "She blames me for Caleb's death. You heard her the day at his funeral and in the hallway yesterday."

"She's hurt, Alex."

"I'm hurt, too!" I sat up, crossing my legs.

The mats shook as Luke rolled onto his side. "She loved Caleb. As impractical as it is for any of us to love someone, she loved him."

"And I loved him. He was *my* best friend, Luke. She blames me for my best friend's death."

"She doesn't blame you anymore."

I smoothed back the tiny hairs that had escaped my ponytail. "When did that happen? In the last twenty-four hours?"

Undaunted, Luke sat up and somehow found my hand in the darkness. "The day she came up to you in the hallway, she wanted to apologize to you."

"That's funny, because I remember her saying something like I needed to rein in my grief." I didn't pull my hand away from his, because it did feel kind of nice for someone to touch me and nothing freaky happen. "Is that a new form of apology I'm unaware of?"

"I don't know what she was thinking. She wanted to apologize, but you wouldn't stop to talk to her," Luke explained softly. "She lost it. She was a bitch about it. Olivia knows that. Then you owning her ass in front of everyone didn't help, either."

The old Alex would have snickered at that, but it didn't make me feel good.

"You need to talk to her, Alex. You both need each other right now."

I pulled my hand free and came to my feet swiftly. The room suddenly felt stifling and unbearable. "I don't need her or anyone."

Luke was standing beside me in an instant. "And that was probably the most childish thing you've ever said."

I narrowed my eyes in his general direction. "And I have something even more childish to say to you. I'm like two seconds from hitting you."

"That's not very nice," Luke teased, stepping around me. "You need friends, Alex. As hot as Seth is, he can't be your only friend. You need girl time. You need someone you can cry to, someone who isn't trying to get in your pants. You need someone who wants to be around you not because of what you are, but who you are."

My jaw hit the mat. "Wow."

Luke must have sensed my stunned response, because he laughed. "Everyone knows what you are, Alex. And most people think it's pretty damn cool. What they don't think is cool—the reason why everyone is avoiding you—is your attitude. Everyone gets that you're hurt over Caleb and what happened with your mom. We understand that, but that doesn't mean we have to tolerate your constant bitchiness."

I opened my mouth to tell Luke that I wasn't the one being the bitch, that it was all of them who'd been treating me like a three-headed dog since I'd returned—and even before then—but nothing came out. Besides spending time with Seth, I had isolated myself from everyone.

And sometimes I was a terrible person. I had reasons—good reasons, but they were just excuses. Weight settled over my chest.

In the silence and darkness surrounding us, Luke found me and wrapped his arms around my stiff shoulders. "Well, maybe we do have to tolerate it a little bit. You are an Apollyon after all." I could hear the smile in his voice. "And even though you've been a giant bitch, we still love you and we're worried."

A lump formed in my throat. I fought it, really I did, but I felt tears stinging my eyes as my muscles started to relax. My head somehow found his shoulder and he patted my back soothingly. For a moment, I could believe that Luke was Caleb and in my head, I pretended that I told him everything that had happened. My make-believe Caleb smiled at me, held me closer, and ordered me to pull my head out of my ass. That no matter what had happened and everything I learned, the world hadn't ended and wasn't going to.

And for the time being, that seemed to be enough.

Aiden was waiting for me when I finally pulled myself out of the sensory room. He didn't say anything as we headed outside. Both of us had said and probably thought too much as it was. There wasn't any awkwardness between us, but there was this vast sense of… uncertainty. Although, it could just've been I was projecting my own feelings onto him.

We made our way up the walkway, heading toward the dorms. The wind kicked up sand and there was a cold, damp feeling in the air as we neared the garden.

Two pure boys were staring at the marble statue of Apollo reaching for Daphne as she changed into a tree. One elbowed the other. "Hey, look. Apollo is getting wood."

His friend laughed. I rolled my eyes.

"Alex." There was something about Aiden's voice, a roughness that told me that whatever he was about to say was going to be powerful. His gaze moved to my face, then behind me. "What the hell?"

Not what I was expecting.

Aiden brushed past me, solely focused on something other than me. Dammit. I whirled around. "You don't—*oh*."

Now I saw what had cut Aiden off.

Two half guys carried a barely conscious Jackson between them—a hardly recognizable Jackson. He looked like he'd woken up on the wrong side of an ass kicking. Every visible inch of his skin was bruised or bloodied—eyes swelled shut, lips split wide open—and the deep, angry mark smeared across his left cheek suspiciously resembled a boot print.

"What happened to him?" Aiden demanded, taking the place of one of the halfs and practically supporting all of the boy's weight.

The half shook his head. "I don't know. We found him like this in the courtyard."

"I… I fell," Jackson said, blood and spit trickling from his mouth. I think he was missing some teeth.

A dubious expression crossed Aiden's face. "Alex, please go straight to your dorm."

Nodding mutely, I stepped out of the way. I was still pissed at Jackson. He had tried to stomp my head in, but what had been done to him was horrific and calculating. Compared to the fist Aiden had planted in his face when Jackson had…

My wide eyes met Aiden's for a second before he carried Jackson off toward the med building. My conversation with Seth came back to me.

"So, who did you spar with in class?" he'd asked.

"I always get paired with Jackson."

My gods, Seth had done this.

It appeared that Seth was avoiding me for the most part, probably because of the whole ham sandwich incident. Our practices were either cancelled or consisted of working on my mental shields. For a whole week, whenever I saw him, I asked him about Jackson. With a look of complete innocence, he'd told me he hadn't done it. I didn't believe him and I'd told him just that.

He'd looked at me, expression beautifully empty and said, "Now why would I ever do such a thing?"

I didn't want to believe that he had, because whoever had done that to Jackson had put him out of commission for a long time. Jackson wasn't talking, literally. His jaw was wired shut, and I'd heard he needed a lot of dental work. Even though he'd heal a lot quicker than a mortal, I knew he still wouldn't talk. The boy had had the ever-loving crap scared out of him.

And even though I didn't want to believe it was Seth, I couldn't shake my suspicions. Who else would do such a thing to Jackson? Seth had motive—a motive that made me feel ill. If he'd done it, it'd been because of what Jackson had done to me in class. But how could he do something so... violent, so unstable? That question haunted me.

The one good thing was that the weird funk that had settled over me like an itchy blanket faded. A tiny part of me missed Seth's company in the evenings and the way he always managed to turn me into a human body pillow during the night, but there was another part of me that was sort of relieved. Like there wasn't anything additional expected from me.

Even though no one tried to drug or kill me, Linard and Aiden still followed me around. And when they were busy, it was Leon's massive shadow that lurked behind me. I'd taken to hanging around the training rooms even on the days Seth and I wouldn't practice. I knew that Aiden would eventually find me there. We didn't talk about being afraid again, but we sort of just... hung out... in the training room.

It sounded lame, but it was like the old times, before everything got so incredibly screwed up. Sometimes Leon popped in on us. He never seemed surprised or suspicious. Not even the last time, when we'd been sitting with our backs against the wall, arguing about whether or not ghosts existed.

I didn't believe in them.

Aiden did.

Leon had thought we were both idiots.

But damn, I looked forward to it. Just sitting there and talking. No training. No trying to tap in and use akasha. Those moments with Aiden, even when Leon decided to join us, were my favorite part of the day.

I hadn't choked Olivia again, but things were super-awkward when I did see her—no big surprise there. But I did start eating my lunch in the cafeteria with Seth. After the second day, Luke joined us, then Elena, and finally Olivia. We didn't talk, but we also didn't yell anything at each other.

Some things didn't change, though. The mortal holidays of Christmas and New Year came and went, along with most of January. Most of the pures still seemed to expect every half to turn into an evil-aether-sucking creature and jump them. Deacon, Aiden's brother, was one of the few who braved sitting next to us in class or talking to us around campus. Another thing that hadn't changed was my inability to write a letter to my father. What was I supposed to say? I had no idea. Each night that I'd been alone, I'd started a letter, and then stopped. Paper balls littered my floor.

"Just write what you're feeling, Alex. You're overthinking it," Aiden had said after I'd complained. "You've known that he's been alive for two months now. You need to just write without thinking."

Two months? It hadn't felt that long. And that meant I had a little over a month before I Awakened. Maybe I was trying to slow time down. Either way, my feelings were all over the place, and if my father was as competent as I believed him to be, I didn't want him to think I had issues.

So after practice with Seth, I gathered up my notebook and headed over to one of the less crowded rec rooms. Curling up in the corner of a bright red sofa, I stared at a blank page and chewed on the end of my pen.

Linard took up position at the door, looking bored. When he caught me watching him, I made a face and returned to gazing at the blue lines on the paper. Luke interrupted a few times, trying to lure me into a game of air hockey.

When his shadow fell across my notebook again, I groaned. "I don't want to…"

Olivia stood in front of me, wearing a thick cashmere sweater I immediately started lusting after. Her brown eyes were wide.

"Uh… sorry," I said. "I thought you were Luke."

She smoothed a hand over her curly hair. "He's trying to get you to play skee ball?"

"No. He moved on to air hockey."

Her laugh was nervous as she glanced over at the group by the arcade games. Then she squared her shoulders as she gestured at the spot beside me. "Can I sit?"

My stomach turned over. "Yeah, if you want."

Olivia sat, running her hands over her jean-clad legs. Several moments passed without either of us speaking. She was the first to break the silence. "So, how… how have you been?"

It was a loaded question, and my laugh came out choked and harsh. I brought the notepad to my chest as I glanced over at Luke. He was pretending not to have noticed us together.

She let out a little breath and started to rise. "Okay. I guess—"

"I'm sorry." My voice was low, words hoarse. I felt my cheeks burn, but I forced myself to keep going. "I'm sorry for everything, especially the thing in the hallway."

Olivia squeezed her thighs. "Alex—"

"I know you loved Caleb and all I've been thinking about is my own hurt." I closed my eyes and swallowed down the lump in my throat. "I really do wish I could go back and change everything that night. I've thought a million times about all the things we could've done differently."

"You shouldn't… do that to yourself," she said quietly. "At first, I didn't want to know what really happened, you know? Like the details. I just couldn't… deal with knowing for awhile, but I finally got Lea to tell me everything about a week ago."

I bit my lip, unsure of what to say. She hadn't accepted my apology, but we were talking.

She drew in a shallow breath, eyes gleaming. "She told me that Caleb saved her. That you were fighting another daimon, and if he hadn't grabbed her, she would've died."

I nodded, clenching the notebook. Memories of the night surfaced, of Caleb streaking past me.

"He was really brave, wasn't he?" Her voice caught.

"Yes," I agreed passionately. "He didn't even hesitate, Olivia. He was so fast and so good, but the daimon… was just faster."

She blinked several times, and her lashes looked damp. "You know, he told me what happened in Gatlinburg. Everything you guys went through and how you got him out of the house."

"It was luck. They—my mom and the others—started fighting. I didn't do anything special."

Olivia looked at me then. "He thought the world of you, Alex." She paused, laughing quietly. "When we first started dating, I was jealous of you. It was like I couldn't live up to everything you guys had together. Caleb really loved you."

"I loved him." I took a breath. "And he loved you, Olivia."

Her smile was watery. "I guess I needed to blame someone. It could've been Lea, or the Guards who failed to keep the daimons out. I don't know. It's just that you're this unstoppable force—you're an Apollyon." Springy curls bounced as she shook her head. "And—"

"I'm not an Apollyon, yet. But I get what you're saying. I'm sorry." I squeezed the wire on the notebook. "I just wish—"

"And *I'm* sorry."

My head jerked toward her.

"It wasn't your fault. And I was a total bitch to blame you. That day in the hallway, I wanted to apologize but it just all came out wrong. And I know that Caleb would hate me for blaming you. I shouldn't have in the first place. I was just so hurt. I miss him so much." Her voice cracked and she turned away, taking a deep breath. "I know those are just excuses, but I don't blame you."

Tears clogged my throat. "You don't?"

Olivia shook her head.

I wanted to hug her, but wasn't sure if that would be cool. Maybe it was too soon. "Thank you." There was more I wanted to say, but I couldn't find the right words.

Her eyes closed. "Want to hear something funny?"

I blinked. "Yeah."

Turning to me, she grinned even though her eyes glistened with tears. "After the day you and Jackson had that fight, everyone was talking about it in the cafeteria. Cody was walking by and said something ignorant. I don't remember what—probably something about how great being a pure-blood is." She rolled her eyes. "Anyway, Lea got up all casually and dumped her entire plate of food on his head." A giggle broke free. "I know I shouldn't laugh, but I wished you'd seen that. It was hilarious."

My mouth dropped open. "Seriously? What did Cody do? Did Lea get in trouble?"

"Cody threw a fit, calling us a bunch of heathens or something lame like that. I think Lea got written up and her sister wasn't too happy with her."

"Wow. That doesn't sound like Lea."

"She's kind of changed." Olivia sobered up. "You know, after everything? She's not the same. Anyway, I have some stuff I need to do, but I'm... I'm glad we talked."

I met her gaze and felt some of the tension leak away. It wouldn't be like before, not for awhile. "Me, too."

She looked relieved as she smiled. "See you in the cafeteria for lunch tomorrow?"

"Sure. I'll be there."

"I'm leaving for winter break next week with my mom. Some kind of Council business she has to attend to and she wants me to go with her, but when I get back, can we do something? Like maybe watch a movie or hang out?"

While mortals had winter break over the Christmas holiday, we had ours the entire month of February, in celebration of Anthesterion. Back in the old days, the festival was only three days and everyone pretty much got drunk in honor of Dionysus. It was like All Souls Night and Carnival rolled into one giant, drunken orgy. At some point the pures had extended the festival to an entire month, calmed it down, and filled it with Council sessions. Slaves and servants used to be able to participate, but that had also changed. "Yeah, that would be great. I'd love to."

"Good. I'll keep you to that." Olivia got up to leave, but stopped at the door. Turning around, she gave me a small wave and a tentative smile before dipping out.

I glanced at my notebook. Some of the hurt and guilt that had lingered after Caleb's death had lifted. I took a deep breath and scribbled a quick note to Laadan, telling her not to worry about the drink incident and thanking her for telling me about my father. Then I wrote two sentences under the brief paragraph.

Please tell my father that I LOVE him.
I will fix this.

Later that night, I sealed the letter and handed it over to Leon, who was hovering outside my dorm, with explicit instructions to give it to Aiden.

"May I ask why you're passing notes to Aiden?" He eyed the letter like it was a bomb.

"It's a love note. I'm asking him to circle 'yes' or 'no' if he likes me."

Leon pinned me with a bland look, but shoved the letter in his back pocket. I gave him a cheeky grin before shutting the door. It felt like a semi-truck was lifted from my shoulders now that I'd written the letter. Spinning away from the door, I darted toward the computer desk. My bare toes smacked against something thick and heavy.

"Ouch!" Hopping on one leg, I looked down. "Oh, my gods, I am so stupid."

The Myths and Legends book stared up at me. I bent quickly and grabbed it. Somehow, during all the craziness, I'd forgotten about it. Sitting down, I cracked open the dusty thing and began searching for the section Aiden had mentioned in New York.

I had no luck in the part written in English. Sighing, I flipped to the front of the book and started skimming the pages covered in what looked like gibberish to me. My fingers stilled about a hundred pages in, not because I recognized any of the writing, but because I recognized the symbol at the top of the page.

It was a torch turned down.

There were several pages written in ancient Greek, completely useless to me. They should be teaching that instead of trig at the Covenant, but what did I know? Then again, the pures were taught the old language.

Aiden knew the old language—kind of nerdy, in a totally hot way.

If I could find out more about the Order, then maybe we could get the evidence needed to prove that something crazy was up with Telly and Romvi. I wasn't a hundred percent sure that it had anything to do with what had happened, but it was much better than Seth's suggestion.

The last thing we needed was an uprising… or one of us killing *another* pure-blood.

CHAPTER 8

LATER THAT NIGHT, WHEN I WAS HALF ASLEEP, I HEARD the familiar click of my door unlocking. I rose onto my elbow, pushing the mess of hair out of my face. The fine shiver tiptoeing down my spine told me it was Seth. Locks didn't stand a chance against him. He either melted them or used the element of air to unlatch them from the other side.

He stopped just inside the doorway. His eyes were a soft, tawny glow in the dark.

Surprised to see him, it took me a few moments to say anything. "You're not supposed to be in my dorm this late, Seth."

"Has that ever stopped me before?" He sat on the edge of my bed and I could feel his gaze on me. "You've been in a much better mood this evening."

"And here I thought I was getting better at blocking you."

"You are. You did really well at practice today."

"Is that why you're here?" I heard him kick off his shoes. "Because I'm less likely to throw food at you right now?"

"Maybe." I could hear the smile in his voice.

"I was beginning to think you found your own bed more appealing."

"You missed me."

I shrugged. "Seth, about Jackson—"

"I've already told you. I didn't have anything to do with that. And why would I do such a bad, bad thing?"

"I don't know why. Maybe because you're psychotic?"

Seth laughed. "'Psychotic' is such an extreme term. That would suggest I don't feel guilty about my actions."

I arched a brow. "My point exactly."

When he pulled back the covers, I scooted over and watched him slide his legs under them. He eased onto his side, facing me. "You do realize I have a guard detail. They'll know you're in here."

"I passed Linard on my way in." He brushed back a stand of hair that had fallen across my cheek, tucking it behind my ear. His hand lingered. "He told me I was breaking the rules. I told him to bite me."

"And what did he say to that?"

Seth's hand dropped to my shoulder, covering the thin strap of my tank top. The cord inside me started to hum softly. "He didn't look too happy. Said he was going to report me to Marcus."

My heart dropped a little. There was no doubt in my mind that meant Aiden would hear about this; Aiden had to be aware of Seth's sleeping habits. Knots formed in my stomach as I stared at Seth. *I'm not with Aiden. I'm not with Aiden. I'm not doing anything wrong.* Tension still dug into my muscles.

"Not that Marcus can really do anything about it." He leaned over, gently guiding me down so that I was lying on my back. His fingers glided under the strap, and I shivered as his rough knuckles brushed over my collarbone. "He's just the Dean."

"And my uncle," I pointed out. "I doubt he likes the idea of boys sleeping in my bed."

"Hmm, but I'm not just any boy." He tipped his head down. His hair fell forward, shielding his face. "I'm the Apollyon."

My chest rose sharply. "The rules… still apply to you and me."

"Ah, I remember this girl who couldn't follow a simple rule even if her life depended on it." He angled his head, which caused his nose to brush mine. "And I think what we're doing, right now, is the least shocking rule you've broken."

I flushed as I put my hands on his chest, stopping him from overcoming that last inch or two that separated us. "People change," I said lamely.

"Some people do." He placed his arm beside my head, supporting himself.

The cord was really starting to go crazy, demanding that I pay attention to it. My toes curled. "Did you come here to talk about the rules I've broken or what?"

"No. I actually had a reason for coming."

"And that is?" I shifted uncomfortably, trying to ignore the way my skin, especially the palms of my hands, started to tingle. Thank the gods he had a shirt on.

"Give me a second."

I frowned. "Why do—"

Seth dipped his head, brushing his lips over mine, and being caught between wanting to clamp my mouth shut and wanting to open for him was a frustrating feeling. I ached to be near him as equally as I did to be away from him.

"That's… that's why you came here?" I asked when he lifted his head.

"It wasn't the main reason."

"Then why are you—" His mouth cut my words off, and the kiss deepened, stealing my protests. The cord tightened as his hand slipped down my arm, over my stomach and under the hem of my shirt.

He smiled against my lips. "I have to travel with Lucian over winter break. I won't return until the end of February."

"What?" The cord's buzzing was getting excessive, making it hard to concentrate. I was kind of surprised that he'd leave so close to my eighteenth birthday, since I'd figured he'd camp inside my room in the weeks leading up to my Awakening. "Where are you going?"

"To the New York Covenant," he answered, sliding his other hand into my hair. "There have been some problems that demand the Council's attention."

Some of the fuzziness receded. "I want to go with you. My father is—"

"No, you can't go. It's not safe for you there."

"I don't care. I want to go. I have to see my father." By the look on Seth's face, I could tell I wasn't gaining any ground. "You'll be there.

Nothing will happen. And I'd be less safe here without you." The last words physically hurt to say, but I threw pride under the bus. Seeing my father was that important.

Seth's lips tipped up, enjoying that little ego stroke. "Marcus has assured Lucian that you'll be well protected. Your darling pure-blood would slit his wrists before he let anything happen to you."

I gaped.

"What?" He moved his hand up until it rested under my rib cage. "It's the truth. And Leon and Linard will be here, watching over you. You'll be fine."

I wasn't scared of being left behind. I just wanted to see my father. "Seth, I have to go."

He kissed my lower lip, which had scarred just a little. "No, you don't. And you're not going. Not even I could get Lucian to agree to take you back to that hellhole."

My mind raced frantically, trying to find a way to convince him.

"And don't even think about sneaking off, because everyone is expecting you to do that. I don't think I'll be able to sense much from you when we're that far apart, but from the moment I leave, someone will be watching you. So don't even think it. I'm serious."

"I don't need a damn babysitter."

"Yes, you do." His lips found my chin next. "The girl who can't follow rules to save her own life is still inside you."

"You're an asshole."

"Been called worse by you, so I'll take that as a compliment." He grinned even though I knew he felt the fury rising in me.

"When do you leave?" I asked, trying to keep my voice steady.

"I'm leaving Sunday night, so you're completely stuck with me until then." He kissed the hollow of my throat.

"Great," I muttered. Classes would be suspended on Wednesday. Almost all the pures left for super-posh vacations, which meant most of the Guards would be gone, protecting them. Some of the halfs would be out of here—anyone who still kept in contact with a mortal parent or was on good terms with a pure-blood one. There was still a chance I could sneak out, but how in the hell would I get to New York? I didn't even have a driver's license, but that was the least of my problems.

I'd have to get to New York without getting killed in the process.

Seth kissed me again and I debated pulling his hair out by the fistful while the bond between us tried its best to choke the living crap out of me.

"Why do you have to go, anyway?" I asked when he took a breather. I needed something—anything—to focus on that would take the edge off the cord that was tightening and tightening.

He twined strands of my hair around his fingers. "There's a problem with the... servants in the Catskills."

"What?" Dread blossomed in my stomach, growing as quickly as a weed. "What do you mean?"

"Some of them disappeared after the attack. Their bodies weren't found and no daimons escaped." Another quick, deep kiss before he spoke again. "And something appears to be wrong with the elixir."

"Do you know anything about the ones who disappeared?" I caught his wrist before the hand crept any higher under my shirt.

"I don't believe your father is among the missing, but as soon as I can confirm that I'll let you know." He lowered himself down, and since I'd grabbed his wrist, there was nothing to stop him. "I don't want to talk anymore. I'm going to be gone for weeks."

His weight made the cord extremely happy, and I struggled to pay attention. "Seth, this... this is important. What happened with the elixir?"

He sighed. "I don't know. It doesn't appear to be working as strongly."

"As strongly?"

"Yeah, the halfs... are becoming self-aware. Kind of like the computers in Terminator."

Odd comparison, but I got what he meant. And whoa—that was some serious stuff right there. The elixir was a mix of herbs and chemicals that worked to keep a half-blood compliant and dazed. Without it, I doubted the halfs in servitude would be thrilled with their lot in life. "It seems to be working here."

"That's the thing. It's working everywhere but there. The Council wants us there to make sure nothing happens in New York, especially after the attack."

"But why do you have to go?"

"I don't know, Alex. Can we talk about this later?" He looked down at me, eyes glowing. "There are other things I want to do."

The cord buzzed its approval. "But—"

Seth kissed me again and the hand against my stomach pressed down. I let go of his wrist, intending on pushing him off, but then I was gripping his shirt. The air around us seemed to crackle. There was something building inside me, a warning that the damn bond was up to no good.

I felt the cord rushing to the surface before I actually opened my eyes. Amber and blue lights cast strange shadows across the wall of my bedroom. I was transfixed by them for a moment. It was so bizarre that we were responsible for them. That they even came from within us.

It freaked me out a little.

But Seth's free hand was everywhere, skimming down my arm, over my leg, and our cords were spiraling together, connecting us. My fingers clenched his shirt and I was pulling him down one second, then pushing him away the next.

Suddenly, the skin under his palm burned. Tiny pricks of pain stole my breath. I felt the rushing building in my stomach, akasha passing through the cords. A brief flicker of sanity reminded me of what had happened the last time we'd held on. Us, moving together on the bed, and there were fewer clothes to be removed this time.

Panic dug its claws deep in me. I wasn't ready for this—with Seth. Letting go of his shirt, I pushed him hard enough that I was able to wiggle out from underneath him, breaking the connection. I scrambled onto my knees, clutching my stomach. "That... hurt."

Seth looked dazed. "Sorry, it kind of just happened."

Hands shaking, I pulled my shirt up far enough to see what I suspected was going to be there. Centered above my navel, right under my rib cage, was a glowing mark that looked like two check marks joined at the top.

"The power of the gods mark," Seth whispered, sitting up. "Damn Alex, that's a big one. Tomorrow, we should try blowing something up. I know you completely sucked at it when you did it the first time, but I bet it would work now."

I couldn't believe how quickly he went from wanting to get it on to wanting to blow something up. Seth seemed more excited about the rune than the other thing. Hell, his eyes had that crazy look again.

He placed his hands around the mark reverently. "There are four marks that appear first: courage, strength, power, and invincibility. But the power one, that's akasha. See how it's placed here?" He went to touch the mark, but I scooted back. He frowned. "Anyway, that's where you pull power from."

It was also where the cord slumbered when it wasn't trying to turn me into one giant, raging hormone. "What happens when you get the fourth mark?"

Seth ran a hand through his hair, tugging it back from his face. Moonlight cut through the blinds, slicing across his face. "I don't know. Mine came all at once, but they appeared in that order: on both of my palms, my stomach, and then on the back of my neck. Then everywhere else."

My mouth suddenly felt dry. I dropped my shirt and backed up to the edge of the bed. "Do you think I'll Awaken early if the fourth one appears?"

He lifted his eyes. "I don't know, but would it be such a bad thing?"

Dizziness swept through me. "Maybe we should stop… touching or whatever until I turn eighteen."

"What?"

"Seth, I can't Awaken ahead of schedule."

He shook his head. "I don't understand, Alex. Things will be so much better once you Awaken. You wouldn't have to worry about Telly or the furies. Hell, the gods won't even be able to touch us. How is that not a good thing?"

It wasn't a good thing, because once I Awakened, there was a strong chance I'd lose myself in the process. Seth had warned me long ago that it would be like two halves coming together, that whatever he wanted would color my choices and decisions. I'd have no control over myself or my future.

And Aiden had been right that day in the sensory deprivation chamber. It terrified me.

"Alex." Seth took my hand carefully, gently. "You Awakening now would be the best thing for... us. We could even try it. See if we can get the fourth mark to appear. Maybe nothing will happen after that. Maybe you'll Awaken."

I pulled my hand free. The eagerness in his voice creeped me out. "Are... are you doing this on purpose, Seth?"

"Doing what?"

"Trying to get me to Awaken early by touching me or whatever?"

"I'm touching you because I enjoy it." Then he reached for me again, but I knocked his hand away. "What is your deal?" he asked.

"I swear to the gods, Seth—if you are doing this on purpose I will destroy you."

Seth's brows furrowed. "Don't you think you're being a tad bit melodramatic here?"

"I don't know." And I really didn't. My palms tingled, my stomach burned, and the cord was finally settling down. "You haven't done anything with me except training in weeks and then you show up tonight, all touchy and feely. Then this happens?"

"I was all touchy and feely because I'm going to be gone for weeks." Seth slid off the bed, standing in one fluid motion. "And I wasn't really avoiding you. I was just giving you some space."

"Then why did you come here tonight?"

"Whatever the reason was, clearly it was a mistake." He bent, grabbing his shoes. "Apparently, I'm just here to use you for my nefarious plans."

I climbed off the bed, hugging my elbows. Was I being paranoid? "What are you doing?"

"What does it look like? I don't want to be where I'm not wanted."

An uncomfortable feeling started to twist my insides. "So why did you come here if it... wasn't because of that?"

His head snapped up, eyes a furious shade of ocher. Like a lion that'd been cornered, caught between wanting to run and attack. "I missed you, Alex. That's why. And I'm going to miss you. Did that ever cross your mind?"

Oh, oh gods. Guilt brought a hot flush to my face. That hadn't even crossed my mind. I felt like the worst kind of bitch.

A moment passed and something flared in his eyes. "It's Aiden, isn't it?"

My heart tripped over itself. "What?"

"It's always about Aiden." He laughed, but there was no humor there.

This wasn't about Aiden—had nothing to do with him. It was about Seth and me, but before I could even say a word, Seth looked away.

"I guess I'll see you when I get back." He started toward the doorway. "Just... just be careful."

"Crap," I muttered. I darted around the bed, blocking the door. "Seth—"

"Get out of the way, Alex."

His words irked me, but I took a deep breath. "Look, this whole marking and Awakening thing freaks me out. You know that, but... but I shouldn't have accused you."

There was no change in his expression. "No, you shouldn't have."

"And this has nothing to do with Aiden." It didn't, or at least that's what I kept telling myself as I grabbed his free hand, and he flinched. "I'm sorry, Seth."

He stared behind me, lips thin.

"I really am sorry." I let go of his hand and placed my head against his chest. Carefully, I wrapped my arms around him. "I just don't want to become someone else."

Seth inhaled sharply. "Alex..."

I squeezed my eyes shut. Bond or no bond, I did care about him. He was important to me and maybe there was more to how I felt about him than what the bond was making me feel. Maybe it was just that I cared for him like I'd cared for Caleb. Either way, I didn't want to hurt his feelings.

He dropped his shoes and swept his arms around me. "You drive me crazy."

"I know." I smiled. "The feeling is mutual."

He laughed and then brushed his lips over my forehead. "Come on." He started pulling me back to the bed.

I stalled a little. Not hurting his feelings did not equal me ending up with a mark on the back of my neck.

Seth dropped down, tugging me forward. "To sleep, Alex. Nothing more... unless..." His gaze dropped to my tank top. "You know, you should wear that more often. It leaves very little to the imagination, which is something I like."

Flushing to the roots of my hair, I quickly climbed over him and pulled the covers up to my chin. Seth laughed as he lay down. He threw an arm around my waist, snuggling close. His breathing was steady. Nothing like mine, which seemed to be racing my heartbeat. And he was smiling easily, as if we hadn't just argued.

"You're such a perv," I said for the hundredth time.

"You've called me worse."

And I had a feeling I probably would in the future, too.

CHAPTER 9

"WOW. LOOK WHO'S SMILING. THE WORLD IS GOING TO end." Two silvery eyes peeked out behind a mop of curly blond hair, and Deacon St. Delphi smirked as he dropped into the seat beside me. "How's it going, my favorite half-blood?"

"Good." I glanced down at my textbook, lips pursed. "Sorry I haven't been real chatty."

He leaned over, nudging me in the side. "I understand."

Deacon did. That's probably why he hadn't pressured me into talking with him since I'd been back. He'd just sat beside me in class, not saying a word. I hadn't realized he'd been waiting for me to come around.

I glanced at him again. That's the thing about Deacon. Everyone, including Aiden, saw him as a lazy party-boy who didn't pay attention to anything, but he was far more observant than anyone gave him credit for. He'd had a real hard time growing up without his parents, and I think he was finally coming out of the "party-boy who doesn't care about anything" stage.

"Are you doing anything for winter break?"

He rolled his eyes. "That would require Aiden taking time off, since he won't let me off this island without him. He's been super-paranoid ever since the whole thing in the Catskills. I think he's expecting daimons or furies to drop in here any minute."

I cringed. "Sorry."

"Whatever," he replied. "It's not your fault. So I'm not going to be doing anything exciting. I hear my esteemed older brother is playing guard for you."

I rolled my eyes.

"You know, I overheard him and the Dean talking when he visited the house."

"What house? Aiden's cabin?"

Deacon arched a brow. "No, like *the* house." He saw my dumbfounded look and took pity on me. "Our parents' house? Well, it's really Aiden's house now. It's on the other side of the Island, near Zarak's."

I had no idea that there was another house. I'd just assumed that Aiden had the cabin and Deacon stayed in the dorm. Come to think of it, why in the hell was Aiden living in that tiny shack if he owned one of those huge, opulent houses on the main island?

As if he knew what I was thinking, Deacon sighed. "Aiden doesn't like to stay at the house. Reminds him too much of our parents, and he hates the whole lavish lifestyle thing."

"Oh," I whispered, glancing at the front of the classroom. Our teacher was always late.

"Anyway, back to my story. I overheard them talking." Deacon's chair and desk made a terrible scratching noise as he scooted closer to me. "Want to know?"

Luke, who had been sitting on Elena's desk, faced us. His brows rose when he saw us. "Sure. Spill it," I said.

"There's something going on with the Council—that has to do with the half-bloods."

"Like what?" I asked.

"Don't know exactly. But I know it has something to do with the New York Council." Deacon looked away, focusing on the front of the class. "I figured you might know, since you were just up there."

I shook my head. There was always something going on with the Council, and it probably had to do with the elixir. Then I realized Deacon was still staring at the front of the classroom. I followed his gaze. He was staring at Luke.

And Luke was staring back at him.

Like in the really intense way I sometimes stared at… Aiden.

My eyes darted back to Deacon. I couldn't see his eyes, but the tips of his ears were pink. After several moments, like too long for one dude to be looking at another dude casually, Deacon leaned back. I thought about the phantom voice I'd heard with Luke in the sensory room. It had sounded familiar… but no way.

"Anyway," Deacon cleared his throat. "I think I might throw a party for those left behind during winter break. You think Aiden will be game?"

"Uh, probably not."

Deacon sighed. "It's worth a try."

I glanced at Luke again. "Yeah, I guess so."

"It's not working."

Seth made an impatient sound in his throat. "Try concentrating."

"I am," I snapped, pushing the windblown hair out of my face.

"Try harder, Alex. You can do it."

I hugged myself, shivering. It was freezing out by the marshes. The cold, damp wind beat against me and the heavy sweater was no help. We'd been at this for the better part of Saturday. When Seth had suggested I try to blow something up, I'd assumed he'd been joking.

I'd been wrong.

Closing my eyes, I pictured the thick boulder in my mind. I already knew the texture, the sandy color, and its irregular shape. I'd been staring at the damn thing for hours.

Seth moved behind me, taking my hand and placing it against the spot the latest mark had appeared. "Feel it in here. Do you?"

Feel the cord? Check. I also liked the fact that he was now blocking the worst of the wind.

"Okay. Picture the cord unraveling, feel it coming alive."

I had a feeling Seth was enjoying this way too much, considering how he was pressed against me.

"Alex?"

"Yeah, I feel the cord." I did feel it opening up, slithering through my veins.

"Good. The cord is not just us," he said softly. "It's akasha—the fifth and final element. You should feel akasha now. Tap into it. Picture what you want in your mind."

I wanted a taco, but I doubted akasha could serve me up some Taco Bell. Gods, I'd do some terrible things for Taco Bell right about now.

"Alex, are you paying attention?"

"Of course." I smirked.

"Then do it. Blow up the rock."

Seth made it sound so easy. Like a toddler could do this. I wanted to elbow him in the stomach, but I pictured the rock and then pictured my cord shooting from my hand. I did this over and over again.

Nothing happened.

I opened my eyes. "Sorry, this isn't working."

Seth moved away, brushing back the shorter stands of hair that fell out of his ponytail. He popped his hands on his hips and stared at me.

"What?" Another gust of biting wind had me shuffling to stay warm. "I don't know what you want me to do. I'm cold. I'm hungry. And I saw that National Lampoon's Christmas Vacation is on TV for some odd reason and I must watch it since you soaked up all the time it was on TV during Christmas."

His brows inched up. "Watch what?"

"Oh, my gods! You do not know of the trials and tribulations of the Griswold family?"

"Huh?"

"Wow. That's kind of sad, Seth."

He waved his hand. "It doesn't matter. Something must trigger your ability to tap into akasha. If only…" A thoughtful look crept over his expression and then he clasped his hands. "The first time you did it, you were pissed. And then when you went all crazy ninja on the furies, you were angry and scared. You have to be *pushed*."

"Oh, no no no." I started backing up. "I know where you are going with this and I'm not doing this with you. I mean it, Seth. Don't you—"

Seth raised his hand and the air element smacked me in the chest, knocking me flat on my back. Fighting the use of the elements was something I had gotten a bit better with. I did tap into the power then and I felt the cord tense, then snap. I buckled, breaking through what felt like hurricane-force winds. Rising up, my hair blew straight back.

I was going to maim Seth.

Then he was on me, using his weight to force me back against the coarse, dead grass. Small pebbles dug into my back as I squirmed under him. "Get off, Seth!"

"Make me," he said, lowering his face to mine.

I tipped my hips, wrapped my legs around his waist and rolled. For a second, I had the advantage and I wanted to wrap my chilled fingers around his neck and choke the living crap out of him. I didn't like being pinned or the ensuing feeling of helplessness. And Seth knew that.

"Not like that," Seth grunted. He grasped my shoulders, flipping me onto my back. "Use akasha."

We struggled, rolling through the small bushes. He was growing more frustrated each time he slammed me back, and I was feeling murderous. Rage, sweet and heady, rushed through me, twisting around the cord. I felt it building. My skin was tingling. The marks of the Apollyon seared and pulsed.

Seth's lips curved. "That's it. Do it."

I screamed.

And then Leon was above us, grabbing Seth by the scruff of his neck and tossing him several feet back. He twisted in midair like a cat, landing in a crouch. The marks of the Apollyon came out all at once, blurring across his skin in dizzying speeds. He zeroed in on Leon. There was something deadly in his eyes—the same look he'd given the Master after he'd hit me. I thought of Jackson.

I jumped to my feet, rushing Seth. "No! No, Seth!"

"You really shouldn't have done that." Seth advanced, his intentions clear.

Leon arched a brow. "You want to try that, boy?"

"You want to die?"

"Stop it," I hissed, squirming between them. I looked over my shoulder at Leon. The pure-blood Sentinel didn't even look concerned. He was crazy. "Leon, we were training."

"That's not what it looked like to me."

Over Seth's broad shoulder, I saw several Guards and Aiden heading our way. I hoped they picked up their pace and got here before one of these idiots did something stupid.

"Leon, he wasn't hurting me," I tried again.

"What do you think you're going to do?" Seth demanded. "To me?"

He stared down at Seth. "You really think you can take me, don't you?"

"I don't think." Akasha, brilliant and beautiful, surrounded his right hand. The air crackled around the ball. "I know."

This was insane. I grabbed Seth's arm and a rush of anger hit me. *I* wanted to attack Leon, needed to show him that he was messing with the wrong person, that I was better than him. He wouldn't dare touch *me* again. I was going to show him.

"Bring it," Leon said, his voice low.

"Hey!" yelled Aiden. "That's enough!"

Seth and Leon moved at the same time, both of them knocking me aside. The combination of their arms sweeping out and hitting me sent me flying backward. I hit the boulder I'd been trying to blow up, tumbling over the top. Twisting so I didn't hit the soggy marsh face first, I landed on my hands and knees. Icy muck saturated my jeans and splashed my face.

Stunned more by the pure rage than anything else, I lifted my head and peered through my hair. What the hell had just happened? The whole pushing me thing had been an accident, but the violence I'd felt had not been my own.

It had been Seth's. It wasn't like those times I'd had those hot flashes. This had been different. I'd *felt* what he'd felt, *wanted* what he'd wanted. Had that happened before? I didn't think so. My hands shook.

The Guards had reached Leon. I wasn't sure if they were trying to protect Leon or Seth. Aiden, though, went after the Apollyon, like I should've known he would the moment I spied him stalking across the wind-tossed sand.

I was sure Aiden knew what had happened had been an accident, but he looked like he wanted to pummel both guys. By the sounds of their arguing and shoving one another, Leon blamed Seth. Seth blamed everyone but himself. The Guards looked increasingly worried.

Staggering out of the marsh, I headed toward them just as Seth tried to sidestep Aiden.

Eyes flashing, Aiden grabbed him by the collar of his shirt and pushed him back several feet. It was like he didn't even see the strongest and deadliest element known to the gods inches away from his body—or he didn't care.

"That's enough," Aiden said, shoving Seth as he let go. "Back off."

"You really want to get involved in this?" Seth asked. "Right now?"

"More than you would ever know."

Akasha fizzled out and Seth pushed Aiden. "Oh, I think I do. And you know what, it's something I think about… *every time.* You get what I'm saying?"

"That's the best you got, Seth?" Aiden went toe-to-toe with the Apollyon. And suddenly, I knew this wasn't just about what had just happened. This was more. "Because I think you and I both know the truth about *that.*"

Oh, dear gods, this was turning into a boy fight.

Seth moved so fast it was hard to see him. An arm cocked back, aiming right for Aiden's jaw. Reacting just as fast, Aiden caught Seth's arm and threw him back again.

"Try it again, and I won't stop," Aiden warned.

A second later they were crashing into each other. Both hit the ground, rolling and throwing punches—a blur of black garb as each one gained and lost the upper hand. I started forward, but stopped short. They weren't even fighting like Sentinels. There was nothing graceful in their punches or blocks. They brawled like two idiots high on testosterone, and I had the strongest urge to walk up and kick them both in the head.

I threw my hands up. "You've got to be kidding me."

The Guards and Leon shot forward, grabbing for the two guys. It took several tries to get Aiden off Seth. A cut marred his right cheek. Blood beaded. There was a split in Seth's lip.

"Are you done?" demanded Leon, shouldering Aiden back a few steps. "Aiden, you need to *stop*."

Aiden wiped the back of his hand over his cheek as he shrugged Leon's hand off. "Yeah, I'm done."

The Guards were saying the same thing to Seth, but when they let go of him, Seth shot around them. "You think I'm scared that you'll turn me in for fighting? Any of you? They can't touch me! I'm the fu—"

"Stop it!" I screamed. "Just stop!" Seth froze, and several sets of eyes centered on me. "Gods! We *were* training. There's no reason to kill each other over this." I glanced at Aiden. "No reason to do *any* of this. Just freaking stop."

Tension still ripened the air, but Seth pulled back and spat out a mouthful of blood. As he straightened his shirt, the marks started to fade. "Like I'd been saying, but apparently all of you are too stupid to understand, we were—"

"Shut up, Seth." I clenched my hands.

His brows rose.

Aiden still looked furious. His eyes were like pools of silver, consuming his entire face.

"It's done and over, okay?" I said, mostly to him. "I'm fine. No one is dead. And if you three can manage not to try to kill each other, I'm going to go and take a shower, because now I smell like ten-day-old butt."

Leon's lips twitched as if he wished to smile, but after the glare I cut his way, his expression returned to the stoic one I was familiar with.

I headed around them, shivering. Icicles were forming on my jeans.

Seth wheeled around. "Alex—"

"No." I stopped. There was no way he was coming back with me. I needed to be away from him, putting some distance between his anger and me before I started throwing punches. I needed to figure out what'd happened back there, why I'd felt what Seth wanted so strongly.

"Alex!" Seth called out. "Come on."

"Leave me alone right now." I started walking again. "I'm done with this for today. I mean it. I'm *done*."

CHAPTER 10

SETH KNEW BETTER THAN TO SEEK OUT MY COMPANY Saturday night. I was grateful for that, because I didn't want to see his face. I did, however, answer the door Sunday evening when he actually knocked. That's how I knew he was feeling apologetic. Seth never knocked.

His hands were shoved into the pockets of his dark cargos. The right side of his lip was swollen. "Hey," he said, staring over my head.

"Hey."

He shifted from one foot to the next. "Alex, I'm… sorry about yesterday. I didn't—"

"Stop," I cut him off. "I know you were just trying to get me to use akasha and you didn't mean to knock me over, but you guys were insane. Not in a good way, Seth."

A sheepish look crept across his face. "I know, but Aiden pissed me—"

"Seth."

"Okay. You're right. It's over and done. And I don't want to argue with you. I'm getting ready to leave." He looked at me then. "I thought it would be nice if you walked with me to the bridge."

"Just let me grab something to put on." I needed to talk with him, anyway. After I grabbed a hoodie, we walked out of the dorm in silence. The campus was dark; only the shadows of the patrolling Guards moved. When I let out my breath, it formed small puffs in the air. "I felt your anger yesterday."

"I'm sure anyone within a ten-mile radius felt my anger yesterday."

"That's not what I meant." We followed the marbled pathway around the dorms, heading toward the bridge by the main Covenant building. "I *really* felt it. I wanted to knock the crap out of Leon. It was like… like it was my anger."

Seth didn't respond as he stared ahead, eyes narrowed.

"It went away as soon as I wasn't touching you, but it was pretty weird." I stopped walking as the bridge came into view. A black Hummer was being loaded with luggage. Exhaust filled the air, and several Council Guards stood post. "You don't have anything to say about that?"

He glanced down at me. "You were so close to tapping into akasha, Alex. If Leon hadn't interfered, it would've happened."

As if that was the most important thing that'd happened. "Seth, did you hear a word I said?"

"I did, and I don't know why you felt my anger so clearly." He took his hands out of his pockets and folded his arms. "Maybe it was because you were tapping into akasha. It made you more in tune with what I was feeling."

What I had felt didn't seem to bother or really surprise Seth. But to me, it was a pretty big deal. "When I Awaken, I'll feel and want what you want. Don't you get what I'm saying? I *wanted* what *you* wanted already."

"Alex." He dropped his hands on my shoulders and pulled me against his chest. "You're not Awakening. Stop worrying."

I frowned and pushed off. He let me go. "But it's really starting to happen, isn't it? With the marks and now this? And I'm only like a month away."

"It's not such a—"

"Alexandria, I am so glad you've come to see Seth off," said Lucian. I turned and was immediately enveloped in a weak hug. The smell of incense and cloves choked me. "I wish it was safe to bring you along. It would ease my worries to have you by Seth's side."

My arms stuck out from my sides awkwardly. Ugh. I hated when Lucian did this.

He patted my back and stepped away, addressing Seth. "How many Guards do you think we should bring?"

Lucian was asking Seth for his opinion? What. The. Hell. I turned to Seth in disbelief.

Seth stood straighter. "At least five, which would leave four behind to help keep guard in case something should arise here."

"Good. You have an eye for leadership, Seth." Lucian patted his shoulder. "If we had more Sentinels like you, we wouldn't have such a serious daimon problem." He paused, smiling. "If we had more men like you on the Council, then our world would be far better."

I wanted to gag. There was no way Seth could be falling for this epic level ass-kissery. It was so obvious from the way Lucian simpered and cooed. It was blatant, but by the gods, Seth looked like he'd just been handed a million dollars and been told he could spend it all on girls and liquor.

"I'd have to agree." Seth's smug smile spread.

I wanted to shake Seth. I was seriously considering it.

Lucian faced me. "You, my dear, are lucky in more ways than most half-bloods. Being blessed as an Apollyon and having this fine young man as your other half."

I scrunched up my face.

Beside me, Seth went still.

"I'll leave you two to say goodbye. We shall be leaving in a few moments, Seth."

I stared at Lucian's retreating form. The white robes flowed out, never quite trailing on the ground. I thought about how he'd stared at Minister Telly's throne while I'd given my testimony in the Catskills. No one loved power more than Lucian.

"You know," drawled Seth, "you don't have to look so shocked by what Lucian said. It could be worse."

I laughed. "Are you serious?"

Seth glowered. "I happen to think I'm a pretty damn good catch."

"You happen to think you're the greatest thing that ever breathed, but that's not what I'm talking about. He was kissing your ass, Seth. He's up to something."

"He wasn't kissing my ass." He folded his arms again. "Lucian happens to think I know what I'm talking about. He also happens to appreciate what I have to say."

"You have got to be kidding me." I tried to not roll my eyes.

"Why is that so hard for you to believe?" Displeasure radiated from his voice and stance. "Let me ask you a question, Alex. If that was Lucian or your uncle saying good things about Aiden, would you find it so hard to swallow?"

"What the hell is that supposed to mean?" And where had that come from? "Aiden is a Sentinel. His ability to make decisions or lead is—"

"What do you think I am?" Seth leaned his head forward, brows lowered. "A joke instead of a Sentinel?"

Yikes. I saw my mistake. "That's not what I meant. You're a Sentinel. A damn good one, but please tell me you don't trust him." I grabbed his forearm and squeezed. "That's all I meant to say."

"I do trust Lucian, and you should, too. Out of everyone around you, he's the only one who's trying to make our world different."

"What?"

"Seth?" Lucian called. "It's time."

"Wait." I held onto his arm. "What do you mean?"

Agitation blew off him as he stared at me intently. "I have to go. Please be careful, and remember what I said the other night. Don't even think about trying to make your way to New York."

I glared at him.

A bit of a smile peeked through. He started to turn away, but stopped. "Alex?"

"What?"

His mouth opened as he ran his hand over his head. "Just be careful, okay?" When I nodded, he reached into his pocket and pulled out something small and slim. "I almost forgot. I picked this up so we could talk while I was gone."

I took the cell phone. It wasn't one of the cheap versions, and I hoped it had a lot of games preloaded on it. "Thanks."

Seth nodded. "My number is programmed in there. I have yours."

There was nothing else to say. When Seth reached the Hummer, Lucian clapped him on the back *again*.

Leon suddenly appeared beside me—my escort back to the dorm, I realized.

Seth climbed into the Hummer, leaving to board a private jet at the airport on the mainland. He glanced back at me as the vehicle began to move.

I forced a smile before Leon guided me away from the bridge, but under the overhead lamps, I saw the brief look of disappointment on Seth's face. And the satisfied smile that was on Lucian's.

It was weird with Seth being gone. The cord in me settled down, and I was pretty sure if a god appeared in front of me, Seth wouldn't have felt a flicker of surprise. It had only been one day since he'd left, but I already felt... *normal*. Like a weight had lifted off my shoulders.

And that was odd, because my backpack was ridiculously heavy with the Myths and Legends book in it. I was carrying it around, hoping to corner Aiden with it whenever he took up babysitting duties. Right now Leon was trailing behind me at a not-so-discreet distance.

I stopped in the middle of the pathway by the garden and turned around. "Aren't you cold?"

Leon glanced down at the short-sleeved shirt he was wearing. "No. Why?"

"Because it's freezing." And it was. I had a tank top, a long-sleeve thermal, and a sweater on, and I was still cold.

Leon stopped beside me. "Then why are you outside if you're so cold?"

"Unfortunately, going outside is the only method of traveling to other parts of the campus, unless you know something I don't."

"You could just do us all a favor and stay in your dorm," he suggested.

Shivering, I hugged my elbows. "Do you have any idea how nice it is to be able to do something other than train or stay in my room?"

"Or spend time with Seth?"

I looked at him closely, trying not to smile. "Was that a joke? Oh, my gods. It was."

His features remained expressionless. "There is nothing about that boy that is a joking matter."

"Okay." I turned around and started walking. This time Leon walked beside me. "You really don't like Seth, do you?"

"Is it that obvious?"

I peeked at him. "No. Not at all."

"Do you?" he asked as we rounded the corner of the training center. The wind off the ocean was unnaturally brutal. "I've heard rumors… that two Apollyons share a powerful bond. It must be hard to know how you truly feel about someone if that's the case."

Now this was awkward. There was no way I was discussing my relationship troubles with Leon of all people.

He sighed deeply as he stared up at the statue of Apollo and Daphne, a distant look on his face. "Emotions that are forced always end in tragedy."

That was deep. Another gust of frigid wind cut through me. The look on Daphne's face was tragic. "Do you think Daphne knew that the only way she could escape Apollo was by dying?"

He didn't answer immediately, and when he did, his voice was thick. "Daphne did not die, Alex. She still remains as she was the day… she was lost. A laurel tree."

"Man, that sucks. Apollo was such a freak."

"Apollo was struck by a love arrow and Daphne was struck by a lead one." He looked down as he gestured at the statue. "Like I said, love that is not organic in nature is dangerous and tragic."

Tucking my hair back, I glanced at the statue again. "Well, I hope I don't have to turn myself into a tree."

Leon tsked. "Then pay attention to what is need and what is want."

"What?" I looked at him sharply, squinting. The sun had begun to set, casting an eerie golden halo over him. "What did you just say?"

He shrugged. "Your other babysitter is here."

Distracted, I turned around. Aiden was strolling up the walkway. I'd kill to see him in jeans again. I winced. Okay, maybe not *kill*, but close. I twisted back around. Leon was gone.

"Dammit," I muttered, scanning the growing shadows creeping across the beach and garden.

"What?" Aiden asked.

My chest fluttered like always as I faced him. There was a slight bruise along his jaw from his scuffle with Seth. "I was talking to Leon and he just up and disappeared on me."

Aiden smiled. "He has a habit of doing that."

"It's just that he said something—" I shook my head. "It doesn't matter. Are you my babysitter for now?"

"Until you decide you're staying in for the evening," he responded. "Where you headed?"

"I was going to the rec center, but I have something I want to show you." I tapped the bottom of my bag. "You up for it?"

His brows rose. "Should I be concerned by what's in your bag?"

I grinned. "Maybe."

"Well, what is life without taking risks? Do we need privacy?"

"Probably."

"I know just the place." He shoved his hands into the pockets of his cargos. "Follow me."

Grasping the strap of my bag, I ordered myself to pull it together. I wasn't talking to him just so I could ogle him or flirt. Or do anything I wasn't supposed to be doing. I had a purpose for this, so there was no reason for my heart to be racing as fast as it was.

No reason at all.

Aiden nudged me with his elbow after a few moments of walking in silence. "You look different."

"I do?"

"Yeah, you look more like…" He fell quiet. By the time he spoke again, the ocean was a golden red as the sun slowly disappeared over the horizon. "You just seem more relaxed."

"Well, I have some time to myself. That's relaxing." I wondered if I did look different. Didn't seem that way when I got ready this morning.

The only thing I really noticed that was different was that the marks hadn't burned or tingled once since Seth left.

"Oh, I almost forgot. Your letter was sent to New York, ahead of the crew that just went up there. Laadan should've received it yesterday or today."

"Really? I hope my father… isn't one of the ones who are missing."

"How do you know about that?" His eyes narrowed. "Never mind. Seth?"

I nodded. "He told me that some of the half servants were missing and that the elixir wasn't working."

A troubled look darkened his eyes. "How much did he tell you?"

"Not much at all."

Aiden nodded curtly. "Of course not. Some of the halfs aren't responding to the elixir. There've been outbreaks of fighting among the servants; they're refusing Masters' orders and disappearing. The Council fears there will be a rebellion, and the New York Covenant has been weakened since the attack. And no one knows exactly how or why the elixir stopped working."

I thought of my father. Was he one of those who'd disappeared, or was he fighting back? I knew he had to be one of the ones the elixir had stopped working on. "I should be there."

"You should be anywhere but there."

"Now you sound like Seth."

His eyes narrowed. "For once, I have to agree with him."

"That's shocking." My gaze fell on the main academy building, and I knew immediately where we were going. "You're taking me to the library."

The smile returned. "It's private. No one is ever in there at this time, and if anyone spots us, you're studying."

I laughed then. "And someone is going to believe that?"

"Stranger things have been known to happen," he replied as we headed up the wide steps.

We passed two Guards posted at the entrance. Ever since the attack here that had taken Caleb's life, and the subsequent one in the Catskills, security had gone through the roof. Back in the day I would've bitched about this because it made sneaking around so much more difficult. But now, after everything, I was relieved to see the increased numbers.

Toasty air greeted us as we entered. Silently, I followed Aiden down the hall toward the library. Several Instructors still lingered in their offices, and we passed a few students heading out.

Aiden stepped forward and opened the door to the library, forever the gentleman. Smiling my thanks, I stepped inside and came to a complete standstill.

Luke and Deacon were emerging from one of the tall stacks, shoulder to shoulder. When they saw us, I'd swear they jumped at least three feet apart.

"Deacon?" Aiden sounded shocked. "You're in the library?"

"Yeah." Deacon brushed the mop of curls off his forehead. "We were studying for trig."

Neither of them had a single book in their hands. I looked at Luke expectantly. He looked away, but his lips twitched.

Aiden eyes widened. "Wow. I'm sort of proud of you. Studying?"

I clamped my mouth shut.

"Turning over a new leaf and all." Deacon bumped into his older brother. "Taking my education seriously."

My tongue was literally burning to say something.

Aiden nodded at Luke. "Keep him out of trouble, Luke."

Oh jeez. By the way Deacon was shifting back and forth on his feet and the size of Luke's grin, I figured Aiden had no idea what kind of "trouble" those two were probably getting into. Same-sex relationships in our world didn't even have a place on the list of taboo things to do. It was the fact that Deacon was a pure and Luke was a half.

And of all the half-bloods in the world, I knew just how stupid and dangerous whatever it was that they were doing was. I glanced at Aiden. He caught my eyes and smiled. My belly flopped. Stupid and dangerous, but it didn't change how I felt.

CHAPTER 11

I WAS STILL STRUGGLING TO KEEP MY MOUTH SHUT when Aiden found an empty study room in the back of the library, somewhere near the Books-I'd-Never-Read and the Books-I've-Never-Heard-Of section. He left the door cracked open, which relieved and disappointed me in the same breath.

Sitting down, I dropped my bag on the table. "That's really cool that Deacon is studying and all."

Aiden took the seat beside me, turning so that his knee pressed against mine and he was facing me. "Can I ask you a question?"

"Sure." I pulled out the massive book and placed it between us.

"Do I look stupid?"

My hand froze over the edge of the book. "Uh, is this a trick question?"

He arched a brow.

"No. You don't look stupid."

"I didn't think so." He reached over, taking the book away from me. His hand brushed mine as he did so, sending little shivers through my fingers. "They were doing the same amount of studying that we're doing."

I wasn't sure how to proceed with this. So I said nothing.

Aiden stared at the book, brows lowered. "I know what my brother is doing, Alex. And you know what? It pisses me off."

"It does?"

"Yes." He looked up, meeting my gaze. "I can't believe he thinks I'd care if he was into guys or whatever. I've always known he's been that way."

"I didn't."

"Deacon is good at hiding it. What am I looking at?" he asked. I reached over, opening the book to the section about the Order of Thanatos. Understanding dawned. He turned a couple of the pages before going back to the beginning of the section. "He's always pretended to be interested in girls, and maybe he is, too. But he never had me fooled."

"He had me fooled." I watched a wavy lock of hair fall over Aiden's forehead. An insane urge to brush it back hit me hard. "So he's never said anything to you about it?"

Aiden snorted. "No. I think he believes I'd be upset or something. And trust me, I've wanted to tell him I don't care, but I think it makes him uncomfortable. You know, talking about it. So I just pretend like I don't see it. I guess he'll talk to me about it eventually."

"He will." I bit my lip. "But... it's Luke."

A muscle popped in his jaw. "I don't like the fact that he may be... involved with a half, but I trust that he won't do anything—" He broke off, laughing. "Yeah, well, I'm not the person to be lecturing on the whole pure and half business."

A flush crept over me. Aiden looked up, and our eyes locked. He opened his mouth, but shut it quickly. He turned back to the book, clearing his throat. "So, the Order of Thanatos? Not exactly fun reading material."

Finding safe ground, I nodded. "Telly had this symbol tattooed on his arm." I pointed at the torch, careful not to touch him. "And so does Romvi—who, by the way, still hates my guts, in case you're wondering. And I remembered in the section that talked about the Apollyon, it mentioned that Thanatos killed Solaris and the First. Maybe this Order business is still going on and they have something to do with what... what happened in the Catskills."

The hand beside the book curled into a fist, but Aiden didn't look up. "As far as I know the Order doesn't exist anymore, but you never know."

"Maybe this can tell us something? But I can't read it."

He smiled briefly. "Give me a few minutes. Reading this isn't exactly easy."

"Okay." Beyond the crack in the door, the library was dark and silent. There was no way I was going out there. I pulled out a notebook and pen. "I'll... pretend to study or something."

Aiden chuckled. "You do that."

I smiled as I started doodling on a blank page of notebook paper. It was hard, because his knee was still touching mine, and it may have been my imagination, but we seemed to be getting closer. His entire lower leg was against mine.

While Aiden read, I sketched a really bad version of the Apollo and Daphne statue outside. Several times, Aiden glanced over and made comments about the drawing. He offered to pay for art classes at one point. I punched him in the arm for that.

Giving up on my masterpiece, I checked to see what page he was on. As I stared at the symbol on each page, I felt a tightening in my throat. Instead of thinking about Telly or Romvi, I thought of the pure I'd killed in the Catskills. Leaning back in the chair, I rubbed my hands over my thighs. The feel of shoving a blade into a pure was much different than shoving one into a daimon, even a half daimon.

There were always choices, and once again, I'd made the wrong decision. Actually, I'd made a string of bad decisions over a short period of time, but that one kind of took the cake. I could've disarmed the pure-blood Guard. I could've done something other than what I had done. I'd killed him and still didn't even know his name.

"Hey," Aiden said softly. "Are you okay?"

"Yep." I lifted my head, forcing a smile. "Find anything out yet?"

He was watching me intently. I could feel it, even after I returned to staring at my hands. "Just why the Order was established," he said. "It appears that they were created by us—the pure-bloods—as an organization to keep the old ways alive and to protect the gods. And it looks like even a few chosen half-bloods were initiated into the Order."

"Great." I smoothed my hands over the table. "Do the gods need protection?"

"It doesn't seem to be in the way you'd think, but more like protecting their existence from mortals and those who might be a threat to the gods." Aiden turned back to the book, flipping several chapters ahead. "It does say the members are marked, which would explain the tattoo if they do belong to the Order. But there is something else."

"What?" I glanced at him. "What is it?"

He took a deep breath and slid the book toward me. "We've all misread it. Understandable since it's how it's phrased. Look at this."

Aiden was pointing at the section on the Apollyon. "'*The reaction from the gods, particularly the Order of Thanatos, was swift and righteous. Both Apollyons were executed without trial*'."

I sat back, understanding sinking in. "It wasn't Thanatos who killed them, but the Order of Thanatos."

Aiden nodded as he turned back to the section on the Order. "That's what it looks like."

"But how? Both Solaris and the First would had been fully Awakened. The way Seth talks, once that happens we become indestructible."

He shook his head. "The Order is very mystical, or at least, that's how it reads in this section." He tapped his finger on something that looked like chicken scratch to me. "The Order is said to be '*the eyes and the hand of Thanatos*.' There's something here about the Order being gifted with 'daggers dipped in the blood of the Titans.'"

"Daggers dipped in the blood of the Titans? Like, literally? Is the Apollyon somehow allergic to Titan blood?" I shook my head. "What I don't get is, if the gods and the Apollyon can both use akasha, then why would the gods—Thanatos—need anyone else to kill the Apollyon? They could just use akasha."

"I don't know," he said, looking at me. His eyes were gunmetal gray. "And I have a hard time believing that Seth wouldn't know, either. Didn't he tell you that, once you Awaken, the knowledge of the previous Apollyons will pass on to you?"

"Yeah, he did. Seth would have to know." An uncomfortable feeling clawed for my attention as I rested my chin on my palm. If Seth knew everything that the previous Apollyons knew, then wouldn't one of them, in all these years, have figured out that they were a product of a union between a pure and a half? And wouldn't one of the Apollyons have to know about the Order, especially if the lives of Solaris and the First had passed to Seth during his Awakening?

"What is it?" Aiden asked quietly.

Anger stirred, poking at the cord. "I don't think Seth is being completely honest with me."

Aiden didn't respond.

I drew in a deep breath. "I don't understand why he would lie about this. Maybe… maybe he just never put two and two together." That sounded lame even to me, but my brain had a hard time accepting that Seth could be hiding something like this. Why would he?

A few moments passed before Aiden spoke. "Alex, if the Order does exist today, then they could be behind the attacks in the Catskills. And if they are the eyes and hand of Thanatos, they've pegged you as a threat."

I thought about what the furie had said before she'd tried to rip my head off—that I was a threat and it wasn't anything personal. But trying to kill me was very personal. "Do you think the furies were there because of the daimon attack, or because… of me?"

"They didn't react until the daimon attack."

Rubbing my temples, I closed my eyes. This was all giving me a headache. "There are just so many things that don't add up—the Order, the furies, Seth. Why did they go after me instead of him?"

Aiden closed the book. "I need to tell Marcus about this. If the Order is still alive and well, then this is serious. And if Telly is a member, then we need to be careful."

I nodded, prying my eyes open. I could feel his gaze on me again. "Okay."

"And I don't want you going to Romvi's class anymore," he continued. "I'll talk to Marcus and I'm sure he'll agree with that."

"That shouldn't be hard. Tomorrow is the last day of classes before break, so I'll skip." I shivered. "Do you think the 'eyes of Thanatos' part is something literal? And daggers actually dipped in real honest-to-gods Titan blood?"

"Knowing the gods, I'd go with a yes." There was a pause, and Aiden reached over, capturing my chin with the tips of his fingers. He slowly turned my head toward him. "What are you not telling me, Alex?"

A frisson of heat shot through me. "Nothing," I whispered, and tried to turn my head, but he kept me still.

"You know you can tell me anything, right? And I know there is something you're keeping from me."

Seth's warning to keep the Apollyon marks quiet was overwhelmed by the desire to tell someone what was happening. And who better to tell than Aiden? He was the one person in this world that I trusted, especially considering how much he'd risked to keep me safe. Seth wouldn't be happy if he knew, but then again, I wasn't particularly happy with Seth at the moment.

"It's happening," I said finally.

Aiden's eyes searched mine. "What's happening?"

"This—the freaky stuff." I lifted my hands, palms up. His gaze dropped without releasing my chin, and when his eyes met mine again, they were questioning. "I've started getting the marks of the Apollyon. You can't see them, but they're there, on both of my palms. And there's one on my stomach."

He seemed taken aback by this, releasing my chin but not moving away. "When did this start happening?"

I looked away. "The first happened while we were in the Catskills. Seth and I were training one day and I got mad. Somehow, I blew up a rock and then the next thing I know there was this cord coming from Seth and I got a rune."

"Why didn't you tell me?"

"Well, we really weren't getting along then and you were busy. And Seth asked me not to say anything until we knew what was going on." Sighing, I told him about the rest of the times and how I'd seen my own cord. Displeasure rolled off Aiden by the time I finished telling him. "It happens when we're... touching sometimes. Seth thinks that, if I get the fourth mark on the back of my neck, then I'll Awaken. Maybe ahead of schedule, and he's all thrilled by that prospect."

"Alex," he breathed unsteadily.

"Yeah, I know. I'm a huge freak even by Apollyon standards." I laughed. "I don't want the fourth mark. You know, I'd kind of like to ride out the rest of being seventeen and not be the Apollyon. But Seth is all like, 'this would be the best thing ever'."

"Best thing for who?" he asked quietly. "You or Seth?"

I laughed again, but my weird humor dried up when I recalled how I suspected Seth of doing the rune things on purpose.

"Alex?"

"Seth says it would be best for me because I'd be stronger, but I think he's... I think he's jonesing for a power boost. Reminds me of Super Mario Brothers power up or something, because I can feel it—akasha—going from me to..." My mouth dropped open. "Son of a bitch."

"What?" Aiden frowned.

My stomach rolled. "The second time I got a mark, I was exhausted for days." I sat up straighter, staring at Aiden as it clicked into place. "Remember the night we all met in Marcus' office? Another rune had appeared right before then and that time had been different than any other time." I felt heat crawl over my cheeks as I remembered how much I'd been down with the whole thing while it was happening. "Anyway, I was really tired and just off after that for days."

Aiden nodded. "I remember. You were pretty crabby."

My crabbiness had led to the sensory deprivation room... and Aiden's whispered fear. "Well, you didn't get it as bad as Seth. I threw a sub at him."

He was trying to fight a smile, but his eyes lightened. "He probably deserved it."

"He did, but gods, is that what's going to happen when I Awaken?" Dread traced icy fingers over my skin. "He's going to drain me. I don't even think he realizes that."

Anger flared in his eyes, dispelling the softness that had gathered in them. His hands curled into fists. "Whatever it is that... you two are doing that's causing those runes to show up, you need to stop."

I looked at him blandly. "I've already decided that, but that isn't going to stop it from happening eventually. And you know what the really messed up thing is? My mom warned me that the First would drain me. I just thought she was being all daimon crazy."

Aiden reclaimed the little distance I'd been able to put between us. "I'm not going to let anything happen to you, Alex. That goes for Seth, too."

Whoa. My heart did a crazy thing there. And he really sounded like he believed he could. "Aiden, you can't stop this. No one can."

"We can't stop you from Awakening, but the power transfer will only happen if you touch after you turn eighteen, right? Then you don't touch."

I couldn't possibly imagine Seth being down with the whole "not-touching" part, but he'd understand once he knew what it could possibly do. "He'll understand," I said. "I'll talk to him when he gets back. This is probably something better to discuss face to face."

Aiden didn't look convinced. "I don't like this."

"You don't like *him*," I pointed out gently.

"You're right. I don't like Seth, but there's something more to this."

"Isn't there always?" I moved slightly and felt his breath over my lips. If I moved an inch, our lips would touch. And Aiden was suddenly staring at my mouth.

"I'll talk to Marcus," Aiden said, voice gruff.

"You already said that."

"I did?" His head angled slightly. "We should head back."

I swallowed. Aiden wasn't moving and every muscle in my body demanded that I cross that tiny space between us. But I pushed back the chair, making a horrible scratching noise. I stood. There didn't seem to be enough air in the little room with faded, pea-green walls. I started toward the door, but stopped when I realized I'd left my bag on the table. I turned around.

Aiden stood in front of me. I hadn't heard him rise or move toward me. He had my bag in hand, book already tucked inside. And he was standing so close that the tips of his shoes brushed mine. My heart was racing and it felt like a dozen butterflies had exploded in my stomach. I was half-afraid to breathe, to feel what I knew I wasn't allowed.

He placed the strap of my bag over my shoulder and then he tucked my hair back behind my ear. I thought that maybe he was going to hug me—or shake me, because that was always a possibility. But then his hand slid over my cheek and his thumb smoothed over my lower lip, careful with the faint scar over the center, even though the pain had long since ceased.

I sucked in a sharp breath. His eyes were liquid silver. My pulse pounded through me. I knew he wanted to kiss me, maybe do other stuff. My skin was tingling with excitement, anticipation, and so much want. And I think he was feeling what I was. I didn't need a stupid cord to tell me that.

But Aiden wouldn't act on it. He had the kind of self-control that rivaled those of the virgin priestesses who'd served in Artemis' temples. And there were all the other reasons why he shouldn't—why I shouldn't.

Aiden closed his eyes and exhaled roughly. When his eyes reopened, he dropped his hand and shot me a quick smile. "Ready?" he asked.

Missing his touch already, all I could do was nod. We walked back to my dorm in silence. I kept stealing glances at him, and he didn't look angry, just lost in his own thoughts and perhaps a little sad.

Aiden walked me straight to my door as if some crazy Order member or a furie was going to jump out of a supply closet. The hall was nearly empty since I shared the first floor with a lot of pures. Their parents had pulled them from class on Monday, getting an earlier start on winter break. He nodded curtly and waited until I closed and locked the door.

Dropping my bag by the couch, I sat and pulled out the cell phone Seth had given me. There was only one contact saved in the address book: *Cuddle Bunny.*

I couldn't help but laugh. There always seemed to be two sides to Seth—the funny and charming side, the one who could be patient and gentle. And then there was a whole different side—the Seth I didn't really know, the one who seemed to only tell half-truths and was the physical embodiment of everything I feared.

Taking a deep breath, I pressed on the name and heard the phone ring once, twice, and then kick over to a standard voicemail greeting.

Seth didn't answer. Nor did he call back that entire evening.

CHAPTER 12

I HAD NO CLUE WHAT SETH COULD BE DOING THAT HE was unable to return a call. It wasn't like I was worried about his safety. Seth could take care of himself. But I did wonder if he was still mad at me. Funny thing was, if he wasn't, he was going to be after I got done talking to him. Pushing Seth out of my mind was surprisingly easy as I entered Technical Truths and Legends.

Deacon glanced up, grinning as I sat beside him. I was surprised to see him on the last day of classes. I figured that, out of everyone, he would have wiggled his way out of class. "How did your library visit go? Get any studying done?"

I peeked at the front of the classroom. Luke was talking to Elena, but he was watching us—Deacon—out of the corner of his eye. "*My* library visit?" I focused on Deacon. "How was yours?"

"Good. Got a lot of studying done." Deacon didn't even miss a beat.

"Wow." I lowered my voice. "Amazing, considering neither of you had any books to study."

Deacon opened his mouth, but shut it.

I winked.

The tips of his ears turned bright red. He tapped his fingers on the top of the desk. "Well, then."

Part of me wanted to tell Deacon that Aiden knew and he had nothing to worry about, but that was so not my place. But maybe I could give it a gentle push in the right direction. "It's not a big deal," I whispered. "Honestly, no one here, pure or half, cares about that."

"It's not like that," he whispered back.

I raised a brow. "It's not?"

"No." Deacon sighed. "I like girls, too, but…" His gaze found Luke. "He's different."

Well, at least I hadn't been completely off-base when it came to Deacon's preferences. "Yeah, Luke sure is different."

Deacon cracked a smile. "It's not what you think. We haven't… done anything."

"Whatever." I grinned.

He leaned over the gap between our desks. "He's a half, Alex. Of all people, I think you know just how dangerous that is."

I jerked back and stared at him.

Deacon winked as a sly grin crossed his face. "But the question is: worth breaking the number one rule or not?"

Before I could even open my mouth to respond to that—and honestly, I had no idea what to say—two Council Guards stepped into the class, silencing the entire room. I shifted back in my seat as my unease blossomed, almost wishing I could slide under the table.

The one with cropped brown hair scanned the room, his lips pressed into a hard line. His gaze landed on me. The blood froze in my veins. Lucian wasn't here, and I didn't recognize the two Guards.

"Miss Andros?" His voice was soft, yet full of authority. "You need to come with us."

Every damn kid in the class turned and stared. Grabbing my bag, I met Deacon's wide eyes. I headed toward the front of the class, forcing a "whateva" smile on my face. But my knees were shaking.

Council Guards calling someone out of class was never a good thing.

There was a low murmur radiating from where Cody and Jackson sat. I ignored them and followed the Guards out. No one spoke as we walked through the halls and up the ridiculous number of steps. Dread continued to weave its way through me. Marcus wouldn't have sent Council Guards to retrieve me. He'd have sent Linard, or Leon, even Aiden.

Covenant Guards opened the door to Marcus' office, and I was ushered in. My gaze traveled over the room, quickly seeking out the occupant.

My step faltered.

Head Minister Telly stood in front of Marcus' desk, hands clasped behind him. Those pale eyes sharpened the moment our gazes locked. The gray seemed to have spread from his temples since the last time I'd seen him, now peppering his hair. Instead of the lavish robes he'd donned during the Council, he wore a simple white tunic and linen pants.

The door shut with a soft click behind me. I spun around. There were no Guards, no Marcus. I was completely alone with Head Minster Douchebag. Great.

"Will you sit, Miss Andros?"

I turned around slowly, forcing myself to take a deep breath. "I prefer to stand."

"But I prefer that you sit," he replied evenly. "Take a seat."

A direct order from the Head Minister was something I couldn't refuse. But it didn't mean I was just going to bend right over for him. I made my way to the chair as slowly as possible, smiling on the inside when I saw the muscle in his jaw begin to tick.

"What can I do for you, Head Minister?" I asked after I made a show of placing my bag by my feet, smoothing out my sweater, and getting comfortable.

Disgust filled his gaze. "I have some questions for you about the night you left the Council."

Acid was eating its way through my stomach. "Shouldn't Marcus be here? And don't you have to wait till my legal guardian is present? Lucian is in New York, where you should be."

"I see no reason to include them in this... unseemly business." He turned his attention to the aquarium, watching the fish for a few moments while I grew more uncomfortable. "After all, both of us know the truth."

That he was a giant asshat? Everyone knew that, but I doubted that was what he was getting at. "What truth?"

Telly laughed as he turned around. "I want to chat with you about the night the daimons and furies attacked the Council, about the real reason you fled."

My heart stuttered, but I kept my face blank. "I thought you knew. The daimons were after me. So were the furies. See, I was terribly popular by the end of the night."

"That is what you say." He leaned against the desk and picked up a small statue of Zeus. "However there was a dead pure-blood Guard found. Do you have anything to add to that?"

A bitter taste formed in the back of my mouth. "Well… there were a lot of dead pures and halfs. And a lot of dead servants that no one gave two shits about. They would've been saved if someone had helped them."

He arched a brow. "The loss of a half-blood is hardly a concern of mine."

Anger was a different taste in my mouth. It tasted like blood. "Dozens and dozens of them died."

"As I said, how would that be a concern of mine?"

He was goading me. I knew it. And I still wanted to punch him.

"But I am here about the death of one of my Guards," he continued. "I want to know how he died."

I feigned boredom. "I'd say it probably had to do with the daimons that were swarming the building. They do tend to kill people. And the furies were ripping through people."

The smirk on his face faded. "He was killed with a Covenant dagger."

"Okay." I sat back in the chair, cocking my head to the side. "Did you know that halfs can be turned now?"

The Head Minister's eyes narrowed.

I slowed my speech down. "Well, some of those halfs were trained as Sentinels and Guards. They carry daggers. And I think they know how to use those daggers, too." Eyes wide, I nodded. "It was probably one of them."

Surprisingly, Telly laughed. It wasn't a nice laugh—more like a Dr. Evil laugh. "What a mouth you have on you. Tell me, is it because you think you're so safe? That being the Apollyon makes you untouchable? Or is it just blind stupidity?"

I pretended to think about that. "Sometimes I do some pretty dumb things. This could be one of them."

He smiled tightly. "Do you think I'm stupid?"

Odd. That was the second time I'd been asked a version of that question within the last twenty-four hours. I gave the same answer. "Is that a trick question?"

"Why do you think I've waited until now to question you, Alexandria? See, I know about your little bond with the First. And I know that this kind of distance negates that bond." His smile became real as my hands clenched the arms of the chair. "So, right now, you're nothing but a half-blood. Do you understand me?"

"Do you think I need Seth to defend me?"

The hollows of his cheeks started to turn pink. "Tell me what happened that night, Alexandria."

"There was this giant daimon attack that I tried to warn you guys about, but you ignored me. You said it was a ridiculous notion that daimons could pull off such a stunt." I paused, letting that jab sink in. "I fought. Killed some daimons and brought down a furie or two."

"Ah, yes. You fought magnificently from what I hear." He paused, tapped his chin. "And then a plot was discovered. The daimons were after the Apollyon."

"Exactly."

"I find that strange," he replied. "Considering that they were trying to kill you in plain sight of Guards and Sentinels. Who, by the way, are loyal to the Council."

I yawned loudly, doing everything to show I wasn't afraid while I was shaking inside. If he saw that, then he'd know he was onto something. "I have no idea what goes on inside the mind of a daimon. I can't explain that."

Telly pushed off the desk, coming to stand in front of me. "I know you killed the pure-blood Guard, Alexandria. And I also know that another pure-blood covered it up for you."

My brain sort of emptied as I stared up at him. Terror, so potent and so strong, knocked the air out of my lungs. How had he known? Had Aiden's compulsion worn off? No. Because I'd be in front of the Council, handcuffed, and Aiden… oh gods, Aiden would be dead.

"You have nothing to say to that?" Telly asked, clearly enjoying this moment.

Pull it together. Pull it together. "I'm sorry. I'm just a little shocked."

"And why would you be shocked?"

"Because that's probably the stupidest thing I've heard in a long time. And have you seen the people I know? That's saying something."

His lips thinned. "You're lying. And you're not a very good liar."

My pulse pounded. "Actually, I'm a great liar."

He was losing his patience quickly. "Tell me the truth, Alexandria."

"I am telling you the truth." I forced my fingers to relax around the chair arms. "I know better than to attack a pure, let alone kill one."

"You attacked a Master at the Council."

Crap. "I didn't actually attack him—I stopped him from attacking someone else. And well, I learned my lesson after that."

"I beg to differ. Who helped you cover it up?"

I leaned forward in the chair. "I have no idea what you're talking about."

"You are testing my patience," he said. "You don't want to see what will happen when I lose it."

"It kind of sounds like you *have* lost it." I looked around the room, forcing my heart to return to normal. "I have no idea why you're asking me these questions. And I'm missing the last day of class before winter break. Are you going to give me an excuse or something?"

"Do you think you're clever?"

I smirked.

Telly's hand snaked out so quickly I didn't even have a chance to deflect the blow. The back of his hand connected with my cheek with enough force to snap my head to the side. Disbelief and rage mixed, rushing through me. My brain flat-out refused to accept the fact that he had just hit me—actually dared to hit *me*. And my body was already demanding that I hit him back, lay him out on his back. My fist practically itched to connect with his jaw.

I gripped the edges of the chair, facing him. That's what Telly wanted. He wanted me to strike him back. Then he'd have my ass on a golden platter.

Telly smiled.

I returned the gesture, ignoring the stinging in my cheek. "Thank you."

Anger flared deep in his eyes. "You think you're tough, don't you?"

I shrugged. "I guess you could say that."

"There are ways of breaking you, dear girl." His smile increased, but it never reached his eyes. "I know you killed a pure-blood. And I know someone—another pure or the First—covered for you."

A shiver ran down my spine, like icy fingers of panic and terror. I shoved it down, sure to revisit it later... if there was a later. I arched a brow. "I have no idea what you're talking about. I've already told you what happened."

"And what you've told me is a lie!" He shot forward, gripping the arms of the chair. His fingers were inches from mine, lips pulled back, face red with fury. "Now tell me the truth or so help me..."

I refused to pull away like I wanted to. "I *have* told you."

A vein popped on his temple. "You are treading on dangerous ground, dear."

"You must not have any proof," I said softly, meeting his enraged stare. "If you did, I'd already be dead. Then again, if I were just a half-blood you wouldn't need much proof. But to take me out, you need the Council's permission. You know, being the *precious Apollyon* and all."

Telly pushed back from the chair, turning his back to me.

I knew I needed to shut up. Taunting him was probably the stupidest thing I could do, but I couldn't stop. Anger and fear were never a good mix for me. "What I don't understand is how you're so certain that I killed a pure-blood. There were obviously no witnesses to his death. No one is pointing a finger at me." I paused, enjoying the way the muscles in his back tensed under the thin tunic. "Why would you...?"

He turned around, face impressively blank. "Why would I what, Alexandria?"

My stomach churned as realization set in. My suspicions had been correct. I stared at his elegant hands. "How can you be so certain unless you ordered someone—a Guard—to attack me? Then I guess you'd be fairly certain if that Guard did turn up dead, but you wouldn't have done that. Because I'm sure the Council would be pretty pissed. You might even lose your position."

So busy gloating, I didn't even see him move.

His hand caught the same cheek. The burst of red-hot pain stunned me. It was no pansy hit. The chair went up on two legs before settling back down. Tears stung my eyes.

"You… you can't do this," I said, voice hoarse.

Telly grasped my wrist. "I can do as I please." Telly hauled me to my feet, his fingers bruising my arms as he dragged me across my uncle's office. He shoved me toward the window overlooking the quad. "Tell me, what do you see out there?"

I blinked back tears, biting down on the fury threatening to boil over. Statues and sand, and beyond that, the ocean rolled and tumbled with rough waves. People were scattered across the campus.

"What do you see, Alexandra?" His grip tightened.

I winced, hating my moment of weakness. "I don't know. I see people and freaking sand. And the ocean. I see lots of water."

"See the servants?" He gestured toward the atrium, where a cluster of them stood waiting for orders from their Master. "I own them. I own all of them."

The muscles in my body locked up. I couldn't pull my gaze from them.

Telly leaned in, his breath hot in my ear. "Let me tell you a little secret about the true nature of your other half's trip to the Catskills. He's been brought in to deal with any servant who is off the elixir and is refusing to submit. Did you know that?"

"Deal with them?"

"Take some of that cleverness from your mouth and apply it. I'm sure you can figure it out."

I could figure it out, but I couldn't believe it. There was a difference between those two things. Because I understood that Telly was claiming that Seth would take down any half-blood who was causing problems, but Seth wouldn't actually agree to something like that. And I also knew that Telly was telling me this to rattle me.

It was working.

"I have something else I want to tell you," Telly said. "I do have a favorite of all the servants, you see. One I personally requested many years ago. Did you know I knew your mother and father?"

I closed my eyes.

"What, Alexandria? Has someone already let that little bird out of the cage?" He let go of my wrist, chuckling. "To think your beautiful mother had tainted herself in that way, to mix with a half-blood. Did they really think they'd get away with it? And do you really think Lucian has forgotten the disgrace she placed upon his head?"

Dad. Daddy. Father. All titles which hadn't really meant anything until I read Laadan's letter. But now they meant everything.

"I know he must mean nothing to you," Telly continued. "You've never known him, but I do know that whoever covered up what you did must mean a lot to you. And what do they say? Like father, like daughter?"

Desperation washed away any relief I felt. Telly wasn't going to use my father against me. He was just going to use Aiden.

Telly left me by the window, returning to the center of the room. "This is your last chance. I will leave the day after tomorrow, before dawn, and if you haven't turned yourself in by then, there will be no more chances. This could end easily."

I didn't even feel the throbbing in my face anymore.

Telly smiled, reveling in my silence. "Admit to killing the Guard, and I won't push on…" his lip curled, "who covered it up. And trust me, I will find out. There are only a few I have noticed who have taken any interest in you, other than the First. What?" He laughed. "Did you think I hadn't been paying attention?"

Air rushed from my lungs so quickly I felt dizzy.

"Let's see." Telly tapped his chin. "There is your uncle, who I think cares for you far more than he lets on. He was in New York. Then there is that one Sentinel—the one who found you that night in the maze. Leon? Then there is the one who graciously offered to train you. I do believe that would be St. Delphi. And then there is Laadan. All of them are suspects, and I will ensure that all of them suffer. As the Head Minister, I can revoke Marcus' position. I can even remove Lucian. I can file charges against the rest. With all the unrest and recent incidents, it would be all too easy."

A lump of horror and frustration formed in my throat. Tears built behind my eyes at the same moment I wanted to smash Telly's head in.

"You'll go into servitude and you will go on the elixir. If you refuse, well, things will end badly."

My hands curled into fists. "You're… revolting."

Telly started toward me, his hand streaking out to hit me again.

I caught his wrist, my eyes meeting his and holding. "I've been hit enough, thank you."

A commotion from the hallway caught Telly's attention and he pulled his wrist free. Marcus' voice rang loud, demanding entry to his office. Telly raised a brow at me. "You have until dawn on Friday."

The walls closed in.

Telly smirked as Marcus' demands grew louder. Neither of us spoke during those moments.

"Why do you hate me so much?" I asked finally.

"I don't hate you, Alexandria. I hate what you *are*."

CHAPTER 13

THAT WAS WHAT THIS HAD COME DOWN TO—BECAUSE I was an Apollyon, because I'll turn Seth into a God Killer. And I knew then, beyond a doubt, that Telly was a member of the Order. In his mind, he was just protecting the gods from a threat, and he saw no wrong in what he did.

The doors swung open as I turned back to the window, struggling for control.

"What is going on in here?" Marcus demanded.

"I had some… unanswered concerns about the night Alexandria left the Council," Telly replied. "At first she was not very cooperative when it came to the questions, but I do believe we worked out an understanding. After that, she was surprisingly helpful."

Yeah, he worked it out on my face.

I wondered how quickly I could rip one of those daggers off Marcus' wall and plunge it into Telly's eye before his Guards could react. The tension in the room escalated, waves rippling out in every direction.

"And why was I not involved in this questioning? Or better yet, why couldn't this wait until Lucian's return?" Marcus said evenly, but I recognized the edge to his voice. Gods knew I'd been on the receiving of it countless times. "He is her guardian and should have been present."

Telly tsked softly. "This wasn't a formal questioning or sanctioned by the Council. I had a few concerns I needed to clear up. Therefore I had no need for Lucian's or your presence. That is, beside the fact that I am the Head Minister and do not need your permission."

He'd effectively put Marcus in his place.

"Alexandria," called Telly. "Please do not forget what we've discussed."

I didn't respond, because I was still weighing whether or not I could stab him before the Guards took me down.

Head Minister Telly excused himself then, giving out pleasantries in such a calm manner I almost found it hard to believe he'd just pulled the world out from underneath my feet.

"Alexandria?" Marcus' voice broke the silence. "What did he want to discuss with you?"

"He had questions about what happened at the Council." My voice was unnaturally thick. "That's all."

"Alex?" Aiden said, and my heart dropped all the way to my toes. Of course, he was here. "What happened?"

Facing them, I used my hair to shield my stinging cheek from them and kept my gaze plastered to the carpet. "Apparently, I have a bad attitude. We had to work through that."

Aiden was suddenly in front of me, tipping my chin back. My hair slid off my cheek. Rage blasted off him, swallowing up the air like a black hole of fury.

"He did this?" His voice was so low I barely heard him.

Unable to answer, I looked away.

"This is unacceptable." Aiden whirled on Marcus. "He cannot do this. She's a girl."

Sometimes Aiden forgot that I was also a half-blood, which pretty much zeroed out the whole "not hitting girls" thing. Like with Jackson. Like with most pure-bloods. Our society—our rules and how we were treated—it sucked. There were no words for it.

And at once, a thousand questions rose up, but one stood out. How could I continue to be a part of this world? Being a Sentinel, in a way, was supporting the social structure, basically saying that I was okay with this, and I wasn't. I hated it.

Shaking my head, I pushed those thoughts out of my head for now. "He's the Head Dick. He can do whatever he wants, right?"

Marcus looked thunderstruck as he continued to stare at me. Was he really that surprised by Telly's violence? If that was the case, he'd just lost some intelligence points. He turned to Leon. "She was supposed to go nowhere by herself. Why was Telly able to reach her?"

"She was in class," Leon responded. "Linard was waiting for her to leave. And no one expected Telly to be here. Not with everything that is happening in New York."

Marcus cut a dangerous look at Linard. "If you have to sit in class with her, then do it."

"It's not his fault," I said. "No one can watch me every second of the day."

Aiden cursed. "Is that all you'll do? She is your niece, Marcus. He hit *your niece* and that's your answer?"

Marcus' eyes deepened to a bright green. "I am well aware of the fact that she is my niece, Aiden. And do not think for one second that I found any of this," he threw his hand toward me, "acceptable. I will contact the Council immediately. I do not care that she is a half-blood. Telly has no right."

I shifted my weight. "The Council is going to care? Seriously? You guys beat the crap out of servants all the time. Why would I be any different?"

"You are not a servant," Marcus said, storming to his desk.

"Does that make it okay?" I shouted, my hands curling into fists. "It's okay to beat servants because of their blood? And it's not okay because I have half—" I cut myself off before I revealed too much. All eyes were on me.

Behind his desk, Marcus took a deep breath and briefly closed his eyes. "Are you okay, Alexandria?"

"I'm just peachy."

Aiden took my arm. "I'm taking her to the clinic."

I pulled my arm free. "I'll be fine."

"He *hit* you," Aiden seethed, eyes flashing.

"And it will just bruise, okay? That's not the problem." I needed to be out of this room, away from all of them. I needed to think. "I just want to go back to my room."

Marcus froze with the phone halfway to his ear. "Aiden, make sure she makes it back to her room. And I want her to stay there until we find out what Telly is up to or until he leaves. I will contact Lucian and the rest of the Council," Marcus said, and his gaze found Aiden's again. "I mean it. She is not to leave the room."

I was too busy going over everything that had happened to care about Marcus sentencing me to my dorm. And if Lucian found out about what'd happened, then that meant Seth would, too. At least there was one bright lining in the cloud of crud. If Seth were here, he'd probably kill Telly.

Marcus stopped me at the door. "Alexandria?"

I turned around, hoping he'd make this fast. Bitch me out for antagonizing Telly, tell me not to do again, and warn me about my bad behavior.

He met my stare. "I am sorry that I was not here to stop him. This will not happen again."

My uncle had an alien in him. I blinked slowly. Before I could say anything, he went back to his phone call. Sort of stunned, I let Aiden guide me out of the office and down the hall.

Once the door in the stairwell closed behind us, Aiden blocked the stairs. "I want to know what happened."

"I just want to go back to my room."

"I'm not asking, Alex."

I didn't answer, and finally Aiden turned around stiffly and went down the stairs. I followed behind him slowly. Classes were still in session, so the stairwell and the first floor lobby were virtually empty with the exception of some Guards and Instructors. We walked back to my dorm in silence, but I knew he wasn't going to let this go. Aiden was just biding his time, so I wasn't entirely surprised when he followed me into my room, closing the door behind him.

I dropped my bag and ran my hands through my hair. "Aiden."

He grasped my chin like he'd done in Marcus' office, tilting my head to the side. His jaw tightened. "How did this happen?"

How bad did it look? "I guess I didn't respond correctly after the first time."

"He hit you twice?"

Embarrassed, I pulled away and sat on the couch. I was trained to fight and defend myself. I'd walked away from daimon battles with scratches. This whole situation made me feel weak and helpless.

"You shouldn't be here," I said finally. "I know Marcus said to make sure I stayed in my room, but it shouldn't be you."

Aiden stood in front of the small coffee table, hands on his hips. His posture reminded me so much of our training sessions—the one he got when he knew I was going to push back on something. He was digging in for the long haul. "Why?"

I laughed and then winced. "You shouldn't be around me. I think Telly has someone watching me—us."

There wasn't an ounce of panic in those silver eyes. "You need to tell me what happened, Alex. Don't even think about lying to me. I'll know."

Closing my eyes, I shook my head. "I don't know if I can."

I heard Aiden move around the table and sit on its edge in front of me. His hand pressed against my other cheek. "You can tell me anything. You know that. I will help you always. How can you doubt that?"

"I don't doubt that." I opened my eyes, ashamed to find they felt damp.

Confusion flickered across his face. "Then why can't you tell me?"

"Because... because I don't want you to worry."

Aiden frowned. "You're always thinking about someone else when you should be more concerned about yourself."

I snorted. "That's so not true. I've been really self-centric lately."

He laughed softly, but when the rich sound faded, so did his brief smile. "Alex, talk to me."

The terror and panic returned. I'm not sure they'd ever really left. The words just came out. "Telly knows."

A slight narrowing of his eyes was his only reaction. "How much?"

"He knows I killed a pure-blood," I whispered. "And he knows either Seth or a pure covered it up."

Aiden said nothing.

I really started to freak out. "He's definitely part of the Order, and I think he's the one who sent the Guard to kill me. It's the only way he could know unless the compulsion—"

"The compulsion hasn't faded." Aiden dragged his hand over his head. Dark waves tumbled through his fingers. "We would know. I'd be arrested by now."

"Then the only way he would know is if he sent the Guard to kill me."

Aiden clasped the back of his neck. "Are you sure he knows?"

I laughed harshly as I gestured at my cheek. "He did this when I wouldn't admit to it."

The silver in his eyes burned. "I want to kill him."

"Me too, but that's not really going to help things."

He flashed me a wild smile. "But it would make us feel better."

"Damn, you've gotten dark. Funny, but dark."

Aiden shook his head. "What did he say, exactly?"

I told him the questions Telly had asked. "You know, the only good thing about this is that he didn't think using my father had any pull on me. But he said that, if I turn myself in, he wouldn't push to find the pure who covered for me. If I didn't tell him, then he would go after every pure who seems to tolerate me: you, Laadan, Leon, even Marcus. I guess he doesn't think he can get Seth or he's afraid of him."

"Alex—"

"I don't know what to do." I pushed off the couch, sidestepping him. I prowled the length of the small living room, feeling caged. I stopped, my back to Aiden. "I'm screwed, you know that, right?"

"Alex, we'll think of something." I felt him come up behind me. "This isn't the end. There are always options."

"Options?" I crossed my arms. "There were options when the Guard tried to kill me, and I chose the wrong one. I made a huge mistake, Aiden. I can't fix that. And you know what? I don't even think he cares about that Guard."

"I know," he replied softly. "I think he sent that Guard knowing that you'd be able to defend yourself, that you would probably even kill the Guard. It makes sense."

I turned around. "It does?"

He nodded, eyes narrowing. "It's the perfect set-up, Alex. Telly sends the Guard to kill you, knowing there would be a good chance that you'd fight back and kill the Guard out of self-defense."

"And self-defense means nothing in this world."

"Exactly. So Telly would have you then. No one could stop him from having you killed or at least placing you into servitude. He puts you on the elixir and you don't Awaken. Problem solved, except Telly didn't expect a pure to use compulsion and cover it up for you."

I nodded. "But he now knows that someone did."

"It doesn't matter," Aiden said. "He may know but he has no evidence without incriminating himself. Telly may be the Head Minister, but he does not wield the kind of power where he can indiscriminately go after pure-bloods. He can accuse us all he wants, but he can't do anything without evidence."

A tiny seedling of hope rooted in my chest. "He has a lot of power, Aiden. He has the Order, too, and gods know how many people belong to it."

"It doesn't matter, Alex." Aiden placed gentle, strong hands on my shoulders. "All he has right now is fear. He thinks he can scare you into admitting the truth. He's using that fear against you."

"But what if he does go after everyone? What about you?"

Aiden smiled. "He can, but he's not going to get anywhere with it. And when you don't admit to anything, then he'll go back to New York. And we'll be ready if he tries something again. This isn't the end."

I nodded again.

Aiden looked me straight in the eyes. "I want you to promise me that you won't do anything stupid, Alex. Promise me that you won't turn yourself in."

"Why does everyone think I'm always going to do something stupid?"

His look said he knew better. "Knee-jerk reaction, Alex. I think we've covered that."

I sighed. "I won't do anything reckless, Aiden."

Aiden stared at me for a moment, then nodded. Instead of relaxing like I thought he would, he seemed to grow more tense. He exhaled roughly and then nodded once again. Whatever he was thinking, I knew it wasn't good.

And when his steely gaze met mine, I knew there was a good chance he didn't believe any of the promises I'd made.

CHAPTER 14

LATER THAT EVENING, I HELD THE CELL PHONE TWO feet from my head and still felt like Seth was yelling in my ear.

"I'm going to kill him!"

"Yeah, you're not the first one to say that." I climbed off the couch, scowling at the door. I didn't need to check to know that Leon stood right outside my room. Thank the gods most of the kids were gone, because having a personal Sentinel guard would make me an even bigger freak. "And it's pretty sad when I'm the voice of reason."

"What else do you suggest?" he asked. "He's the Head Minister, Alex. It's obvious that he ordered that Guard to attack you."

"Yeah." I headed to my bathroom, turning my head to the side. The left side of my cheek was red and slightly swollen. A bit of blue lined my jaw. Jackson had done worse. Telly hit like a girl. I started to smile. "But Aiden said that he doesn't—"

"Aiden's an idiot."

I rolled my eyes. "Anyway, why didn't you answer the phone last night?"

"Are you jealous?"

"What? No. It was just weird."

Seth laughed. "I was busy and it was too late by the time I had a chance to call you. Did you miss me or something?"

Not really. I pushed away from the mirror and went into the bedroom. "Seth, what are you really doing up there?"

"I already told you." Static filled the line for a few seconds. "Anyway, is that really important right now? You should be worried about Telly."

I sat on the edge of the bed. "Telly said that you were there to deal with the halfs who were causing problems and weren't responding to the elixir. Is that true?"

Silence.

Knots started to form in my stomach. "Seth."

He sighed into the phone. "Alex, that isn't the problem right now. Telly is."

"I know that, but I need to know what you're doing up there." I plucked at a loose thread in the bedspread. "My dad... I know he wasn't responding to the—"

"I haven't even seen your father, Alex. Granted, I really don't know what he looks like and Laadan isn't telling. He could be here. He could be gone."

Anger and frustration rushed to the surface. "What are you doing to the halfs who aren't responding to the elixir?"

A sound of exasperation traveled through the phone. "What I've been ordered to do by the Council, Alex. Take care of them."

Blood froze in my veins. "What do you mean by 'take care of them'?"

"Alex, that isn't important. Look, they're just half-bloods—"

"What the hell do you think we are?" I stood and started pacing. Again. "We are half-bloods, too, Seth."

"No," he replied evenly. "We are the Apollyons."

"Gods, I wish you were in front of me."

"I knew you missed me," Seth said. I could hear his smile.

"No. If you were in front of me, I'd kick you in your junk, Seth. You cannot be okay with... *taking care* of those halfs! Wrong doesn't even sum up what that is. It's disgusting—revolting."

"I'm not *killing* anyone, Alex. Gods, what do you really think of me?"

"Oh." I stopped, feeling my cheeks turn red.

A couple of moments passed in silence. It sounded like Seth was walking somewhere fast. "I'd like to be in your head for just one hour," he laughed. "No. Forget that. I don't. You'd kill my self-confidence."

"Seth—"

"Let's focus on the important stuff here, which is Telly. I don't believe he doesn't have a damn thing. He wouldn't hold that threat of going after the pure responsible for the compulsion without having something."

Fear spiked. "You seriously think he has something?"

"Telly is a lot of things, but he isn't stupid. He waited until he knew that neither Lucian nor I were anywhere near you before he made his move. I wouldn't be surprised if Telly didn't screw with the elixir weeks ago as a fallback plan. He needed a distraction and he got one. And Aiden isn't stupid, either," he said. "He's telling you what you need to hear to stop you from doing something stupid."

Feeling dizzy, I sat back down. "Shit."

"Listen to me, Alex. None of them—your uncle or Aiden—is important. Stay away from Telly. Let him act on his threat, whether he has proof or not."

"What?" I stared at the phone as if he could somehow see me, which was kind of dumb. "They're important to me, Seth."

"No. Aiden is important to you. In reality, you could care less about the rest," he corrected.

"That's not true!"

Seth laughed, but there was no humor in it. "Alex, you're a terrible liar."

What the hell? Did everyone think I was prone to acts of stupidity *and* a terrible liar? But I wasn't lying. Laadan and Marcus were important to me. Even Leon, though he was kind of weird.

I took a deep breath. "So, you think Telly does have something?"

"I don't think Telly would make idle threats and hope you fall for them. Look at all that he's done so far."

I dropped my head into my open palm. "Seth, I can't let him go after them."

"You can and you will. They. Are. Not. Important. You are. We are."

"I hate it when you say things like that," I seethed.

"Because it's true, Alex. Why? Because once you Awaken, we can change things." Seth paused and then his voice lowered. "You have no idea what the majority of the Council wants done to the half-bloods up here. Luckily, my presence seems to be keeping most of them in line, but they do want them killed, Alex. They see the half-bloods as a problem that they don't have the time or manpower to deal with. Especially now that the daimons have no qualms about attacking the Covenants."

"I thought you didn't care about the half-bloods." I lifted my head and stared at the blank wall across from the bed.

"Not losing sleep over their crappy lives and being okay with exterminating them are two different things, Alex."

"Gods, Seth." I shook my head. "Sometimes I don't even know you."

"You never tried to," he said, without a trace of anger. "And it really doesn't matter right now. All that matters is that you stay safe. Look, I got to go. Just stay in your room, at least until Telly leaves. I know he has to be back here by Friday because they are having a session."

"All right," I said. "Seth?"

"What?"

I bit my lip, having no idea what I wanted to say to him. There was just so much, and none of it was anything I was willing to get into right now. "Nothing. I'll… I'll talk to you later."

Seth hung up, without making me promise to stay out of trouble. I think he knew my word was just as good as his.

The next twenty-four hours crept by painfully slowly. I wasn't allowed to leave my room. Food was brought to me by one of my babysitters. Besides them, I had no visitors. Bored out of my mind, I cleaned my bathroom and started to rearrange my closet, which ended with clothes strewn across the floor.

There was a moment when panic punched a hole through my chest. Was I making the right decision by not turning myself in?

I tried calling Seth a few times but that was a total bust. He eventually called back just after I'd changed for bed. We didn't talk for long or about anything important. I think he was just surprised that I was still in my dorm and hadn't done anything dumb yet.

It took hours of tossing and turning to drift off to sleep. But I didn't stay asleep for long. I woke up while it was still dark, the comforter twisted around my legs.

I watched slivers of light slice across the ceiling, disappearing when the moon dipped behind a cloud outside my window. My brain immediately kicked into hyperdrive, replaying everything that had happened with Telly, then with Aiden and Seth. What if Seth had been right and Telly had a way of finding out that it was Aiden? Or even if he didn't, what if he did go after him? And it wasn't just Aiden I cared about. What would it say about me if I let others be harmed so I skated through until the next time? Because there would be a next time—I knew it. And who would risk their future and their life then?

It wasn't right or fair.

Sitting up, I swung my legs off the bed and stood. Cool air spread goosebumps over my bare legs. I grabbed a long, chunky sweater off the corner of my bed and slipped it over my tank top. Creeping to the window, I pried the blinds apart and peered outside. I couldn't see anything in the darkness and I wasn't even sure what I was looking for.

"What am I doing?" I asked myself.

"Absolutely nothing if I have anything to do with it."

Shrieking, I dropped the blinds and spun around. Heart pounding, I squinted at the tall outline taking up the entire doorway to my bedroom. Once I recognized who it was, it did nothing to calm my racing heart. "Holy daimon babies! You gave me a heart attack."

Aiden stepped forward, folding his arms. "Sorry about that."

I pulled the sweater closer, staring at him. "What are you doing in my dorm?"

"You have a problem with guys in your dorm now?"

"Ha. Ha." I hurried over to my bedside table and flipped on the lamp. A soft glow filled the room. "Actually, I never invited Seth in here. He just kind of made himself at home."

A ghost of a smile appeared on his face. As always, he was in his Sentinel garb. Then it struck me. My mouth dropped open.

"You're working, aren't you?" I demanded.

"Well, there was a good chance that you'd try to sneak out and turn yourself in before Telly could leave in the morning. We were taking precautions just in case you did."

"We?" I sputtered. "Is anyone else in here?"

"No, but Leon was in right after you fell asleep. Linard is patrolling the outside." He paused. "I just switched shifts with Leon. I'm sorry if I woke you."

I stared at him, dumbfounded. "You guys have been switching off in here while I slept? Last night, too?"

He nodded. "Thankfully, Marcus suggested the idea. Otherwise I have a feeling Linard would've been chasing you across the quad and stopping you before you ran off."

"I'm not stupid." My fingers curled around the edges of my sweater. "Do you really think I'd just up and go turn myself in to Telly in the middle of the night?"

He cocked his head to the side. "This is coming from the girl who once snuck out of the Covenant to find a daimon."

Touché. "Whatever. I wasn't planning to do anything like that again."

"You weren't?"

I shook my head. There had been a part of me that had been considering it. "I couldn't sleep. There's a lot going on in my head."

"That's understandable." His eyes drifted over me, settling on my cheek. "How is it?"

I tipped my head, shielding my face. "It's fine."

He looked away a moment, then his gaze swung back to me. "You've been through worse, I know, but still. You should've never had to deal with what you did... or with Jackson. Any of this really."

"What do you mean?"

"Nothing—I'm just rambling." Aiden's shoulders relaxed as he glanced around the room. "It's been a long time since I've been in here."

I followed his gaze, which had landed on the bed. A warm flush went from my hair to the tips of my toes. A dozen or so vivid images danced in front of my eyes—all of them completely wrong considering everything that was going on.

"It was your first day back here," he said, and a small grin appeared. "There were clothes on the floor then, too."

Surprised, I focused on him—the real, completely clothed Aiden. Of course, he'd been in my living room area, but he was right. He hadn't ventured any further than the couch. "You remember that?"

He nodded. "Yeah, I was lecturing you."

"After I pulled Lea out of her chair by her hair."

Aiden laughed and the sound warmed me. "You finally admit to it."

"She kind of deserved it then." I bit my lip as he looked up, his gaze meeting mine. What was he thinking right now? I sat on the edge of the bed. "I'm not going to do anything, even though I should. You don't have to stay in here."

Aiden was silent a couple of moments, then he made his way to where I was sitting and sat beside me. The air in the room suddenly got heavier, the bed smaller. The last time we'd been on a bed—and I'd been this close to being undressed—had been the night in his cabin. Impossibly, I grew warmer at the memory, and nervous—a lot more nervous. I should've stayed asleep.

"Why do you think you need to turn yourself in, Alex?"

I scooted back and tucked my legs under me. The distance helped a little. "Seth said that there's a good chance Telly can prove that it was you or that he will make a move against everyone he suspects."

He twisted around, facing me. "It doesn't matter if he does, Alex. Going to Telly means the end of you. Don't you understand that?"

"Not going to Telly could mean the end of you—of anyone who he thinks may have helped me."

"It doesn't matter."

"You sound like Seth—like no one else's life is important but mine. That's bullshit." I rose to my knees, dragging in a deep breath. "What if Telly does something to you? Or to Laadan or Leon or Marcus? You expect me to be okay with that? To live with that?"

Aiden's eyes darkened. "Yes, I expect you to live with that."

"That's insane." I climbed off the bed, feeling the spicy rush of anger. "You're insane!"

He watched me calmly. "It's the way it is."

"You can't say that my life is more important than yours. That's not right."

"But your life *is* more important to me."

"Do you hear yourself?" I stopped in front of him, hands shaking. "How can you make that decision for other people—for Laadan and Marcus?"

"Look," Aiden said, his hands rising into the air. "Get mad at me. Hit me. It doesn't change anything."

I moved toward him, to push him but not actually hit him. "You can't—"

Aiden caught both my wrists and hauled me into his lap, switching my wrists to one hand. He sighed. "I didn't mean for you to *actually* hit me."

Too stunned to respond, I just stared at him. Our heads were only inches apart. My legs tangled with his, and then he reached up with his free hand, smoothing the mess of hair back from my face. My breath caught as my heart sped up. Our gazes locked and his eyes turned to quicksilver.

He cupped the nape of my neck. I heard his sharp intake of breath. Then he let go of my wrists and grasped my hips. Before I could blink, I was on my back, and Aiden hovered over me. Using one arm to support himself, he lowered his head and brushed his lips over my swollen cheek.

"How do we always end up like this?" he asked, voice rough as his gaze traveled away from my face and down my body.

"I didn't do this." Slowly, I lifted my hands and placed them against his chest. His heart jumped under my palm.

"No. This was all me." The lower half of his body shifted down. Our legs were flush. His eyes searched mine. "It gets harder every time."

My brows rose and I bit back a giggle. "What does?"

Aiden grinned and his eyes lightened. "Stopping before it's too late."

In a second, everything—the rift that had come between us the day I'd given him that stupid pick, what I'd seen in the Catskills, the mess we were in, and even Seth—everything vanished. The words came out of me in a rush. "Don't stop."

CHAPTER 15

AIDEN'S EYES SEEMED TO GLOW FROM WITHIN AS HE stared down at me. Like in the library, I knew he wanted to kiss me. His resolve was cracking and the hand against my cheek trembled.

I slid my hands down his taut stomach, stopping above the band of his pants. More than anything I wanted to lose myself in him, to forget about everything. I wanted him to lose himself in *me*.

He sucked in air, lips parted. "It probably would be a good idea if Leon or someone else was watching you during the night."

"Probably."

His lips tipped into a crooked smile as his hand drifted away from my cheek, down my neck and under the collar of my sweater. I jumped a little when his hand skimmed over my shoulder. "People say hindsight is always twenty-twenty," he said.

I didn't care about people's eyesight. All I cared about was his hand on my skin, pushing the sweater down my arm. "When… when does the next babysitter arrive?"

"Not until morning."

Butterflies went crazy in my stomach. Morning was several hours away. A lot of things could go down in those hours. "Oh."

Aiden didn't respond. Instead, his fingers skimmed over the tags on my arm and then he closed his eyes. A shudder rolled through his entire body, shaking me to my core. Then his head dipped and dark waves of hair fell forward, but not quick enough to shield the hunger in his stare.

I tensed, my chest tightening. His breath was warm and tantalizing on my lips, and then they brushed across mine so softly. That simple act stole my breath, my heart. But even as he pulled away, I realized that he couldn't steal something he already had.

Aiden rolled onto his side, pulling me along with him. He eased one arm under me, cradling me to his chest so tightly I could feel his heart thundering. There was something under his shirt that pressed against my cheek. I realized it was his necklace.

"Aiden?"

He lowered his chin to the top of my head and drew in a deep breath. "Go to sleep, Alex."

My eyes snapped open. I tried to lift my head, but I couldn't move an inch. "I don't think I can sleep now."

"Well, you better try."

I tried to wiggle free, but he moved his leg, clamping one of mine between his. My fingers curled into his thermal. "*Aiden.*"

"Alex."

Frustrated, I pushed on his chest. Aiden's laugh rumbled through me, and even though I wanted to smack him, I started to smile. "Why? Why did you kiss me? I mean, you did just kiss me, right?"

"Yes. No. Sort of." Aiden sighed. "I wanted to."

My smile started to turn giddy. It was like there was a part of me that had no perception of the outside world or all the consequences—the part that was completely controlled by my heart. "Okay. Then why did you stop?"

"Can we talk about anything other than that? Please?"

"Why?"

His hand moved up my back, delving into my hair and sending shivers over my skin. "Because I asked you nicely?"

Being this close to him wasn't helping. Every time I breathed, it was full of his aftershave and the scent of sea salt. If I moved, it only brought us closer. There was no way in hell I was sleeping any time soon. "This is so wrong."

"That's the truest thing you've said this evening."

I rolled my eyes. "And this is completely your fault."

"Not going to argue with that." Aiden shifted onto his back, and I ended up pinned to his side. I tried to sit up, but he locked his arms together. My head ended up on his shoulder with my arm trapped against his stomach. "Tell me something," he said after I stopped struggling.

"I don't think you want me to tell you something right now."

"True." He laughed. "Where do you want to be assigned when you graduate?"

"What?" I frowned. Aiden repeated the question. "Yeah, I heard you, but that's such a random question."

"So? Answer it."

Giving up on trying to get free and jump him, I decided to make the best of this weird situation and snuggled closer. I'd probably regret it later, when he came to his senses and pushed me away. Aiden's arms tightened in response. "I don't know."

"You haven't thought about it?"

"Not really. When I first returned to the Covenant, I didn't even think I was going to be allowed back in and then I learned about the whole Apollyon thing." I paused, because I wasn't sure why I hadn't really given it much thought. "I guess I just stopped thinking it would even be an option."

Aiden unlocked his hands and began to trace an idle circle over my upper arm. It was ridiculously soothing. "It's still an option, Alex. Awakening doesn't mean your life is over. Where would you go?"

Wishing we'd had the foresight to turn off the light before our impromptu cuddle-fest, I closed my eyes. "I don't know. I guess I'd pick some place I'd never been, like New Orleans."

"You've never been there?" Surprise colored his voice.

"No. Have you?"

"I've been there a couple of times."

"During Mardi Gras?"

Aiden picked up my hand that was on his stomach, threading his fingers through mine. My chest fluttered. "Once or twice," he answered.

I smiled, picturing Aiden carrying beads. "Yeah, so maybe some place like that."

"Or Ireland?"

"You remember the weirdest things I say."

His fingers closed over mine. "I remember everything you say."

Warmth stole through me and I savored it. He'd said the same thing the day at the zoo, but somehow I'd forgotten that in the mess of everything that had happened after that. "That's kind of embarrassing. I say a lot of stupid things."

Aiden laughed. "You do say some pretty weird things."

I couldn't argue with that. We lay there together in a companionable silence for a little while. I listened to the even sounds of his breathing. "Aiden?"

He tilted his head toward me. "Yeah?"

I finally put voice to something that had been nagging me for a while. "What... what if I don't want to be a Sentinel anymore?"

Aiden didn't answer immediately. "What do you mean?"

"It's not that I don't see the purpose behind being a Sentinel and I still have that need, but sometimes I feel like being a Sentinel is agreeing with the way things are." I took a deep breath. Saying this aloud was damn near close to heresy. "It's like being a Sentinel means I'm okay with how half-bloods are treated and I'm... I'm not okay with that."

"Neither am I," he said softly.

"I feel... terrible for even thinking this, but I just don't know." I squeezed my eyes shut, partially ashamed. "But after I saw those dead servants in the Catskills, I just can't be a part of this."

There was a pause. "I see what you're saying."

"There's a but, isn't there?"

"No. There's not." Aiden squeezed my hand. "I know becoming the Apollyon isn't something you want, but you will be in the position to change things, Alex. There are pures who will listen to you. And there are some who want things to change. If this is something you feel strongly about, then you should do what you can."

"It doesn't mean I'd be shirking my duties as a Sentinel?" My voice sounded tiny. "Because the world needs Sentinels and Guards, and the daimons—they kill indiscriminately. I can't just—"

"You can do what you want." Sincerity rang in his tone, and I wanted to believe him, but that wasn't the case. Even as the Apollyon, I was still a half-blood and I couldn't do what I wanted. "And it's not shirking your duty," he said. "Changing the lives of hundreds of half-bloods will do more than hunting daimons."

"You think so?"

"I know so."

A little bit of the pressure eased and I yawned. "What if someone sees us?"

"Don't worry about it." He brushed my hair back over my shoulder. "Marcus knows I'm here."

I doubted that Marcus knew Aiden was in my bed. Maybe all of this was a dream, I decided. But my lips still tingled from the brief kiss. I wanted to ask him why he was here, like this. It didn't make sense, but I didn't want to kill the warmth between us with questions rooted in logic. Sometimes logic was just overrated.

Slowly, I pried my eyes opened and blinked. The dusky rays of early morning sunlight filtered through the blinds. Little dots of dust floated in the stream of light. A heavy arm lay over my stomach and a leg was thrown over mine, as if he'd wanted to make sure I couldn't escape while he slept.

Not that a god could make me move from this bed or his arms.

I delighted in the feel of him pressed against my side, the way his breath stirred the hair at my temple. Last night hadn't been a weird dream. Or if it had been, I wasn't sure I wanted to wake up. Maybe he hadn't been afraid of me running off when he slept. Perhaps he'd hungered for my closeness the way I sought his.

My heart rate picked up even though I hadn't moved. Lying here, staring at the tiny particles of dust, I wondered how many times I'd dreamt of falling asleep and waking up in Aiden's arms. A hundred or more? Definitely more. My throat tightened. It didn't seem right that I'd be teased like this, given a taste of what a future with Aiden could be like, something I could never have.

An ache filled my chest. Being in his arms like this hurt, but there wasn't an ounce of regret. In the silence of the early morning, I admitted that there was no getting over Aiden. No matter what happened from here on out, my heart would remain his. He could settle down with a pure and I could go leave this island forever and it wouldn't matter. Against all odds and common sense, Aiden had slipped under my skin, wrapped himself around my heart and embedded himself into my bones. He was a part of me and…

All of me—my heart and my soul—would always belong to him.

And I was foolish to believe otherwise, to even entertain a different scenario. I thought of Seth then and that ache in my chest spread, turned inward and burned like a daimon tag. Whatever I had going on with Seth wasn't fair to him. If he truly cared for me, he expected to have some kind of hold on my heart and feelings.

Careful not to disturb Aiden, I reached down to the hand that rested on my hip and spread my hand over his. I'd remember this morning forever, no matter how short or long forever turned out to be.

"Alex?" Sleep roughened Aiden's voice.

"Hey." My smile was watery.

Aiden stirred beside me, lifting up on one arm. He didn't speak as he turned his hand over and clasped mine. His silvery gaze moved over my face and he smiled at me, but it never reached his eyes. "It'll be okay," he said. "I promise you."

I hoped so. Telly would've left by now, without me. I bet he was ticked. There was no way of knowing what he'd do now. And if anything happened to any of them, it was on my head. I rolled onto my side, but the position was a little uncomfortable since Aiden still held onto my hand.

"You hate this—this not doing anything when you feel responsible for what's happened."

I sighed. "I *am* responsible for this."

"Alex, you did it to save your life. This isn't your fault," he said. "You understand that, right?"

"Do you know if Telly has left?" I asked instead of answering.

"I don't know, but I assume so. Before I came here last night, Linard had said he hadn't left the main island since he was at the Covenant."

"You guys have been watching him, too?"

"We needed to make sure he wasn't up to anything. The Guards who serve Lucian who remained behind have been an asset. Telly has been watched so closely I know he had steamed lobster for dinner last night."

I frowned. Last night I'd had a cold-cut sub. "You all should start your own spy business."

Aiden chuckled. "Maybe in a different life, and if I got cool gadgets out of it."

I cracked a smile. "The 007 type of gadgets?"

"He has this BMW R1200 C motorcycle in *Tomorrow Never Dies*," he said, sounding wistful. "Man, that bike was sweet."

"Never seen it—the movie."

"What? That's sad. We'll have to fix that."

I rolled over. The smile Aiden wore now reached his eyes, turning them a soft heather gray. "I have no desire to watch a James Bond movie."

His eyes narrowed. "What?"

"Nope. Those movies sound boring to me. So do Clint Eastwood movies. Yawn."

"I don't think we can be friends any longer."

I laughed and his smile spread. Those dimples appeared, and oh man, it'd been so long since I'd seen them. It felt like forever. "You don't smile enough."

Aiden arched a brow. "You don't laugh enough."

There hadn't been much to laugh about recently, but I didn't want to focus on that stuff. Aiden would leave soon and all of this was like a fantasy. One I wasn't ready to let go of just yet. We stayed like that for a little while, talking and holding hands. When the time did come to face reality, Aiden climbed out of the bed and went into the bathroom. I lay there with a goofy grin on my face.

This morning had been full of opposites: sadness and happiness, desperation and hope. All of those varying emotions should've left me exhausted, but I felt ready to go… running or something.

And I never felt ready to go running.

A knock at the door drew me from my thoughts.

"That's probably Leon," Aiden said from behind the bathroom door. The rest of what he said was drowned out by a rush of water in the sink.

Groaning, I got out of bed and pulled my sweater around me. The clock in the living room said it was only thirty minutes past seven. I rolled my eyes. Second day of winter break and I was out of bed before eight in the morning. There was something cosmically wrong with that.

"Coming!" I yelled when he knocked again. I opened the door. "Good morning, sunshine."

It was Linard who stood in the hall, his hands clasped behind his back. His eyes drifted over my head, scanning the room. "Where's Aiden?"

"In the bathroom." I stepped aside, letting him in. "Did Telly leave?"

"Yes. He left just at dawn." Linard turned to me, smiling. "He waited, like he offered, but you did not come."

"I bet he was pissed."

"No. I think he was more… disappointed than anything."

"Too bad. So sad." I hoped Aiden hurried up, because I really needed to brush my teeth.

"Yes," Linard said. "It is too bad. Things could've ended easily."

"Yeah…" I frowned. "Wait. Wh—"

Linard moved fast, like all Guards were trained to. There was a brief second when I recognized that I'd been in this position before, except that time there'd been adrenaline pumping through my veins. Then red-hot pain exploded just below my ribs, near the power rune, and all thought fled. It was the kind of pain that was sharp and sudden, stealing your last breath before you even realized you'd taken it.

Stumbling backward, I looked down as I tried to pull air into my lungs and make sense of the nerve-racking pain firing through my body. A black dagger was slammed all the way to the hilt, imbedded deep within my body. In a far corner of my mind, I knew that this blade wasn't an ordinary dagger. It was dipped in something—most likely Titan blood.

I wanted to ask why, but when my mouth opened, blood bubbled and trickled out.

"Sorry." Linard yanked the blade free. I slumped over, unable to make a sound. "He gave you a chance to live, at least," he whispered.

"Hey, I was expecting Leon—" Aiden came to a halt, just a few feet from us, and then he slammed into Linard. An inhuman, animalistic sound tore from Aiden as he wrapped an arm around Linard's throat.

My back hit the wall beside the counter and my legs gave out on me. I slid down as I clutched at my stomach, trying to staunch the flow. Warm, sticky blood gushed between my fingers. There was a yelp and then a sickening crunch that signaled the end of Linard.

Aiden screamed for help as he dropped beside me, knocking my trembling hands out of the way and pressing his own down on the wound. Aiden's stricken face loomed over mine, his eyes wide with horror. "Alex! Alex, talk to me. Talk to me, dammit!"

I blinked and his face formed again, but it was fuzzy. I tried to say his name, but a hoarse, wet cough racked my body.

"No! No. No." He looked over his shoulder at the door. Guards had gathered, drawn by the commotion. "Get help! Now! Go!"

My hands spasmed at my sides and then a numbness settled deep in my bones. Nothing hurt really, except my chest, but it ached for a different reason. The way he looked when he turned back to me and his eyes darted to my stomach. He pushed down harder. His gaze was frantic, shocked, and terrified.

I wanted to tell him that I still loved him—that I always had—and I wanted to tell him to make sure Seth didn't lose it. My mouth moved, but no words came out.

"It's okay. Everything is going to be okay." Aiden forced a smile, eyes glistening. Was he crying? Aiden never cried. "Just hold on. We're getting help. Just hold on for me. Please, *agapi mou*. Hold on for me. I promise—"

There was a popping sound, followed by a flash of light, brilliant and blinding. And then there was nothing but darkness and I was falling, spinning, and it was all over.

CHAPTER 16

THE GROUND UNDER MY CHEEK WAS DAMP AND COLD—
a musky, wet scent filled the air, one that reminded me of being deep
inside a mossy cavern. Come to think of it, shouldn't I feel cold? This
place was dark and dank, the only light being provided by tall torches
thrusting out of the ground, but I felt okay. Sitting up, I brushed the hair
out of my face as I stood on shaky legs.

"Oh… oh, hell to the no…"

I was on a riverbank, and across from me were hundreds, if not
thousands, of people—*naked people*—shivering as they huddled
together. The onyx-colored river separating us rippled and the mass of
people surged forward, reaching out and howling.

I shuddered, wanting to cover my ears.

People on my side of the bank milled about, some dressed in Sentinel
garb and others in casual clothing. Their conditions varied. The ones
waiting by the edge of the river seemed the happiest. Others looked
confused, faces pale and their clothing splattered with blood and gore.

Men dressed in leather tunics rode black horses, herding the most
unfortunate-looking into groups. I figured they were guards of some
sort, and by the way a few of them were watching me, I had the distinct
impression that I wasn't supposed to be here—wherever here was.

Wait. I turned back to the river, trying to ignore the poor… *souls…
on the other*—oh, gods dammit. This was the River Styx, where Charon
ferried souls to the Underworld.

I was dead.

No. No. No. I couldn't be dead. I hadn't even brushed my teeth, for crying out loud. There was no way. And if I were dead, what would Seth do? He was going to go crazy when he found out—if he hadn't already figured it out. Our bond diminished with distance, but could he have felt my loss? Maybe I wasn't dead.

Pulling open my sweater, I looked down and cussed.

The entire front of my tank top was drenched in blood—my blood. Then I remembered everything: the night before and this morning with Aiden that'd seemed so perfect. Aiden—oh gods—he'd begged me to hold on and I'd left.

Anger rushed through me. "I can't be dead."

A soft, feminine laugh came from behind me. "Honey, if you're here, you're dead. Like the rest of us."

I turned around, ready to clock someone in the face.

A girl I'd never seen before squealed loudly. "I knew it! You're dead."

I refused to believe I was dead. This had to be a bizarre, pain-induced nightmare. And seriously, why was the chick so happy that I was dead? "I'm not dead."

The girl was probably in her twenties, wearing a pair of expensive-looking jeans and strappy sandals. She clutched something in her hand. I pegged her for a pure-blood, but the open and sympathetic look in her gaze told me I had to be wrong. "How'd you die?" she asked.

I hugged my sweater around me. "I didn't die."

Her smile didn't waver. "I was shopping with my Guards at night. Like these shoes?" She stuck out her foot, angling it so I got a good view of them. "Aren't they divine?"

"Uh, yeah. The shoes are great."

She sighed. "I know. I died for them. Literally. See, I decided I wanted to wear them out, even though it was getting late and my Guards were getting nervous. But seriously, why would there be a bunch of daimons on Melrose Avenue?" She rolled her eyes. "They drained me dry and here I am, waiting for Paradise. Anyway, you look a little confused."

"I'm fine," I whispered, looking around. This couldn't be real. I couldn't be stuck in the Underworld with Buffy. "How come you don't look like them?"

She followed my gaze and winced. "They haven't been given this yet." A shiny gold coin lay in her open palm. "They can't cross over until they have passage. Once it's placed on their body, they'll look all kinds of fresh and new. And they'll be able to catch the next ride."

"And what if they don't get a coin?"

"They wait until they do."

She meant the souls on the other side of the river. Shuddering, I turned my back to them and realized that I… I didn't have a coin. "What happens if you don't have a coin?"

"It's okay. And some of them just got here." She placed an arm around my shoulders. "It takes a couple of days in most cases. People like to hold funerals and stuff, which totally sucks for us because we have to wait here for what feels like eternity." She paused and laughed. "I didn't even tell you my name. I'm Kari."

"Alex."

She frowned.

I rolled my eyes. Even dead people needed an explanation. "It's short for Alexandria."

"No. I know your name." Before I could question how she knew my name, Kari steered me away from a group of angry-looking Guards who were examining my ruined clothing. "It does get kind of boring down here."

"Why are you being so nice to me? You're a pure-blood."

Kari laughed. "We're all equal down here, honey."

My mom had said that once. Funny. She had been right. Gods, I didn't want to believe it.

"And besides, when I was alive… I wasn't a hater," she went on, smiling softly. "Maybe it was because I was an oracle."

Shock forced my mouth to gape. "Wait—you're the oracle?"

"It runs in my family."

I leaned closer, inspecting the deep hue of her skin and those dark eyes that suddenly looked way too familiar. "You're not related to Grandma Piperi, are you?"

Kari laughed throatily. "Piperi is my last name."

"Holy…"

"Yeah, weird, right?" She shrugged, dropping her arm. "I had the huge purpose in life, but my love for shoes kind of ended it all. Takes the term 'killer shoes' to a whole new level, right?"

"Yeah," I said, totally wigged out. "So, are you the oracle that came into… whatever when Grandma Piperi passed?"

A few moments passed and then she sighed. "Yes, I did… unfortunately. I was never big on Fate and destiny, you see? And visions… well, they suck most of the time." Kari looked at me, her obsidian eyes narrowing. "You're supposed to be here."

"I am?" I squeaked. Aw, man…

She nodded. "You are. This—I've seen this. Like I knew I was going to meet you, but I had no idea it would be *here*. See, oracles don't know when the passing of their own time will be, which blows." She laughed again. "Gods, I know what's going to happen."

Now that caught my attention. "You do?"

Her smile turned secretive.

My fingers dug into my sweater. "And are you going to tell me?"

Kari fell quiet, and did it matter now that she was making little sense? She was an oracle and I was dead. Wasn't a thing I could do about anything, right? Shaking my head, I took in the rest of my surroundings. I couldn't see where the river led to; it flowed to where was nothing but a deep, black hole. To our right there was a small opening, and a strange, bluish glow emanated from whatever was beyond this place.

"Where's that go?" I asked, pointing at the light.

Kari sighed. "Back up there, but it's not the same. You're a shade if you go that way, and that's even if you can get past the guards."

"The guys on the horses?"

"Yep. Going down or up, Hades does not like to lose any souls. You should've been here when someone tried to make a run for it." She shivered delicately. "Gross."

A commotion by the river had us turning around. Kari clapped her hands together. "Sweet gods, finally!" Kari took off toward the ever-increasing throng of people by the river.

"What?" I hurried after her. The guards on the horses were forcing people into lines on both sides of the river. "What's going on?"

She looked over her shoulder at me, smiling. "It's Charon. He's here. It's Paradise time, baby!"

"But how do you know where you're going?" I struggled to keep up with her, but when I reached the fringes of the group, I froze. *Oh, crap.*

"You just know," Kari said, pushing past those who I assumed had no money for passage. "It was nice meeting you, Alexandria. And I'm about ninety-nine percent sure we'll meet again." Then she disappeared into the crowd.

Too busy with the scene unfolding before, I didn't pay attention to what she said. The boat was larger than they showed in paintings. It was *massive,* like the size of a yacht, and a lot nicer-looking than the busted old canoe image I was familiar with, painted a bright white and trimmed in gold. At the helm was Charon. Now he looked like I expected.

Charon's slight form was swallowed by a black cloak that covered his entire body. In one bony hand he held a lantern. His shrouded head turned toward me and even though I couldn't see his eyes, I knew he saw me.

Within seconds the boat was swarmed and gliding down the River, disappearing through the dark tunnel. I had no idea how long I stood there, but finally I turned away and hurried through the crowd. Everywhere I looked, there were faces. Young and old. Expressions bored or stunned. There were dead people wandering around everywhere and I was alone, utterly alone. I tried to make myself as small as possible, but I bumped a shoulder here, an arm there.

"Excuse me," an old woman said. A gaudy pink nightgown dwarfed her frail form. "Do you know what happened? I went to sleep and… I woke up here."

"Uh." I started backing off. "Sorry. I'm as lost as you."

She looked perplexed. "You went to sleep, too?"

"No." I sighed, twisting away. "I was stabbed to death."

Once those words left my mouth, I wanted to take them back, because they made everything real.

I stopped outside the throng of people and stared down at my bare feet. I wanted to smack myself. I really was dead.

Lifting my head, my eyes found the strange blue light. If what Kari said was true, then that was the way out of this… holding area. Then what? I'd be a shade for eternity? But what if I wasn't really dead?

"You're dead," I muttered to myself. But I started toward the blue light. The closer I got to it, the more drawn to it I was. It seemed to offer everything—light, warmth, *life.*

"Don't go toward the light!" A voice yelled, followed by laughter—mischievous, beloved laughter. "They lie about the light, you know. Never go toward the light."

I froze and if my heart still had been beating, which I wasn't sure about, it would've stopped right then and there. As if moving through cement, I turned slowly, I couldn't believe—didn't want to believe what I was seeing because if this wasn't real…

He stood only a few feet away, wearing a white linen shirt and pants. His shoulder-length, blond hair was tucked back behind his ears and he was smiling—actually smiling. And those eyes, the color of the summer sky, were brilliant and alive. Not like the last time I'd seen him.

"Alex?" Caleb said. "You look like you've seen a ghost."

All my muscles sprang into action at once. I took off toward him and jumped.

Laughing, Caleb caught me around the waist and swung me around. It was like a dam bursting open. I turned into a fat, bawling baby in under a second. My whole body shook; I couldn't help it. It was Caleb—*my* Caleb, *my* best friend. *Caleb.*

"Alex, come on." He set me on my feet, but still held me close. "Don't cry. You know how I get when you cry."

"I'm… sorry." Nothing in this world was going to break my boa constrictor hold on him. "Oh, my gods, I can't believe… you're here."

He smoothed my hair back. "Missed me, huh?"

I lifted my head. "It's not the same without you. Nothing is the same without you." I reached up, placing my hands on his cheeks and then in his hair. He was flesh and bone. Real. There were no shadows under his eyes and his gaze didn't hold that weary look they'd had after Gatlinburg. The tags were gone. "Oh gods, you're really here."

"It's me, Alex."

Pressing my cheek against his chest, I started crying again. Never in a million years did I think I'd get to see him again. There was so much I wanted to say. "I don't understand," I murmured against his chest. "How can you be here? You haven't been waiting this entire time, have you?"

"No. Persephone owed me one. We were playing Mario Kart Wii, and I let her win. I cashed in my favor."

I pulled back, wiping the tears off my face with the back of my hand. "You have the Wii down here?"

"What?" He grinned, and oh gods, I'd thought I'd never see that grin again. "We get bored. Especially Persephone, when she's down here during these months. Usually Hades doesn't play, thank the gods. He freaking cheats."

"Wait. You play Mario Kart with Hades and Persephone?"

"I'm kind of a celebrity down here, because of you. When I first… arrived, I was taken straight to Hades. He wanted to know everything about you. I guess I kind of grew on him." Caleb shrugged and then he pulled me back in for another one of his mammoth hugs. "Gods Alex, I wanted to see you again. I just didn't think it would be like this."

"You're telling me," I said dryly. "What… what is it like?"

"It's not bad, Alex. Not bad at all," he said softly. "There are things I miss, but it's like being alive, only not."

Then it struck me. "Caleb, is… is my mom here?"

"Yes, she is. And she's really nice." He paused, pursing his lips. "Really nice considering she hasn't tried to kill me this time around, you know."

I felt nauseous, which was strange since I was supposed to be dead. "You've talked to her?"

"Yes. Seeing her the first time was really weird, but what she was when she had us isn't who she is now. She's your mom, Alex. The mom you remember."

"You sound like you've forgiven her."

"I have." He wiped away the fresh tears gathering on my cheeks. "You know, I wouldn't have in life, not really. But once you finally accept the whole dying thing, it kind of enlightens you a bit. And she was forced into becoming a daimon. They really don't hold that against you down here."

"They don't?" Oh, gods, I was going to start crying again.

"Not at all, Alex."

Some of the guards were gathering close to us. I focused on Caleb, hoping they weren't going to pull us apart. "I have to see her! Can you take—?"

"No, Alex. You can't see her. She doesn't even know you're here, and that's probably for the best right now."

Disappointment swamped me. "But—"

"Alex, how do you think your mom would feel if she knew you were here? There's only one reason why you'd be here. It would upset her."

Dammit, he had a point. But I was here, which meant I was dead. Wouldn't I be seeing her soon anyway? So that logic failed with me.

"I've missed you," he said again, and it brought me back to him.

I clenched the front of his shirt, and words I wanted to say spilled forth. "Caleb, I'm so, so sorry for everything. What happened in Gatlinburg and… and I didn't really pay attention to what you were going through afterward. I was so stuck on myself."

"Alex—"

"No. I am sorry. Then what happened to you. It wasn't fair. None of it was. And I'm so sorry."

Caleb lowered his forehead to mine and I swore his eyes glistened. "It wasn't your fault, Alex. Okay? Never think that."

"I just miss you so much. I didn't know what to do after you… left. I hated you for dying." I choked up. "And I just wanted you back so bad."

"I know."

"But I don't hate you. I love you."

"I know," he said again. "But you need to know that none of that was your fault, Alex. This was meant to happen. I understand that now."

I laughed thickly. "Gods, you sound so wise. What the hell, Caleb?"

"Death made me smart, I guess." His gaze searched my face. "You don't look any different. It just seems so... so long since I last saw you."

"You look better." I traced my fingers down his face, pressing my lips together. Caleb looked marvelous to me. There wasn't a hint of all that he'd suffered. He seemed at peace, fulfilled in a way he hadn't been when he was alive. "I just miss you so much."

Caleb squeezed me tighter and he laughed. "I know, but we need to stop with this friendship bonding crap, Alex. First we're tortured by daimons together and now we've both been stabbed. That's taking the 'we do everything together' to an all-new high."

Tears streamed down my face, but I laughed again. He felt so warm and real. Alive. "Gods, I really am dead."

"Yeah, you sort of are."

I sniffled. "How can I be sort of dead?"

Caleb pulled back and tipped his chin down. A mischievous smile tugged at his lips. "Well, there's this really big, blond god raising all kinds of hell with Hades right now. Apparently you're still in limbo or something. Your soul is still up for grabs."

My insides knotted, and I blinked. "What?"

He nodded. "You're not going to be dead for very long."

I wiped under my eyes. "I've been here for hours. I'm so dead."

"Hours here is only seconds there," he explained. "When I came up here I was worried it was too late, that Hades had already released you."

"I'm not going... to stay dead?"

"No." Caleb smiled. "But I had to see you. There's something I need to tell you."

"Okay." A twinge of pain in my stomach startled me. I jerked against him. "Caleb?"

"It's okay." His lanky arms held me still. "We don't have much time, Alex. I need you to listen to me. Sometimes we hear things down here... about what is going on up there. It's about Seth."

A burning kindled deep inside me. "What... what about Seth?"

"He doesn't really know, Alex. He thinks he's in control, but he's not. Don't... don't believe everything you hear. There's still hope."

I tried to laugh, but the burning was turning into a full-blown fire. "You're still… such a Seth fanboy."

Caleb made a face. "I'm being serious, Alex."

"Okay," I breathed, clutching my stomach. "Caleb, something's… wrong."

"Nothing's wrong, Alex. Just remember what I said. Sometimes people have a hard time remembering everything after these kinds of things. Alex, can you do me a favor?"

"Yes."

"Tell Olivia that I would've picked Los Angeles." Caleb placed his lips against my forehead. "She'll understand, okay?"

I nodded although I didn't understand why as I held onto his shirt for dear life. "I'll… I'll tell her. I promise."

"I love you, Alex," Caleb said. "You're like the sister I never wanted, you know?"

My laugh was cut off by the fire tearing apart my insides. "I love you, too."

"Never change who you are, Alex. It's your passion—your reckless faith—that will save you, save both of you." He held me tighter. "Promise me you won't forget this."

As the pain grew and my vision clouded, I held onto Caleb. "I promise. I promise. *I promise. I prom*—"

I was ripped away from him, or at least, that was how it felt. I was spinning and spinning, coming apart and slamming back together. Pain was everything. It swamped my senses, fueling the terror. My lungs burned.

"Breathe, Alexandria. *Breathe.*"

I gulped in air as my eyelids fluttered open. Two all-white eyes—no pupil or irises—stared back at me. The eyes of a god.

"Oh, *gods*," I whispered, and then I lost consciousness.

CHAPTER 17

PEOPLE MOVED AROUND ME. I COULDN'T SEE THEM, but I could hear their feet smacking on the tile, their voices hushed. Someone hovered near the bed. Their breathing was even and steady, lulling. I caught the scent of burning leaves and sea salt.

A door opened, and the person beside my bed shifted.

I faded out after that, slipping back into the pleasant haze. When I opened my eyes finally, they felt like they'd been sewn shut, and it took a few tries to get my vision to work. White walls surrounded me—plain and boring white walls. I recognized the med room. There were no windows, so I had no idea if it was night or day. There were faint memories of Linard and pain, then a flash of light and a feeling of falling. After that, things were hazy. I remembered a musty smell and there was more, but it seemed to exist just on the fringe of my thoughts.

My mouth felt as dry as cloth, my limbs wooden. A dull ache throbbed in my sternum. I drew in a deep breath and winced.

"Alex?" There was movement on the other side of my bed, and then Aiden came into view. Dark shadows bloomed under his eyes. His hair was a mess, falling every which way. He sat on the bed, careful not to move me. "Gods Alex, I... I never thought..."

I frowned and reached over to take his hand, but the motion pulled at my stomach. Tender skin stretched, sparking a sharp sting. I gasped.

"Alex, don't move around too much." Aiden placed his hand on mine. "He patched you up, but you need to take it easy."

I stared at Aiden, and when I spoke, my throat felt raw. "Linard stabbed me, didn't he? With damn Titan blood?"

Aiden's eyes flashed to a dark, thunderous gray. He nodded.

"Rat bastard," I croaked.

His lip twitched at what I said. "Alex, I'm… I'm so sorry. This shouldn't have happened. I was there to make sure you remained safe and—"

"Stop. This wasn't your fault. And obviously I'm okay for the most part. I just didn't expect Linard—Romvi, yes. But Linard?" I started to move, but Aiden was faster, gently pushing my shoulders down. "What? I can sit up."

"Alex, you need to lie still." Exasperated, he shook his head. "Here, drink this." He held a cup in front of my face.

I took the straw, glaring at him over the rim of the cup. The peppermint-flavored water did feel absolutely divine, easing the soreness in my throat.

Aiden stared back at me, drinking me in as if he'd never expected to see me again. An image of him leaning over me, stricken and pleading, flashed through me. An array of emotions flickered over his face now: amusement, weariness, but most of all, relief.

He pulled the cup away from me. "Easy."

I pushed the covers down, surprised to find that I wore a clean shirt and the gray sweats that the Covenant usually handed out. Ignoring the twinge of pain, I pulled up the hem of my shirt. "Oh crap."

"It's not as bad—"

My hands trembled. "Really? Because I think this would make your James Bond proud." The angry red line was two inches long and at least an inch wide. The skin around the mark was pink and puckered. "Linard tried to gut me."

Aiden took my hands and pried them away from my shirt. Then he pulled it down and fixed the blankets around me carefully. It never failed to amaze me how… careful and gentle Aiden was with me even though he knew I was tough to the core. It made me feel feminine, small, and cherished. Protected. Cared for.

For someone like me who was born and trained to fight, his gentle handling undid me.

A muscle flexed in his jaw. "He did."

I stared at Aiden, sort of in awe. "I'm like a cat. I swear I have nine lives."

"Alex." He looked up, meeting my eyes. "You used all those lives, and then some."

"Well…" The musty scent came back to me.

Aiden cupped my cheek, and warmth sped through me. His thumb smoothed over my jaw. "Alex, you… you died. You died in my arms."

I opened my mouth, but closed it. The bright light and the sensation of falling hadn't been a weird dream and there was more… I knew it.

His hand trembled against my cheek. "You bled out so quickly. There wasn't enough time."

"I… I don't understand. If I died, then how am I here?"

Aiden glanced at the closed door and exhaled slowly. "Well, this is where things kind of get strange, Alex."

I swallowed. "How strange?"

A brief smile appeared. "There was a flash of light—"

"I remember that."

"Do you remember anything after that?"

"Falling—I remember falling and…" I scrunched up my face. "I can't remember."

"It's okay. Maybe you should get some rest. We can talk about this later."

"No. I want to know now." I met his gaze. "Come on, this sounds like it's going to be interesting."

Aiden laughed, dropping his hand. "Honestly, I wouldn't have believed it if I hadn't seen it."

I started to roll onto my side, but remembered the whole no moving thing. Staying still was going to be a challenge. "The anticipation is killing me."

He inched closer, his hip bushing my thigh. "After the flash of light, there was Leon crouching over us. At first, I thought he'd just gotten to the room, but he… he didn't look right. He reached for you, and I thought he was going to check your pulse, but he put his hand on your chest instead."

My brows lifted. "You let Leon cop a feel?"

Aiden looked like he wanted to laugh again, but shook his head. "No, Alex. He said that your soul was still in your body."

"Uh."

"Yeah," he replied. "Then he told me I needed to get you to the med clinic and make sure the doctors started surgery to stop the bleeding, that we weren't too late. I didn't understand, because you... you were dead, but then I saw his eyes."

"All-white eyes," I whispered, remembering a brief glimpse of them.

"Leon's a god."

I stared at Aiden, unable to come up with any response to that. My brain pretty much shut down with that little piece of information.

"I know." He leaned over me, smoothing my hair back with one large hand. "Everyone pretty much had the same expression when I brought you in here. Marcus had arrived then... and the doctors were trying to get me to leave. Some were closing off the wound. Others were just standing there. It was chaos. You had to have been.... gone a couple of minutes—the time it took me to get you from your dorm to the med clinic, and freaking Leon just popped into the med room. Everyone froze. He walked up to you, put his hand on you again, and told you to breathe."

Breathe, Alexandria. Breathe.

"And you breathed," Aiden said, his voice hoarse as he cradled my cheek. "You opened your eyes and whispered something before going unconscious."

I was still stuck on the whole god part. "Leon's a... god?'

He nodded.

"Well," I said slowly, "holy daimon butt."

Aiden laughed—really laughed. It was deep and rich, full of relief. "You... you have no idea..." Averting his eyes, he ran a hand through his hair. "Never mind."

"What?"

Jaw tensed, he shook his head.

I reached up and the moment my hand touched his, he threaded his fingers through mine and looked at me. "I'm okay," I whispered.

Aiden stared at me for what seemed like eternity. "I thought you were gone—you *were* gone, Alex. You had *died*, and I was… I was holding you and there was nothing I could do. I never felt pain like that. His breath caught. "Not since I lost my parents, Alex. I never want to feel that again—not with you."

Tears rushed to my eyes. I didn't know what to say. My mind was still reeling from everything—total brain overload. And he was holding my hand, which was not the most shocking event of the day by any means, but it affected me just the same. I'd died. And a god who was apparently a Sentinel here had brought me back, and all that jazz. But it was the way Aiden was staring at me, like he'd never expected to talk to me again, see my smile, or hear my voice. He looked like a man who had stood at the edge of despair and had been pulled back at the very last second, but was still feeling all those terrible emotions, still not quite believing that he hadn't lost something—that *I* was still here.

I realized something so important, so powerful then.

Aiden could tell me he didn't feel the same way I did. He could fight what lay between us night and day. He could speak only in lies from here on out. It didn't matter.

I would always, *always* know differently.

Even if space separated us, or a dozen rules were imposed to keep us apart, and we could never be together, I would always know.

And gods, I loved him—loved him so much. It would never change. There were so many things I was unsure of, especially right now, but that I knew. Before I could stop it, a single tear escaped, running down my cheek. I squeezed my eyes shut.

He drew in another breath, this one much sharper, more broken. The bed dipped as he moved, and his hand slid into my hair, where his fingers curled around the strands. His lips were warm and smooth against my cheek, kissing the tear away.

I became very still, afraid that any movement would send him away. He was like some kind of wild creature about to break.

When he spoke, his breath danced over my lips, sending shivers through me. "I can't feel that way again. I just can't."

He was so close, still holding my hand tightly in his while his other slipped out of my hair and traced an invisible line over my face.

"Okay?" he said. "Because I can't lose—" He cut off, looking toward the door. The sound of footsteps grew closer. His lips pressed into a tight line as he turned back to me. He dropped my hand and straightened. "We'll talk more, later."

I sat there dumbly, my heart fluttering spastically, and said the most eloquent thing I could. "Okay."

The door opened, and Marcus walked through. His shirt was half-tucked in and his usually-pressed trousers were wrinkled. Like Aiden, he looked a mess, but relieved. He stopped beside my bed, exhaling loudly.

I cleared my throat. "You're wrinkled."

"You're alive."

Aiden stood. "That she is. I was just filling her in on everything."

"Good. That's good." Marcus stared at me. "How are you feeling, Alexandria?"

"Okay, I guess, after dying and all." I shifted, uncomfortable with the attention. "So about this Leon god thing? I don't know of any gods named Leon. Is he like the red-headed stepchild god that no one claims?"

Aiden retreated to the corner of the room, a much more appropriate distance for a pure-blood. I immediately missed his closeness, but he kept his eyes on me. It was like he was afraid I'd disappear. "That's because Leon isn't his real name," he said.

"It's not?"

Marcus sat in Aiden's spot. He reached out, but stopped and lowered his hand into his lap. "Do you want some water?"

"Um, sure." Weirded out a little, I watched him refill my cup and hold it for me to drink. The alien in my uncle had obviously taken full control. Soon, it would claw its way out of his stomach and tap dance across my bed.

Aiden leaned against the wall. "Leon is Apollo."

I choked on the water. Wheezing, I clutched my stomach with one hand and waved the other in front of my face.

"Alexandria, are you okay?" Marcus set the cup down and glanced over his shoulder at Aiden, who was already beside the bed. "Go get one of the doctors."

"No!" Eyes watering, I dragged in air. "I'm fine. Water just went down the wrong pipe."

"You sure?" Aiden asked, looking torn between wanting to drag a doctor in here and taking my word for it.

I nodded. "Yeah, that just surprised me. I mean, whoa. Are you guys sure? Apollo?"

Marcus watched me carefully. "Yes. He's definitely Apollo."

"Holy…" There weren't enough words in the world to do that justice. "Did he explain anything?"

"No." Marcus tucked the loose blanket back around me. "After he brought you back, he said he needed to leave and that he'd be back."

"He kind of popped out of the room." Aiden rubbed his eyes. "We haven't seen him since."

"And that was yesterday," Marcus added.

"So I've been sleeping for an entire day?" My gaze darted between the two. "Have either of you slept this entire time?"

Aiden looked away, but Marcus was the one who answered. "A lot has been going on, Alex."

"But you guys—"

"Don't worry about us," Marcus interrupted. "We'll be fine."

Not worrying about them was easier said than done. Both of them looked terrible. "Is… Linard is dead."

"Yes," Marcus said. "He was working with this… this Order."

I glanced at Aiden, now remembering that sickening crunch I'd heard. If I was expecting remorse in his steady gaze, I didn't find it. Actually, the look on his face said he'd do it again. "What about Telly?"

"He never landed in New York. Right now, we have no idea where he is. Instructor Romvi has also disappeared." Marcus dropped his hands into his lap again. "I've made some calls and I have a few trusted Sentinels looking for Telly right now."

"Trusted like Linard?" As soon as those words came out of my mouth, I wished I hadn't said them. My cheeks started to burn. "I'm... sorry. That wasn't right. You didn't know."

Marcus' green eyes flashed. "You are right. I didn't know. There were a lot of things I wasn't aware of. Like the real reason you left New York and the fact that you've already been receiving the Apollyon marks."

Oh, no. I didn't dare look at Aiden.

"It wasn't until a few nights ago that I was even aware that the Order of Thanatos could be involved," Marcus continued, his shoulders stiffening. "If I had known the truth, this could've been prevented."

I squirmed as much as I could. "I know, but if we'd involved you in what happened in New York, then you'd be at risk."

"That doesn't matter. I need to know when these kinds of things happen. I'm your uncle, Alexandria, and when you kill a pure-blood—"

"She did it out of self-defense," Aiden said.

"And you compelled two pure-bloods to protect her." Marcus shot a glare over his shoulder at Aiden. "I get that, but that doesn't change the fact that I needed to know. All of this created a perfect storm for something like this to happen."

"You're not... mad at Aiden? You aren't going to turn him in?"

"Sometimes I doubt his critical thinking abilities, but I understand why he did it." Marcus sighed. "The law requires that I do, Alexandria. It even requires that I turn you in, and by not doing so, I'll face charges of treason. Just as Aiden will face charges of treason if anyone discovers what he did."

Treason equaled death for them. I swallowed. "I'm sorry. I'm sorry I dragged all of you into this."

Aiden softened. "Alex, don't apologize. This isn't your fault."

"It's not. You can't help... what you are. And all of this is because of what you are." Marcus' lips curved into a half smile. "I don't agree with a lot of the decisions you've made or the fact that both of you have kept very important things from me, but I cannot blame Aiden for doing what I would've done in the same situation. I'm your uncle, Alexandria, and I will be tough on you, but that doesn't mean I don't care for you."

Stunned into silence, I stared at him. Could I've totally misinterpreted everything about this man? Because I seriously would've bet my life that he couldn't stand me. But had it just been his version of... tough love? Blinking back tears, I suddenly wanted to hug him.

The look on Marcus' face told me he probably wouldn't be comfortable with that.

Okay. We definitely weren't on hugging terms yet, but this... this was good. I cleared my throat. "So... wow. Leon is Apollo."

Aiden grinned.

Grinning back at him, I suddenly felt panicked and it took me a second to realize why. "Oh, my gods." I started to sit up, but Marcus stopped me. "I need to call Seth. If he suspects anything, he'll go crazy. You don't even know."

Aiden's grin faded. "If he'd known—felt it through your bond, then he'd have already gone crazy. He doesn't know."

He had a point, but I still needed to talk to him.

"We think it's best that he doesn't know, not until he is here with you," Marcus said. "Right now, we cannot afford for him to lose it. And he did call for you last night. Aiden told him you were sleeping."

Aiden rolled his eyes. "After he complained about *me* answering the phone that *he* gave you, he hung up. If he felt anything, he doesn't know why."

Sounded like Seth. Relieved, I settled back down. "Can someone grab my phone, though? If he doesn't hear from me, he'll suspect something and blow someone up."

"That can be arranged."

"I'll get it," Aiden said, sighing.

"Good. And while you go get it, why don't you take a shower and get some rest. You haven't slept since yesterday morning," Marcus said. "Lucian's Guards are outside the door. No one will get past them."

The only reason I trusted Lucian's Guards was the fact that there was only one person who wanted me to Awaken more than Seth, and that was Lucian. "Does Lucian know what happened?"

Marcus stood. "Yes, but he agreed that it would be wise to keep Seth in the dark for a little while."

"And you trust Lucian?"

"I trust that he understands that we cannot afford any acts of retaliation from Seth. Other than that, not particularly, but he needed to know about Telly. He has some of his people looking for the Head Minister," He paused, running a hand down the side of his face. "Don't worry about things like that right now. Get some rest. I'll be back later."

There were still a lot of questions, like who were the Sentinels that Marcus trusted? And how in the world could we keep a secret like this from Seth? But I was tired and I could tell that both of them were, too.

Aiden lingered after Marcus left. He came to my bedside, his silvery gaze drifting over me.

"You haven't left this room, have you?" I asked.

Instead of answering, he bent and placed his lips against my forehead. "I'll be back shortly," he promised. "Just try to get some rest and don't get out of the bed until someone is with you."

"But I'm not tired, not really."

Aiden laughed softly as he pulled back. "Alex, you may feel fine, but you lost a lot of blood and you just had surgery."

And I'd died, but I figured there was no point in adding that. I didn't want Aiden to worry any more than he did, especially when he looked so exhausted. "All right."

He moved away from the bed and stopped at the door. Looking back at me, he smiled. "I won't be gone long."

I eased onto my side carefully. "I'm not going anywhere."

"I know. Neither am I."

CHAPTER 18

I SLEPT LONGER THAN I'D EXPECTED. WHEN I AWOKE, the room was empty and my cell phone had been placed on the bedside table. I hoped that Aiden was getting some rest, and that Marcus was, too. Pushing into a sitting position, I winced as the movement pulled at the skin around the stitches.

Curious, I inspected the jagged scar again. Half-bloods were notoriously fast healers and Covenant blades were designed to cut cleanly, but it had to have done some internal damage. Had Apollo somehow patched me up more? Because I doubted that the doctors could've reversed that kind of damage. Other than feeling lethargic, I felt... okay.

But as I glanced around the room, something poked at the recesses of my memories. I was forgetting something—something hugely important. It was on the tip of my tongue, just like when I'd been under a compulsion before. This was different, though. It was like waking up and not being able to remember a dream.

Sighing, I reached over and snatched up the cell phone. There was only one missed call from Cuddle Bunny. Scooting down, I called him back.

Seth answered on the second ring. "So, you're alive?"

My heart flipped over heavily. "Yeah, why wouldn't I be?"

"Well, I haven't spoken to you in about two days." He paused. "What have you been doing?"

"I've been sleeping, not doing much."

"Sleeping for two straight days?"

I poked at my scar and winced. "Yeah, that's about all."

"Interesting…" There was a muffled sound, like something had been pulled over the phone. "You've been sleeping but Aiden had your phone?"

Crap. "He's been babysitting me. I don't know why he answered the phone when you called." There was another muffled sound, and then Seth grunted. "What are you doing?"

"Pulling on my pants and it's hard when you're holding a phone."

"Um, do you want me to call you back? Like when you're not naked?"

Seth laughed. "I'm not naked now. Anyway, maybe we have some weird Apollyon malaise. I've been exhausted for about two days, but feel fine now."

So he had felt something. I chewed on my lip. "Can I ask you something?"

"Hit me."

"You said that when I Awaken, I'll know what the past Apollyons knew, right?"

There was a pause. "Yes, I said that."

Unease twisted my insides. "Then how did you not know about the Order of Thanatos, and that they'd killed Solaris and the First? Wouldn't you've seen what they've seen?"

"Why are you asking?" Seth asked.

I took a deep breath. "Because it doesn't make sense, Seth. You should've known. And how did you not know that a half and pure made an Apollyon? None of the Apollyons in the past had ever figured that out?"

"Why are you asking about this—" A distinctive, very feminine giggle cut off his words. When Seth spoke again, it sounded far away and sounded an awful lot like the word, "behave."

I sat up, sucking in air sharply as my stomach screamed in protest. "Who are you with, Seth?"

"Why? You jealous?"

"Seth."

"Hold on a second," he replied, and then there was a sound of a door shutting. "Dammit, it's cold out here."

"Better be careful. Don't want anything to freeze and fall off."

He laughed. "Oh, that was bitchy. I think you just might be jealous."

Was I jealous that he was so obviously with a girl and he'd been naked? Shouldn't I be? But I wasn't jealous—more like annoyed. Annoyed because I'd been getting stabbed and dying while Seth was screwing around. And how could I be mad? I was the one in love with another guy. I really had no room to talk. But I hadn't gotten naked with that guy, not in several long months. Not since I'd decided to see what could happen with Seth.

Gods, I was so confused and I had no idea what was going on and why it was happening now.

"I'm not doing anything wrong," Seth said after a stretch of silence.

"I didn't say you were. Wait. You're with Boobs, aren't you?"

"Do you really want to know, Alex?"

Not when he put it like that. I chewed on my lip, unsure of what to say. Suddenly I heard Caleb's voice in my head. *There's still hope.* Weird.

"We never said we were in a relationship, and besides, whatever. You're there. I'm here. And in a week or so, I'll be back. And it's not going to even matter."

I blinked. "Really, it's 'whatever'?"

Seth sighed. "I know he was by your side the minute I left, doing his annoying brooding thing, trying to figure out a way to be with you. And he's answering your phone while you're sleeping? Yeah, it's 'whatever'."

My mouth dropped open. "That is totally not what is happening here."

"Look, it doesn't matter. I've got to go. I'll talk to you later." Then he hung up on me.

I stared at the phone for several minutes, shocked and a bit disturbed. Had he just given me permission to do "whatever" with Aiden because he's doing "whatever" with Boobs? My gods, had I died and come back into an alternative universe?

The door opened then, and Aiden walked through. Setting the phone aside, I was happy to see that he looked a lot more refreshed. Damp hair curled around his temples and the shadows under his eyes had lessened.

"Hey, you're awake." He sat beside me and the bed shifted us closer together. "How are you feeling?"

I leaned away from him. "Gross."

Aiden frowned. "Gross?"

"I haven't brushed my teeth or washed my face in days. Don't come near me."

He laughed. "Alex, come on."

"Seriously, I'm gross." I put my hand over my mouth.

Ignoring my protests, he leaned over and brushed my stringy hair back. "You're as beautiful as always, Alex."

I stared at him. He must not get out much.

Aiden arched a brow. "Did you call Seth?"

Unwilling to lower my hand, I nodded.

His eyes danced. "Did he seem suspicious?"

"No," I said from behind my hand. "He was actually with Boobs."

He looked confused. "Boobs?"

"It's this girl from New York," I explained.

"Oh." Aiden leaned back. "What do you mean by he was with this girl?"

"What do you think?" I lowered my hand.

"Oh, Alex, I'm sorry."

I made a face. "Why are you sorry? It's 'whatever.' Seth and I aren't in a relationship." But he had been behaving himself since he'd returned to the Covenant with me. Pushing that out of my mind, I focused on something more important. "I need to get out of this bed."

Something flickered across Aiden's face and then he shook his head. "Alex, you really shouldn't."

"I *really* need to."

He held my stare and then he seemed to get it. "Okay, here, let me help you."

The idea of him getting close to me when I felt this gross didn't appeal to me, but there was no arguing with him. Aiden helped me out of the bed and then insisted on guiding me to the little bathroom. I half-expected him to follow me inside.

Closing the door behind me, I did my thing and eyed the shower stall longingly. Aiden would have a fit if I turned it on. I glanced at the door, debating whether or not he'd dare busting in here. Aiden was way too saintly.

I decided to test that theory out.

The second after I turned the water on, he yelled. "Alex, what are you doing?"

"Nothing." I pulled off my clothes, wishing I had something clean to put on.

"*Alex.*" Bemused frustration colored his tone.

I grinned. "I'm taking a quick shower. I'm gross. I need to be clean."

"You shouldn't be doing that." The door handle jingled. It wasn't locked. "Alex!"

"I'm naked," I warned.

Silence and then, "Is that supposed to make me not want to come in there?"

A warm flush covered my body as I stared at the door.

There was an audible sigh. "Make it quick, Alex, because I *will* come in there if you are not done in less than five minutes."

I took the quickest shower of my life. Drying off and dressing quickly, I reveled in the feeling of being clean again, but showering had taken whatever energy I'd had left in me. I sat in front of the sink, because the toilet seemed too far away, and started brushing my teeth. My mouth no longer felt like a woolly mammoth, but as I eyed the sink and realized that I'd have to get back up again, I kind of wished I'd stayed in bed.

I know he was by your side the minute I left, doing his annoying brooding thing, trying to figure out a way to be with you.

Closing my eyes, I clutched the plastic toothbrush and stretched out my legs.

Whatever. You're there. I'm here. And in a week or so, I'll be back. And it's not going to even matter.

Foamy toothpaste trickled down my chin. It wouldn't matter because Seth would be around? Or it wouldn't matter because in five weeks, I'd Awaken? Was that what Seth was trying to say in between whatever Boobs was doing?

"Alex?" Aiden knocked on the bathroom door. "Are you okay in there?"

I tipped my head toward the closed door. More toothpaste dribbled from my mouth. "I'm tired."

The door opened. Aiden's gaze dropped and his brows went up. A slow smile crept over his face, softening the hard look that had been in his eyes since I woke up. Aiden laughed.

Something fluttered in my chest. "Laughing at a dead girl isn't nice."

"I told you that you should've stayed in bed." The light didn't go out of his eyes as he knelt. He reached over, wiping the toothpaste off my chin with his thumb. "But you never listen. Hold on."

It wasn't like I was going anywhere, so I watched him glance at the sink and then rise. Aiden disappeared back into the room, returning with two small plastic cups and some paper towels a few seconds later.

Prying the toothbrush out of my hands, he tossed it in the sink after filling up the cup. "Here you go."

Cheeks flaming, I took the cup and swished the water in my mouth.

Aiden handed me another empty cup. "Rinse and repeat."

I glared at him, but secretly did a happy dance in my head when he laughed again. Once I didn't have toothpaste falling out of my mouth anymore and my hands were empty, Aiden bent and carefully slid an arm around me. "I can stand without help," I grumbled.

"Sure you can." Aiden's hair tickled my cheeks. "That's why you're sitting on a bathroom floor. Come on, back to bed."

The door in the main room opened. "What's going on?" Marcus' voice carried through the room. "Is Alexandria okay?"

Crimson stained my entire face.

"She's fine." Aiden easily hauled me to my feet. The tender skin pulled a little, but I kept my expression blank. Didn't want him having a heart attack. "She just wore herself out," he continued, grinning as he let go. "You okay to make it back to the bed?"

I nodded. "It's not my fault. Leon—Apollo—whoever he is—didn't fix me right. Godly powers my—"

"I did fix you, but you were dead. Give me some credit," Apollo said.

I jumped, smacking my hand on my chest. Apollo sat on the edge of the toilet seat, one leg crossed over the other.

Beside me, Aiden bowed stiffly. "My master."

"Oh, my gods," I said. "Seriously. Are you trying to kill me again by giving me a heart attack?"

Apollo tipped his head at Aiden. "I've already told you. You don't need to do the 'master' and bowing business with me." Little sparks of electricity rimmed those all-white eyes. "Why are you out of bed? Doesn't getting stabbed warrant some downtime?" He smiled at Aiden, who was now standing. "She really is hard to take care of, isn't she?"

Aiden looked a little pale. "Yeah…"

"I… I felt gross."

Apollo disappeared from the bathroom and popped up behind Aiden. Marcus took a step back, his eyes wide. He bowed too, and I really thought for a moment that Marcus was going to drop to his knees.

"Good gods," Aiden said under his breath as he led me out of the bathroom.

I stared at the hulking god in the corner of the room as I climbed back into bed. "Did anyone know about this?"

Apollo glided to the bed. It was strange looking at him and seeing some traces of Leon. The face was basically the same, but more refined, sharper. Hair that looked like spun gold replaced the short crew cut Leon had favored, falling just below his broad shoulders. And he seemed taller, if that was even possible. He was achingly beautiful, lacking the rougher edges, but his eyes… they creeped me out. There were no pupils or irises, just white orbs that seemed full of electricity.

The Sun God.

I was staring at the mother effin' Sun God… and yet, it was like staring at Leon. It was bizarre that a god would even be on earth, but to be as comfortable as Apollo seemed was unreal.

Apollo arched a brow as he slowly turned his head to Marcus. "I know this is a little… shocking, but what I was doing required that I disguise who I was."

Marcus blinked, as if he was coming out of a daze. "Are there more like you here?"

Apollo smiled. "We are always around."

"Why?" Aiden asked, dragging his fingers through his hair. He looked a little out of it also.

"Things are complicated," Apollo said.

"So, was Leon a real person? Did you like, take over his body or something?" I folded my legs under the blanket. "Or have you been Leon this entire time?"

The corners of Apollo's lips twitched. "We are one in the same."

Slowly, I reached over and poked his arm. It felt like real flesh, warm and hard. Disappointed, I poked him again. I was expecting something amazing—celestial—by touching him. Instead all I got were weird looks from everyone in the room, including Apollo.

"Please stop touching me," Apollo said.

I jabbed his arm again. "Sorry. It's just that you're real. I mean, I just thought you guys weren't really around here."

"Alex." Aiden sat on the edge of the bed. "You should probably stop touching him."

"Whatever." I dropped my hand into my lap. I still wanted to touch him, though, which was really weird. I kind of wanted to rub all over him like a cat or something… and that was more than weird, and a little uncomfortable.

"Usually we're not," Apollo said, frowning at me. "When we are on earth our powers are limited. Everything about this place drains us. We tend to stay away and if we do visit, it is only for a short while."

"Long enough to hook up with some mortal chicks?"

"Alexandria," Marcus snapped.

Apollo faced me. "No. We haven't spawned any demigods in centuries."

I shuddered when my gaze met his. "Your eyes are really freaking creepy."

He blinked, and in a nanosecond, his eyes were a brilliant, intense cobalt. "Better?"

Not really. Not when he was staring at me like that. "Sure."

Marcus cleared his throat. "I'm really at a loss of what to say."

Apollo waved his hand dismissively. "We've worked together for months. Nothing has changed."

"We didn't know you were Apollo." Aiden folded his arms. "That changes things."

"Why?" Apollo smiled. "I just don't expect you to be as willing to spar with me now."

The skin around Aiden's eyes crinkled as he smiled. "Yeah, you can be sure of that. All of this is just... I mean, how did we not know?"

"Simple. I did not want any of you to know. It made things easier... blending in."

"I'm sorry," I interrupted. Apollo arched a brow, waiting. I felt my cheeks flush. "This is just really awkward."

"Do tell," Apollo murmured.

"I mean, I've like insulted you every which way from Sunday to your face. Multiple times. Like when I accused you of chasing boys and girls and how they turn themselves into trees to get away—"

"Like I said before, some of those things are not true."

"So Daphne didn't turn into a tree to get away from you?"

"Oh, my gods," Aiden muttered, rubbing a hand along his jaw.

A muscle popped on Apollo's jaw. "That was not all my fault. Eros shot me with a damn arrow of love. Trust me, when you are hit with one of those things, you cannot help what you do."

"But you cut off some of *her* bark." I shuddered again. "And wore it as a wreath. That's like a serial killer collecting their victim's personal items... or fingers."

"I was in love," he replied, as if being in love explained away the fact that the chick turned herself into a tree to get away from him.

"Okay. What about Hyacinth? The poor boy had no idea—"

"Alexandria," Marcus sighed, looking near apoplectic.

"Sorry. I just don't understand why he hasn't smited me or something."

"The day is still young," Apollo said, grinning when my eyes widened.

Marcus glanced at me. "You're here because of her."

Apollo nodded. "Alexandria is very important."

This was weird to me. "I thought the gods weren't fans of the Apollyons."

"Zeus created the first Apollyon thousands of years ago, Alexandria, as a way to ensure that no pure-blood would become too powerful and threaten the mortal race or us," he explained. "They were created as a system of checks and balances. We are neither fans nor enemies of the Apollyon, but see them only as a necessity that will be needed one day. And that day has come."

CHAPTER 19

"WHY NOW?" I ASKED WHEN NO ONE ELSE SPOKE. I think the pures were a little star-struck. Apollo was a rock star to them, but even with his otherworldly beauty he was still just Leon to me.

"The threat has never been greater," Apollo answered. Seeing my confusion, he sighed. "Perhaps I should explain a few things."

"Perhaps you should," I muttered.

Apollo drifted over to the bedside table and picked up the pitcher of water. Sniffing it, he placed it back down. "My father has always been… paranoid. All that power, but all Zeus has ever feared is his children doing what he did to his parents. Overthrowing him, conquering Olympia, slaughtering him in his sleep—you know, the same old family drama."

I shot Aiden a look, but he was riveted by Apollo.

"Anyway, Zeus decided that he should keep his enemies close. That is why he called all the demigods back to Olympus and destroyed the ones who didn't heed his call, but he forgot about their children." Apollo smirked. "All that power, and sometimes I wonder if Zeus had been dropped on his head as a baby. He forgot about the Hematoi, the children of the demigods."

I laughed, but Marcus glanced up at the ceiling as if he expected Zeus to strike Apollo with a bolt of lightning.

"The Hematoi," Apollo looked at Marcus and Aiden pointedly, "are watered down versions of the demigods, but you are very powerful in your own way. Your numbers frankly outnumber the gods by thousands. If there was ever a cohesive attempt to overthrow us, it might just succeed. And the mortals, they would not stand a chance against the Hematoi."

"I thought you guys were, like, all-knowing. Wouldn't you know if you were about to be overthrown?"

Apollo laughed. "Legends, Alexandria, are hard to separate from the truth. There are things we know, but the future is never set in stone. And when it comes to any creature living on this planet, we cannot see or interfere with them. We do have… tools we use to keep an eye on things."

"That's why the oracle lived here," Aiden said.

Again, there was a tickle in the back of my head. Something about an oracle poked at my fuzzy memories. It stayed out of reach.

"Yes. The oracle answers to me and only me."

"Because you're a god of prophecy… among five hundred other things," I added, picking back up on the conversation.

"Yes." He came back to the bed, tilting his head to the side. "Once Zeus realized that he had forgotten about the Hematoi, he knew he had to create something that was powerful enough to control the Hematoi but could not populate like the Hematoi did."

Marcus sat in the only spare chair in the room. "And so the Apollyon was created?"

Apollo sat beside Aiden, which really crowded the bed. "An Apollyon can only be born when the mother is Hematoi and the father is a half-blood. It is the aether of a female pure combined with that of a half-blood which creates the Apollyon. It is similar to the way a minotaur is born. Apollyons are nothing more than monsters in the scheme of things."

I frowned at his back. "Gee. Thanks."

"Mixing of the two races was forbidden to ensure that there would not be many and the Hematoi were ordered to kill any offspring of a pure and a half."

My mouth dropped open. "That's terrible."

"That it may be, but we could not have a dozen Apollyons running around." He looked over his shoulder at me. "Two are considered bad enough. Can you imagine if there were a dozen? No. You cannot. And besides, one slipped through every generation as planned. Though, we do make mistakes every once in awhile."

I was really beginning to dislike Apollo. "So I'm a monster and a mistake?"

He winked. "The perfect kind of mistake."

I scooted away from him a little.

The grin reached his vibrant eyes. "As long as the Apollyon behaves himself, he is left alone to do his duty. But when there is a second in the mix, it ups the power of the First. This was something we had not accounted for. Zeus thinks it is a kind of cosmic joke."

Marcus leaned forward. "But why do you even allow the second to live if one is such a threat?"

I shuddered.

Apollo stood again, apparently suffering from a hyperactivity disorder. "Ah, you see, we cannot touch the Apollyon. The markings are... wards against us. Only Thanatos' Order can carry out a successful attack on the Apollyon and, of course, an Apollyon can kill another Apollyon."

My head was starting to hurt. "And Seth would know this, right?"

"Seth would know all of this."

I exhaled loudly. "I may just kill him."

Apollo arched a brow. "Mankind and the Hematoi have something greater to fear than the daimon... issue. And by the way, the whole daimon problem can totally be blamed on Dionysus. He was the first to discover that aether could be addictive and he just had to show someone. Once Dionysus got so high off the stuff, he actually showed himself to a King of England. Do you know how many problems that caused?"

It was official. The gods were overgrown children. "That's good to know, but can we get back to the whole greater fear thing?"

"The oracle had a prophecy upon your birth, that one would bring the true death to all of us and the other would be our savior."

"Oh geez," I muttered. "Grandma Piperi strikes again."

Apollo ignored that. "She could not tell which one, though. And I grew curious. When Solaris came around, there had been no such prophecy. What made this time so different? So I checked in on you both throughout your lives. There was nothing particularly remarkable about either of you."

"You're really doing wonders for my self-esteem."

He shrugged. "It is only the truth, Alexandria."

"You did not tell the rest of the gods about Seth and Alexandria?" Marcus asked.

"No. I should have, and my decision not to has not made me many fans." He folded his arms. "But then three years ago, the oracle foresaw your death if you stayed at the Covenant, which led to your mother leaving to protect you, although her prophecy did come true."

It struck me then. "Because I came back to the Covenant…"

"And you did die," Aiden finished, his hands curling into fists. "Gods."

"The oracle is never wrong," Apollo said. "I kept an eye on you up until the night before the daimon attack in Miami. I thought you had sensed me once. You were returning from the beach and you stopped just outside your door."

My eyes widened. "I remember feeling something weird, but I… didn't know."

"If only I had stayed around…" He shook his head. "When I learned that the Covenant was actively seeking you, I disguised myself as Leon to see what was going on. I had no idea Lucian was aware of your true identity."

"I never told him," Marcus said. "I only knew because my sister confided in me before she left. Lucian already knew by then."

"Interesting," Apollo murmured. "I do believe I am not the only god hanging around."

"Wouldn't you know if there were other gods around?" Aiden asked.

"Not if they did not want me to know," he answered. "And we could be moving in and out at different times. Although, I do not know what any god would have to gain by ensuring that the two Apollyons were brought together."

"Do any of you want revenge?" I asked.

Apollo laughed. "When do we not want revenge against one another? We are constantly irking one another out of boredom. It would take no stretch of the imagination for one to take it all too seriously."

"But what is the fear, Apollo?" Marcus asked. "Why would the Order try to take out Alexandria when she has done nothing?"

"It is not Alexandria they are trying to stabilize."

"It's Seth," I whispered.

Aiden stiffened. His eyes turned a thundercloud gray. "It's always about Seth."

"But he hasn't done anything," I protested.

"Yet," Apollo replied.

"Have you, I don't know, foreseen him doing something?"

"No."

"Then this is all based on crazy Grandma Piperi?" I tucked my hair back. "And that's all?"

Marcus' eyes narrowed. "It does sound extreme."

Apollo rolled his eyes. "You cannot tell me that Seth is not primed for disaster. He already has an ego of a god, and trust me, I would know. The kind of power that a God Killer can harness is astronomical and unstable. He is already feeling the effects of it."

"What do you mean?" Aiden asked.

"Alex?" Apollo said softly.

I shook my head. There were moments when I questioned Seth's sanity and even his intentions. Then there was Jackson. I couldn't prove that it had been him, but... I shook my head. "No. He would never do something so stupid."

"It is sweet." In a second, Apollo was in front of me and at eye level. "That you would defend him even though I know you do not trust him entirely. Maybe at one point you did, but not anymore."

I opened my mouth, but closed it. Lowering my gaze to my palms, I bit my lip. Once again, something poked at my memory. I swallowed.

"I must leave now," Apollo said quietly.

I looked up, meeting his gaze. Apollo creeped me out and made me really question just how cool I was, but I sort of liked him. "Will you be back?"

"Yes, but I cannot be Leon anymore. My cover is… blown, and I must answer for not informing Zeus of what I have been doing."

"I will probably be grounded." He laughed at his own joke. I just stared at him. "I am Apollo, Alexandria. Zeus can kiss it."

Marcus once again looked like he wanted to crawl under the bed.

"I will check in when I can." He turned to Marcus. "I will also see if I can track Telly down. Oh, and see if you can have Solos Manolis transfer up here from Nashville. He is a half-blood you can trust."

"I've heard of him," Aiden spoke up. "He's quite… outspoken."

Apollo smiled and then, without so much as another word, disappeared from the room.

"Well, he sure knows how to make an exit." Aiden stood, shaking his head.

Marcus and Aiden made plans to contact this Solos, but I was only half-listening. Curling on my side, I thought about what Apollo had said about Seth. Part of me flat-out refused to believe that Seth could be dangerous, but when I was being honest with myself, I wasn't so sure about that. There were moments he'd proven that I really didn't know what was going on in his head or what to expect from him. I couldn't even figure out why he was so trusting of Lucian—a man who was as plastic as they came.

I hadn't even realized Marcus had left until Aiden sat and placed his hand on my cheek. I wondered if he realized how much he'd been touching me lately. It was almost like an unconscious move on his part. Maybe he did it to remind himself that I was alive…

Suddenly, the fog cleared around my memories. I sat up so quickly that I gasped.

"Alex? Are you okay?" Aiden's eyes were wide. "Alex?"

It took me several seconds to say it. "I remember… I remember what happened when I died."

The look on his face said he hadn't expected me to say that. His hand slid around the nape of my neck. "What do you mean?"

Tears clogged my throat. "I was in the Underworld, Aiden. There were all these people there, waiting to pass over and guards on horses. I even saw Charon and his boat—and his boat is much, much bigger and nicer. There was this girl named Kari who'd been killed by daimons while shopping for shoes and…"

"And what?" he asked, gently wiping away a tear.

"She said she was an oracle. That she knew we'd meet but not like this. And I saw Caleb. I got to talk to him, Aiden. Gods, he looked so… so happy. And he plays Wii with Persephone." I laughed and wiped at my face. "I know it sounds crazy, but I saw him. And he said my mom was there and that she was happy. He told me that a big blond god was arguing with Hades over my soul. He must've meant Apollo. It was real, Aiden. I swear."

"I believe you, Alex." He cradled me against his chest. "Tell me what happened. Everything."

I pressed my cheek against his shoulder, squeezing my eyes shut. I told him everything that Caleb had told me, including what he'd said about Seth. When I asked Aiden to get Olivia's number so I could pass on his message, he shook his head, expression pained.

"I know you want to tell her," he said, "and you will, but right now, we don't want a lot of people knowing what happened. We don't know who we can trust."

In other words, it wasn't Olivia we needed to be worried about, but we couldn't run the risk of things being repeated. I hated the idea of not telling her right now, because it was important, but how could I tell her without giving away what happened? I couldn't.

"I'm sorry, Alex." His hand smoothed along my back. "But it has to wait."

I nodded.

Part of me ached worse after realized I'd been with Caleb, because his loss was fresh again. But as Aiden held me long after I'd quieted down, the tears that came, in spite of everything, were joyful ones. The pain of Caleb's loss was still there, but it was lessened by the knowledge that he was truly at peace, and so was my mom. And right now, that was all that mattered.

CHAPTER 20

MY HEART WAS RACING, PUMPING BLOOD THROUGH my body way too fast for someone who'd died and all. I tried and failed not to stare at Aiden as a Guard carried my bags into his parents' house. It was the middle of the night, and I should've felt cold, but I felt ridiculously hot. Especially after Deacon met us in the foyer with a funny little grin on his face.

"This is probably the safest place to stash you until we find Telly and are able to determine if anyone else here is tied to the Order." Marcus dropped his arm on my shoulders. "Once I get back from Nashville, you'll stay with me, or with Lucian, once he returns from New York."

"She should be kept as far away from Lucian's house as possible," Apollo said, appearing out of nowhere. Several of the Guards backed off, eyes wide and faces pale. Apollo grinned at them. "Anywhere Seth will be, I suggest Alexandria should not be."

Every pure and half bowed at the waist. I did too, forgetting the stitches that were healing, and grimaced.

"We need to put a bell on him," Aiden muttered.

I pressed my lips together to keep from laughing.

"Actually," Apollo drawled slowly. "She is probably the safest here."

Deacon sounded like he choked.

Marcus recovered quicker than he had last time. "Have you found something?"

"No." Apollo glanced at Deacon curiously before his gaze settled on Marcus. "I wanted to speak with you privately."

"Of course." Marcus turned to me. "I'll be back in a few days. Please listen to what Aiden tells you and… try to stay out of trouble."

"I know. I'm not allowed to leave his house unless Apollo tells me to." Those were Marcus' exact words. No one else could remove me from this house other than Apollo, Aiden, or Marcus. Not even Lucian's Guards. If anyone else tried, I'd been given permission to kick some butt.

Marcus nodded at Aiden and turned to leave. Passing by, Apollo gave us a two-finger salute that just looked bizarre coming from him. Over the past two days, I'd grown used to his random appearances. It seemed he took great pleasure in scaring the crap out of everyone when he did it.

"You ready?" Aiden asked.

Deacon arched a brow.

"Shut up," I said as I walked past Deacon.

"I haven't said a single thing." He spun around and followed me in. "We're going to have so much fun. It's like a slumber party."

A slumber party at Aiden's house? Oh gods, the images I came up with made me blush.

Aiden closed the door behind the others as they left and shot his brother a look.

Deacon rocked back on his heels, grinning. "Just so you know, I get incredibly bored quite easily and you will be forced to be my source of entertainment. You'll kind of be like my own personal jester."

I flipped him off.

"Well, that wasn't funny at all."

Aiden brushed past me. "Sorry. You're probably going to wish you'd stayed in the med clinic."

"Oh, I'd wager that's not the case." Deacon met my glare with an impish grin. "Anyway, did you celebrate Valentine's Day when you were slumming with the mortals?"

I blinked. "Not really. Why?"

Aiden snorted and then disappeared into one of the rooms.

"Follow me," Deacon said. "You're going to love this. I just know it."

I followed him down the dimly-lit corridor that was sparsely decorated. We passed several closed doors and a spiral staircase. Deacon went through an archway and stopped, reaching along the wall. Light flooded the room. It was a typical sunroom, with floor-to-ceiling glass windows, wicker furniture, and colorful plants.

Deacon stopped by a small potted plant sitting on a ceramic coffee table. It looked like a miniature pine tree that was missing several limbs. Half the needles were scattered in and around the pot. One red Christmas bulb hung from the very top branch, causing the tree to tilt to the right.

"What do you think?" Deacon asked.

"Um… well, that's a really different Christmas tree, but I'm not sure what that has to do with Valentine's Day."

"It's sad," Aiden said, strolling into the room. "It's actually embarrassing to look at. What kind of tree is it, Deacon?"

He beamed. "It's called a Charlie Brown Christmas Tree."

Aiden rolled his eyes. "Deacon digs this thing out every year. The pine isn't even real. And he leaves it up from Thanksgiving to Valentine's Day. Which thank the gods is the day after tomorrow. That means he'll be taking it down."

I ran my fingers over the plastic needles. "I've seen the cartoon."

Deacon sprayed something from an aerosol can. "It's my MHT tree."

"MHT tree?" I questioned.

"Mortal Holiday Tree," Deacon explained, and smiled. "It covers the three major holidays. During Thanksgiving it gets a brown bulb, a green one for Christmas, and a red one for Valentine's Day."

"What about New Year's Eve?"

He lowered his chin. "Now, is that really a holiday?"

"The mortals think so." I folded my arms.

"But they're wrong. The New Year is during the summer solstice," Deacon said. "Their math is completely off, like most of their customs. For example, did you know that Valentine's Day wasn't actually about love until Geoffrey Chaucer did his whole courtly love thing in the High Middle Ages?"

"You guys are so weird." I grinned at the brothers.

"That we are," Aiden replied. "Come on, I'll show you your room."

"Hey Alex," Deacon called. "We're making cookies tomorrow, since it's Valentine's Eve."

Making cookies on Valentine's Eve? I didn't even know if there was such a thing as Valentine's Eve. I laughed as I followed Aiden out of the room. "You two really are opposites."

"I'm cooler!" Deacon yelled from his Mortal Holiday Tree room.

Aiden headed up the stairs. "Sometimes I think one of us was switched at birth. We don't even look alike."

"That's not true." I fingered the decorative garland covering the marble banister. "Your eyes are the same."

He smiled over his shoulder. "I rarely ever stay here. Deacon does every once in a while, and visiting Council members will stay here sometimes. The house is usually empty."

I remembered what Deacon had said about this house. Wanting to say something, but at a loss for what to say, I trailed behind him quietly. Over the last two days, Aiden had stayed by my side constantly. Like before the whole stabby incident, we'd talked about stupid, inane things. And he hadn't been able to get Olivia's number for me. All he had access to was her mom's.

"Deacon stays in one of the bedrooms downstairs. I'll stay here." He gestured at the first room, drawing my attention.

The urge to see his room was too much to resist. I peeked inside. Like the one in the cabin, there were just the bare essentials. Clothes were folded neatly on a chair beside the full-size bed. There were no pictures or personal effects. "Was this your room when you were younger?"

"No." Aiden leaned against the wall in the hallway, watching me through hooded eyes. "My room used to be the one Deacon stays in. It's hooked up with all the stuff Deacon requires. This was one of the guest rooms." He pushed off the wall. "Yours is down the hall. It's a nicer room."

I tore myself away from his room. We passed several closed doors, but one had locked double doors decorated with titanium inlays. I suspected that had been his parents' room.

Aiden pushed open a door at the end of the carpeted hall and turned the light on. Sliding past him, my mouth dropped open. The room was huge and beautiful. Plush carpet covered the floors, heavy curtains blocked the bay window, and my bags of personal items had been stacked neatly by a dresser. A flat-screen TV hung from the wall and the bed was big enough for four people. I spied a bathroom with a huge tub and my heart went all fluttery.

Seeing my love-struck expression, Aiden laughed. "I figured you'd like this room."

I looked inside the bathroom, sighing. "I want to marry that bathtub." I turned around, smiling at Aiden. "This is like going to one of those super-expensive hotels, except everything is free."

He shrugged. "I don't know about that."

"Maybe not to you and all your endless wealth." I drifted off to the window and parted the curtains. Oceanside view. Nice. The moon reflected off the still, onyx-colored waters.

"That money isn't really mine. It's my parents'."

Which did make it his and Deacon's, but I didn't push it. "The house is really beautiful."

"Some days it's more beautiful than others."

I felt my cheeks flush. I pressed my forehead against the cool window. "Whose idea was it for me to stay here?"

"It was a joint effort. After... what happened, there was no way you could've stayed in the dorm."

"I can't stay here forever," I said quietly. "Once school is back in, I need to be on the other island."

"We'll figure something out when that time comes," he said. "Don't worry about that right now. It's past midnight. You have to be tired."

Dropping the curtains, I faced him. He stood next to the door, hands curled into fists. "I'm not tired. I was stuck in that hospital room and that bed for what felt like eternity."

He cocked his head to the side. "How are you feeling?"

"Fine." I patted my stomach. "I'm not broken, you know."

Aiden was quiet for a few moments, and then he smiled a little. "Want something to drink?"

"Are you trying to booze me up, Aiden? I'm shocked."

He arched a brow. "I was thinking more along the lines of hot chocolate for you."

I grinned. "And what about you?"

Turning around, he headed out of the bedroom. "Something I'm old enough to drink."

I rolled my eyes, but followed him out of the room. Aiden did make me hot chocolate—with tiny marshmallows—and he didn't drink anything other than a bottle of water. He then took me on a quick tour of the house. It was similar to Lucian's—lavishly grand, more rooms than anyone would ever need in a lifetime, and personal property that was probably worth more than my life. Deacon's room was by the kitchen, accessed through a titanium-trimmed door under the stairs.

Sipping my drink, I laughed when Aiden tried to right the bulb on Deacon's MHT tree. I drifted around the room, looking for some sort of personal effects. There wasn't a single picture of the St. Delphi family. Nothing that proved they even existed.

Aiden stood in front of a closed door—a room he hadn't shown me on the mini-tour. "How's the chocolate?"

I smiled. "It's perfect."

He set his water down on the coffee table and folded his arms. "I've been doing a lot of thinking about what Apollo said."

"Which part of crazy are you thinking about?" I watched him over the rim of my mug, loving the way he smiled in response to the stupid things that came out of my mouth. That had to be true love, I decided.

"You shouldn't stay at Lucian's when he returns."

I lowered my mug. "Why?"

"Apollo has a point about Seth. You're in danger because of him. The further away from him you are, the safer you'll be."

"Aiden—"

"I know you care about him, but you've suspected that Seth hasn't been honest with you." Aiden strode forward and dropped into a chair. His gaze lowered and heavy lashes fanned his cheeks. "You shouldn't be around him—not when he can come and go at Lucian's."

Aiden had a point. I'd give him that, but I seriously doubted that was the whole reason. "And you feel this way all because of what Apollo said?"

"No. It's more than that."

"You don't like Seth?" I asked innocently, setting my mug down.

He flashed his teeth. "Besides that, Alex, he hasn't been honest about a lot of things. He lied about knowing how an Apollyon was created, about the Order, and there's a good chance he's... giving you those marks on purpose."

"Okay, besides all those reasons?"

He stared up at me. "Well, I don't like that fact that you're settling for him."

I rolled my eyes. "I hate when you say that."

"It's the truth," he said simply.

Irritation started to burn below my skin. "That's not the truth. I'm not settling for Seth."

"Let me ask you a question, then." Aiden leaned forward. "If you could have... who you wanted, would you be with Seth?"

I stared at him, somewhat shocked that he'd even throw that out there. And it really wasn't a fair question. What could I say to that?

"Exactly." He sat back, smiling smugly.

A fierce emotion blasted through me. "Why can't you just admit it?"

"Admit what?"

"That you're jealous of Seth." It was one of those times I needed to shut up, but I couldn't. I was angry and thrilled all at once. "You're jealous of the fact that I can be with Seth if I want to be."

Aiden smirked. "There. You just said it yourself. You'd be with Seth *if* you wanted to be. Obviously you don't, so why *are* you with him? You're settling."

"Ugh!" My hands curled into fists and I wanted to stomp my foot. "You are absolutely the most frustrating person I know. Fine. Whatever. You're not jealous of Seth or the fact that he's been sleeping in my bed for the last two months, because of course you haven't wished that was you at all."

Something dangerous flared in his silvery eyes.

Cheeks flaming, I wanted to smack myself. Why had I said that? To piss him off or to make myself look like a total ho-bag? I'd accomplished a little of both.

"Alex," he said, voice low and deceptively soft.

"Just forget it." I started past him, but his hand shot out as fast as a snake striking. One second I was walking and the next I was in his lap, straddling him. Eyes wide and heart thundering, I stared at him.

"Okay," he said, grasping my upper arms. "You're right. I'm jealous of that little punk. Happy?"

Instead of basking in the glory of having him admit that I was right, I placed my hands on his shoulders and basked in something totally different. "I… I keep forgetting how fast you can move when you want to."

A strange small smile played over his lips. "You haven't seen anything yet, Alex."

My pulse went into cardiac arrest territory. I was done arguing—done talking in general. Other things were on my mind. And I knew he was thinking the same. His hands moved down my arms to my hips. He tugged me forward, and the softest part of me pressed against his hardness.

Our mouths didn't touch, but the rest of our bodies did. Neither of us moved. There was something primal in Aiden's gaze, wholly possessive. I shivered—the good kind of shiver. All I could think about was how good, how right his body felt pressed against mine.

I cupped his face and then slid my fingers through his hair, amazed that the intensity of what I was feeling was stronger than any bond with Seth. Delicious sensations rolled through me as his hands tightened around my hips, and when he rocked against me, the way his hands trembled and the powerful way his body coiled completely undid me.

"There's something I need to tell you," he whispered, his eyes searching mine. "That I should've told you—"

"Not right now." Words would ruin things. They brought logic and reality into the game. I lowered my mouth to his.

A hallway light turned on outside the room.

I sprang away from Aiden as if he'd caught fire. From several feet away, I struggled to catch my breath as my eyes locked with Aiden's. He came out of the chair, his chest rising and falling sharply. There was a second when I thought he was going to say the hell with it and pull me back into his arms, but the sound of encroaching footsteps knocked some sense into him. Closing his eyes, he tipped his head back and exhaled loudly.

Without saying a word, I spun around and left the room. I passed a sleepy, confused-looking Deacon in the hallway.

"I'm thirsty," he said, rubbing his eyes.

Muttering something that resembled good night, I fled upstairs. Once inside the bedroom, I collapsed on the bed and stared at the vaulted ceiling.

Things just weren't meant to happen between us. How many times had we been interrupted? It didn't seem to matter how strong our connection was—our attraction. Something always got in the way.

Fully clothed, I rolled onto my side and curled up into a ball. I wanted to spin-kick everyone who thought me staying with Aiden was a good idea. We—I—had enough problems right now without throwing myself at Aiden.

Not that I'd really thrown myself at him this time… or the last time. *Oh hell…*

I reached under my shirt and felt the scar below my ribcage. The act served as a painful reminder that my love problems—or lack thereof—were not my greatest.

CHAPTER 21

THE FIRST THING I DID WHEN I WOKE UP WAS TAKE A nice, luxurious bath in the garden tub. I stayed in that thing until my skin started to wrinkle and even then it was hard to pull myself out of it.

It was heaven in a bathroom.

After that, I went downstairs and found Deacon sprawled across a couch in the rec room. Knocking his legs aside, I sat down. He was watching *Supernatural* reruns. "Good choice," I commented. "They're two brothers I'd like to meet in real life."

"True." Deacon knocked wild curls out of his eyes. "It's what I watch when I'm not in class or pretending to be in class."

I grinned. "Aiden would kill you if he knew you skip class."

He kicked up his legs and dropped them in my lap. "I know. I've cut back on the skipping class thing."

He'd also cut back on the drinking thing. I glanced at him. Maybe Luke was a good influence on him. "You doing anything special for Valentine's Day?" I asked.

His lips pursed. "Now why would you ask that, Alex? We don't celebrate V-Day."

"But you do. You wouldn't have that… tree if you didn't."

"Are you?" he inquired, his gray eyes dancing. "I'd swear I saw Aiden at the jewelry—"

"Shut up!" I hit him across the stomach with the throw pillow. "Stop saying things like that. Nothing is going on."

Deacon grinned, and we watched the rest of the shows he'd recorded. It wasn't until the afternoon that I worked up the nerve to ask where Aiden was. "He was outside with the Guards the last time I checked."

"Oh."

Part of me was glad that Aiden was doing his babysitting outside. My cheeks caught fire just thinking about us in the chair last night.

"So you two were up pretty late," Deacon said.

I kept my expression blank. "He was showing me the house."

"Was that all he was showing you?"

Shocked, I laughed as I twisted toward him. "Yes! Deacon, geez."

"What?" He sat up and swung his legs off my lap. "It was just an innocent question."

"Whatever." I watched him stand up. "Where are you going?"

"Over to the dorms. Luke's still there. You're more than welcome to come, but I doubt Aiden will let you out of this house."

Pures and halfs could be casual friends, especially while they were in school together, and a lot of them were, although not so much since the daimon attacks at the beginning of the school year. Zarak hadn't thrown any of his huge parties lately. But for a half to be hanging out at a pure's house would raise questions.

"What are you two doing?" I asked.

Deacon winked as he backed out of the room. "Oh, I'm sure the same thing you and my brother were doing last night. You know, he's going to show me around the dorm."

✝

Several hours later, Deacon returned and Aiden finally reappeared inside. Avoiding my gaze, he went straight upstairs. Deacon shrugged and coaxed me into making cookies with him.

When Aiden finally came downstairs he lingered in the kitchen while Deacon and I made cookies. I sort of gaped at him—dressed down in jeans and a long-sleeved shirt—so long that Deacon elbowed me in the side. Once Aiden loosened up, he joked around with his brother. Every so often our eyes would meet, and electricity danced over my skin.

After eating our weight in raw cookie dough, we all ended up in the living room, sinking into couches bigger than most people's beds. Deacon controlled the TV for four straight hours before ambling off to bed and Aiden went outside to check in with the Guards—why, I had no idea. I roamed around the house. What had Aiden wanted to talk about before I told him to stop talking? Had he been ready to talk, like he'd hinted when I was still in the med clinic? Restless, I found myself in the MHT tree room.

I poked the bulb, smiling as it swayed back and forth. Deacon was so bizarre. Who had a Mortal Holiday Tree? So weird.

It was late, and I should've been in bed, but the idea of sleeping was unappealing. Full of restless energy, I drifted around the room until I came to a stop in front of the door. Curious, and with nothing else better to do, I tried the handle and found it unlocked. Glancing over my shoulder, I pushed open the door and crept inside the softly lit room. At once I realized why Aiden had kept this room off his tour.

Everything personal was crammed into the circular room. Pictures of Aiden lined the walls, chronicling his childhood. There were photos of Deacon as a precocious-looking little boy, head full of blond curls and chubby cheeks that hinted at delicate features.

I stopped in front of one of Aiden and felt my chest tighten. He must've been six or seven. Dark curls fell across his face instead of the looser waves he had now. He was adorable, all gray eyes and lips. There was a photo of him with Deacon. Aiden was probably around ten or so and he had one lanky arm draped over his younger brother's shoulders. The camera had captured both boys laughing.

Moving around an overstuffed couch, I slowly picked up the titanium picture frame that was on the fireplace mantel. My breath caught.

It was his father—his mother and father.

They stood behind Deacon and Aiden, their hands on the boys' shoulders. Behind them the sky was a brilliant blue. It was easy to tell which boy favored which parent. Their mother had hair the color of corn silk that fell past her shoulders in springy curls. She was beautiful, as all pures were, with delicate features and laughing blue eyes. It was shocking, though, how much Aiden looked like his father. From the almost-black hair and piercing silver eyes, he was an exact replica.

It didn't seem fair that his parents were taken so young, robbed of watching their boys grow up. And Aiden and Deacon had lost so much.

I ran my thumb over the edge of the frame. Why had Aiden closed off all these memories? Did he ever come in here? Looking around the room, I spied a guitar propped beside a stack of books and comics. This was his room, I realized. A place where he thought it was okay to remember his parents and maybe to just get away.

I turned my attention back to the photo and tried to picture my mother and father. If pures and halfs had been allowed to be together, would we've had moments like these? Closing my eyes, I tried to picture the three of us. My mom wasn't hard to remember now. I could see her before she turned, but my father had the mark of slavery on his forehead and no matter what I did, it wouldn't go away.

"You shouldn't be in here."

Startled, I spun around, clutching the frame to my chest. Aiden stood in the doorway, arms straight at his sides. He stalked across the room and stopped in front of me. Shadows hid his expression. "What are you doing?" he demanded.

"I was just curious. The door wasn't locked." I swallowed nervously. "I haven't been in here long at all."

His gaze dropped and his shoulders stiffened. He pried the picture from my fingers and set it back on the mantel. Without speaking, he bent and placed his hands over the kindling. Fire sparked and grew immediately. He grabbed a poker.

Embarrassed and stung by his sudden coldness, I backed away. "I'm sorry," I whispered.

He prodded at the fire, his spine stiff.

"I'll leave." I turned, and suddenly he was in front of me. My heart tumbled over.

He clasped my arm. "Don't leave."

I searched his eyes intently, but couldn't gain anything from them. "Okay."

Aiden took a deep breath and let go of my arm. "Would you like something to drink?"

Hugging my elbows, I nodded. This room was his sanctuary, a silent memorial to the family he'd lost, and I'd invaded it. I doubted even Deacon dared to tread in here. Leave it to me to just bust on in.

Behind the bar, Aiden pulled two wine flutes out and sat them down. Filling the glasses, he glanced up at me. "Wine okay?"

"Yes." My throat was dry and tight. "I really am sorry, Aiden. I shouldn't have come in here."

"Stop apologizing." He came around the bar and handed me a glass.

I took the glass, hoping he didn't notice how my fingers shook. The wine was sugary and smooth, but it didn't settle in my stomach right.

"I didn't mean to snap at you like that," he said, moving toward the fire. "I was just surprised to see you in here."

"It's… uh, a nice room." I felt like an idiot for saying that.

His lips tipped up at the corner.

"Aiden…"

He stared at me for so long I thought he'd never speak and when he did it was not what I expected. "After what happened to you in Gatlinburg, it reminded me of what it'd been like for me… after what happened to my parents. I had nightmares. Could hear… hear their screams over and over again for what felt like years. I never told you that. Maybe I should have. It could've helped you."

I sat on the edge of the couch, clenching the fragile stem.

Aiden faced the fire, taking a sip of his wine. "Do you remember the day in the gym when you told me about your nightmares? It stuck with me—your fear of Eric and his return," he continued. "All I kept thinking was, what if one of the daimons had escaped the attack on my parents? How would I've gone on?"

Eric was the only daimon to escape from Gatlinburg. I hadn't stopped thinking about him, but to hear his name knotted up my stomach. Half of the tags on my body were thanks to him.

"I thought getting you out of there, taking you to the zoo would help get your mind off things, but I had… I had to do more. I contacted some of the Sentinels around here. I knew Eric wouldn't have gone far, not after he knew what you were and had tasted your aether," he said. "Based on Caleb's and your description, it wasn't hard to find him. He was just outside of Raleigh."

"What?" The knots grew larger. "Raleigh is like, less than a hundred miles from here."

He nodded. "As soon as it was confirmed that it was him, I left. Leon—Apollo—went with me."

At first I couldn't figure out when he could've done this, but then I remembered those weeks after I'd told him I loved him and he'd ended our training sessions together. Aiden had had time to do this without me ever knowing. "What happened?"

"We found him." He smiled humorlessly before turning back to the fire. "I didn't kill him outright. I don't know what that says about me. By the end, I think he truly regretted ever learning of your existence."

I didn't know what to say. Part of me was awed by the fact he had gone to such great lengths for me. The other part was sort of horrified by it. Underneath the calm and controlled persona that Aiden wore like a second skin was something dark—a side of him I'd only glimpsed. I stared at his profile, suddenly realizing that I hadn't been fair to Aiden. I'd set him upon this incredibly high pedestal, where he was absolutely flawless in my mind.

Aiden wasn't flawless.

I swallowed a sip of my wine. "Why didn't you tell me?"

"We really weren't on talking terms then, and how could I've told you?" He laughed harshly. "It wasn't like a normal daimon hunt. It wasn't a precise and humane kill like we're taught."

The Covenant basically taught us not to play with our kills, so to speak. That even though the daimon was beyond saving, he'd once been a pure-blood… or a half-blood. Still, as disturbing as learning that Aiden had most likely tortured Eric, I wasn't disgusted by it.

Gods know what that said about *me*.

"Thank you," I said finally.

His head jerked toward me sharply. "Don't thank me for something like that. I didn't do it just—"

"You didn't do it just for me. You did it because of what happened to your family." And I knew I was right. It wasn't so much that he'd done it for me. It was his way of taking revenge. It wasn't right, but I understood it. And in his shoes I would've probably done the same thing and then some.

Aiden went still. The flames sent a warm glow over his profile as he stared down at his glass. "We were visiting friends of my father in Nashville. I didn't know them very well, but they had a daughter who was about my age. I thought we were just vacationing before the start of school, but as soon as we got there, my mother practically pushed me in her direction. She was a tiny thing, with pale blonde hair and these green eyes." He took a breath, fingers tightening around the fragile stem of the glass. "Her name was Helen. Looking back, I know why my parents arranged that I spend so much time with her, but for some reason, I just didn't get it."

I swallowed. "She was your match?"

A rueful smile appeared. "I really didn't want to have anything to do with her. I spent most of my time shadowing the half-blood Guards while they trained. My mother was so upset with me, but I remember my father laughing about it. Telling her to just give me some time, and let nature run its course. That I was still very much just a boy and that men fighting would interest me more than pretty girls."

There was a lump forming in my chest. I sat back, the glass of wine forgotten.

"It was night when they came." His thick lashes fanned his cheeks as his eyes lowered. "I heard the fighting outside. I got up and looked out the window. I couldn't see anything, but I just knew. There was a crash downstairs, and I woke up Deacon. He didn't understand what was happening or why I was making him hide in the closet and cover himself with clothes.

"It all just happened so fast after that." He took a healthy swallow of the wine and then sat his glass on the ledge. "There were only two daimons, but they had control over fire. They took out three of the Guards, burning them alive."

I wanted him to stop, because I knew what was coming, but he had to get this off his chest. I doubted he'd ever put that night into words, and I needed to deal with it.

"My dad was turning the element back on them, or at least, trying to. The Guards were dropping left and right. Helen was awakened by the commotion, and I tried to get her to stay upstairs, but she saw one of the daimons attack her father—ripped his throat open right in front of her. She screamed—I'll never forget that sound." A distant look crept across his face as he continued, almost like he was there. "My father made sure my mother got up the stairs, but then I couldn't see him anymore. I heard him scream and I just," he shook his head, "stood there. Terrified."

"Aiden, you were just a boy."

He nodded absently. "My mom yelled at me to get Deacon and get him out of the house with Helen. I didn't want to leave her, so I started down the stairs. The daimon came out of nowhere, grabbing her by the throat. She was staring at me when he snapped her neck. Her eyes... just glossed over. And Helen... Helen was screaming and screaming. She wouldn't stop. I knew he was going to kill her, too. I started running up the stairs, and I grabbed her hand. She was panicking and fighting me. It slowed us down. The daimon reached us and he grabbed for Helen first. She went up in flames. Just like that."

I gasped. Tears burned my eyes. This... this was more horrific than I'd imagined, and it reminded me of the boy the daimon had burned in Atlanta.

Aiden turned to the fire. "The daimon went after me next. I don't know why he spared me the fire and knocked me to the ground, but I knew he was going to drain my aether. Then there was this Guard who'd been burned downstairs. Somehow, through what had to have been the worst kind of pain, he made it up the stairs and killed the daimon."

He faced me and there wasn't any pain in his expression. Maybe sorrow and regret, but there was also a bit of wonder. "He was a half-blood. One of the ones I'd been following around. He was probably my age now, and you know, in all that horrific pain, he still did his duty. He saved my life and Deacon's. I found out a few days later that he had succumbed to the burns. I never got a chance to thank him."

His tolerance of half-bloods made sense. That one Guard's actions had changed centuries of beliefs in one little boy, turning prejudice into awe. It was no wonder that Aiden never saw the difference between halfs and pures.

Aiden made his way over to me and sat. He met my stare. "That's why I chose to become a Sentinel. Not so much because of what happened to my parents, but because of that one half-blood who died to save my life and my brother's."

I didn't know what to say or if there was anything I could. So I placed my hand on his arm as I blinked back tears.

He placed his hand over mine as he looked away. A muscle worked in his jaw. "Gods, I don't think I've ever talked to anyone about that night."

"Not even Deacon?"

Aiden shook his head.

"I feel… honored that you'd share that with me. I know it's a lot." I squeezed his arm. "I just wish you'd never had to experience any of that. It wasn't fair to any of you."

Several moments passed before he answered. "I had justice for what those daimons did to me. I know it's different from what you dealt with, but I wanted to give you that justice. I wish I'd told you before."

"A lot of stuff was going on then," I said. We hadn't been talking, and then Caleb's death happened. My heart didn't clench as badly as it used to at his name. "I understand what happened with Eric."

He smiled a little. "It was a knee-jerk reaction."

"Yeah." I searched for something to take our minds off everything. We both needed it. My gaze found the acoustic guitar propped against the wall. "Play something for me."

He rose and picked up the guitar reverently. Walking back to the couch, he sat on the floor in front of me. He tipped his head down and locks of hair fell forward as he fiddled with the knobs along the headstock. His long fingers plucked a pick out from the taunt strings.

He peered up, his lips tipped in a half-smile. "Treachery," he murmured. "You knew I wouldn't refuse you."

I eased down on my side. My stomach rarely ached, but I'd grown accustomed to being careful. "You know it."

Aiden laughed as he thrummed his fingers on the strings lightly. After a few more moments of adjusting the tone, he started playing. The song was as haunting as it was soft, pitching high for a few strands, and then his fingers slipped down the chords. My suspicious were confirmed. Aiden could play. There wasn't one wrong slip or falter.

It entranced me.

Resting my head on the throw pillow, I curled up and closed my eyes, letting the melody filling the room drift over me. Whatever he was thrumming on the guitar was soothing, like the perfect lullaby. A smile pulled at my lips. I could totally see him sitting in front of a packed bar, playing tunes that enchanted everyone in the room.

When the song ended, I opened my eyes. He was staring back at me, eyes so soft, so deep, that I never wanted to look away. "That was beautiful."

Aiden shrugged and gently placed the guitar beside him. He reached up, carefully taking the barely-touched glass of wine from my fingertips. His eyes watched me as he took a sip, and then he set the glass aside, too. Minutes could've passed as we stared at each other, neither of us talking.

I didn't know what came over me, but I reached out and placed a hand on his chest, beside his heart. Under my right hand, there was something hard and teardrop-shaped tucked under his shirt. I'd felt the necklace before and never really paid it much attention, but now there was something… familiar about it.

I sucked in a sharp gasp as comprehension shot through me. Aiden stared back, his eyes incredibly bright. A shiver ran down my spine, spreading across my skin with dizzying speed. I reached up, sliding my fingers under the thin chain.

"Alex," Aiden ordered, pleaded really. His voice was thick, gruff. "Alex, please…"

I hesitated for an instant, but I had to see it. I just had to. Carefully, I tugged the chain up. My breath caught in my throat as I lifted the chain until it was completely out from underneath his shirt.

Dangling from the silver chain was the black guitar pick I'd gotten him for his birthday. The day I had given it to him he'd told me he didn't love me. But this… *this* had to mean something, and my heart was swelling, in danger of bursting.

Speechless, I ran my thumb over the polished gemstone. There was a tiny hole in the top, where the chain threaded through.

Aiden placed his hand over mine, closing my fingers around the guitar pick. "Alex…"

When my eyes met his, there was a brutal level of vulnerability in his stare, a sense of helplessness that I shared. I wanted to cry. "I *know*." And I did. I knew even if he never spoke those words, even if he refused to, I'd still know.

His lips parted. "Couldn't fool you for that long, I guess."

I squeezed my eyes shut, but a tear wiggled its way free, gliding down my cheek.

"Don't cry." He caught the tear with his finger as he pressed his forehead against mine. "Please. I hate when you cry because of me."

"I'm sorry. I don't want to be all weepy." I wiped at my cheeks, feeling foolish. "It's just that… I never did know."

Aiden clasped the sides of my face, pressing a gentle kiss to my forehead. "I wanted a piece of you with me always. No matter what."

I shuddered. "But I don't… I don't have anything of you."

"Yes, you do." Aiden brushed his lips over my damp cheek. A soft smile filled his voice. "You'll have a piece of my heart—all of it, really. Forever. Even if your heart belongs to someone else."

My heart tumbled over, but I stilled. "What do you mean?"

He dropped his hands, leaning back. "I know you care about him."

I did care about Seth. But he wasn't my heart. When Aiden was there, in front of me, the connection between us was something more than prophecy. My true fate—real and not an illusion. Prophecies are just dreams; Aiden was my reality.

"It's not the same," I whispered. "It never has been. You have my heart… and I only want to share my heart with you."

Aiden's eyes were back to liquid silver. I saw that before he lowered his gaze. Moments passed before his eyes flicked up, meeting mine.

There seemed to be some sort of internal battle he struggled with. When he spoke, I wasn't sure if he'd won or lost. "We should go to bed."

A shock ran through me, flushing my skin. But *wait*—was he suggesting that we go to bed together or that we go to bed in separate beds? I really had no idea, I was too afraid to hope, and oddly, I was frightened by the idea. It was like being offered what I'd waited for so long and suddenly having no idea what to do with it.

Or how to do it.

His lips quirked, and then he stood. Clasping my boneless hands in his, he tugged me to my feet. My legs felt weak. "Go to bed," he said.

"Are… are you coming, too?"

Aiden nodded. "I'll be up in a few."

I couldn't breathe.

"Go," he urged.

And I went.

CHAPTER 22

I WAS SURE I WAS GOING TO HAVE A HEART ATTACK. Rarely did mortal illnesses plague us, but since I had a cold already, I figured nothing was impossible.

I still couldn't really breathe.

I brushed my teeth and got the tangles out of my hair. I stared at the obscenely large bed in the middle of the room. I couldn't decide what to wear. Or should I wear nothing? Oh gods, what was I thinking? It wasn't like he said he was coming up to have sex. And if he wasn't and he saw me lying on the bed naked, that would be a whole lot of awkward. Perhaps he just wanted to spend more time with me. Seth issue aside, there was still the whole glaring issue of us not being able to be together.

But he had the pick. He'd had *the* pick hovering over his heart this entire time.

I pulled on a tank top and sleeping shorts, then started toward the bed. Then I looked down at my arms. In the moonlight streaming in through the window, I could still see the patchy, irregular skin. I didn't want Aiden to see that. So I changed quickly, pulling on a thin, long-sleeved shirt. I kept the bottoms on. Then I jumped in the bed, pulled the covers up to my chin, and waited.

There was a soft knock on the door a few minutes later. "It's okay." I winced at the way my voice croaked.

Aiden came in, shutting and locking the door behind him. He'd changed, too, wearing a pair of dark sleeping pants and a gray tank top that showed off muscular arms. I swallowed nervously and willed my heart to slow down before I spazzed out.

He faced me and went rigid. The room was too shadowed for me to see his expression, and I wished I could, because then I could've tried to figure out what he was thinking. Wordlessly, he went to the windows first and drew the blinds. The room was cast into utter darkness, and my fingers dug into the rich comforter. I heard him padding around the room, and then a soft glow appeared. Aiden brought a candle to the bed, setting it down on a small table. He looked at me, expression softened by the candlelight. He smiled.

I started to relax, the blanket easing away from my fingers.

Carefully, he pulled back the covers on his side and climbed in, never once breaking eye contact with me. "Alex?"

"Yeah?"

He was still smiling. "Relax. I just want to be here with you... if that's okay?"

"It's okay," I whispered.

"Good, because I really don't want to be anyplace else."

Oh, the warmth that flooded my chest could've had me floating to the stars. I watched him stretch out beside me. My gaze darted to the closed door even though I knew Deacon was nowhere near us. And it wasn't like he didn't already suspect something. Or like he cared. I bit my lip, daring a quick look at Aiden. He chin was tipped up and his eyes burned silver, bright, and intense. I couldn't look away.

Aiden drew in a shallow breath, lifting the arm closest to me. "Come?"

Heart pounding, I scooted over until my leg brushed his. His arm came up, wrapping around my waist. He guided me down so that I was nestled against him, my cheek on his chest.

I could feel his heart racing just as fast as mine. We lay in silence for a little while, and in those minutes, it was like being in paradise. The simple pleasure of being beside him felt so right it really couldn't be wrong.

Aiden brought his other arm across him, cupping my cheek in his hand. His thumb smoothed over my jaw. "I'm sorry for that day in the gym. For how I talked to you, for how much I hurt you. I just thought I was doing the right thing."

"I understand, Aiden. It's okay."

"It's not okay. I hurt you. I know I did. I want you to know why I did that," he said. "After you told me how you felt, at the zoo... it... it shattered my self-control." Didn't seem that way, I thought as he continued. "I knew I couldn't be around you anymore, because I knew I would touch you and I wouldn't stop."

I lifted up, staring down at him and opened my mouth to say something that probably would've ruined the moment, but I never had the chance. Aiden's hand found the nape of my neck and pulled me down. His lips met mine, and like every time before, there was this indefinable spark that coursed through us. He made a sound against my lips, kissing me harder and harder.

He pulled back just enough so that his lips brushed mine when he spoke. "I can't keep pretending that I don't want this—that I don't want you. I can't. Not after what happened to you. I thought... I thought I'd lost you, Alex, forever. And I would've lost everything. You *are* my everything."

Many emotions rose in me all at once—awe, hope, and love. So much love that everything outside of us vanished in that instant. "This... this is what you've been trying to tell me."

"It's what I've always wanted to tell you, Alex." He sat up, bringing me along with him. "I've always wanted this with you."

I slid my hands to his cheeks, meeting his heated gaze with my own. "I've always loved you."

Aiden made a strangled sound and his lips were on mine again. His hand buried in my hair, holding me still. "This wasn't my intention... coming in here."

"I know." My lips brushed his as I spoke. "I know."

As he kissed me again, he eased onto his back. My heart was hammering against my ribs as his fingers left my face and traveled down. He lifted himself up just enough for me to take off his shirt and toss it aside. My hands splayed across each hard ripple and I kissed my way down until his chest heaved under my lips and he whispered my name in a pleading sort of way. He gripped my arms and pulled me back to his lips.

I shrugged out of his grasp and lifted my arms without speaking. He obeyed the silent command and tossed my shirt aside. Without any warning, I was on my back, staring up at him. His hands slipped over my bare skin as his lips dipped down my throat and over the curve of my shoulder. Each scar was kissed tenderly, and when he came to the one Linard's blade had left, he shuddered.

My fingers sifted through his hair as I held him to me. His kisses were doing crazy, strange, and wonderful things to me. I whispered his name over and over again like some kind of mad prayer. Then I was moving against him, being guided by some primal instinct that told me what to do. The rest of our clothes ended up in a pile on the floor. The moment our bodies were flush with one another, a sense of wildness came over me.

Our kisses deepened, his tongue swept over mine, and I rocked against him. All of this was wonderful, exquisitely pleasing. Aiden dropped kisses all over my flushed skin. I was lost in the heady sensations, completely unprepared for it. This may not have been what we intended, but this… this was happening.

Aiden lifted his head. "Are you sure?"

"Yes," I breathed. "I've never been more sure."

His hand trembled against my flushed face. "Have you gotten…?"

He was asking if I'd had my shot—the Council-mandated birth control for all half-blood females. I nodded.

The silver eyes flared. His hand trembled against my cheek again and as he lifted up, his eyes roamed over me. My newfound courage all but disappeared under his scalding stare. Somehow sensing my nervousness, his kiss was gentle and sweet. He was patient and perfect, coaxing away the shyness until I wrapped myself around him.

There was a near-panicked edge to him, driven by the knowledge that there was no pulling back, no stopping this time. With a thrusting kiss that left me shaken, his hand drifted with such exquisite detail. His kisses followed the same pattern and when he paused, his eyes begged for permission. That simple moment, that tiny act brought tears to my eyes.

I couldn't—didn't want to—deny him anything.

Aiden was everywhere—in every touch, every soft moan. When I thought I couldn't take anymore, that I would surely break, he was there to prove that I could. When his lips descended on mine again, they did so with a fevered pitch.

"I love you," he whispered. "I have since the night in Atlanta. I always will."

I gasped against his skin. "I love you."

He broke. Whatever control he had wrapped around him finally slipped away. I reveled in it, the pure simplicity of being in his arms and knowing that he felt the same keen madness that I did. Supporting himself with his forearm as his kisses took on the same sense of urgency that I felt, he lifted his mouth to whisper something in a beautiful language I didn't understand. I was nearly over the edge, rushing towards a glorious ending.

We were surrounded by our love for one another. It became a tangible thing, electrifying the air around us until I was sure we both would ignite under its power. Then in a mindless moment of pure beauty, we weren't a half-blood and a pure-blood, we were simply just two people madly, deeply in love.

We were one.

I awoke some time later, tucked in Aiden's arms. The candle still flickered by the bed. The sheet had tangled around our legs, and the comforter was pushed to the floor. I realized that I'd been more or less using him as a pillow. I lifted my head and drank him in. I could never grow tired of looking at him.

His chest rose evenly under my hands. He looked so young and relaxed while he slept. Locks of dark waves tumbled against his forehead and his lips were parted. I leaned down and placed a soft kiss against those lips.

His arms immediately tightened, betraying that he was not as deeply asleep as I'd originally thought. I grinned at being caught. "Hello."

Aiden's eyes fluttered open. "How long have you been staring at me?"

"Not long."

"Knowing you," he drawled lazily, "you've been staring at me since I fell asleep."

"That's not true." I giggled.

"Uh huh, come here." He tugged me down. My nose brushed against his. "Not nearly close enough."

I shifted closer. My leg wrapped around his. "Close enough?"

"Let me see." His hands slid down my back and rested over the curve of my waist with the slightest pressure. "Ah, that's better."

I flushed. "Yes… yeah, it is."

Aiden grinned wolfishly and a wicked glint filled his silver eyes. I should've known at that point he was up to something, but this side of Aiden—this playful and sensual side—was unknown to me. His hand glided lower, eliciting a pleased gasp of surprise. He sat up in one fast fluid motion and I found myself unexpectedly in his lap.

I didn't have a moment to consider much. Aiden kissed me, scattering all thoughts or responses. The sheet slipped away and I melted against him. It was quite some time later, when the sun was about to rise and the candle had long since gone out, that Aiden gently roused me.

"Alex." He brushed his lips over my forehead.

I opened my eyes, smiling. "You're still here."

His hand caressed my cheek. "Where else would I be?" Then he kissed me, and my toes curled. "Did you think I'd just leave?"

I marveled at the fact that I could run my hand up his arm without having him pull away. "No. I don't know, actually."

He frowned as he traced the shape of my cheekbone. "What do you mean?"

I snuggled closer to him. "What happens now?"

Understanding flared in his gaze. "I don't know, Alex. We have to be careful. It's not going to be easy, but… we'll figure something out."

My heart skipped a beat.

A relationship was going to be damn near impossible anywhere we'd go, but I couldn't stop the hope swelling inside me or the tears building in my eyes. Was it wrong to hope for a miracle? Because that's what we would need to make this work.

"Oh, Alex." He gathered me into his arms, holding me tightly against him. I burrowed my face in the space between his neck and shoulder, inhaling deeply. "What we did—it was the best thing I've ever done and it wasn't just some sort of fling."

"I know," I murmured.

"And I'm not going to let you go—not because some stupid law says we can't be together."

Dangerous words, but I melted along with them, cherished them. I wrapped my arms around him, trying to keep old fears and worries at bay. Aiden was taking a huge risk to be with me—so was I—and I couldn't deny our feelings because of what'd happened to Hector and Kelia. That fear wasn't fair to Aiden or to me.

Aiden rolled onto his back, fitting me to his side. "And I'm not going to lose you to Seth."

The air hitched in my lungs. Somehow, being so lost in Aiden, I'd completely forgotten the unforgettable—the fact that I'd be Awakening in two weeks—and all the ramifications of that. Fear tasted like blood in the back of my throat. What if that changed the way I felt about Aiden?

Crap. What if the bond twisted those feelings back to Seth?

And how in the hell had I forgotten about Seth in the first place? "Out of sight and out of mind" was totally not justifiable. The thing was I did care for Seth—a lot. Part of me even loved him, even though I wanted to hurt him most of the time. But my love for Seth was nothing like what it was for Aiden. It didn't consume me, didn't make me want to do crazy things, be reckless, and in the same breath, be safer and more cautious. My heart, my body didn't respond in the same way.

Aiden's hand skimmed over my arm. "I know what you're thinking, *agapi mou, zoi mou.*"

I took a shallow breath. "What does that mean?"

"It means, 'my love, my life'."

I squeezed my eyes shut against the rush of tears as I remembered the first time he'd said "*agapi mou*" to me. My gods, Aiden hadn't lied. He had loved me since the very beginning. Knowing that filled me with steely resolve. I rose up and stared down at him.

He smiled, and my heart jumped. He reached up, tucking my hair back behind my ear. His hand lingered. "What are you thinking now?"

"We can do this." I leaned down and kissed him. "We will do this, dammit."

His arm circled around my waist. "I know."

"Gods, I know this sounds really lame, so please don't laugh at me." I grinned. "But I've been… terrified of this Awakening, of losing myself. But… but I'm not anymore. I won't lose myself, because… well, how I feel about you, it would never let me forget who I am."

"I'd never let you forget who you are."

My grin spread. "Gods, we're crazy. You know that, right?"

Aiden laughed. "I think we're pretty good at crazy, though."

We stayed in each other's arms longer than we should have. I was reluctant to let him leave and I think he was, too. Rolling onto my side, I watched him throw his clothes on. He grinned when he caught me. I wiggled my brows. "What? It's a nice view."

"Wicked," he said, sitting beside me. His hand skimmed over my hip. There was something fierce in his gaze. "We will do this."

I snuggled closer to him, wishing he didn't have to leave. "I know. I believe that."

Aiden kissed me once more and whispered, "*Agapi mou.*"

CHAPTER 23

EVERYTHING AND NOTHING CHANGED AFTER HAVING sex. I didn't look any different. Well, there was the goofy smile plastered over my face that I couldn't get rid of. Other than that, I looked the same. But I did feel different. I ached in places I had no idea someone could even hurt. My heart also did that fluttering thing every time I even thought his name, which was so girlie and I loved it.

Letting my heart instead of my hormones decide when to do it made what Aiden and I'd done special. And when we passed each other throughout the day, the looks we stole suddenly meant more. Everything meant more, because we both were risking it all and neither of us regretted that.

I spent the better part of the afternoon and evening playing Scrabble with Deacon. I think he regretted asking me to play, because I was one of *those* Scrabble players—the kind who played three-letter words every chance I got.

There was a part of me that kept expecting the gods to zap one of us for finally breaking all the rules. So when Apollo popped in on our fourth round of Scrabble, I about had a heart attack.

"Gods!" I clutched my chest. "Can you stop doing that?"

Apollo looked at me strangely. "Where is Aiden?"

Slowly rising to his feet, Deacon cleared his throat and bowed. "Um, I think he's outside. I'll go get him."

I glared at Deacon's retreating form. Left alone with Apollo, I wasn't sure what to do. Should I stand up and bow, too? Was it considered rude to sit in the presence of a god? But then Apollo sat beside me, cross-legged, and started messing with the letters on the board.

Guess not.

"I know what's happened," Apollo said after a few seconds.

My brows furrowed. "What are you talking about?"

He nodded at the board.

My gaze dropped to the game and I nearly passed out. He'd spelled SEX and AIDEN with those stupid little squares. Horrified, I shot to my knees and swept the letters off the board. "I-I have no idea what you're talking about!"

Apollo tipped his head back and laughed, like, chortled really loudly.

I think I hated him, god or not.

"I've always known." He leaned back against the couch, folding his arms. His blue eyes burned unnaturally, lit from within. "I'm just surprised you two made it this far."

My jaw hit the floor. "Wait. That night Kain came back? You… you knew I was in Aiden's cabin, didn't you?"

He nodded.

"But… how do you know now?" My stomach dropped. "Oh, my gods, have you been doing some kind of creepy peeping-god thing or something? Did you see us?"

Apollo's eyes narrowed as he tilted his head toward me. "No. I *do* have better things to do."

"Like what?"

His pupils started to burn white. "Oh, I don't know. Maybe track down Telly, keep an eye on Seth and, if I get lucky, bring you back from the dead. Ah, and I forgot making a few appearances at Olympus, so that I don't have every one of my siblings curious about what I'm doing."

"Oh. Sorry." I settled down, feeling chagrined. "You are really busy."

"Anyway, I can smell Aiden on you."

My face caught fire. "What? What do you mean, you can *smell* him? Dude, I showered."

Apollo leaned over, his gaze meeting mine. "Every person has a unique scent. If you mix yours enough with that person, it takes a lot to get their smell off you. Next time you might want to try Dial soap instead of those girly body washes."

I covered my flaming face. "This is so wrong."

"But it does amuse me greatly."

"You... you're not going to do anything about it?" I whispered, lifting my head.

He rolled his eyes. "I believe that is the least of our problems at the moment. Besides, Aiden is a good guy. He will always put you first, above all else. But I am pretty sure he will get overprotective at some point." Apollo shrugged while I stared, open-mouthed, at him. "You will just have to set him straight."

Was Apollo giving me relationship advice? This was officially the weirdest moment of my life, and that was saying something. Thankfully Aiden and Deacon returned then, and I was saved from dying of humiliation.

Deacon shoved his hands into his pockets. "I'm just going to go busy myself with... something. Yeah." Spinning around, he closed the door on his way out.

There was something really weird about Deacon's reaction to Apollo. For his sake, I seriously hoped he hadn't done anything with Apollo. He might end up a flower or a tree stump.

Aiden strolled into the living room and bowed. "Is there news?" he asked upon straightening.

"He knows about us," I said.

A second later, Aiden hauled me to my feet and shoved me behind him. In both of his hands were Covenant daggers.

Apollo arched a golden eyebrow. "And what did I say about the whole overprotective bit?"

Well, he did call it. Cheeks flaming, I grabbed Aiden's arm. "He doesn't seem to care, apparently."

Aiden's muscles tensed under my hand. "And why should I believe that? He's a god."

I swallowed. "Well, probably because he could've killed me already if he was going to have a problem with it."

"That is true." Apollo stretched his legs out, crossing them at the ankle. "Aiden, you cannot actually be shocked that I know. Do I need to remind you of our special hunt in Raleigh? Why else would a man hunt down someone like that unless it was for love? And trust me, I know the crazy lengths people will go to for love."

The tips of Aiden's cheeks flushed as he relaxed by a fraction. "I'm sorry for... pulling these on you, but—"

"I understand." He waved his hand dismissively. "Have a seat, cop a squat, whatever. We need to talk, and I do not have long."

Taking a deep breath, I sat where I'd been before. Aiden took the arm of the couch behind me, remaining close. "So what's going on?" I asked.

"I was just with Marcus," Apollo answered. "He's gotten Solos on board."

"On board for what?" I glanced at Aiden. He looked away. Equal parts curious and angry, because I knew that meant he was keeping something from me, I elbowed his leg. "On board for what, Aiden?"

"You have not told her, have you?" Apollo scooted further away. "Don't hit me."

"What? I don't just hit people." Both stared at me knowingly. I folded my arms to keep from hitting them. "Fine. Whatever. What's going on?"

Apollo sighed. "Solos is a half-blood Sentinel."

"Gee. I've figured that part out." Aiden pushed me in the back with his knee. I shot him a death glare. "What does he have to do with any of this?"

"Well, I am trying to tell you." Apollo rose to his feet fluidly. "Solos' father is a Minister in Nashville. He's actually the only son of the Minister; he has been doted on and raised with a lot of knowledge of the politics of the Council."

"Okay," I said slowly. Pures caring for their half-blood children wasn't unheard of. Rare, yes, but I was an example of that.

"Not everyone on the Council is a fan of Telly, Alex. Some would even like to see him removed from his position," Aiden explained.

"And if I remember correctly, he was outvoted when it came to placing you into servitude." Apollo glided over to the window. "Word of what he's involved in will not sit well with those members of the Council, including Solos' father, who, by the way, is a softie when it comes to the treatment of half-bloods. Having them on our side can only help."

"What do you mean, his father is a softie?"

Apollo faced me. "He is one of those who do not believe that half-bloods should be forced into servitude if they do not fit the mold of a Sentinel or Guard."

"Well, you have no one to blame for that rule but yourself." Anger sparked inside of me. "You're responsible for the way we've been treated."

Apollo frowned. "We have had nothing to do with that."

"What?" Surprise colored Aiden's voice.

"We are not responsible for the subjugation of half-bloods," Apollo said. "That was all the pure-bloods. They decreed the separation of the two breeds into castes centuries and centuries ago. All we asked was that pures and halfs not mix."

Those words pulled the world out from underneath my feet. Everything I'd been taught to believe was no longer true. Since I was a small child, I'd been told that the gods saw us as lesser and our society acted on that belief. "Then why... why haven't you guys done anything?"

"It was not our problem," Apollo responded blithely.

Rage whipped through me like a red-hot bullet and I shot to my feet. "It wasn't your problem? The pure-bloods are your children! Just like we are. You all could've done something years ago."

Aiden caught my arm. "Alex."

"What did you expect us to do, Alexandria?" Apollo said. "The lives of half-bloods are literally a step—a small step—above those of mortals. We cannot interfere in such trivial things."

The slavery of thousands and thousands of halfs was a trivial thing?

Breaking free of Aiden, I charged Apollo. Looking back, not a good idea, but I was so angry, so shocked that the gods had stood by since the beginning and *allowed* the pures to treat us like animals they could herd. A small, rational part of my brain knew not to take it personally, because this was how the gods were. If it didn't involve them directly, they didn't care. It was as simple as that. The pissed part beat out the rational part.

"Alex!" Aiden yelled, reaching for me.

I was so much faster when I wanted to be. He couldn't stop me. I made it about a foot in front of Apollo before he held up his hand. I smacked off an invisible wall. The force blew my hair back.

Apollo smiled. "I do like your feisty temper."

I kicked the shield. Pain fired through my foot. I hobbled back. "Ouch! Dammit, that hurt!"

Aiden got a secure grip around me. "Alex, you need to calm down."

"I am calm!"

"Alex," Aiden chided, obviously trying not to laugh.

Apollo lowered his hand, appearing contrite. "I do… understand your anger, Alexandria. The half-bloods were not treated fairly."

I took several deep, calming breaths.

"By the way," Apollo said, "the next time you charge a god, and it is not me, you will be destroyed. If not by that god, then by the furies. You are lucky the furies and I do not get along. They would love to see my entrails strung upon the rafters—"

"Okay. I get the picture." I eased my aching foot down. "But I don't think you really understand. That's the problem with you gods. You created all of this and then just left it. Taking no responsibility for what happened. You guys take 'self-centered' to a whole new epic level. And all of our problems—the daimons and even the Apollyon crap—are the gods' fault. You said it yourself! If you ask me, you guys are freaking useless 99% of the time."

Aiden placed his hand on the small of my back. I expected him to tell me to shut up, because I was yelling at a god, but that's not what he did. "Alex has a point, Apollo. I didn't even know… the truth. Even we are taught that the gods decreed the separation of the two breeds."

"I do not know what to say," Apollo said.

I smoothed my hair down. "Please don't say you're sorry, because I know it wouldn't be true."

Apollo nodded.

"Okay. Now that we've gotten this out of our systems, let's get back to the point of this visit." Aiden pulled me to the couch, forcing me to sit down. "And seriously, Alex, no hitting."

I rolled my eyes. "Or what? You're going to put me in a time out?"

Aiden's grin was daring, as if he was up for the challenge and might even enjoy it.

"Solos and his father will be assets in making sure Telly is removed from the Head Minster position and that an extensive investigation is done to determine how many Order members may be out there. And before you ask me why, as a god, I cannot just see that, I must remind you that we are not omniscient."

"Why were you guys worried about how I'd react to that?" I asked, confused. "Sounds like a good thing."

"It's not everything." Aiden took a deep breath. "Solos' father owns extensive property throughout the states, places where we can hide you until all the Order members are uncovered."

"Not just that," Apollo added. "We can keep you safe until we know how to deal with Seth and your Awakening."

I blinked, positive I hadn't heard them right. "What?"

"The worst thing that can happen right now is for Seth to take on your power and become the God Killer." Apollo folded his arms. "Therefore, we need to make sure you are far enough away that when you do Awaken, the bond is severed by distance and you cannot connect with him. He cannot be trusted."

"Why? Why can't he be trusted? What has he done?"

"He's lied to you about a lot of things," Aiden pointed out.

I shook my head. "Besides the lying about the Apollyon stuff, what has he done?"

"It is not what he has done, Alexandria, but what he will do. The oracle has seen it."

"You're talking about that whole 'one to save and one to destroy' crap? Why? Why would that be the case with Seth and me, when we aren't the first set of Apollyons?" I tucked my hair back, frustrated and full of the need to… protect Seth's name. Not like he had a good name, but come on.

Suddenly, Apollo was kneeling in front of me at eye level. Aiden stiffened beside me. "I did not waste my time trying to keep you safe, and argue with Hades over your soul, only to have you throw it away based on foolish and naïve trust."

I squeezed my hands into balls. "Why do you even care, Apollo?"

"It's complicated," was all he said.

"If all you can say is that 'it's complicated' then you can forget that. What about school?"

"Marcus ensured us that you'd graduate on time," Aiden said.

"You knew about this?"

He nodded. "Alex, I think it's the smart thing to do."

"Running is the smart thing to do? Since when do you believe that? Because I remember you telling me that running solved nothing."

Aiden's lips thinned. "That was before you were murdered, Alex. Before I—" He cut himself off, shaking his head. "That was before."

I knew what he meant and I hurt for that. I ached, because he had to worry about me, but that still didn't completely extinguish my anger. "You should've told me this was what you guys were planning. It's the same as Seth and Lucian planning to whip me away to some distant country. I should be included in these plans."

"Alexandria—"

"No." I cut Apollo off and stood before Aiden could stop me. "I'm not going into hiding because there's a *chance* that Seth might do something."

"Then forget the issue with Seth." Aiden stood, folding his arms. "You need to be protected from the Order."

"We can't forget about Seth." I started pacing, wanting to pull out my hair. "If I up and disappear, what do you think Seth's going to do? Especially if we don't tell him, which I know is what you guys are thinking."

Apollo rose to his feet and tipped his head back. "This would be so much easier if you had an agreeable personality."

"Sorry, buddy." I stopped, meeting Aiden's steely eyes. "But I can't go along with this. And if you really think that the Order is going to try something again, then we need Seth's help."

Aiden turned halfway, his broad shoulders tensed as he growled under his breath. Typically, I'd be annoyed with the testosterone display, but yeah, I kind of found it hot.

The Sun God sighed. "For now, you win, but if I so much as think that this will end badly—"

"How can things end badly?" I asked.

"Besides the obvious?" Apollo frowned. "If Seth does what is feared, the gods would bring their wrath down upon all pures and halfs to make a point. And as I was saying, if it was even to get to that point, you will have no choice."

"Then why don't you just let the Order kill me? That would solve all your problems, wouldn't it?" Not that I wanted to die, but it did make sense. Even I could see that. "Seth wouldn't become the God Killer then."

"Like I said, it is complicated." Then Apollo simply vanished.

"I hate when he does that," I glanced at Aiden. He stared back at me, brows furrowed, jaw tight. I sighed. "Don't look at me like I've kicked a baby pegasus into the street."

Aiden exhaled slowly. "Alex, I don't agree with this. You have to know that we are only looking out for what is best for you."

Hot or not, there went my tenuous grip on my temper. "I don't need you looking out for what's best for me, Aiden. I'm not a child!"

His eyes narrowed. "I of all people know you're not a child, Alex. And I sure as hell didn't treat you like one last night."

My cheeks flushed a hot mix of embarrassment and something far, far different. "Then don't make decisions for me."

"We're trying to help you. Why can't you see that?" Then his eyes deepened to a tumultuous gray. "I will not lose you again."

"You haven't lost me, Aiden. I promise you." Some of the anger seeped out of me. Fear was behind his fury. I could understand that. It was what drove my tantrums on a regular basis. "You haven't and you won't."

"That's not a promise you can make. Not when there are so many things that could go wrong."

I didn't know what to say to that.

Aiden crossed the room, sweeping me up in a tight embrace. There wasn't a word spoken for several moments, just the ragged rise and fall of his chest.

"I know you're mad," he began, "and that you hate the idea of anyone trying to control you or force you into doing something."

"I'm not mad."

He pulled back, arching a brow.

"Okay. I'm mad, but I understand why you think I should go into hiding."

He led me back to the couch. "But you're not going to go along with this."

"No."

Aiden pulled me into his lap, circling his arms around me. My heart did a flip and it took me a few seconds to get accustomed to this openly affectionate Aiden who didn't pull away and keep his distance.

"You are the most frustrating person I know," he said.

I rested my head on his shoulder, smiling. "None of you are giving Seth a chance. He hasn't done anything, and I don't have any reason to fear him."

"He's lied to you, Alex."

"Who hasn't lied to me?" I pointed out. "Look, I know that's not a great excuse, and you're right, he has lied to me. I know that, but he hasn't done anything that warrants me running off and hiding. We have to give him a chance."

"And what if we take that risk and you were wrong, Alex? Then what?"

I hoped that wouldn't be the case. "Then I'll have to deal with it."

His shoulder tensed under my cheek. "I'm not okay with that. I've already failed you once and—"

"Don't say that." Twisting in his embrace, I met his gaze and cupped his cheeks. "You had no idea Linard was working for the Order. You are not at fault for that."

He pressed his forehead against mine. "I should've been able to protect you."

"I don't need you to protect me, Aiden. I need you to do what you're doing now."

"Hold you?" His lips twitched. "I can do that."

I kissed him, and my chest squeezed. Never in a million years would I get used to being able to kiss him. "Yes, that, but I just need... your love and your trust. I know you can fight for me, but I don't need you to do that. These problems—they're mine, not yours, Aiden."

His arms tightened around me, so tight, I found it hard to breathe. "Because I love you, we share each other's problems. When we fight, we fight together. I'm going to be by your side no matter what, whether you like it or not. That's what love is, Alex. You never have to face anything alone again. And I get what you're saying. I don't agree with it, but I will support you in any way I can."

I was struck silent. There was really nothing I could say to that. I wasn't that great with words, not those kinds of words. So I wrapped myself around him like a super-friendly octopus. When he leaned back, I settled over him, not caring that he was still in his Sentinel gear, daggers and all. Quite some time passed before either of us spoke.

"Seth's not really a bad guy," I said. "He can be prone to moments of great douchery, but he wouldn't do something like take out the Council."

Aiden's fingers slipped over my cheek. "I wouldn't put anything past Seth."

I decided not to respond to that. Since the phone call after Linard's attack, I hadn't even heard from Seth. And now that I had calmed down a bit, I started to think logically about what Apollo had said. "Everyone fears Seth—the gods, the pures, and the Order—because he'll become the God Killer, right?"

"Right," he murmured. His hand drifted to my shoulder, brushing my hair back.

"Well, what if he doesn't become the God Killer?"

His hand stilled. "You mean if we stop the transfer of power? That's what we're trying to do by keeping you away from Seth."

"I seriously doubt that's the sole purpose of keeping me away from Seth."

"You got me there," he said, and I could hear the smile in his voice.

Tipping my head up, I decided it was way past time to clear the air. Aiden first… and then Seth, because the last thing I wanted was for anyone to be hurt over this. "I care about Seth—I do. He's important to me, but it's not the same. You know you don't have anything to worry about, right? What Seth and I had… well, I don't even know what we had. It wasn't a relationship, not really. He asked to try and see what happens. And this is what happened."

Aiden caught a strand of my hair between his fingers. "I know. I trust you, Alex. But that doesn't mean I trust him."

There was no winning this with him. "Anyway, I can talk to Seth and let him know what's going on with the Order and what people fear."

"And you think he'll go along with that?"

"I do. Seth won't force me into anything by using the… connection against us." I wiggled up Aiden's chest and kissed his chin. "Seth once told me that if things ever became… too much, he'd leave. So there is a way out."

"Huh, he actually said that?" His eyes burned silver. "Maybe he's not so bad."

"He's not."

"I don't like this, but like I said, I will support you any way that I can."

"Thank you." I kissed his cheek again.

A sigh shuddered through him. "Alex?"

"What?"

He leaned back, watching me through heavy lashes. "Did you guys eat all the cookie dough last night or did you actually make any cookies?"

I laughed at the turn in conversation. "We made some. I think there might be a few left."

"Good." He placed his hands on my hips and tugged me forward, pressing our bodies together. "What's Valentine's Day without cookies?"

"I think the mortals put a lot of emphasis on chocolate this time of the year." I placed my hands on his shoulders, and the stuff with angry gods, Order members, Seth, and everything else took the back seat. "But cookies work."

One hand slid up the curve of my spin, slipping under the mass of tangled hair and sending a fine shiver over my skin. "So there's no lame Christmas tree involved?"

"There's no such thing as a Mortal Holiday Tree." My breath caught as he guided my mouth toward his, stopping just as our lips brushed. "But… but I'm sure the mortals would appreciate the thought of that kind of tree."

"You do?" He pressed his mouth to one corner of my lips and then the other. Eyes drifting shut, my fingers dug into his shirt. When he kissed me slowly, pouring all his unstated passions into that one act, his powerful body tensed under mine.

I couldn't remember what we were talking about. There was just the heady, wild rush of feelings that stormed through me. This was Aiden—the man I'd loved for what felt like forever, in my arms, under me, against me, and touching me.

"Happy Valentine's Day," he murmured.

Aiden held me close and still, and in those moments, he showed rather than told me just how much we were in this together.

CHAPTER 24

I'D FANTASIZED SO MANY TIMES ABOUT WHAT IT would be like to be in a relationship with Aiden. There had been days, not too long ago, that I would've smacked that dream right out of my head because it seemed so hopeless. But for a week I lived that fantasy to the fullest.

We stole as many moments alone as we could, filling them with deep kisses and quiet laughter. And plans, we actually made plans.

Or at least we tried to.

My back arched and a giggle escaped.

"Oh, so you *are* ticklish?" Aiden murmured against the flushed skin of my neck. "This is a very interesting development."

It seemed that, when we were together, we could never keep our hands off each other for very long. Aiden had to be touching some part of me. Whether it was just a slight contact of skin, his hand wrapped around mine or our bodies flush with our legs tangled lazily, we were *always* touching.

Maybe it was because he'd fought it for so long or maybe we both were crazy, intoxicated by the simple act of just lying together, and we were addicted to it. Our legs pressed together and our heads rested on the arm of the couch in the room with the family portraits. It was safe in here as no one dared to enter it. What had once been Aiden's sanctuary had become ours.

Today was no different.

But it wasn't all fun. As the days passed and I knew Seth's return was approaching, anxious energy built inside me. There was also barb-tipped guilt that sank in deep. Sometimes, when I thought of him, I remembered those glimpses of vulnerability he'd shown after our midnight swim in the Catskills and the day after I'd been given the brew. Seth was a lot of things, almost a complete enigma at times, but under it all, he was a guy who… who cared, and he cared about me. Maybe more than I did for him. Maybe not, but I didn't want to hurt him.

I wiggled on the couch beside Aiden, trying to shake the sudden dark cloud that'd settled over me. Talking to Seth wasn't going to be easy. Then again, I had no idea how he would respond. He'd been with Boobs…so maybe it wouldn't be that hard.

"So tell me," Aiden continued idly, drawing me back to the present—to him. "Where was that spot again? Was it here?" He trailed his fingers over my stomach.

"No." My eyes closed as my heart jumped and tiny shivers skated through me.

"Here?" His fingers danced over my ribs.

Beyond words, I shook my head no.

"Now where was that spot?"

His agile fingers skipped over my stomach and along my side. I clamped my mouth shut, but my body shook as I tried to restrain my natural reaction.

"Aha! Is this it?" He increased the pressure slightly.

I squirmed, but he was relentless. He laughed when I jackknifed, and I would've tumbled to the floor if it weren't for his quick movement. "Stop," I gasped in between fits of giggles, "I can't take it."

"All right, maybe I should be nice." Aiden pulled me back to his side and leaned over me. He plucked a strand of hair and twisted it around his two fingers. "Anyway, back to the question at hand. What place other than New Orleans?"

I ran my hand down his arm, loving the way his muscles seemed to clench under the skin I touched. "How about Nevada? There're no Covenants nearby. The closest is the University."

He leaned down, brushing his lips over my cheek. "Are you suggesting Las Vegas?"

I fixed an innocent look on my face. "Well, there'd be a lot of daimons, since you pures like to party there, but no real Hematoi establishments of any kind."

"First New Orleans and now Las Vegas?" He brushed his lips back and forth as his fingers tipped my head back. "I'm starting to see a trend here."

"I don't know." My breath caught as he pressed down. "Maybe you can't handle Las Vegas."

Aiden smirked. "I love a challenge."

I giggled, but all humor fled the moment his lips touched mine again. I could go on just kissing him forever. They were gentle kisses at first, soft and questioning. My fingers sank through his hair, clenching him closer, and the kisses deepened. I shifted and wrapped my arms around him, wanting to be able to push the stop button on time. I could stay here forever, feeling his body molded to mine, melting together—I froze against him.

The feeling slithering down my spine was unmistakable. The three runes that had been dormant since Seth left now woke up with a vengeance, burning and tingling. The cord snapped alive, responding to its other half.

His lips moved down my neck, over my collarbone. "What is it?"

There was no stop button for time. Dammit. "Seth's here, like he's right outside."

Aiden lifted his head. "Seriously?"

I nodded stiffly.

He swore under his breath and sprang to his feet. I started to get up, but he held out his hand. "Let me just check this out first, Alex."

"Aiden—"

Swooping down, he clasped my shoulders and kissed me until I almost forgot about the way the cord was unraveling in the pit of my stomach. "Just let me check this out, okay?" he whispered.

I nodded and watched him prowl toward the door. With a quick reassuring smile, he left the room. It was probably a good thing that he was going out to greet Seth. I needed a few moments to collect myself after that last kiss.

Nervous energy rushed me and the cord thrummed happily. Agitated, I rose to my feet within a minute and crossed the room. Seth was near. I knew it deep in my bones. I stopped in front of the cracked door and held my breath.

They were in the hallway, alone. And of course they were arguing already. I rolled my eyes.

"You think I don't know?" I heard Seth say in a smug, knowing way. "That I didn't know this entire time I've been gone?"

"Know what?" Aiden sounded surprisingly calm.

Seth laughed softly. "She may be here with you, right now, but that's just a moment in time in the big scheme of things. And all moments end, Aiden. Yours will, too."

I wanted to throw open the door and tell Seth to shut up.

"Sounds like something on the back of a twisted Hallmark card," replied Aiden. "But perhaps your time has already ended."

There was a stretch of silence and I could picture the two of them. Aiden would be coolly looking down on Seth, who would be smiling arrogantly and secretly enjoying the whole confrontation. Sometimes I wanted to smack them both.

"It doesn't really matter," said Seth. "That's what you don't get. She can love you and it still doesn't matter. We belong together. It's fated. Have your moments, Aiden, because in the end, it really won't mean a damn thing."

That was it. I threw open the door and stormed out into the hallway. Neither of them even turned around, and I knew they heard me fly out of the room. Beyond them I could see the shadows of the Guards through the tiny square windows on each side of the door.

"You really think that?" Aiden cocked his head to the side. "If so, then you're a damn fool."

Seth smiled. "I'm not the fool here, pure-blood. She doesn't belong to you."

"She belongs to no one," Aiden growled as his hands flexed by his hips, where his daggers normally hung.

"Debatable," Seth said, so low I wasn't even sure I'd heard him correctly.

I shoved between the two idiots before one of them did some damage. "You don't own me, Seth."

Seth finally looked at me, his eyes a cool amber. "We need to talk."

That we did. I glanced at the furious pure-blood beside me. This wasn't going to be pretty.

"In private," Seth added.

"What can you possibly need to say that you can't say in front of me?" Aiden asked.

"Aiden," I groaned. "You promised, remember?" I didn't need to say any more. Aiden knew. "I do need to talk to him."

"Nothing will happen to her. Not when she's with me."

I spun around. "Just let me get my hoodie. Try not to kill each other."

"No promises," Seth smirked.

Grabbing my hoodie off the back of the couch, I quickly hauled it on and hoofed it back to the hallway. Gods knew a second of those two together was a second too long. I passed Aiden a meaningful look as I followed Seth to the front door. He looked severely unhappy, but nodded.

Brutal temperatures sucked away my breath as I stepped outside. I was unable to remember the last time it'd been this cold in North Carolina. Seth wore just a black thermal and cargos. Nothing else. I wondered if I got built-in weather padding once I Awakened.

The Guards immediately stepped aside, revealing the strong winter sun glaring off the still waters. At first I was surprised, but then I remembered whose Guards they were—Lucian's.

Aiden moved uneasily. His hands opened and closed at his sides.

Seth feigned a look of sympathy. "Don't look too happy about this, Aiden."

I kicked Seth in the shin.

"Ouch," he hissed, blasting me with a look. "Kicking is not nice."

"Antagonizing people isn't nice," I shot back.

Aiden sighed. "You have twenty minutes. Then we'll come looking for you."

Backing down the steps, Seth bowed at Aiden and then pivoted around. Wind caught and tossed his hair around. Sometimes I forgot how… beautiful Seth was. He could give Apollo a run for his money. Both of them had this type of cold beauty that didn't seem real, because it was flawless both far away and up close.

I fell into step beside him, shoving my hands into the center pocket of my hoodie. "I wasn't expecting you back so soon."

Seth arched a golden eyebrow. "Really? I'm not surprised by that."

My cheeks flushed. There was no way he could've known what had happened between Aiden and me. The bond didn't work over that many miles. Taking a deep breath, I womaned up. "Seth, I have to—"

"I already know, Alex."

"What?" I stopped, pushing my hair out of my face. "You know what?"

He faced me and leaned in, bringing his face mere inches from mine. The cord went crazy inside me, but it was manageable… as long as he didn't touch me. Oh gods, this wasn't going to be easy. "I know everything."

"Everything" could mean a lot of things. I hunched my shoulders, squinting against the harsh glare. "What exactly do you know?"

His lips tipped into a small smile. "Well, let's see. I know about *that*," he gestured to the St. Delphi house, "back there. I knew that was going to happen."

I went hot and cold all at once. "Seth, I'm really sorry. I don't want to hurt you."

He stared at me a moment, then laughed. "Hurt me? Alex, I've always known how you've felt about him."

Okay. I must've been on crack when I thought I'd seen vulnerability in Seth before. Silly me, he was the boy with no feelings or something. But even for the cocky, annoying version of Seth, he was taking this surprisingly well—too well. My suspicions skyrocketed. "Why are you so okay with this?"

"Am I supposed to be upset? Is that what you want?" He tipped his head to the side, brows slanted. "Do you want me to be jealous? Is that what it takes?"

"No!" I felt my face flush again. "I just didn't expect you to be so… okay with it."

"Well, I wouldn't say I'm okay with it. It is what it is."

I stared at him and then a thought struck me. "You're not going to turn him in, are you?"

Seth slowly shook his head. "How would that benefit me? You'd be in servitude and on the elixir."

And I wouldn't Awaken, which it always seemed to come down to, and I was big enough person to admit that stung. I wondered what bothered Seth more—my life being virtually over or my Awakening not happening. I looked away, biting my lip. "Seth, I found some stuff out while you were gone."

"So did I," he responded evenly.

That was cryptic. "You had to know about the Order and how an Apollyon is made."

His expression didn't change. "Why is that?"

Frustration flared. "You once said that when you Awakened, you knew everything from the previous Apollyons. One of them would've known about the Order, and about how they were born. Why didn't you tell me?"

Seth sighed. "Alex, I didn't tell you because I didn't see a point."

"How could you not see a point after everything that happened to me in New York? If you'd told me about the Order, I could've been better prepared."

He looked away, lips pursing.

"And I asked you while we were there if you knew what that symbol meant," I said. Anger and so much disappointment swamped me. I didn't even try to shield my emotions from him. "You said you didn't know. When I asked if you knew about a half and a pure mixing, you said you guessed your father had to be a half. You knew the truth. What I don't get is why you didn't tell me."

"I was told not to."

"What?" Seth started walking, and I hurried to catch up with him. "Who told you not to tell me?"

He stared up the beach. "Does it matter?"

"Yes!" I practically shrieked. "It does matter. How can we have anything if I don't trust you?"

His brows shot up. "What *do* we have exactly, Alex? I do remember telling you that you had a choice. I didn't ask for labels or expectations."

I remembered that, too. The night in the pool seemed forever ago. Part of me missed that playful Seth.

"And you made your choice," Seth continued softly. "You made your choice even when you said you chose me."

I also remembered that fleeting, satisfied look when I had said that I'd chosen him. Shaking my head, I searched for something to say. "Seth, I—"

"I don't want to talk about this." He stopped where the sand faded into pavement, reached down and brushed his knuckles across my cheek. I jerked back, startled by the contact and the electric shock that followed. Seth lowered his hand, staring at the backs of the small shops lining the main road. "Anything else you want to talk about?"

He hadn't answered a damn question, but I did have one more. "Did you see my father, Seth?"

"No." He met my eyes.

"Did you even look for him?"

"Yes. Alex, I couldn't find him. That doesn't mean he wasn't there." He pushed back the shorter strands that had been blown free. "Anyway, I brought you back a gift."

I wasn't sure I'd heard him right, but then he repeated it, and my heart sank. "Seth, you shouldn't have brought me anything."

"You'll change your mind once you see it." A wicked grin pulled at his lips. "Trust me, this is a once-in-a-lifetime type of gift."

Great. This was making me feel better. If he handed me the Hope Diamond, I was going to throw up. He and I had never been in a relationship, but guilt still twisted at my insides. When I looked at him, I saw Aiden. And when Seth touched me, I felt Aiden. The worst thing of it all was that Seth knew.

"Alex, just come on."

"Okay." I drew in a deep breath and then pressed my lips together. The wind that kicked up from the ocean was shockingly cold, and I huddled down in my hoodie. "Why in the world is it so cold? It never used to be this cold here."

"The gods are pissed," Seth said, and then laughed.

I frowned at him.

Seth shrugged. "They are putting all their focus into this little piece of the world. It's because of us, you know. The gods know change is coming."

"Sometimes you really kind of freak me out."

He laughed.

I made a face. We walked in silence after that. I kept expecting him to turn toward the Covenant-controlled island and when we didn't, then I thought we'd head toward Lucian's house, but he led me straight through town and toward the courthouse, which was used by the Council members.

"My gift is in the courthouse?"

"Yes."

Honestly, I never knew what to expect from Seth. Even with the bond, I didn't have a clue what went on in his head half of the time.

The normal number of Council Guards stood just inside the Courthouse, hidden from mortal tourists; beyond them, three of Lucian's Guards blocked a door. They stepped aside, opening the door for us.

I halted, knowing where the door and the stairs led to. "Why are we going down to the cells, Seth?"

"Because I'm going to lock you up and get all freaky."

I rolled my eyes.

Taking my elbow, he tugged me forward. Down we went. My eyes adjusted to the darkness of the stairwell. Old boards creaked under our feet. The cells weren't underground. They were actually on the first floor. The main entrance opened up to the second floor, but it still felt like we were walking down into some dank, dark place.

Dim light lit the hallway. Over Seth's shoulder, I could make out several cells lining the narrow corridor. I shuddered, picturing myself stuck in one of them. Gods, how many times had I come close to that?

Ahead of us, two Guards stood in front of the very last cell. Seth walked up to them and snapped his fingers. "Leave us."

I gaped as the two Guards left. "Do you have special Apollyon finger-snapping powers?"

He tipped his head toward me. "I have a lot of special Apollyon finger powers."

I shoved him. "Where's my gift, perv?"

Seth backed up, grinning. He stopped in front of the barred door and spread his arms. "Come look."

Okay. I was curious. Stepping forward, I stopped in front of the door and peered through the bars. My mouth dropped open as my stomach hollowed.

Huddled in the middle of the cell, with his hands tied to his ankles, Head Minister Telly stared back at us with blank eyes. His face was battered, barely recognizable, and his torn, dirtied clothing hung off him.

"Oh, my gods, Seth."

CHAPTER 25

STUNNED, I JERKED BACK FROM THE CELL DOOR.
Everything Apollo had warned me about rushed to me at once. Everyone
had been afraid of something like this happening—everyone but me,
and still I had a hard time believing that this was actually happening.

"What have you done?" I asked.

"What? I brought you a gift—Telly."

I turned to him, shocked that I had to explain all the things wrong
with this. "Seth, most guys bring girls roses or puppies. Not people,
Seth. Not the Head Minister of the Council."

"I know what he did, Alex." He placed his hand over the scar Linard
had left behind. "I know he ordered this."

Through the heavy material, I could feel Seth's hand. "Seth, I…"

"I felt something when it happened… like our bond had completely
disappeared," he said quietly and quickly. "I couldn't feel your emotions
but I knew you were there… and then you weren't for a few minutes. I
knew. Then Lucian told me. My first reaction was to bring just his head
back to you, but I did the next best thing."

I felt physically ill as I stared at Seth. And when I looked at Telly in
the cell, I saw Jackson's battered face. I should've known. Good gods, I
should've known he'd know… and he'd do something like this.

"It didn't take much for me to find him," he continued casually. "And
I know people were looking for him. Leon," Seth laughed, "or should I
call him Apollo? Yeah, I beat him to the punch on this one. Those two
days you didn't call me? That's all it took for me to find him."

The air flew right out of my lungs. Ice drenched my veins.

He frowned. "He ordered your death, Alex. I figured you'd be happy to know that we have him and he's not going to be a problem anymore."

I turned back to the cell. "Gods, how have the furies not reacted to this?"

"I'm not stupid, Alex." He moved to stand beside me, shoulder to shoulder. "Lucian ordered this and had his Guards carry it out. I was only… along for the ride. Clever, aren't I?"

"Clever?" I gasped, stepping away from the cell—from Seth. "So this was Lucian's idea?"

"Does it matter?" He folded his arms. "Telly tried to have you killed—he *did* have you killed. For that, he has to be punished."

"That doesn't make this okay! Look at him!" I pointed at the cell, feeling sick. "What *is* wrong with him?"

"He's under a rather strong compulsion not to talk." Seth tapped his chin thoughtfully. "I'm not sure he's even thinking. Actually, I think he's sort of fried."

"Gods, Seth. Hasn't anyone ever told you two wrongs don't make a right?"

Seth snorted. "Two wrongs always make a right in my book."

"This isn't funny, Seth!" I tried to calm down. "Who's going to kill him? The pure-blood Council?"

"No. The new Council will."

"The new Council? What the hell is that?"

Frustration flared in his amber eyes. "You just need to understand why this is happening. This man serves the gods who want you—us—dead. He has to be taken out."

I ran my hands over my head, wanting to pull my hair out. "Seth, was this Lucian's idea or not?"

"Why does that matter? What if it was? He only wants to keep us safe. He wants change and—"

"And he wants Telly's throne, Seth! How can you not see that?" Coldness seized my insides as I stared at Seth. Lucian wanted power and taking Telly out was one way to achieve that, but that didn't mean he could take complete control of the Council… or did it? I shook my head. "There's no way the gods would allow this. They don't want what Telly did."

"The gods are the enemy here, Alex! They don't speak to the Council, but they do speak to the Order."

"Apollo saved my life, Seth! Not Lucian!"

"Only because they have plans for you," he said, stepping forward. "You don't know what I know."

My hands curled into fists. "Then tell me what you know!"

"You wouldn't understand." He turned toward the still form in the cell. "Not yet. I don't even blame you for it. You have too much pure in you—now more than ever before."

I flinched. "That wasn't... wasn't fair."

His eyes closed and he ran the heel of his palm over his forehead. "You're right. That wasn't fair."

Taking the moment of clarity, I seized it. "You can't keep him here, Seth. You're right. He has to be punished for what he did, but he needs a trial. Keeping him like this, under a compulsion in a cell, is wrong."

Gods, it was a messed up day when *I* was the voice of reason.

Seth turned to me. He opened his mouth, but closed it. "I already have too much invested in this."

Dread inched down my spine. I started toward him, but stopped. I folded my arms over my chest. "What do you mean?"

He reached out toward me, but I jerked away. Confused, he lowered his hand. "How can you want him to live?"

"Because it's not our place to decide who lives or dies."

His brows furrowed. "And what if it will be?"

I shook my head. "Then I don't want any part of that. And I know you don't, either."

Seth sighed. "Alex, you're training to be a Sentinel. You'll make life-and-death decisions all the time."

"That's different."

"Is it?" He inclined his head toward me, a smug smile washing away any hesitation.

"Yes! As a Sentinel, I'll kill daimons. That's not the same as playing jury and executioner."

"How can you not see I'm doing what needs to be done, even if you're too weak to do it yourself?"

Who in the hell was this person beside me? It was like reasoning with a lunatic…now I knew how people felt when they tried to reason with me. Irony was a cruel, cruel foe. "Seth, where are the keys to the cell?"

His eyes narrowed. "I'm not letting him out."

"Seth." I took a tentative step toward him. "You can't do this. Neither can Lucian."

"I can do as I damn well please!"

I shoved past him, reaching for the handle on the door, and then I was against the opposite wall with Seth in my face. Fear blossomed low in my stomach as the cord hummed madly. "Seth," I whispered.

"He's staying in there." His eyes flashed a dangerous ocher. "There are plans for him, Alex."

I swallowed down the sudden taste of bile. "What plans?"

His gaze dropped to my lips, and a whole new fear took root. "You'll see soon enough. You don't have to worry, Alex. I'm going to take care of everything."

Planting my hands on his chest, I shoved him back several feet. Shock and then anger flashed across his features. "You're freaking insane, Seth. Don't go down this road."

Whirling around, he stormed back to the cell and pointed at Telly. "So, you'd rather see this thing free? Free to enslave half-bloods, to order them killed? Free to continue his assassination attempts on you? And then we are to wait for a trial—a trial rigged to protect the pure-bloods? They'd just slap him on the hand. Hell, they might even order you to apologize for screwing up his plans to kill you!"

Anger flooded me. I stepped forward, toe-to-toe with Seth. "You don't care about what happens to the half-bloods! It has nothing to do with what you're planning! And you know that. What you're doing— what you're agreeing to is wrong. And I'm not—"

"Go," he cut me off, his voice furious and low.

I stood my ground. "I'm not going to let you do this, Seth. I don't know what Lucian's said that's convinced—"

"I said *go*." Seth shoved me—shoved me *hard*. I barely caught myself. "Maybe next time I'll bring you roses or puppies."

That raised my hackles, and so did the smile he gave me. It took every ounce of my self-control to turn and walk away. I hurried up the stairs. Like a thousand times in my life, I didn't plan on listening to what I'd been told to do. But for the first time, it was probably the right thing to do. Aiden and Marcus needed to know what Seth and Lucian were up to. Maybe they could stop this, before it became too late—before Seth took part in killing the Head Minister and sealed both our fates.

There still had to be hope for Seth. Sure, what he was taking part in was crazy, but not *epically* crazy. Technically, Seth hadn't done anything *yet*. Like Caleb had said, there was still hope. Whatever Lucian had on Seth, however he was pulling his strings, had to be broken before history repeated itself.

I pushed open the doors of the Courthouse and came face to face with the root of all my problems.

Lucian was flanked by several Council Guards, all dressed in those ridiculous white robes. The smile that spread across his face never quite reached his eyes. "I thought I'd find you here, Alexandria."

Before I knew what was happening, his Guards surrounded me. Oddly, the Guards were all pure-bloods. Smart move, I'd give him that. "What's going on, Lucian?"

"When will you call me 'Father'?" He came up the final step, stopping in front of me. Wind blew his robes, giving an appearance that he was floating.

"Um, how about next to never?"

His pleasant smile remained. "One day that will change. We will be one big happy family, the three of us."

Now that was disturbing. "You mean Seth? He's as much a part of you as I am."

Lucian tsked softly. "You will return to my house, Alexandria. There is no need to stay at the St. Delphi residence any longer."

My mouth opened to argue that, but I clamped it shut. There was no way of knowing if Lucian was aware of my feelings for Aiden, or if Seth had told him anything. Putting up a fight would only arouse his suspicions. There was nothing I could do to stop this. Lucian was my legal guardian. Swallowing down my anger and distaste, I stepped forward. "I just need to get my stuff."

Lucian stepped aside, motioning for me to follow. "That will not be necessary. Your belongings will be retrieved by Seth."

Damn him. I stiffened as Seth came out the door. He didn't spare me a glance as he brushed past me.

Lucian clapped Seth on his shoulder. "Meet us back at our house."

Seth nodded and went down the steps. On the sidewalk, he looked up and gave me a sardonic grin before heading off toward one of the Hummers parked along the curb.

"Now, my dear, you will come with me," Lucian said.

Fuming, but unable to do a damn thing about it, I followed Lucian into the other Hummer. Gods forbid that Lucian actually walk to his house. Once he climbed in the back seat with me, I was crawling out of my skin to get out of the car.

Lucian smiled. "Why is it that you're so uncomfortable around me?"

I turned away from the window. "There is just something about you."

He arched a brow. "And that would be?"

"Well, you're like a snake, but slimy."

He leaned back against the seat as the Hummer moved. "Cute."

I smiled tightly. "Let's cut the bull, Lucian. I know about Telly. Why would you do something that even I think is reckless and stupid?"

"The time for change is upon us. Our world needs better leadership."

My laugh escaped before I could stop it. "Are you high?"

"For too long we've been expected to live by the old laws, existing beside mortals as if we are no better than them." Disgust dripped from his words. "They should take the place of half-bloods, serving our every need or whim. And when they do, we—the new gods—will rule this earth."

"My gods, you are insane." There was nothing else I could say. And worse of all, Grandma Piperi had been right, but like always, I hadn't understood. History was on repeat, but in the worst possible way. And evil had hidden in the shadows, acting like a puppet master pulling strings. Grandma Piperi had been referencing Seth and Lucian. I felt sick. If I'd only figured this out earlier, I could've prevented it from going this far.

"I don't expect you to understand, but Seth does. That's all I need."

"How did you get Seth to go along with this?"

He studied his fingernails. "The boy never had a father. His pure-blood mother wanted very little to do with him. I suppose she regretted her relations with the half, but had been unable to get rid of him while he was still in her womb."

I flinched.

"It's safe to assume that she wasn't a very kind mother," Lucian continued. "But that boy still managed to impress the Council and gain entrance into the Covenant. He had a tough childhood, always alone. I suppose all Seth has ever wanted is to be loved." He looked at me. "Could you do that? Give him the one thing he's always wanted?"

Suddenly, I knew beyond a doubt, Seth hadn't told Lucian about Aiden. But why? Removing Aiden from the equation would only benefit Seth. Could it be that Seth hadn't because he knew it would hurt me? If that was the case, then Seth was still *thinking*. He wasn't a lost cause, after all.

"I do hope so. Seth is a good boy."

My eyes widened. "You sound... sincere."

Lucian sighed. "I've never had a child of my own, Alexandria."

Shock rippled through me. Lucian actually cared for Seth. And Seth saw him as a father. But it didn't change what Lucian was doing. "You're using him."

The Hummer rolled to a stop behind Lucian's house. "I'm offering him the world. The same thing I'm offering you."

"What you are offering is certain death for anyone who goes along with this."

"Not necessarily, my dear. We have supporters in the most... unlikely of places—a very powerful supporter."

My door opened before I could respond. A Guard waited for me to exit, carefully watching me as if he expected me to sprint away, which was what I'd considered but knew I'd never get away with it. I was led into the house quickly and then left in the opulent foyer with my stepfather.

"It's a shame that you have to make this so difficult, Alexandria."

"Sorry to rain on your crazy parade, but I'm not going to go along with this. No one else will, either."

"Is that so? Do you doubt my impassioned words?" His gaze settled on his half-blood guards. "I want to see a better life for the half-bloods."

"Bull," I whispered, and my gaze moved to the Guards. The condemnation that filled their expressions when they looked at me said that they did believe Lucian. And the real question was how many halfs were behind Lucian? The numbers could be astronomical.

Lucian laughed. It was a cold, grating sound. "You really have no control over this."

"We'll see about that." I reached for the doorknob, but froze when it turned and locked in my hand. I loathed the air element with all my heart. Slowly, I faced him. "You can't keep me in here. Let me out."

Lucian laughed again. "I'm afraid you will not be allowed any visitors until your Awakening. And do not hope that Apollo will arrive, either. He will not be able to enter my house."

I frowned. "You can't stop a god."

Lucian looked pleased as he stepped aside. My gaze fell behind him and up the wall that Seth had once pinned a Guard to. There was a mark there—a crudely drawn symbol of a man with a snake's body.

"Apollo cannot enter any home that bears the mark of the Python of Delphi. It was created so long ago as a punishment for breaching the rules of Olympus. Funny, I never knew that until recently."

I swallowed. The drawing looked like it had been done in blood. "How… how did you figure that out?"

"I have many friends… of great power and consequence." Lucian gazed at the drawing, a slight smile on his angular face. "I have many friends that would surprise you, my dear."

I felt the walls closing in, squeezing the breath out of my lungs. I was trapped here until my Awakening. My breath hitched. I should've listened to Aiden and never left his house. "You can't do this."

"Why can't I?" He drifted toward me. "I am your legal guardian. I can do with you as I please."

My temper stretched and snapped. "Really? When has that worked out for you in the past?"

"In the past I did not have Seth, nor were we so close to the Awakening." He caught my chin, digging his bony fingers in. "You can fight me on this all you want, but in a few days, you'll Awaken. First, you will connect with Seth, and what he desires, you will desire. And then your power will transfer to him. You can't stop that."

I blanched. "I'm stronger than that."

"You think so? Think about that, my dear. Think about what that means and whether or not there is even a point in fighting what's about to happen."

Unease crept over me, but I kept my expression blank. "If you don't release me, I will break your arm."

"You would, wouldn't you?" His breath was warm against my cheek. Bile rose in my throat. "There was only one thing that Telly and I ever agreed on."

"What was that?"

"You need to be broken down." He released me, the same damn smile plastered across his face. "Except he went about it all the wrong way. I will not make the same mistake that I made with your mother. I allowed her too much freedom. As of now, you're mine. Just like Seth is. And you would do very well to remember that."

I recoiled from him. "You're a bastard."

"That may be the truth, but in a few days, I'll control both of the Apollyons. Then we'll be unstoppable."

CHAPTER 26

DINNER WAS AWKWARD FOR SEVERAL REASONS. THERE were only three of us clustered at the end of the long rectangular table, eating by candlelight as if we'd been thrust into medieval times. Seth alternated between chumming it up with make-believe-daddy Lucian and glaring at me. I refused any attempt Lucian made at luring me into conversation. And I couldn't even bring myself to eat the mouthwatering steak, which really sucked.

This was going to be my last dinner.

I knew it. What I was planning as I watched the two would surely end up with me being killed, but it was either go out this way or be part of something as heinous as destroying those who did not agree with Lucian and enslaving mankind. Because that's what they planned—or at least, Lucian planned. Lucian needed the Apollyons—at least, the God Killer—to achieve this. It made sense. The Apollyons had been originally created to keep the pures in line, but if he controlled the Apollyons then he had nothing to fear. Once I Awakened, Seth could take down any god that went after Lucian, making Lucian practically invincible. It was a brilliant plan. One that I knew Lucian probably had worked on from the moment he became aware that there were two Apollyons in one generation.

They'd give Council members an option. Stand with them or fall. With Seth at full Apollyon power—the God Killer—he'd be able to zap any god who came gunning for him. Not that Lucian believed any gods would. Once Seth became the God Killer, no god would be stupid enough to come within a mile of him. The only threat would be members of the Order, but they too would have one hell of a time taking Seth down. Lucian already had Sentinels searching for the remaining members. I shuddered at what I knew they would do to them.

And yet, as much as they talked, I felt there was something they weren't sharing. There was more to this, just as I felt there was more to why Apollo had been so adamant about keeping me safe.

"How did the Order kill the First and Solaris?" I asked, speaking for the first time.

Lucian raised his brows at Seth as he twirled the crystal flute.

"They caught them unexpectedly." Seth glanced down at his plate. "At the same moment, they were stabbed through the heart." He cleared his throat. "Why do you ask?"

I shrugged. Mostly because I was curious since it wasn't like killing two Apollyons was an easy feat. When I didn't give an answer, they resumed their talking. I resumed my plotting.

I was going to do something I never thought I'd do again. I was going to kill a pure-blood—Lucian. My fingers curled around the steak knife. It was the only way to stop this. Take out Lucian and then Seth would be freed from his freakish parental influence. And I'd be dead, but maybe… maybe Aiden and Marcus could prove Lucian's insanity. It was worth a shot. I couldn't let this happen, and it would happen if they kept me here, and then there would be no stopping them.

This was possibly the craziest, most spontaneous and reckless thing I'd ever planned, but what other choice did I have? Lucian already controlled Seth and he could control me through him if Seth willed it. That was everyone's fear—my worst fear.

I had to do something.

"May I be excused?" I asked.

"You haven't eaten anything." Seth frowned. "Are you feeling sick?"

Gee, could it be I'd lost my appetite because I was surrounded by lunatics? "I'm just tired."

"That's fine," Lucian said.

Trying not to think about what I was doing, I placed my napkin over the steak knife and slid it, handle first, up my sleeve. I stood on weak knees. Killing in battle or when I needed to protect myself was totally different than this. Part of me screamed that this was wrong— just as wrong as what they intended to do to Telly, but one life to protect countless more? It seemed worth it.

Okay. Two lives, because I seriously doubted I was going to get away with this. Guards waited just outside the dining room. If they didn't kill me, the Council Lucian sought to betray would. Ironic.

I walked around the table slowly, calming my breathing and blocking my emotions. I had enough strength to shove this knife through his back, severing his spinal cord. It would be easier to go for the throat or eye, but gods, I was grossing myself out just thinking about it.

Just do it. I reached Lucian's side and drew in a deep breath as I let the knife slide out from my sleeve. Then a freight train slammed me to the ground.

I hit the tiled floor with a hard crack. Seth pinned my legs as he twisted my wrist until I cried out and was forced to drop the knife. As I tried to twist out of his grasp, Guards rushed into the room, but Lucian held his hand out, stopping them.

"What is wrong with you?" Seth asked furiously, giving me a little shake when I didn't answer fast enough. "Are you insane?"

My heart pounded against my ribs. "I'm not the crazy one here!"

"Really—you're not the crazy one?" His gaze went to the knife. "Do I need to explain this to you?"

"Deal with her." Lucian stood and threw down his cloth napkin, voice eerily calm. "Before I do something I regret."

Seth exhaled harshly. "I'm sorry, Lucian. I'll fix this."

So shocked, I couldn't speak. He was apologizing to Lucian? I was in crazy land and there was no escape.

"She needs to accept this," Lucian said. "I will not live in fear of being murdered in my own home. Either she complies or I'll have her locked up."

Seth's eyes met mine. "That won't be necessary."

I glared at him.

"Good." Lucian sounded more disgusted than afraid. It was like I had spit on him instead of trying to kill him. "I'm retiring for the evening. Guards!"

In a rush of activity, they followed Lucian out of the room. Some of them were pures. Had he promised them something worth going against the Council and risking death? I knew what he'd offered the halfs.

Seth still held me to the floor. "That was possibly the stupidest thing you'd ever tried to do."

"Too bad it didn't work."

Appearing incredulous, he hauled me to my feet. The moment he let go, I bolted for the door. He caught me before I made it out of the room, clamping his arms around me. "Stop this!"

I threw my head back, narrowly missing his. "Let me go!"

"Don't make this hard, Alex."

I struggled in his viselike grip. "He's using you, Seth. Why can't you see that?"

His chest rose against my back. "Is it so hard for you to accept that Lucian cares for me—for you?"

"He doesn't care about us! He just wants to use us." I kicked my legs out to use the wall, but Seth anticipated this and spun me around. "Damn you! You're smarter than this!"

Seth sighed and started dragging me toward the hall. "You're such a little fool sometimes. You will want for nothing, Alex. Nothing! Together we will be able to change our world. Isn't that what you want?" We had reached the bottom of the steps, and I kicked for the statue of some god I didn't recognize. "Gods! Knock it off, Alex. For someone who's so short, you're freaking heavy. I don't want to have to carry you up these stairs."

"Gee. Thanks. Now you're calling me fat."

"What?" His arms slackened.

I slammed my elbow into his stomach hard enough that the impact rattled my entire body. Seth doubled over, but didn't let go. Cursing wildly, he flipped me around and bent at the waist. He clamped his arm down on my waist and hauled me over his shoulder. Before I could kick him where it counts, he caught my legs and held them down.

"Put me down!" I pounded on his back with my fists.

Seth grunted as he started up the stairs. "Seriously, I can't believe I have to do this."

I continued my assault on his back to no avail. "Seth!"

"Maybe you deserve a spanking, Alex." Laughing, he rounded the landing as I jabbed him in the kidneys. "Ouch! That hurt!"

We were making enough noise to rouse every Guard in the house, but no one intervened. I recognized the upside-down hallway and the door Seth pushed open. It was my old bedroom in Lucian's house.

Seth stormed across plush white carpet that so had not been in my bedroom when I'd stayed in this house. Back then, I'd had bare floors that had been cold in the winter. He dumped me unceremoniously on the bed and then planted his hands on his hips. "Behave."

I sprang to my feet. Seth caught me around the waist and pushed me back down with little effort on his part. An incredible amount of rage filled me with energy, sweeping through me like a rush of roiling waves. And I let the fury swell and spread like the rising tide.

"You're being ridiculous, Alex. And you need to calm down. You're making me wish I had some Valium."

My hands balled into fists. "He is using you, Seth. He wants to control us so he can overthrow the Council. He wants to be greater than the gods. You know they'll never allow that! That's why the Apollyons were created in the first place."

Seth arched a brow. "Yeah, Alex, I know why the Apollyons were first created. To make sure no pure-blood achieved the power of the gods and blah blah. Let me ask you a question. Do you think any of the gods care if you die fighting a daimon?"

"Obviously they care, because they brought me back."

He rolled his eyes. "What if you weren't the Apollyon, Alex? What if you were just a normal half? Would they care at all if you died?"

"No, but—"

"Do you think that's right? That you're forced to be either a slave or a warrior?"

"No! It's not right, but the gods didn't decree that. The pures did, Seth."

"I know, but don't you think the gods could've changed that if they wanted to?" He moved closer, lowering his voice. "Change needs to happen, Alex."

"And you think Lucian is really going to bring that kind of change?" I willed Seth to understand. "That once he takes complete control of the Council, he'll free the servants? Relieve the halfs from their duty?"

"Yes!" Seth dropped to his knees in front of me. "Lucian will."

"Then who will fight the daimons?"

"There will be those who volunteer, just like the pures who do now. Lucian will do this. All we have to do is support him."

I shook my head. "Lucian has never cared about the halfs. All he has ever cared about is himself. He wants ultimate power—to enslave the mortals instead of the halfs. He said so himself."

With a disgusted humph, he stood. "Lucian has no intentions of doing such a thing."

"He told me in the car!" I grasped his hands, ignoring the way the cord jumped. "Please, Seth. You have to believe me. Lucian will do none of the things he's promised you."

He stared at me a moment. "Why would you even care if enslaving mortals was his ultimate plan? I don't get it. You couldn't stand living among them when you did. Why would you want to protect the gods when the Order killed you—*killed you*—to protect them? And you have a problem with a few pures dying along the way? Look at how they've treated you. I don't get it."

Sometimes I didn't get it myself. The pures treated us halfs like crap. And the gods, well, they were as much to blame as the pures. They'd allowed this to happen. But this was more wrong. "Innocent people will die, Seth. And what do you think the gods will do? They may not be able to touch you and me, but they can be vengeful and downright sadistic. They'll start slaughtering halfs and pures by the busload. Apollo has said so."

He squeezed my hands. "Casualties of war—it happens."

I pulled my hands free. My stomach turned over. "How can you be so uncaring?"

"It's not that I'm uncaring, Alex. It's called strength."

"No," I whispered. "That has nothing to do with strength."

Seth moved away from me, running his hand through his hair, pulling strands free from the leather tie. Had he always been like this? There had always been a degree of coldness to him, but nothing like this.

"It will be okay," he said finally. "I promise. I'll take care of you."

"It's not going to be okay. You have to let me go. We have to be apart from each other."

"I can't, Alex. Maybe in time you'll forget about him and…"

"This isn't about Aiden!"

Facing me, his lips twisted into a bitter, cynical smile. "It's always about Aiden. You don't care about the mortals. If you could still have him and let us have our way, you wouldn't care."

"I do care. You're going to have to kill innocent people to do this, Seth. Can you seriously live with that? Because I can't."

"What pure is truly innocent?" he asked instead of answering my question.

"There are pures who don't want to see halfs enslaved. And yeah, the gods are a bunch of dickheads, but that's what they are."

"We've already been over this, Alex. We aren't going to agree. Not yet, at least. But your birthday is only days away. You'll understand then."

I gaped. "Seth, please listen to me!"

A cool mask slipped over his face, locking him down. "You don't really get it, Alex. I can't—won't let you go."

"Yes, you can! It's quite simple. You just let me walk out of this house."

Seth was in front of me within a second. He gripped my hands, pressing his palms against mine. "You don't know what it feels like now, but you will. The more marks you take, the more akasha drains into me. Nothing—nothing feels like that. It's pure power, Alex. And you haven't even Awakened! Can you imagine what it will be like then?" His eyes took on that crazed, overly-passionate gleam I'd seen and disregarded before. "I can't give that up."

"Gods, do you hear yourself? You sound like a daimon craving aether."

He smiled. "It's nothing like that. It's better."

That was about when I realized that between Lucian's influence and the allure of akasha Seth had been twisted into something dangerous. Apollo had been right. Dammit. Grandma Piperi had been right.

And I had been so, so wrong. I was in a precarious, bad position. Anything was possible and my heart rate doubled. I wanted to smack myself for not letting Apollo stash me away, but when he'd made that suggestion, all I could think was that was what Lucian had wanted to do. I was disgusted with myself for the time I'd wanted to throw the towel in. Running was not something I ever did.

But now I needed to run, because that was the only smart thing to do.

"I want you to leave my room." I forced my knees to stop shaking and I stood. "Now."

"I don't want to leave," he replied evenly.

My heart leapt into my throat. "Seth, I don't want you in here."

He cocked his head to the side, eyes heating up a notch. "Not too long ago you had no problem with me being in your bedroom… or your bed."

"You have no right to be in here. You're not my boyfriend."

Seth's brows flew up. "You speak as if what we are can be simplified with little labels. We aren't boyfriend and girlfriend. You're right about that."

I pushed away from the bed, eyes desperately searching for a way out of the room. There was only a bathroom, closet, and one window. And my old dollhouse… what the hell was that still doing here? Perched atop the house was a creepy porcelain doll I'd hated as a child and still did.

Sneaking up behind me, he whispered in my ear. "We *are* the same person. We want and need the same things. You can love whoever you want and you can tell yourself whatever you want. We don't have to love one another; we don't even have to *like* each other. It doesn't matter, Alex. We're stuck with one another, and the connection between us is far stronger than whatever you feel in your heart."

Whirling around, I put space between us. "No. This is it. I'm calling on that promise you made me. I don't want to do this. You need to leave. I don't care where you go. Just go—"

"I'm not leaving."

Dread turned into something far worse and far more powerful. Fear snaked its way into me, biting deep and spreading through my veins like venom. "You promised me, Seth. You swore that you would leave if this became too much. You can't take that back!"

His eyes met mine. "It's too late for that. I'm sorry, but that promise is null and void. Things have changed."

"Then I'll leave." I took in a deep breath, but it did nothing to calm the pounding in my chest. "You can't keep me here! I don't care that Lucian is my legal guardian."

He tipped his head to the side, his stare becoming almost curious. "Do you think there is any place in this world that I couldn't find you if I wanted to?"

"Gods, Seth, do you even know how stalkerish that sounds—how creepy?"

"I'm just pointing out the truth," he replied blithely. "When you turn eighteen, which is in what? Five days? You don't have any control over that."

My hands balled into fists. Gods, I hated when he was right. Especially when he was scary right and Seth was pretty damn scary right now. I couldn't—I refused to show that. So I relied on anger. "You don't have any control over me, Seth!"

Seth arched one eyebrow. A slow, wicked smile spread across his face. Recognizing that look, I shot back, but he was so incredibly fast. His arm snaked out, catching me around the waist.

Instinct took over. My brain switched off and I flipped into fight mode. Letting my legs go limp, I became dead weight in his arms. Seth cussed and as he dipped to catch me, I sprang up, slamming my knee into his midsection. A whoosh of air left his lungs as he stumbled back.

Spinning around, I threw out my arm, catching him across the chest. It wasn't a meek hit. I put everything into it and Seth went down on one knee.

I darted toward the door, ready to fight my way out of the house and down the street if necessary.

I never made it—not really.

My fingers wrapped around the doorknob the same second I felt a rush of power in the room that raised the tiny hairs all over my body. Then suddenly, I was off my feet, flying backward. Hair blew around my face, clouding my vision.

Seth's arms went around my waist and he tugged me against his chest. "You know, I like you better when you're furious. Do you want to know why?"

I struggled in his embrace, but he held on, and it was like trying to move a semi-truck. "No. I really don't care, Seth. Let me go."

He chuckled deeply, and the sound rumbled through me. "Because when you're angry, you're always one step from doing something irrational. And that's how I like you."

Seth let go without any warning and I spun around. I saw it in his eyes then, in the way his lips parted. Panic froze the blood in my veins. "Don't—"

Seth's hand shot out, wrapping around my neck. The marks of the Apollyon spread across his skin with dizzying speed. What existed in me, that part that had been created to complete him, responded in a heady rush. The marks flew down his arm, reaching over his fingers. A second later, amber light crackled in the air, and then a weaker sheen of blue. His hand circled, pressing down, burning the skin on the back of my neck, creating the fourth rune.

There was a second, right before my brain overloaded with sensation, an instant where I regretted ever allowing Seth to get close to me, to forge the bond between us into something that seemed unbreakable. He had planned this all along.

And then I wasn't thinking anymore.

Deity

CHAPTER 27

SETH'S EYES GLEAMED AS THE PRESSURE INSIDE ME shifted through the cord, leaving me and flowing into him. Suddenly, light flared from four points: my stomach, both palms, and now the back of my neck. Pain pricked along my skin like an angry wasp and then dulled. My head grew heavy, legs weak as the pleasant tug and pull continued.

His free arm caught me just as my legs buckled. I must've blacked out, for how long, I didn't know. I was flat on my back when the room came back into focus. A thick haze settled over me, dragging me down through the bed.

"There you are," Seth said. The hand he smoothed through my hair trembled slightly.

There was a strange, almost metallic taste in the back of my throat. "What... what happened?"

Seth slipped his hand out from my hair. "You didn't Awaken, but..." He grabbed my hand and pressed down on my palm.

The response was immediate. My back arched. It felt like something had reached down into my core, grabbed hold and then *yanked*. It wasn't painful but not pleasant either. "Seth..."

When he let go, the invisible strings were cut. I collapsed, boneless and weak and Seth... he sat back on his haunches, holding his hand in front of his face. An awed, childlike expression filled his face as the bright blue light covered his hand, burning brighter than ever before.

"Akasha… this is good, Alex. This is more… I can feel you under my skin."

Dazed, I watched the ball of light dull and the excitement went out of Seth's eyes. Somehow I knew, even as his dipped and pressed his lips to my cheek, that Seth had harnessed the kind of power needed to kill a god, if only for a few moments.

Lightning struck outside the window, but still no more brilliant than the glimpse of the end. I knew I needed to get out of here, but when I tried to sit up, I felt like I was glued to my bed.

He smiled as he settled beside me, moving his hand back to my cheek, turning my head toward him. His thumb trailed over my lower lip. "Did you see that?"

I wanted to look away, but I couldn't and I felt sick to my soul. Thunder drowned out the beating of my heart.

"It was beautiful, wasn't it? So much power. Lucian will be disappointed that you didn't Awaken after the fourth mark, but something happened."

What did that mean? I didn't understand and my thoughts were too fuzzy. The cord jumped as his hand slipped under my head and drifted back to the rune on my neck. "This is the rune of invincibility," he explained. "When you Awaken, it will be activated. Then the gods cannot touch you."

I met his eyes and forced my heavy tongue to work "I don't… want you to touch me."

Seth smiled and the marks returned, gliding over his golden complexion. I knew the moment our marks touched. He lowered his head till a breath separated our lips. My senses went crazy. Electricity jolted across my skin and down.

"You're so beautiful like this," he murmured, and pressed his forehead against mine.

What was in me, what lay between us, was ugly. How hadn't I noticed that before? There had been signs from the beginning. The night I'd discovered what I was and Seth had remained behind, with Lucian. Seth's need for power and how my response to him seemed out of my control, even when we first stood beside the courtyard months ago and again, several times over. I thought of that fleeting look of satisfaction I'd seen as I stood by the pool and chose to see what happened with him—I'd chosen him. All that time he'd been spending with Lucian…

I'd been so blind.

Seth's lips pressed against my wildly beating pulse and I shuddered, revolted, angry, terrified, and helpless.

"Don't," I begged, before the twisted connection between us spun so tightly that I couldn't tell where he began and I ended.

"You don't want this? You can't deny that a part of you does need me."

"That part isn't real." My body was tingling, throbbing, and yearning for him, but my heart and soul were shriveling up, growing cold. Tears filled my eyes. "Please don't make me do this, Seth." My voice broke. "*Please.*"

Seth froze. Confusion clouded his eyes, the hard glint of amber fire shattering with pain. "I'd… I'd never force you, Alex. I wouldn't do that." His voice was curiously fragile, vulnerable, and unsure.

I started crying. I didn't know if it was the relief from the fear or that deep down the Seth I knew was still in there somewhere. For now.

Seth sat up, running a hand through his hair. "Alex, don't… don't cry."

My hands felt like blocks of cement as I lifted them and wiped under my eyes. I knew not to cry in front of daimons, to show weakness, and Seth… he was no different.

He reached down, but stopped. Several seconds passed before he spoke. "It'll get easier. I promise."

"Just leave," I said hoarsely.

"I can't." He eased down beside me, keeping a discreet distance between us. "The moment I leave this room you'll do something stupid."

Truth be told, I was too tired to stand, let alone stage a daring escape. I managed to roll onto my side, away from him. Sleep didn't come easy that night. The only comfort I took was that, when I closed my eyes, I pictured Aiden. And even though the image did him no justice, his love did the one thing I'd asked for. Not to protect me, but to give me strength to figure a way out of this mess.

Seth rarely left my side the next two days, having food brought to the room, and it took those two days for me to regain any real strength. The last rune had taken more from me than the others, and I knew, just like Seth had said, that something was different.

He'd only pulled akasha from me once more, when he'd brought Lucian in to witness.

Seth had been right. Lucian had been disappointed that I hadn't Awakened, but he'd been pleased by the new power Seth gained, even though it had been temporary.

And gods, Seth had beamed like a kid showing his father his prized science fair project. I thought I'd feel sickened by Seth, but during the long afternoons he spent talking to me while I tried to convince him to let me go, I began to feel sorry for him.

There were two sides to him, and the side I had held close to my heart was losing out to the one that craved power like a daimon thirsted for aether. I wanted to fix him somehow, save him.

I also wanted to strangle him, but that was nothing new.

During the evening of the second night, a commotion downstairs roused me from the bed. Recognizing Marcus' deep booming voice, I stood on weak legs and ambled toward the door.

Seth was beside me in an instant, placing a hand on the door. "You can't."

I blinked away the dizziness. "He's my uncle. I want to see him."

"Since when?" Seth grinned, and I sucked in a breath, because it reminded me of the other Seth—one who wouldn't hold me hostage. "You hate him."

"I… I don't hate him." At that moment, I realized I'd been a giant douche to my uncle. Granted, he wasn't the warmest of people, but he wouldn't shut me in a room with a potential sociopath. I swore I'd be different… if I ever got to see him again. "Seth, I want—"

"Why would you refuse to let Marcus see his niece? Is something wrong?"

My breath caught in my throat as I pressed my hands against the door, under Seth's. Aiden's voice was like a burst of sunlight and warmth. I was *this* close to kicking Seth in the junk just to make him move, and he must've anticipated that, because the warning in his eyes told me not to even think it.

"She is resting, but fine. There is no need for concern," I heard Lucian say and then his voice faded out.

Drawing in a shallow breath, I closed my eyes. Aiden was so close and yet I couldn't get to him. I knew he had to be worried, assuming the worst. If I could just see him, let him know that I was okay… it would ease some of the aching around my heart.

"You really love him?" Seth asked quietly.

"Yes." I opened my eyes. His gaze was downcast. Thick lashes fanned his cheeks. "I do."

He slowly lifted his eyes. "I'm sorry."

I seized the moment. "And I care about you, Seth. I really do. Seeing what you're doing—what you're becoming—is killing me. You're better than this, stronger than Lucian."

"I am stronger than Lucian." He leaned against the door, watching through heavy lidded eyes. "I'll be stronger than a god soon."

And that was that. Seth didn't move away from the door, and eventually I went to the window, hoping I could catch a glimpse of my uncle and Aiden. The terracotta roof over the library blocked the view.

We didn't talk again.

Time was running out and I had to do something.

Seth was antsy the following morning, unable to sit still for longer than a few minutes. His constant pacing and jerky movements were so at odds with his normal otherworldly grace. He had my nerves stretched thin and each time he looked my way, I felt a lump of dread and fear inch up my throat. But he never approached me and he didn't touch me again. Seth would just turn away and stare out the window silently, waiting.

The morning after Marcus' visit, I had to see the rune on the back of my neck again. With my energy at normal levels, I found a hand-held mirror and craned my neck, twisting until I caught a glimpse in the bathroom mirror. It was faint blue, shaped like an S that closed at the end. The invincibility rune. I reached back and touched it. The skin on my fingers tingled from the contact.

I lowered the mirror to the counter and turned around. My eyes looked way too wide, scared almost. There were shadows forming under them, dulling the brown irises. Not that my brown eyes were extraordinary in the first place, but *geesh.*

The skittish look in my eyes hadn't gone away, even after I'd showered. Weight settled on my shoulders, squeezed my chest. Seth had been trying to Awaken me this entire time, like I'd feared. He'd lied. I pushed my damp hair back. Luckily he hadn't succeeded, but there was undeniably something different. I could feel it just below the skin.

There was a knock on the bathroom door. "Alex?" Seth called, and knocked again. "What are you doing in there?"

Gathering up my strength, I focused on the neon pink walls and reinforced the mental shields, blocking him out.

His sigh was audible. "You're just blocking me to tick me off, Alex."

I gave my reflection a weak smile and then I opened the door. Brushing past him, I tossed my dirtied clothes in the corner.

"So you're not going to talk to me?" he asked.

I sat in the chair and picked up a comb.

Seth knelt in front of me. "You know, you can't stay silent forever."

Combing out the tangles, I decided I could try.

"Do you know how long we're going to be together? This is going to get boring and old real quick." When I didn't answer, he grabbed my wrist. "Alex, you're being—"

"Don't touch me." I jerked my arm free, ready to turn the comb into a deadly weapon if need be.

He smiled as he stood. "You're talking."

I threw the comb down and shot to my feet. "You've lied to me over and over again, Seth. You *used* me."

"How did I use you, Alex?"

"You got close to me just so you could try to Awaken me! You used this stupid connection against me." I sucked in a sharp breath. Betrayal sat like stones in my stomach. "Did you plan this all along, Seth? Was this what you were thinking when we were in the Catskills? When you asked me to make a choice?"

He whirled on me, eyes a fierce, angry ocher. "That was not the sole reason, Alex. Not that it matters now. You made your choice. You chose Aiden, as pointless as that was."

I didn't even think. Full of rage and sorrow, I swung at him.

Seth caught my fist before it connected with his face. "We are not training, Alex. We are not playing around. Swing at me again and you will not like the consequences." He released me.

I stumbled back, half-tempted to test out his warning with a kick to the face. A knock on the bedroom door interrupted our stare-down. One of the Guards was on the other side, speaking too low for me to understand.

Seth nodded and then faced me. "We're leaving in five minutes."

My heart stuttered. "Leaving? Going where?"

"You'll see." He paused, his gaze dropping over me. "You have five minutes to put something decent on."

"Excuse me?" I was wearing jeans and a black turtleneck. "What's wrong with what I'm wearing?"

"You will be an Apollyon… my mate, so to speak. You should wear something nicer—classy."

I didn't know which part of what he said made me want to punch him again most. "First off, you don't tell me what to wear. Secondly, I am not your 'mate'. Thirdly, there is nothing wrong with what I'm wearing. And finally, you're insane."

"You now have four minutes." Seth spun around and left the room, locking the door behind him.

A whole minute passed while I stared at the closed door. Then I sprang into action. I raced to the bedroom window and pushed it open.

When I'd been younger, I'd used my bedroom window to climb out on the roof above the library and stargaze. I knew I could make the jump. It was actually shorter than the one I'd made in Miami.

Wasting no time, I wiggled out on the ledge. The muscles in my arms screamed as I slowly lowered myself down. Gods, my upper body strength could use some work. My feet dangled about half a foot from the roof. I felt like a ninja spy in that moment. I started to smile, but the familiar tingle spreading over my skin quickly knocked it right off my face.

I let go.

Hands clamped down on my forearms and hauled me up, back through the window. Kicking and lashing out, I struggled like a wild animal until Seth set me back on my feet.

I spun around. "I still had three minutes."

A reluctant grin appeared on his face. "Yeah, and about a minute after I left your room I realized you'd probably try to escape. Throwing yourself out a window is a better choice than putting on something nice?"

"I wasn't *throwing* myself out the window. I was escaping."

"You were in the process of breaking your neck."

My hands curled. "I would've made the jump, asshat."

Seth rolled his eyes. "Whatever. We don't have time now. We're needed now."

"I'm not going anywhere with you."

Frustration rolled off him. "Alex, I'm not asking."

I folded my arms. "I don't care."

Groaning low in his throat, he shot forward and grabbed my arm. "You always, *always* have to make everything so damn difficult." He started dragging me toward the door. "I don't know why I expected anything less from you. Part of me—and this is sick, I know—is somewhat excited about the idea of you fighting me. It's amusing. Better than you sitting there not speaking."

I dug at his fingers, but there was no releasing them. "Let go of me."

"Yeah, not going to happen."

We were already to the end of the hall, at the top of the stairs. Below I could see a small army of Guards waiting. "What the hell?" I dug my feet in and grabbed the railing with my free hand. "What's going on?"

Exasperated, Seth grabbed me around the waist. Using brute strength, he yanked me away from the railing. "Now you're just being cute." He started down the steps, carrying me easily even though my sneakers hit every step.

Unease lined only a few of the faces of Lucian's Guards as Seth dragged me past them. Cold, bright sunlight met us outside, and Seth didn't release me until he shoved me into the back of a waiting Hummer. And then, he climbed in right after me and caught both my wrists in one hand.

"Sorry. There's a good chance you'll try to throw yourself out of a moving car."

I glared at him, our faces inches apart. "I hate you."

Seth lowered his head until his cheek pressed against mine. "You keep saying that, but we both know it's not true. You can't hate me."

"Is that so?" I elbowed him in the stomach. It did very little. The Hummer started moving. "What I'm feeling right now is definitely not warm and fuzzy."

He laughed, stirring the hair around my temple. "You can't hate me. You weren't built that way. And soon, we will be the same person. You were created to be mine by the very gods we're going to take down, starting today."

CHAPTER 28

SETH'S WORDS STUNNED ME INTO SILENCE. OLD FEARS, never too far away, resurfaced. I had no control in this… fate. No sense of myself. My heart was racing painfully. I couldn't be built for him. He wasn't my existence.

I was my own existence.

I kept telling myself that as Seth led me from the Hummer and into the back entrance of the Courthouse on the main part of Deity Island. I had a sick feeling about this, knowing that Telly was in a cell in this building and that something horrific was about to happen. I could feel it and there was nothing I could do.

Holding my hand in a tight grip, he led me through the narrow halls to the waiting room just outside the glass-domed session area. Through the open door, I could see the place was packed. Every pure who remained on the island during break seemed to be there, as were many of the half-blood Guards and Sentinels. But even more strange was the presence of the halfs who had remained behind at school. Luke sat toward the back with Lea; both of them appeared just as curious as everyone else—even a bit awkward, like they felt out of place. What were they doing here? Half-bloods were never allowed to attend Council unless they'd been summoned to do so.

"What's going on?" I asked.

Seth kept his hand on mine, as if he knew I would bolt if given the chance. "Lucian has called an emergency Council meeting. See?" He gestured toward the front of the square room. "Everyone is here."

The Council filled the titanium-trimmed dais. Easily recognizing Dawn Samos' coppery head in the sea of white robes, I felt my stomach twist.

My eyes scanned over their curious expressions and then I turned to the audience. In the back was my uncle. He was standing, arms folded across his chest. There was a hard, cold look to his emerald gaze. Beside him was a man I'd never seen him before, a tall half-blood built like a Sentinel. Lean and coiled muscles flexed under the black uniform. His brown hair was on the longish side, pulled back in a ponytail. His skin was a mix of ethnicities, deeply tanned. He would've been handsome if it wasn't for the jagged scar slicing from above his right eyebrow down to his jaw.

The doors opened suddenly in the back, and more entered the room. Aiden was among them. My heart thundered in my chest as he stopped beside my uncle. He leaned over, his mouth moving quickly. Marcus stared straight ahead, but the stranger nodded. Then Aiden straightened and turned, looking straight at where I was standing.

Seth pulled back before Aiden could see us. I scowled at Seth, and he smiled back at me. "We're special guests," he said.

"That you are, my boy." Lucian strode through the waiting room. His gaze settled on me and cooled. "Has Alexandria been amicable?"

"What do you think?" I snapped before Seth could respond.

Lucian graced me with one of his plastic smiles. "You're not as wise nor strong as you think you are, Alexandria, but soon you will be."

I shot toward him, but Seth pulled me back and slipped an arm around my waist. That left my arms completely free and, boy, did I try to get hold of Lucian's hair… face… whatever I could grab.

"You are lucky that no one can see what you just tried to do," Lucian hissed. He stopped by the open door, his Guards blocking the entrance. "Or I'd be forced to do something about it. Make sure she behaves, Seth. And that she understands the consequences of acting rashly."

Seth held me, my back against his chest, waiting until Lucian and his Guards reached the dais. "Alex, don't do anything you'll regret."

I struggled against him, getting nowhere. "I'm not the one who's about to do something they'll regret."

His chest rose sharply. "Alex, please. If you try to run while we're out there or if you do anything crazy, I'll be forced to stop you."

My movements ceased. Wariness crept over me and I felt like I could never be warm again. "You would do that… to me?"

It seemed like forever before he answered. "I wouldn't want to, but I would." He paused and another breath shuddered through him. "Please don't make me."

A lump formed in my throat. "I'm not making you do anything."

"But you have," he whispered in my ear. Mixed shivers ran down my spine. "Since the first time I met you. You just didn't know, so how can I really blame you?"

Lucian was taking center stage, starting the Council session. All eyes were on him. No one knew of the drama playing out just behind the walls.

"I don't understand." I closed my eyes against the rush of tears. "Seth, please…"

"It's this." Seth shifted slightly, pressing his hand on my stomach, above where I felt the cord, close to the jagged scar. "You don't know what's it's been like. To feel your power and mine together, to know that it will only grow stronger. It's the aether, yes, but it's also the akasha. It sings to me like a siren."

My breath hitched and I swallowed hard as the cord responded to him.

Seth rested his chin atop of my head. "I can even feel it now—I know how to use it. Together, we'll do this together."

I opened my eyes. "Gods, you sound… insane, Seth."

His fingers curled into my sweater. "One man's insanity is another man's sanity."

"What? That doesn't even make sense."

He laughed softly. "Come on. It's starting."

Just like that, Seth changed. He tugged me to the door, where we remained hidden but could hear what was happening. His grip on my hand loosened, but I knew better than to try to make a run for it. I really believed that he'd stop me—painfully, if necessary.

The members of the Council were talking among themselves, and then they quieted.

Lucian glided to the front of the dais, clasping his hands together in front of him. An elderly, stately Minister spoke first, her voice raspy but strong. "Has there been additional evidence indicating more daimon attacks?"

"Or is it the elixir?" another asked, his hands clasping the arms of a titanium-trimmed throne. "Are we having problems here?"

There was an immediate hum of questions from the crowd and the Ministers. Some of the faces were panicked. Daimon attacks had come too close to home, and the idea of the elixir not working probably horrified those who relied on halfs to do everything for them.

I stiffened and the worst—absolutely worst—idea took hold.

"What are you thinking?" Seth's voice was low, soothing, and at complete odds with what he was capable of.

Marcus had suspected that the daimons who attacked the Council had help, and Seth had suggested that Telly had messed with the elixir to cause a distraction, but as I stared at Lucian, I wondered how much Seth really knew.

Lucian, the perfect pure-blood in his pristine white robes, gazed over the near chaotic crowd with a tight, well-practiced smile on his face. Had Lucian been behind all of this? To create chaos? Because I remembered one of my lessons in Myth and Legends—of how all the societies that had been on the brink of upheaval were the easiest to control, shape, and manipulate... and overthrow.

"Alex?"

Sucking in breath, I shook my head.

"I did not call this session to discuss those things," Lucian began. "Today is a day of discoveries, my fellow Councilmen. Our world is on the brink of great change. A change that is needed, but feared by some. Today, those who fear change, those who have worked in the shadows to stop it, will be unmasked and prosecuted."

My breath caught. *Telly.* But I didn't see him anywhere.

"What are you speaking of, Lucian?" asked a Minister. Her voice was clear but strained. "What fear and change is so great that we were called back early, away from our families and our vacations?"

I almost rolled my eyes at the last part.

Lucian remained staring straight ahead. It was then when I realized at least half of the twelve were smiling. They knew—they supported Lucian. This did not bode well.

But the others had no idea.

"We have been taught to fear the possibility of two Apollyons," Lucian said. "Taught to see them as a threat against our very livelihood and the gods, but I am here to tell you that, instead of fear, we should feel joy. Yes! Joy that we will have the God Killer to protect us in just a few days."

"Protect them against what?" I muttered. "Crazy-ass Ministers?"

"Shh." Seth glared at me.

My jaw ached from clenching my teeth so hard.

"But first, we must deal with something that is both unsavory and," he clapped his hand over his chest, "close to my heart. Guards!"

The door on the other side opened, and in an ironic twist of fate, Guards led Head Minister Telly out to the center of the dais. I couldn't help but remember when Kelia Lothos, the half who'd loved pure-blooded Hector, had been brought before him, half-naked and shackled.

Karma was a bitch.

That didn't make what was happening right, though. I itched to run out there and warn all of them what was about to happen, what I could feel building under my skin.

There was a collective gasp from the audience and half of the Council when Telly was forced to kneel. He lifted his head, but his glazed-over eyes didn't focus on any one thing in particular.

"This man has plotted against the Council's own decision and against my stepdaughter." Lucian's voice hardened as his lips pulled back. "And I have evidence."

"What evidence do you have?" Dawn spoke up, her eyes darting from Lucian to the silent Head Minister.

Seth's breath danced along the back of my neck. I tried to step away, but he pulled me back. My temper, my nerves—everything was stretching too thin.

"During the November Council session, my stepdaughter was unfairly targeted. She'd been asked to attend to give her testimony based on the unfortunate events in Gatlinburg. However, Head Minister Telly proved to have nefarious motives."

No one on the Council looked too concerned. I wasn't sure if I was supposed to feel angry or sad about that.

Lucian turned to Telly. A real smile—a satisfied one—appeared on Lucian's face. "My stepdaughter was a victim of several attacks. Some of you," he glanced over his shoulder at the Council, "may find this of no concern. But she is not just a half-blood; she will be the next Apollyon."

"What attacks?" asked an elderly male minister. The cane he clutched in his left hand was just as weathered as his face.

"She was placed under an unlawful compulsion and left in the cold to die. When that failed, he attempted to coax the Council of Twelve to have her placed on the elixir and enslaved," Lucian announced. "When the Council found no reason for doing so, a pure-blood was compelled to give her the Brew."

"Oh gods," I muttered, feeling my cheeks burn.

"Alexandria was unaware of this," Lucian continued, now appealing to the females on the Council. "It is believed that she was set up to be found in a… compromising position with a pure-blood."

"Son of a bitch," I whispered. The bastard was pulling the family card.

"Not very nice," Seth murmured.

I ignored him.

Dawn looked pale as she watched Lucian. "That… that is most revolting."

"And that is not all." Lucian turned back to the audience. "When all of these things failed, Head Minister Telly ordered a pure-blood Guard to kill her after the daimon attack. If it wasn't for Aiden St. Delphi, who used a compulsion on two pure-bloods, the Head Minister would've succeeded."

My heart slammed against my ribs as my mouth dropped open. I so got what Lucian had just done. He'd let out the cat out of the bag, making it sound like Aiden was some kind of hero to him while knowing what it meant for Aiden.

A Minister eyed Aiden with open disgust. "That is an act of treason against our kind and must be dealt with immediately. Guards!"

No. No. No.

Several people turned toward where I knew Aiden stood. Guards rushed forward, as if Aiden now was the greatest threat. They surrounded Aiden within seconds, daggers out and ready to be used.

Aiden stood remarkably still. There wasn't a flicker of emotion in his face or eyes as the Guards closed in on him.

There was no way I was letting this happen. I started forward, but Seth stopped me. "Don't, Alex."

"How could you? They'll execute Aiden for this." Raw panic tasted like metal in my throat. "He's turned the *entire* society against him with those words, Seth."

Seth said nothing.

"Wait." Lucian's voice traveled, stopping everyone. "The pure is not a concern at this moment. The Head Minister's attempts in the Catskills failed numerous times, but he did not cease in his actions. He sought her out, leaving the New York Covenant in a state of disarray to continue to threaten her with servitude."

"What happened to the Guard who supposedly attacked her?" asked the female Minister who'd spoken first.

"He has been dealt with," Lucian responded, pushing on before that could be further examined. "Head Minister Telly went against the Council's wishes and still tried to force her into servitude. She was even attacked here, stabbed by a half-blood Guard ordered to do so by him."

"And the proof?" the elderly Minister asked. "Where is the proof?"

Lucian turned back to Telly. "The proof is in his own words. Isn't it, Head Minister?"

Telly lifted his head. "It is true. I went against the majority vote and ordered the assassination of Alexandria Andros."

There were a few stunned gasps. I knew it wasn't for my benefit, but more so that Telly would admit to it so easily. They didn't know what I did—that Telly's brain was most likely fried from a powerful compulsion.

An argument broke out among the Ministers for several minutes. Some immediately wanted Telly impeached. Those were the ones who'd smiled earlier. Others, those who I doubted knew what Lucian was up to, didn't see how what he'd done to me was a crime. There were very few laws protecting halfs.

"There will be no impeachment," Lucian's voice silenced the arguing. "Head Minister Telly will be dealt with today."

"What?" Several of the Ministers demanded at once.

"It has come to my attention that the Head Minister is involved in the Order of Thanatos and several of those members are en route to free him." There was another pause. Lucian knew how to shock and awe. "There is no time for anything else. Alexandria's safety is of the upmost importance."

And now I understood Seth's nervousness—all the Guards this morning. Lucian couldn't have the Order ruining his plans. He'd strike first. And my safety? It wasn't about my safety. Lucian was worried that I'd misbehave before he went out on the dais because Seth didn't have full control of me… *yet.*

"This wasn't supposed to happen now, was it?" I whispered.

Seth said nothing.

My mouth was dry. "You all wanted to wait until after I Awakened, but you're doing this because of the Order."

Because wouldn't that suck for Lucian if the Order arrived before I Awakened and ended up killing one of us? All of his plans for nothing,

Lucian motioned toward where we were hidden. "This is a time of change. That change starts now."

"That's us," Seth said, his hand tightening around mine. "And dear gods, please behave."

I didn't have much time to respond to that. Seth started walking, and I had no choice but to follow him out into the session room.

Silence so thick it choked me descended when we appeared. All eyes were on us as we made our way up the marble steps. We stopped just short of Lucian and Telly.

Everyone started talking at once.

The Council quickly grew uncomfortable, shifting in their seats. A murmur swept through the crowd, escalating as the seconds ticked on. Some were standing, their faces showing shock and terror. "No reason to fear two Apollyons," my happy butt. They knew—some out there in the audience recognized the danger.

My heart was trying to come out of my chest, and even though I tried to stop myself, I looked for Aiden. He had gone still. I wasn't sure he was even breathing. Our gazes locked, and in an instant, there was relief and then rage in his steely eyes as his gaze dropped to where Seth held my hand tightly. Then he moved, taking a step forward. Marcus threw out an arm, stopping him. I wasn't sure Aiden was going to pay him any heed, but he did.

I let go of a breath I didn't realize I'd been holding.

"What is this about?" cried a Minister. I'd stopped trying to keep track of them.

Lucian just smiled. I hated that smile. "It is our time to take back what is rightfully ours—a world where we rule and do not answer to a sect of gods who do not care whether we prosper or die. A world where half-bloods are not enslaved, but stand beside us—" several startled gasps cut him off there, go figure "—but where mortals kneel at our feet like they should. We are gods in our own right."

And that was right about when half of the audience came to their feet. Words like "blasphemy," "treason," and "insanity" were tossed around. Some of the half-bloods watched Lucian curiously; his words held a certain appeal to them. But they'd be fools to believe him.

Lucian's Guards and some I recognized from around the Covenant moved to the back doors, blocking anyone from escaping. I almost laughed. We'd thought the Order had infiltrated deep within the Covenant, but Lucian had really outdone himself. It was *he* who had infiltrated the Covenant and Council.

"This is a time for a new era." Lucian's voice resonated through the large courthouse. "Even the lowest half-bloods who stand with us will flourish. Those who do not will fall."

Several members of the Council stood and stepped back. Five of them—the five who supported Lucian—and at least two-dozen Guards... and Sentinels.

I caught a glimpse of Aiden and the stranger moving closer to the dais, but then I lost sight of them. Focusing on what was going on in front of me, as I felt anger and alarm take hold.

"Seth," Lucian said quietly. "This man has attempted to end Alexandria's life several times. Is he worthy of life?"

The elderly Minister came to his feet, leaning heavily on the cane. "He has no say in this matter! Apollyon or not, he does not decide life or death. If Head Minister Telly has gone against the Council of Twelve's wishes, then he is to be tried by that very Council!"

He was ignored.

I stared up at Seth. "No," I whispered. "No. Don't answer that question."

And I was ignored.

Seth tipped his chin up as the marks of the Apollyon broke out across his face, swirling and moving down his neck, under the collar of his shirt. "He is not worthy of life."

Pride filled Lucian's eyes. "Then he is yours to deal with."

Panic punched a hole straight through my chest. I pulled away from Seth, throwing my entire weight into breaking his grip. He only held on tighter. I knew what he intended to do.

"No!" I cried out, still trying to pull free and break the contact. "Telly is a douche, but we don't decide who dies, Seth. That is not what we are—not what the Apollyon is."

"Silly girl," Lucian murmured loud enough for only us to hear. "That is not what an Apollyon decides, but what a God Killer does."

"Don't listen to him," I pleaded, and jerked as his mark burned against mine. "You're not like this. You're better than this. *Please.*"

Seth glanced at me. There was a moment—brief but there. Hesitation and confusion flitted across his face. Seth didn't fully believe he was doing the right thing. Hope seized me.

I clutched his arm. "Seth, you don't want to do this. I know you don't. And I know this isn't you. It's the akasha—I get it. And it's him. He's using you."

"Seth," Lucian urged. "You know what you have to do. Do not fail me—do not fail *us*."

"Please," I begged, holding his gaze while wanting to leap over Telly's defeated, hunched form and snap Lucian's neck. "Don't do this to us—to me, to yourself. Don't become a killer."

Seth's lips quirked up and then he turned away from me, facing Head Minister Telly. "He cannot live. That is my gift to you."

Horror stole my breath. And it struck me then. That was the difference between Aiden and Seth. No matter how badly Aiden would want to strike back or how much he wanted something, he would never risk me. And dammit, Seth would.

He did.

His hand tightened around mine. My body snapped inward as he tore akasha right out from underneath me. I doubled over, catching only a flash of amber light as it enveloped Telly. The last I'd seen Seth use akasha, it had been blue, but that was before the four marks, before he could pull the power of the fifth from me.

Shrieks filled the air—not from Telly, but from the Council and the audience. Telly didn't have a chance to make a sound. Once akasha hit him, charged from both Seth and me, he simply ceased to exist—obliterated.

Glass shattered from the dome overhead. Shards of glass rained down, slicing through the air and those not quick enough to move out of the way. Three winged shapes came through the opening, howling in rage.

The furies had arrived.

CHAPTER 29

THE FURIES WERE IN FULL-OUT UGLY MODE. THEIR SKIN was gray and milky. Snakes snapped from their heads. Fingers extended into sharp points. Those claws could rip through tissue and bone with ease.

They were headed straight for us.

Only a second or two had passed from the moment Seth had charged up and taken out Telly. One furie broke free from her sisters, arcing over the audience, emitting shrill screams.

Seth raised his arm. Akasha streaked from his hand, streaming through the air at incredible speed. He hit the first furie in the chest before the amber light sputtered out. Shock flickered over her monstrous face and then her jaw slackened. The furie dropped, spinning like a downed bird as her wings sliced through air. The furie landed in a lifeless pile of white chiffon, gray skin, and unmoving flesh a few feet in front of us.

The remaining two furies hovered by the broken window. Their mortal skins slipped over the monsters inside, and horror pinched their beautiful features.

"It's not possible," one shrieked, pulling at her blonde hair until strands hung from her clawed fingers. "It cannot be!"

"But it is." The other grabbed her sister's arm. "He has killed one of us."

Weak in the legs, I straightened and swayed unsteadily. Seth's actions had weakened me, leaving me no match for a groundhog, let alone one of the furies, if they attacked. Realizing Seth had released me,

I stumbled to the side of the dais. I was going to die. I was sure of it. My screams would join those of the audience… except the furies didn't attack.

"You've made war against the gods," one hissed. Her wings cut through the air noiselessly. "Make no mistake they will make war against you."

The other spread her muscled arms wide. "You risk them all to gorge yourself with power that never was yours. What a path… what a path *you* have chosen."

And then they were gone.

Chaos reigned supreme below the dais and on it. Telly was gone. There wasn't even a pile of ashes. Bile rose in my throat as I turned away from the spot where he'd knelt.

Toward the back, I heard sounds of fighting as Guards and Sentinels went after the ones blocking the doors. A Guard near us was overtaken. One of his daggers hit the floor. I lurched for it, wrapping my numb fingers around the hilt. I had to stop this—stop Lucian. He was pulling Seth's strings.

I whirled around, finding Lucian speaking to the Council, spouting more crazy stuff that was going to get us all killed.

Seth was on me before I could even take a step toward Lucian. Our eyes met before he wrenched the dagger from my hand. He tossed it aside as he advanced on me. Coldness had crept upon his features. I didn't recognize the look in his eyes. They glowed violently, nearly luminous. That awe was there again. But it wasn't awe… I'd mistaken that look.

It was a craving, a greed for more. The same thing I'd seen time and time again in the eyes of a daimon.

Weaponless and weak, I knew when to retreat. My spine hit the wall. Desperately, I searched for something and found a titanium candelabrum. I grabbed it and threw it at him using both arms.

Lighting quick, he caught the candelabrum and tossed that to the side, too. "Always throwing things," he said, voice thick and different. Gone was the musical quality. "Such a naughty, naughty Alex."

I inhaled raggedly. "This… this is not you."

"It is me." He reached for me. "And this is us."

Dawn's voice distracted him. "This is treason!" she said. Terror filled her amethyst eyes. She was trembling, hugging her elbows. Other Ministers stood behind her, faces pale. "This is treason against the gods, Lucian. What you ask from us cannot be given."

"Do you think change is not needed?" Lucian asked.

"Yes!" She unfolded her arms and raised them in front of her, as if she was shielding herself. "Change is needed. Half-bloods need more freedom and choice. There is no doubt to that. I have a half sister. I love her dearly and want a better life for her, but this... this is not the way."

Lucian cocked his head to the side as he smoothed his hands over his white robes. "And what about the gods, my dear?"

Her breath came out ragged as her spine straightened. "They are our only masters."

All my nightmares were coming true, as were the Order's. History *was* on repeat. Seth stepped to the side, facing the Council members who would not bow to Lucian's will.

Lucian smiled.

"No!" My voice came out ragged as I slid along the wall, away from Seth. "Seth, don't!"

But Seth was on autopilot. He grabbed my hand again. Mark pressed against mark. Pressure filled me and then the cord snapped again, pushing akasha through the bond. There was no reaching him when the power took over, no compassion.

Seth was just Lucian's killing machine.

The brilliant amber light erupted from his hand a second time.

Screams rose above the pandemonium. I swore I could hear Lea's above them all. I knew that couldn't be true, because everyone was screaming. I was screaming.

Seth released his hold, and I dropped to my knees, gagging and choking on the smell of burnt cloth and... flesh—burnt flesh. Where the seven had once stood, only three remained huddled together as they stared at Seth in horror. One whimpered, clutching a blackened arm.

Lea's sister—Dawn—was gone.

He had done it—attacked the Council. My cheeks were damp. When had I started crying? Did it matter? I didn't know.

Lea's sister was gone.

I pressed my hand to my mouth, ordering myself to pull it together. Something had to be done. This was bad—horrendous—but it would get worse once I Awakened. In the chaos, I could escape. I couldn't break down now. Struggling to my feet, I held my breath and edged toward the stairs as Seth's back was to me. I reached the steps and arms went around my waist, lifting me over the edge. Warmth immediately surrounded me, my body—my heart—telling me who it was who'd grabbed me. Sweet relief flooded me.

"I've got you." Aiden set me on my feet. His eyes searched mine intently. "Can you run?"

I heard him as though through a tunnel, and I think I nodded.

Within seconds, we were surrounded.

"Shit." He let go of my hand, blocking my body with his. Coiled tension rolled through his body.

I wished I'd had the foresight to find the lost dagger, because then I'd at least have something to ward off Lucian's Guards. Not that I'd be able to do much with it. It was taking everything in me to stand, to push through the nearly overwhelming exhaustion that'd come when Seth tapped into my power.

Then Aiden sprang. Spinning around, his boot connected with the jaw of the closest Guard, and then he dipped under the outstretched arm of another. Coming up, his fist struck the second in a fierce uppercut. Without missing a beat, he caught another with a kick to the chest, knocking the Guard back several feet.

It had been so long since I'd seen him fight. Forgetting how graceful and fast he was, I stared in awe. Not a single Guard made it past him. He mowed them down with just his hands and kicks.

One, however, did creep up behind us.

The Guard grabbed me from behind and started to pull me back toward the dais, toward Seth and Lucian. With my arms pinned to my side, I was only able to slam my foot down on his. He grunted and his grip loosened, but that was about it.

Aiden turned, seeing my predicament. Our eyes met for a brief second, and then his gaze dropped. I let my legs collapse. Aiden moved so fast the air stirred around me. A second later the Guard hit the ground, unconscious.

"Nice," I croaked as Aiden tugged me to my feet.

His smile was tight as he grabbed hold of my hand again, and we were running up the center aisle. My uncle and the stranger were making short work of the Guards by the door. On the floor, Luke was holding Lea, rocking her back and forth as he kept an eye on the battle. When he saw us, he stood and pulled Lea to her feet. She was hysterical. I didn't think she even knew what was going on around her, not even when the stranger with the scar threw a dagger and took out a Guard right beside her.

"Who… who are you?" I asked.

He bowed at the waist and grinned. "Most call me Solos."

"Solos from Nashville?"

Solos nodded, spun around and punched the living crap out of a Sentinel who'd made a run at us. The punch knocked the guy off his feet. It was pretty epic.

"Are we getting out of here?" Luke asked. He held Lea close to him, his movements near frantic. "We've got to get out of—"

The air popped and crackled. Light followed, flashing over the entire room. When it receded, Apollo stood in the middle of the aisle. "Go," he said. "Get off the island now. I will hold him off, give you enough time."

"Alex!" roared Seth.

Cold shivers went down my spine.

"Whatever you all do, do not stop. Do not stay to help," Apollo ordered before he turned around. "Go."

"Come on." Aiden had me again. "We have a car waiting down the street, by the beach."

"You can run, Alex!" Seth's voice carried over the uproar. "Run all you want! I will find you!"

Aiden dragged me toward the front doors. I looked back, seeing Seth standing in the center of the dais, his chest heaving. The body of the furie lay at his feet like a sick trophy.

"Stop them!" Lucian ordered, moving behind Seth. "Don't let her out of here."

The Guards in front of the dais turned and froze. Then they scattered like roaches.

Apollo moved up the aisle. "Yeah, that's what I thought."

"I will find you! We're connected. We are one!" Seth was still screaming. His gaze fell to the god. He sneered. "You want to fight me now, in your true form?"

"I will fight you in any form, you little punk-ass brat."

Seth laughed. "You can't kill me."

"But I *can* beat the living snot out of you."

That was all I heard. We were out of the courthouse, into the sunlight. Pures and halfs streamed out behind us. We kept running. I struggled to keep up with Aiden, breathing harshly. I could barely feel my legs. Stumbling more than once, Aiden caught me each time, urging me on. Then Marcus appeared at my side, and without a word, swooped me up in his arms.

Indignation swept through me. I loathed the idea of being carried, but I was more of a hindrance on my feet. Only then did I realize that my runes were still burning, the skin throbbing. My stomach started to roll violently.

"I'm going to be sick," I gasped out.

Marcus stopped immediately, placing me on my feet. I hit my knees, and the contents of my stomach emptied on the sidewalk outside a coffee shop. It was quick and powerful, over as soon as it started, leaving my insides aching.

"Alex!" Aiden tracked back to us.

"She's okay." Marcus helped me to my feet. "She's all right. Aiden, go ahead. Make sure your brother is there and get those kids to safety."

Aiden hovered. "I'm not leav—"

"I'm fine. Go."

Obviously reluctant to do so, it took Aiden a few more seconds before he spun around and took off.

"Are you okay?" Marcus asked. "Alexandria?"

I nodded slowly. My hands trembled. "Sorry. I'm so sorry."

Marcus' eyes softened, possibly for the first time since I'd known him. He stepped forward, wrapping his arms around me. It was a brief hug, but tight and everything it should've been. And oddly, I discovered it was something I'd been yearning for.

"Good gods, girl," he choked out, releasing me. "Do you think you can run? It's not very far. We have to get back to the St. Delphi's."

Tears clawed at my throat as I nodded. It wasn't far, but the poor man would die carrying me the whole distance. Hoping my stomach didn't decide to jump out of me again, I started running as fast as I could.

The run ended up nearly killing me. When we finally reached the sand, and were running into the wind, my muscles screamed and protested. I kept going, almost crying out when I saw the two black Hummers… and Aiden.

He met us halfway, thrusting a bottle of water in my hands as I slowed down. "Drink slowly."

I sipped the water as Aiden clasped my shoulders. I wanted to tell him that I was okay, that I wasn't who he should be worried about, but we were moving again.

Deacon was pacing at the rear of the Hummer. "Is someone going to tell me what the hell is going on?" He followed us past the first car. "Lea is hysterical. Luke won't talk. What the hell happened?"

"Did you get the bags in the cars?" Aiden asked, taking the bottle from me before I forgot about the sipping rule. "All of them, like I said?"

"Yes." Deacon ran his hands through his curls, eyes wide and intense. "What happened?"

Solos jogged up to us. "It'll take about eight hours to get where we're going. We should have at least half of that time in before we stop for gas."

"Agreed," Aiden said. He took hold of my limp arm in a gentle grasp, taking on most of my weight. I hadn't realized I'd leaned against the Hummer. His worried gaze kept falling back to me.

"Tell me what happened!" Deacon yelled.

"Seth… Seth attacked the Council." I winced at the words.

Deacon stared incredulously. "Oh my gods."

I broke free of Aiden and looked inside the Hummer. Piled in the back were suitcases. They'd had it all planned. Pushing away from the back of the car, I watched for Seth. How long could Apollo hold him off?

They were finalizing plans, and I was still staring at the suitcases. Obviously they'd hoped to grab me at the Council somehow, not knowing the kind of chaos that was going to erupt. What would they have risked to get me out of there? Life and limb, most likely.

The wind picked up.

Aiden headed back to me, all determination and purpose. "We have to leave now."

Solos called out to Marcus. "You ready for this?"

"Let's get out of here," Marcus replied, casting a long look at me. "You holding up?"

"Yeah," I croaked, and then cleared my throat.

"This is crazy." Deacon opened the back door and started to climb in. "Everything is going bat—"

"No!" Aiden pushed Deacon toward the Hummer being driven by Solos. "We're the ones they will target. Go with Marcus. Luke, stay with him."

All business, Luke nodded and gathered a still-sobbing Lea close to him. I wanted to go to her. She'd lost everything… and each time had had something to do with me. First my mother had taken her parents, and now Seth had taken her sister. Razor-sharp guilt dug in.

Deacon stalled. "No. I want—"

Aiden grabbed his younger brother in a fierce hug. Words were whispered between them, but I couldn't hear anything over the wind. Pushing my hair out of my face, I turned back toward the Covenant-controlled part of the island.

Something was happening. I could feel it. Electricity filled the air, raising the tiny hairs on my arms.

Deacon stumbled back from his brother and turned away. Tears had gathered in his eyes. He feared for his brother's life and he should. When Seth came for us, which he would, he wouldn't pay them any attention.

Seth would come for Aiden and me, and even as strong as he was, it was doubtful Aiden would walk away from that confrontation.

My heart sank. I couldn't do this to them. "Aiden, you can't go with me. You can't do this."

"Don't start," Aiden growled as he grabbed my arm. "Get in the—"

Lightning erupted from the sky, streaking above us and down, slamming just off the coast of the Covenant. Despite our distance from the impact point, the flash of light still blinded me.

Solos stopped, halfway behind the driver's seat. "What the...?"

The wind just stopped. It was unnatural... and so was the silence that descended on Deity Island. Then a rush of seagulls took flight, streaming and squawking in a panic. Hundreds and hundreds of them flew overhead, away from the island.

"What's happening?" Lea whispered. "Is it him? Is he coming?"

"No," I said, feeling it in my core. "This isn't Seth."

"We need to go *now*." Aiden started pulling me toward the passenger side of the car.

In a flurry of activity, everyone jumped into their respective cars. Behind us, people were gathering on the decks of their homes. Guards were scattering across the beach. All were staring across the stretch of ocean that separated the two islands.

I had a really bad feeling about this.

Aiden slammed his door shut and threw the Hummer into drive. He grabbed my hand. "Everything is going to be okay."

Famous last words.

A bone-shaking boom blasted around us, rattling the car. A stream of water jetted into the air on the other side of the island, taller than the highest Covenant building, thicker than two of the dorms. The wall of water stilled, reminding me of how Seth had played with the water in the pool.

This wasn't going to be good.

Another stream burst into the sky and then another... and another until over a dozen walls of water dotted the landscape. Power rippled through the air, sliding over my skin, curling around the cord inside me.

And in the center of each of the streams, I could make out a form of a man.

"Oh, shit," I whispered.

Aiden slammed on the gas and the Hummer lurched forward. "Poseidon."

I twisted around in the seat, watching the ocean from the back window. Beyond the formidable Covenant buildings, the walls started spinning into the funnels. A shadow of a giant trident fell over the Covenant and the sharpened points touched the main island, spelling doom and death for all who remained. Poseidon, the God of the Sea, the great earth-shaker, was very angry.

"Aiden…"

"Turn around, Alex."

My hands clenched the back of the seat. The funnels formed giant cyclones—tornados over water. "They're going to destroy everything! We have to do something."

"There is nothing we can do." With one hand, Aiden grabbed my arm as we crested the bridge to Bald Head Island. "Alex, please."

I couldn't turn away. From the way the cyclones moved in, it appeared Poseidon would spare the mortal island, but as the first funnel reached the Covenant, my chest seized. "They can't do this! Those people are innocent!"

Aiden didn't answer.

Water crashed through the structures. Marble and wood sliced through the air. Screams from those on the main island crawled deep into my soul where the sound would remain for an eternity.

We flew through the streets of Bald Head, narrowly avoiding the stunned pedestrians watching the freakish outburst of nature. And as we reached the bridge leading to the mainland, I saw the great walls of water recede. No building remained on Deity island. There was nothing. All of it was gone. The Covenant, buildings, statues, pures and halfs… everything had been wiped into the ocean.

CHAPTER 30

HOURS PASSED IN STUNNED SILENCE. I FELT SICK, COLD. How many had been on the island? Hundreds of servants and Instructors had remained at the Covenant during winter break, and people had been in their homes. Hands shaking, I smoothed my hair back as Aiden fiddled with the radio until he caught another station.

"...Meteorologists are saying that the earthquake several hundred miles off the coast of North Carolina had produced at least a thirty-foot wall of water. However, residents on neighboring islands remained unscathed. Some have reported seeing a cluster of up to a dozen cyclones, but those reports have not been substantiated by the National Oceanic and Atmospheric Administration. A state of emergency has been declared..."

Aiden turned the radio off. He then reached over, running his fingers over my arm, my hand. He'd been doing that since we got in the car, as if he was reminding himself that I was sitting next to him, that I was still alive after so many lives had been lost.

I pressed my forehead against the window and closed my eyes. Had Poseidon gone after Seth and Lucian, or had Apollo somehow managed to prevent total destruction? All I did know was that Seth was still breathing, because the connection was still there.

Like I'd done during the last couple of hours, I pictured my pink and glittery walls again and reinforced them with all my strength.

"How are you feeling?" Aiden asked quietly.

I peeled my head off the window and looked at him. Everything about him was stiff and tense, from the way he held the steering wheel to the line of his jaw. "How can you even think about how I'm feeling right now?"

"I saw how you reacted when… he pulled power from you." He glanced at me, eyes silvery. "Did they… did he hurt you when you were with him?"

I was exhausted. My head ached and I was pretty sure my toes were numb, but I was alive. "No. He didn't hurt me. And I'm fine. You shouldn't worry about how I'm doing. All of those people…" I shook my head, swallowing against the sudden tightening in my throat. "What Lucian did by telling them you used a compulsion… I'm so sorry."

"Alex, you have no reason to apologize. It wasn't your fault."

"But how can you go back? Being a Sentinel—"

"I'm still a Sentinel. And with everything that's happened, I'm sure what I did is the last thing they'll be thinking about." He glanced at me. "I knew the risks when I did it. I don't regret it. You understand?"

Aiden didn't regret it now, but what about later—if there was a later—and he was tried for treason? Even if he wasn't, he'd be stripped of his Sentinel duties and ostracized.

"Alex?"

"Yes. I understand." I nodded for extra benefit. "Where are we going?"

His knuckles were bleached white. "We're going to Athens, Ohio. Solos' father has a place on the edge of Wayne National Forest. It should be far enough from… him as long as Apollo has given us enough time."

"I don't feel him." We'd stopped referring to Seth by name out loud, like doing so would somehow make him reappear or something.

"Do you think you can shield him, keep him out?"

I glanced at the side mirror; the other Hummer followed close behind. How were they holding up? Lea? "The distance… he shouldn't be able to connect through the bond, if that's what you're worried about. I mean, he couldn't feel anything when he was in New York, so…"

"That's not all I'm worried about," Aiden responded quietly. "It's about an eight-hour drive." He brushed his hair out of his eyes as he squinted into the fading sunlight. "We'll stop along the way, most likely in Charleston, to get gas and something to eat. You think you can hold out that long?"

"Yeah. Aiden... all of those people." My voice broke as my throat tightened. "They didn't stand a chance."

Aiden grasped my hand. "It's not your fault, Alex."

"It's not?" Tears burned my eyes. "If I'd listened to you and Apollo when you suggested that I leave before he came back, this wouldn't have happened."

"You don't know that."

"Yes, I do." I tried to pull my hand free, but Aiden held on. I hoped he was a good one-handed driver. "I just didn't want to believe that he... would do something so terrible."

He squeezed my hand. "You had hope, Alex. No one can ever be faulted for hope."

"You once told me that I needed to know when to let hope go. I was way past the expiration date on hope then." I tried to smile and failed. "I won't make that same mistake twice. I swear."

Bringing my hand to his lips, he placed a sweet kiss against it. "*Agapi mou*, don't hold this kind of guilt too close. A different path could've been chosen, but in the end you did what you felt was right. You gave him a chance."

"I know." I focused on the road ahead, willing the tears away. "It's gone, isn't it? The entire Covenant—even Deity Island?"

He took a shuddering breath. "It could've been worse. That's what I keep telling myself. If classes had been in... just a few more days..."

The loss of life would have been astronomical. "What are we going to do? I can't stay hidden forever."

What was unspoken lay between us. In other words, unless Seth came to his senses, which seemed highly unlikely, he would eventually find me.

"I don't know," Aiden said, merging into the other lane. "But we're in this together, Alex, to the end."

Warmth returned to my heart. His hand felt right in mine, and even though everything around us was so incredibly screwed up, we *were* in this together. To the end.

†

It was the middle of the night when we reached Charleston, West "by gods" Virginia and it was snowing lightly. The vehicles rolled to a stop by the pumps in front of one of those travel centers that are the size of a small Wal-Mart. We needed gas and food, and maybe one of those 5-Hour Energy things, too.

"Hold on." Aiden reached in the seat behind us and pulled out one of the sickle blades. "Just in case."

Collapsed, it fit in my pocket with only half of it sticking out. "Thanks."

His eyes met mine as he slipped me a couple of tens. "Don't take too long, okay? Looks like Solos is going in with you."

I glanced back. He was already waiting by the passenger side. Marcus was fiddling with the gas pump like he'd never used one before. "What do you want?"

"Surprise me." He smiled. "Just be careful."

Promising that I would, I climbed out of the Hummer and nearly ate the pavement as my foot slipped on a patch of ice. "Gods!"

"Alex?" Aiden called out.

"I'm fine." I tipped my head back and closed my eyes, letting the tiny flakes of snow fall upon my face. It had been so, so long since I'd seen snow.

"What are you doing?" Solos asked, killing the moment.

I opened my eyes and forced them to his chest. "I like snow."

"Well, you're going to see a lot of snow where we're going." We started across the parking lot, mindful of the patches of ice that were bound and determined to take me out. "Probably have a foot or more in Athens."

For a moment, I fantasized about snowball fights and sled rides. Stupid of me to do so, but it helped keep me from freaking out.

"You're not what I expected," Solos said as we reached the snow-covered sidewalk.

I shoved my hands into my pockets. "What were you expecting?"

"I don't know." He smiled, softening the scar. "Someone taller."

A small smile pulled at my lips. "Don't let my size fool you."

"I know. I've heard tales about your many escapades, especially how you fought during the attack on the New York Covenant. Some say it's because of what you are that makes you fight so well."

I shrugged.

"But I say it has more to do with your training than anything." Solos glanced behind him and then his shrewd gaze settled on me. "You and St. Delphi seem to be very close."

I schooled my expression blank as I shrugged again. "He's pretty cool for a pure-blood."

"Is that so?"

"Hey! Wait up!" Deacon hit a patch of thick ice and slid to our sides like a pro skater, eyes wide. "Lea wants to eat something. Luke's going to stay with her."

Saved by Deacon. "How's she doing?"

Solos grabbed the door, holding it open for us. "She slept most of the way here," Deacon answered. "Since she woke up, she hasn't really been talking. Luke convinced her that she should eat something, so we're going to share some Cheetos."

I felt for Lea and understood her pain. So did Deacon. My presence probably wouldn't be the best, but Deacon… he'd be good for her.

I shook off the snow once inside the warm, brightly-lit travel center. With the exception of the greasy-haired and scrawny cashier who was reading what looked like a smut magazine, the place was empty. Stomach growling, I headed toward the coolers. Aiden would want water, of course, but I was in need of some caffeine.

Solos stayed with Deacon, because if a random hillbilly daimon appeared, Deacon would be the one needing help. Grabbing a bottle of water and a Pepsi, I scanned the store. The cashier yawned and scratched his chest, never once looking up. Snow was starting to fall in larger flakes. Sighing, I ignored the desire to watch the snow and shuffled toward the chip aisle. The made-to-order sandwiches part of the store wasn't open, so our options were severely limited.

A heavy musky, wet scent flooded the air. I sniffed, finding the smell oddly familiar. I passed Deacon with his arms full.

"You better hurry up. Solos is getting nervous about the mortal."

I glanced back at the front of the store. "What? There's only one guy in here."

"I know."

Shaking my head, I grabbed a packet of beef jerky and a bag of dill-flavored chips. I looked down at my goodies and decided I needed something sweet. After a quick stop in the candy bar area, I returned to the front.

"Nice of you to join us," Solos muttered. A bag of peanuts and an energy drink were in his hands.

I ignored him as Deacon checked out. The cashier glanced up as I handed over my feast of calories, but said nothing. People were super-friendly around these parts.

"That will be $10.59," the man grunted.

Good gods. What did I buy? I dug in my pocket for the cash Aiden had given me. Suddenly, the musky smell returned, but much stronger. And then I remembered that smell. It was the same mossy scent from the Underworld. The overhead fluorescent lights flickered once, then twice.

"Oh man," I whispered, and my heart dropped.

Solos stiffened beside me. "What is it?"

"Y'all don't worry," the clerk said, glancing up at the lights. "It happens all the time with the snow. Drivers hit poles in that black ice out there. Y'all must not be from around here."

The air thickened around us, filling with the same electricity that had enveloped Deity Island moments before Poseidon's arrival. The mortal couldn't feel it.

There was a pop and sparks flew. The security camera by the door stopped blinking red as smoke wafted from it.

"What the hell?" The clerk leaned over the counter. "Now I ain't seen nuttin' like that before."

I ain't seen nuttin' like that, either.

Solos grabbed Deacon's arm. "Time to go."

Wide-eyed, Deacon nodded. "Whatever you say, man."

Leaving my items on the counter, we started for the door. Food be damned. There was definitely something going on, something… godly.

"Hey! Where y'all going? You didn't—"

A deep growl cut off his words. We halted about ten feet from the door. My heart leapt into my throat. The smell of wet dog grew strong, and the fine hairs on my body rose. I turned around slowly, my gaze darting over the store. I reached down, wrapping my hand around the handle of the sickle blade.

Beside the display of Twinkies and cupcakes, the air shimmered. Distinctive shapes of large, booted footprints appeared, blackening the vinyl flooring, filling the air with wisps of smoke and sulfur. The white travel star painted on the vinyl bubbled and smoked.

Two leather-encased legs, then narrow hips, and a broad chest appeared out of thin air. By the time my gaze traveled to his face, I think I'd stopped breathing. "Darkly handsome" didn't do him justice. "Sinfully beautiful" wasn't even in the ballpark when trying to describe this raven-haired god. The smell of sulfur and smoke gave away his identity.

Hades was sort of hot for a god, and I was sure he was there to kill me.

A shotgun blasted, deadening my ears and causing me to jump.

"I don't want none of this bad shit up in here." The clerk cocked the gun again. "Next time I won't—"

Hades raised a hand, and the clerk's eyes rolled back into their sockets. He hit the floor without so much as another word. Hades smiled, flashing a perfect set of ultra-white teeth. The Underworld had a hell of a dental plan.

"Now, we can do this the easy way or the hard way," Hades said, charmingly enough. Weirdly, he seemed to have a British accent. "All I want is the girl."

Solos edged Deacon back against the counter, blocking him in, and casually placed his peanuts and energy drink down. "That's going to be a problem."

Hades shrugged. "Then this will be the hard way."

CHAPTER 31

THE HARD WAY DIDN'T SOUND OR LOOK FUN WHEN Solos tried to get Deacon out of the convenience store and found that the doors wouldn't open. On the other side, Aiden and Marcus desperately tried to open the doors, going as far as to try to throw a bench at the reinforced glass, but to no avail.

Things went from bad to really screwed-up within seconds. Hades wasn't alone—not that we'd forgotten the smell and animalistic growl from earlier. Behind Hades, the air shimmered before two massive, three-headed dogs appeared.

One was black and the other was brown, but both were as ugly as hell. Matted hair covered everything but their long, hairless snouts. Each head had a mouth on it that could swallow a baby whole and their claws looked vicious and sharp. Six sets of eyes glowed ruby red. At the end of each rat-like tail was what looked like a military flail—a morning star type of weapon, rough and full of spikes.

They flanked Hades, snarling and snapping at the air.

We were so screwed.

"Meet Death," Hades gestured at the black dog, "and Despair. Cerberus is a proud papa to his two boys."

"Nice names," I croaked, and then released the two sharp edges of the sickle blade.

"You wanna play, luv?" Hades cocked his head to the side.

"Not really." I wasn't sure which of them I should keep an eye on.

"It's really nothing personal," Hades said. "But we cannot allow the First to become what has been feared. He's already made his choice, and now we must make ours."

Trying to kill me was as personal as it got. I saw Hades' chin go up about an inch and I jumped to the side just as Despair charged me. Darting down the candy aisle, I hoped that Solos was able to protect Deacon. I grabbed hold of a rack and threw it to the floor. Despair went right over the numerous candy bars, his claws ripping through wrappers and chocolate. Hanging a quick right, I glanced over my shoulder.

Despair lost his balance and slid into the standup cooler, crashing through the glass. Bottles of soda flew through the air, fizzing upon impact. Taking advantage of the situation, I spun around and brought the sickle edge down on the closest head.

The blade went clean through muscles and tissue, and a yelp later, Despair became a two headed dog... until the stump started to grow into another freaking head. Fully restored, Despair bared his fangs and pawed at the ground.

I backed up. "Nice doggy. Good doggy."

Despair crouched, each of his mouths snapping at the air.

"Bad doggy!" I took off running, knocking over cases of beer and anything I could get my hands on. Over the shelves I could see Deacon backed up against the front doors, Aiden and Marcus' horrified expressions on the other side. Solos was squaring off with Death, dispatching heads left and right.

And Hades, well, he was just standing there in his big bad god glory.

"Go for the heart!" Solos yelled over the chaos. "The heart in the chest, Alex!"

"Like I don't know where the freaking heart is!" I just didn't want to get that close to the thing. I picked up speed when I saw the dining area, getting an idea—not a good one, but better than running laps around the store with a mutant pitbull chasing after me.

I leapt over the set of chairs and landed on the table. Spinning around, I grabbed the metal chair and held it, legs up. Despair jumped, clearing the mess of chairs and landed on top of me. He shrieked and thrashed as the metal legs embedded themselves deep into his underbelly. The impact busted the table and we both went down, his claws narrowly missing my face. All three heads snapped inches from my nose, its hot, putrid breath setting off my gag reflex.

Tipping my hips, I rolled Despair and sprang to my feet. Despair flopped on his back, legs flailing in the air. Pushing down the urge to vomit, I jumped on the seat of the chair. My weight sent the metal spokes down, piercing the protective plate of bone.

A second later the dog was nothing but a pile of shimmery, blue dust. Lifting my head, I whirled around. "One down…"

Hades let out a roar of fury that shook the shelves and sent overpriced items of every shape and size falling to the floor.

And then he vanished.

"Well, that was easy." I flipped the blade, watching Solos dodge one of Death's heads. "Did you see that? Hades totally just chicken—*oh crap*."

Shelves flew through the air, chairs and tables slid across the floor, flung aside by an unseen force. The floor shook under my feet as I backed up. That was about when I remembered that Hades could become invisible. Terror washed through me like a dark, oily wave of heat.

"No fair," I said, and then whipped the sickle blade through what I hoped wasn't empty space.

An invisible hand caught my arm and twisted. Crying out in pain and surprise, I dropped the sickle. Hades reappeared. "Sorry, luv, all is fair in war."

A blinding light filled the store, followed by a popping sound. Then something zinged past my cheek. I caught a glimpse of silver before Hades released my arm and snatched an arrow out of the air.

"Artemis, that wasn't very nice." Hades snapped the arrow in two and tossed it aside. "You could take an eye out with one of those things."

The soft feminine laugh that followed sounded like wind chimes. A few feet behind us, legs widespread and a silver bow in one hand, stood Artemis. Instead of the white chiffon many goddesses were known for, she wore straight-up combat boots and hot-pink camouflage pants. A white tank completed her badass ensemble.

She reached behind her, pulling another arrow from her quiver. "Back down, Hades."

Hades' lips thinned.

She placed the arrow on her bow. "You will not catch the next one, Hades. And you will not take her."

I slowly backed away from the god smackdown-in-progress, having no idea why Artemis would come to my aid. Out of the corner of my eye, I saw Death finally go down. I picked up my sickle blade.

Hades stepped forward, tile peeling and smoking under his boots. "Why are you intervening, Artemis? You know what will happen. All of us are at risk."

"That is my twin's lineage standing there and she belongs to us." Artemis pulled the arrow back, tossing her waist-length blonde hair over her shoulder. "Which means she is my flesh and bone. So I will say it one more time, just in case Persephone has befuddled that brain of yours—*stand down*."

My mouth dropped opened. Apollo's lineage? *Oh no…oh, hell to the no…*

"I do not care if she is the heir to the bloody throne, Artemis! We must prevent the First from gaining complete power!"

Artemis' fingers twitched. "She is not to be harmed, Hades. That is it."

An incredulous look settled over his darkly handsome face. "I would not harm her… not really. I could take her to the Underworld. It would not even hurt. Artemis, we cannot allow this threat to continue. Be reasonable."

"And I cannot allow you to hurt her. It is not up for discussion."

"So you would risk more destruction? Did you see what Poseidon did today? Or were you too busy hunting and playing with your consorts?"

Artemis smirked. "You really do not want to piss me off right now, Hades. Not when I have an arrow pointed between your eyes."

He shook his head. "You know what Zeus will do if the First becomes the God Killer. You risk it all—the lives of our offspring and the mortals—and for what? Watered-down familial bonds?"

"We will risk it all for everything," she responded quietly. "You know what the funny thing is about prophecies, uncle?"

"That they are always changing?" Hades sneered. "Or that they are nothing more than a load of rubbish?"

Any other time I would've clapped, but seeing that Hades wanted to kill me, I wasn't about to celebrate our shared opinions when it came to the oracle.

Artemis cocked back her arm. "So be it."

Fury rolled off Hades in swamping waves. Swallowing down rightful fear, I took a step back. I expected an all-out royal rumble between the two.

"I should never have allowed her soul to be released," Hades spat. "Apollo promised me that it would never come to this."

"There is still hope," Artemis said.

Those words sparked something in me. *There is still hope.* Was there? I'd seen the look in Seth's eyes, how far gone he'd been when he'd pulled the akasha from me and taken aim at the Council. Poseidon had leveled the Covenant, and there would be more that would go down. More innocent people would die. People that I loved would surely die—all to protect me.

I glanced back at the doors, seeing Aiden's pale face beside Marcus'. I'd been created, like a pawn, to give Seth complete power. There was nothing that could be done about it. None of us could spend our lives hiding. It wouldn't work. I would Awaken in little over a day. Seth would find me. And everything would be over.

Numbness crept through me as I turned back to the two gods and lowered the sickle. "Wait." My voice came out barely a whisper, but everyone froze.

"No!" Deacon yelled, trying to get past Solos. "I know what she's going to do! Alex, no!"

Tears sprang to my eyes as I took in his horrified expression. "I can't… I can't let what happened back there happen again."

Deacon struggled against Solos, his eyes burning a fierce silver, like his brother, so much like him. "I don't care. It'll kill…" He swallowed, shaking his head. "You can't do this, Alex."

It would kill Aiden.

Hades clapped his hands together. "See. Even she understands."

My heart cracked.

Artemis' eyes widened. "Alexandria, please, I understand that the mortal part of you demands that you become a martyr, but you really need to shut up."

"People are going to continue to die. And Seth will find me." I pressed the button on the handle, and the blades collapsed. "I saw him. He's…" I couldn't finish. Saying that Seth was lost was too final and, in a way, it broke my heart.

Hades turned those eyes to me. They snapped with electricity. For a moment, I missed Apollo. At least he toned down those eyes around me, making them seem normal. Hades would do no such thing. "You are doing the right thing," he cooed softly. "And I promise you, you will not feel a thing." He held out his hand to me. "It will be easy, luv."

The crack in my chest spread, and I blinked back tears. This wasn't fair, but it was right. It would hurt Aiden—and Marcus and my friends—but it would also protect them. One day I hoped they'd understand. Over the pounding of my blood, I heard Solos yell for me. Slowly, I raised my hand.

"That is it," Hades whispered. "Take my hand."

Our fingers were only inches apart. I could feel their strange mix of heat and bone-chilling cold. I forced my mind empty. I couldn't afford to think about what I was doing because I'd chicken out.

"Hades," Artemis called out.

He turned slightly. "Stay—"

Artemis released the arrow and it struck where she'd intended—smack dab between Hades' eyes. Then he just poofed—like Grandma Piperi had poofed in the garden the day she'd given me her last prophecy. The overwhelming scent of damp walls and caverns vanished, and the arrow clattered onto the linoleum.

I clamped my hand over my mouth to stop my scream. "Is… did you kill him?"

"No." Artemis scoffed. "I just put him out of commission for a while." She lowered the bow and flicked her wrist. The front doors swung open. Marcus and Aiden rushed in, coming to a halt when they spied Artemis. Neither of the pures seemed to know what to do.

Artemis replaced the arrow back in her quiver and gave Aiden a sexy little grin. "They just keep getting yummier," she purred.

Too stunned to get jealous, I stared at her. "Why? He was right. I'm too much of a risk. I *understand* that."

Artemis focused on me with all-white eyes. "My brother has not risked the wrath of Zeus to protect you, for you to just throw your life away."

I tried to ignore the cyclone of fury building behind me. Dealing with Aiden was not something I was looking forward to. "I don't get it. No one can hide me forever. Seth will find me, and then what? He'll become the God Killer and another god is going to freak out and wipe out an entire city."

Artemis glided toward me, her elegant movements completely at odds with her combat-princess attire. "Or you will turn the tables on the First and all those who think they can overthrow the gods."

"What do you mean?" Marcus spoke, flushing a bright red when Artemis turned to him. He bowed deeply and then straightened. "How can Alexandria turn the tables? If Seth so much as lays a finger on her once she Awakens, he will become the God Killer."

"Not necessarily," she replied evenly.

I blinked rapidly. "Care to explain that?"

Artemis smiled. Impossibly, she became more beautiful... and creepier. "It is true that my brother... holds affection for you, but you are a valuable asset to us. Some wish to see you dead, it is true. Hades will be back... eventually, as will the remaining furies. But you will Awaken soon and you are strong—stronger than you realize."

All my normal smartass responses would probably earn me an arrow in the head, so I had no idea what to say.

She stopped in front of me. When she reached out and clasped my chin with smooth, cold fingers, I wanted to flinch away. She tipped my head back. "You have a reckless sort of passion about you. It guides you. Some would see it as a weakness."

"It's not?" I whispered, unable to look away.

"No." She studied me as if she could see into me, through me. "You have the eyes of a warrior." Her hand dropped and she took a step back. "Prophecies always change, Alexandria. Nothing in our world is set in stone. And power never flows just one way. The key is finding a way to reverse it."

Then she just disappeared.

I touched my chin. The skin tingled. Slowly, I turned to Aiden. "You should've seen those dogs."

Aiden grabbed both my arms, his eyes like liquid silver. I could tell he wanted to shake me. He'd seen through the glass what I'd tried to do and Artemis had pretty much thrown me under the bus. As he stared at me, it was like he'd forgotten everyone else in the store, that my uncle was there, his brother, and Solos. He was that angry.

"Don't you *ever* think about doing something so stupid again."

I looked away. "I'm sorry—"

"I understand that you thought you were doing the right thing," he said through clenched teeth. "But you weren't, Alex. Sacrificing yourself was not the right thing to do. Do you understand me?"

Marcus placed a hand on his shoulder. "Aiden, this is not the place. We need to go."

My breath caught as my eyes darted between the two. "I just don't know how we're going to win this."

"No one wins if you kill yourself," Marcus said quietly. "We must go."

Drawing in a deep breath, Aiden dropped his hands. His look warned that there would be a later, most likely the moment we stepped back in the car. Solos waited by the door, his sharp gaze narrowed on Aiden as he took a sip of his energy drink.

"Are you okay?" Aiden asked Deacon.

He nodded slowly. "Yeah, I'm great. Nothing like witnessing a death match between gods when I'm trying to get some Cheetos."

My lips twitched. Poor Deacon. He clutched that bag to his chest, too.

The cashier's soft snores were the only sound. Remembering the whole purpose of coming to this place, I hastened back to the counter.

"What are you doing?" Aiden asked.

I dropped some cash on the counter and grabbed my bag. "I'm hungry."

Aiden stared a moment, then a slow smile crept across his face. Maybe I wouldn't get bitched out too badly. On the way out, he picked up a package of Hostess CupCakes off the floor and caught my look. "Me, too," he said.

"At least I paid for my stuff."

CHAPTER 32

I DID GET BITCHED OUT—A LOT. AND I DESERVED IT. Aiden had been through the wringer when it came to me lately. He understood why—my motives—but he didn't agree with me. But I knew what I'd been thinking, and it still made sense. I didn't want to die, but I didn't want to see anybody else hurt when handing myself over would stop everything.

Halfway into the second part of the trip, as the tires ate away the miles, he grabbed my hand and held onto it. He hadn't forgiven me, but he didn't want to shake me anymore. That was progress. I still wasn't sure if Artemis shooting Hades in the head was a good move or not by the time we reached Athens.

Tall pines and mounds of snow greeted us when we reached the lodge nestled at the edge of the national forest. Without Marcus and the air element, there would've been no way that we would've made it up the remote road. Even so, it took him over an hour to clear the road.

The lodge was magnificent, made of logs and surrounded by a wraparound deck. If I hadn't been so exhausted, I would've appreciated its beauty much more.

"Do you know that Athens is one of the most haunted locales in Ohio?" Solos said as he opened the door.

"She doesn't believe in ghosts." Aiden lugged our bags over his shoulder, cheeks flushed from the cold. I could barely feel it. All I wanted was a bed to sleep the rest of the day away in.

"Really?" Solos grinned. "We'll have to take you down to the old Athens Lunatic Asylum and see if that changes your mind."

"Sounds like fun," I murmured, watching Luke and Deacon usher Lea inside. "How will we be safe here? What's stopping any god from carpet-bombing us?"

Solos' brows furrowed. "We're safe here."

"How so?"

"Look up there." Aiden shifted the bags and pointed above the front door. Carved into the wood was the same S-shaped rune that was on my neck. "Apollo said no god who means ill will against persons in this house can pass through."

"The invincibility rune." I rubbed the back of my neck absently as I stepped over the threshold. "Didn't know you could just rune up a house. That's pretty handy."

Inside was just as beautiful. Wide windows let in the last of the sunset and the wood floors had been buffed until they shined. It sort of reminded me of the cabin in Gatlinburg. I shuddered.

"You okay?" Aiden whispered, coming up behind me.

I swallowed. "Yeah, I'm just really tired."

Solos showed us to the rooms. Lea was placed downstairs, along with Marcus and Luke. Deacon grabbed the loft above the rec room and the rest of us got rooms upstairs. Everyone huddled in small groups or, like Marcus, stared out one of the windows, appearing lost in deep thought.

Aiden carried my bags into a cozy, rustic-looking bedroom and placed them by the bed. Turning around, our gazes locked. Since the day I'd left with Seth, we hadn't been alone together. The car ride didn't count. We'd been running for our lives after witnessing a tragedy. Kissing and touching hadn't been on our minds.

It kind of returned with a vengeance then.

He crossed the distance, cupping my cheeks in his hands. They were elegant fingers, but calloused from years of training. I loved his hands. He angled his head to mine, his lips hovering just within distance. "Later," he promised, and then he pressed his lips to mine.

The kiss was gentle, sweet, and way too quick. My lips tingled awhile after he'd left the room. Later? How could there be a "later" in a house full of people? I took a hot shower and let the water ease my aching muscles once I figured out how to use the three showerheads without drowning myself. Afterward, I changed into sweats and sent the bed a yearning glance on the way out of the room. I had something to do before I rested.

Lea was sitting on the bed, legs crossed as she stared down at her phone. When I knocked on the open door, she glanced up. "Hey," I said.

She watched me for several long seconds and then cleared her throat. "I texted Olivia in Vail, told her we were okay."

"Does she know what's she going to do?" I sat on the bed beside her, running my hands through the wet tangles in my hair. I thought about Caleb's message to her. Hopefully, I could tell her soon.

"No. Her mom..." her voice caught and she swallowed. "Her mom is freaking out. I think they're going to New York."

Thinking of my father, I felt my chest tighten. Would I ever see him again? Then I felt bad for even thinking that. Lea had lost all of her family. "Will they be safe there?"

Long, coppery hair I'd envied for years shielded her face as she tipped her head down. "She thinks so. She'll let me know once her mom knows more."

I nodded, dropping my hands to my lap. "Lea, I'm so sorry for what happened."

She drew in a breath of air that seemed to shake her entire body. "We've been here before."

"I know."

Lea lifted her head. Her amethyst-colored eyes glittered with tears. "I know it's not your fault. What your mom did or what... what Seth did. Every death that I've seen or been around has had to do with you. They're not your fault, but they still happened."

I looked away, feeling the weight of the last ten months settle over me. Ten months of death, starting with my mom in Miami, and I knew it wasn't over. With the gods involved as they were, with my birthday tomorrow, and with Seth out there looking for us, it wasn't over. But still, what I was feeling was nothing compared to what Lea was going through.

"And I can't... I can't look at you without seeing all those faces," Lea whispered. "I'm sorry. I don't blame you, but I... I just can't look at you right now."

I nodded stiffly and stood. "I'm sorry," I said again. It was the only thing I could say.

"I know."

Leaving her room didn't diminish the guilt. Crawling into bed didn't make any of what happened disappear. And my guilt wasn't like what I'd felt after Caleb's death. This was like having a child who had done something terrible and everyone was staring at me, wondering where it all had gone wrong. Guilt by association.

I rolled onto my side, facing the window. Snow continued to fall outside. Nature was at its best when it was both beautiful and deadly.

Watching the snow cleared my mind of everything that was happening, leaving behind a thin layer of static until exhaustion claimed and pulled me under.

A feathery light kiss woke me up sometime later, drawing my eyes open. Aiden smiled down at me as his thumb traced the shape of my cheekbone. "What are you doing?" I asked sleepily. "What if someone finds you in here?"

"Solos took Deacon and Luke to the store since the snow has let up a little. Lea is resting and Marcus is keeping an eye on things." He curled around me, finding my hand and threading his fingers through it. "And I think the cat's pretty much out of the bag on this."

I tipped my head back, my eyes searching his intently. "What do you mean?"

"We're in a house full of halfs, with the exception of Marcus and my brother. Deacon surely doesn't care and Marcus—"

"My uncle's a stickler for rules," I whispered.

Aiden brushed his lips over the tip of my nose. "Marcus knows, Alex. He's not blind."

"He's okay with it?"

"I wouldn't say *okay*." Aiden grinned. "He actually punched me when he figured it out."

I stared. "What?"

He chuckled under his breath. "Yeah, he punched me right in the face when he got back from Nashville—twice."

"Oh my…" I pressed my lips together to keep from laughing. It wasn't funny, but it was.

"The first hit was because you were with Seth and Lucian. The second one was after he figured out about us."

"How did he find out? We were careful." And we had been.

"I think he's suspected something for awhile," he mused. "But it was when you were gone he figured it out. I think I was pretty transparent during those days."

I wanted to ease the lines of concern that'd appeared on his forehead. We'd talked about my time spent in Lucian's house on the way here and I'd reassured him a dozen times or more that I hadn't been harmed there, but it still bothered him. Just like when I'd died, it was something that would linger with Aiden.

"What did he say to you?" I finally asked him.

"I don't think you want to know. It was one of the only times I've heard Marcus cuss."

I smiled as I lowered my cheek back to the pillow. Gods know I was all too familiar with Marcus being angry. "You don't seem too worried about him knowing."

"I'm not. Right now, there are more… pressing issues to focus on."

Wasn't that the truth? "Part of me wishes tomorrow wouldn't come."

He kissed the top of my head. "Everything will be okay, Alex."

"I know." I closed my eyes and snuggled in. "I just don't know what to expect, you know? Will I automatically turn into a super badass tomorrow or something? Or will I be accidentally blasting people with akasha?" Or would I connect with Seth? That I didn't want to put into words.

"Whatever happens, you'll still be Alex... you'll still be *agapi mou*, my life. Just... just don't ever scare me like you did today, okay? We're still in this together."

"To the end?"

"To the end," he whispered.

Damnable tears rushed to my eyes. I was such a girl, but those words were perfect, what I needed to hear. "Let's make plans again. I liked that." My brows rose when he laughed again. "What?"

"It's just that you are the last person who plans anything."

I grinned, because he had a point. "But I like these kinds of plans."

"Okay." He moved his thumb along the inside of my palm. "I've been thinking about the future—our future."

I loved the sound of that—"our future." When Aiden said it, it seemed possible. "What did you come up with?"

"It's more like something I've decided." He pulled his hand free and smoothed back my hair. "Let's say everything blows over with the compulsion thing, okay?"

Not likely, but I nodded.

"I don't want to stay in our world."

I caught his hand, lowering it to where my heart pounded as I twisted around in his embrace. "What? What do you mean?"

Thick lashes shielded his eyes. "If we stayed in this world, the Hematoi world, we couldn't be together. There will be some who don't care, but... it's too much of a risk, even if we did manage to get assigned to the same area."

Air left my lungs as I stared at him. "But if you left you couldn't be a Sentinel anymore, and you need that."

He looked up, meeting my eyes. "I do need that. Being a Sentinel is important to me, but it's not my world, my life, or my heart. You are. And I want you in my life, really in my life. It's the only way."

I suddenly wanted to cry. Again. I couldn't even form a coherent word, and I knew he could feel my heart slamming itself against his palm, but I didn't care.

Aiden leaned in, brushing his lips over mine. "I love you, Alex. I'd give it all up for you, and I know you've been thinking about it, too, but that's up to you."

Could I give it up… this almost inherent need to become a Sentinel? Could I let go of the desire driven by years of having duty ingrained in me, and the need to somehow make up for what'd happened to my mother? Leaving this world would require assimilating back into the mortal world, something I had totally sucked at for three years. Old fears rose in that moment as years of never fitting in, of always being the freak, flashed before me. Mortals, for the most part, were naturally uncomfortable and drawn to us in the same breath. It was hard being around them, always pretending.

But I had been thinking about a future that didn't include the Covenant or being a Sentinel. I just never thought it could be possible, but when I looked into Aiden's eyes and saw only love—love for me—I knew I could do it. *We* could do it. Aiden was worth it. Our love was. Living like a mortal had choked me before, but now it could provide the type of freedom I yearned for. And together, anything seemed possible.

Tipping my head up, I met his silvery gaze. I could always tell what Aiden was feeling by the color of his eyes and right now, he was laying everything out there and still giving me the choice.

"Yes. I could do it," I whispered. "I would do it."

A shudder rocked Aiden's body. "I was almost afraid you'd say no."

Misty-eyed, I cupped his cheek. Day-old stubble grazed my palm. "I could never tell you no, Aiden. Not that I would ever want to. But… but what about Deacon and Marcus? How can we do it?"

"I think they could know. We could trust them."

There were so many "what ifs" with this plan. How could we escape the Covenant and the society that probably would be very unwilling to let either of us go? We needed a plan, a good one if we even had a chance to make it work, but right now, the idea itself flooded me with warmth and so much hope. And hope, it was a fragile thing, but it kept me going.

Aiden lowered his head, bringing his mouth to mine. He made a sound in the back of his throat as the kiss deepened. The tentative touch gave way to something infinitely more. When he rolled his body, fitting it against mine like a warm blanket, my heart thundered. I was feeling so much and not enough—never enough. There was a yearning, devastating and raw, that would never go away. I lost track of Aiden's hands and how many times we kissed as our bodies moved, and in those moments, we finally found a way to make time stop.

CHAPTER 33

NOTHING… AMAZING HAPPENED ON MY BIRTHDAY.

All morning, everyone watched me as if they expected me to sprout a second head or start floating to the rafters. And I didn't feel any different from last night. No additional marks of the Apollyon popped up. The existing ones didn't tingle. I tried to levitate a chair in the kitchen— it didn't happen and I just felt stupid afterward. By the afternoon, the whole Awakening thing seemed very anticlimactic.

"Hey." Aiden popped his head into the bedroom. "You busy, birthday girl?"

I looked up from the magazine Luke had brought back from the store. "No. I'm just sort of hiding."

Aiden closed the door behind him quietly and smiled. "Why are you hiding?"

Shrugging, I closed the magazine and tossed it to the floor. "I kind of feel like an Apollyon failure."

"Why?" He sat beside me, eyes a soft heather gray.

"Everyone keeps watching me, waiting for something to happen. Earlier, Marcus stared at me so long his eyes crossed. And while Solos was making lunch, he asked if I could heat up the soup with the fire element."

Aiden looked like he was trying not to laugh.

I smacked him on the arm. "It's not funny."

"I know." He drew in a deep breath, but his eyes danced with mirth. "Okay. It is kind of funny."

My eyes narrowed on him. "I can take you, you know?"

He leaned over, lips curving into a wolfish smile. "You can't take what you already have."

A heady feeling came from knowing that, but I socked him on the shoulder anyway. "Stop trying to sweet-talk me."

"I have something I wanted to show you." He reached into his pocket and pulled out a small box. "And then you have to come downstairs and stop hiding."

My eyes were glued to the box. It was plain white, but there was a red bow tied around it. Thoughts of jewelry stores danced in my head. "What is that?"

Aiden placed it in my hand. "It's your birthday, Alex. What do you think it is?"

I looked up, meeting his gaze. "You didn't have to get me anything."

"I know. I wanted to."

I slid off the lid, hooking that soft material of the satin ribbon with my pinky. Upon opening the box, I immediately choked up. "Oh, wow. This... this is so beautiful."

Nestled against more satin, a dark-red crystal had been intricately designed into a rose in bloom, carved as if the petals were reaching up toward the sun. It hung from a delicate silver chain that complemented its beauty. I plucked it from the box. Lights winked and danced off the precious stone and it immediately warmed to my skin.

"Aiden, it's... where did you find something like this?"

"I made it." The tips of his cheeks flushed. "Do you like it?"

"You *made* this?" My eyes widened. I breathed a little harder. It was remarkable that he could craft something so astonishing. "I love it! When did you make something like this?"

"A while back," he said, cheeks reddening further. "After you gave me the pick, actually. I wasn't sure I'd ever... get to give it to you. I mean, I just started making it one day and the more it took shape, I thought of you. I was just going to leave it in your dorm, but then everything happened..." He trailed off, looking contrite. "I'm just going to stop talking now."

I stared at him wordlessly.

"Are you sure you like it?"

Climbing to my knees, I threw my arms around his neck. I clenched the rose in my hand as I kissed his cheek. "I love it, Aiden. It's perfect. Beautiful."

He laughed softly, gently untangling my choke-hold. "Here, let me help you put it on."

I popped around obediently and held up my hair. Aiden clasped the chain behind my neck, letting the crystal rose settle above my chest. The weight of it felt wonderful. I reached up, running my fingers over the delicate edges. Then I sprang around and tackled Aiden.

Laughing, he caught me before we both tumbled off the bed. "I guess you do like it."

I pushed him down and kissed him. "I love it. I love you."

Aiden reached up, tucking my hair back as his molten stare pierced me to my core. "I know what you're thinking."

"Great minds think alike."

"Later," he growled.

I started to protest, but he rolled me to my feet. "Boo."

He gave me a cheeky grin. "You have to come downstairs."

"I do?"

"Yes. So don't argue with me."

"Fine. Only because you're wonderful and this necklace is beautiful." I paused, nudging him with my hip. "And because you're sexy."

Aiden ushered me out of the room after that. Before I reached the stairs, I tucked the necklace under my shirt. People may know or suspect something, but I wasn't about to broadcast it, even though I wanted to shove the necklace in everyone's face and make them coo over it.

I followed Aiden into the kitchen. My steps slowed as I saw *everyone* gathered around the table. "What's going...?"

Deacon and Luke stepped to the side. "Happy Birthday!" they cried in unison.

My gaze fell to the table. There sat a birthday cake, decorated with eighteen burning candles and... *Spider-man?* Yep, it was Spider-man. Red and blue tights and all.

"It was either that or My Little Pony," Luke said, grinning. "We figured you'd appreciate Spider-man more."

"Plus he's all wicked cool with the whole climbing buildings stuff," Deacon added. "Maybe one day, when you decide to Awaken, you'll be just as cool."

"I lit the candles," Solos said, shrugging. "All by myself."

"I gave them the money." Marcus folded his arms. "Therefore I was the key part of all of this."

"And we got grape soda." Luke gestured at the bottles of soda. "It's your favorite."

"This… this is… wow." My eyes found Lea, sitting behind Solos. Her hair was pulled back from her face, eyes still swollen. She caught my eyes and smiled just a little. "This is great. You guys are awesome. Really."

Deacon grinned. "You've got to blow out the candles and make a wish."

What to wish for? I smiled. That was easy. As I crept to the table, I blew out the candles and wished that all of us made it out of this alive, including Seth.

"I want the spider web!" Deacon yelled as I stepped back, producing a supersized knife.

"Yikes." I stepped back into Aiden.

"It's her birthday," Luke took the knife from him. "She gets to pick what piece she wants first."

I laughed. "It's okay. He can have the spider web. I'll take the head."

We set about carving the cake and passing around grape soda. I was overwhelmed by everyone. I hadn't expected much of anything on my birthday except weird looks, but this was amazing. It was easy to forget about everything and what today symbolized. Here, surrounded by friends, things were sort of… normal.

Normal for a bunch of halfs and pures celebrating a birthday.

Okay. It wasn't normal at all, but it was just my kind of abnormal.

Huddled around the table, we laughed as we shared cake and grape soda. Lea perked up a little, nibbling on the frosting. The boys continued to give me crap about not Awakening yet, which Aiden tried to put a stop to. It was cute watching him try not to be overly defensive or protective of me. Not like I needed him to, though I think it was just second nature to him. He was the same with Deacon… when Deacon wasn't wielding a six-inch knife.

Toward the end of the birthday celebration, there was a distinctive *pop!* from the rec room. We all twisted around. I prayed the rune worked on the house, because there was definitely a god here.

Apollo strolled into the kitchen. The first thing I noticed was that his eyes were blue and not that creepy white. "How is my birthday girl?"

For some reason, I blushed to the roots of my hair. "Doing good, grandpa."

He smirked as he slid into the seat beside me, easily prying the knife from Deacon's fingers. "I do not look nearly old enough to be what I am to you."

That was true. He looked like he was in his mid-twenties, which made it all the freakier. "So when were you going to tell me that you spawned me?"

"I did not spawn you. I spawned a demigod centuries ago who eventually spawned your mother."

"Can you guys stop saying 'spawn'?" asked Luke.

Apollo shrugged as he carved off an edge of the cake. He handed the knife back to an oddly subdued Deacon. "I did not find it necessary to tell you. It is not like I am going to be bouncing little Alex babies on my knee."

The soda caught in my throat, and I almost spit it back up. Someone chuckled, and it sounded like Luke. "Yeah, that's not going to happen."

"My sister should have kept that to herself." He took a bite of the cake, made a face, and then pushed his plate away. "Our familial tie is not what is important here."

I frowned.

"You know what, guys?" Solos clapped his hands on Deacon and Luke's shoulders. "I bet I can take you both at air hockey and make you call me mama."

Luke snorted. "Not likely."

Deity

Solos dragged the boys from the room, but Lea sat back in the chair and folded her arms. Her eyes dared anyone to tell her to leave. Now that was the Lea I was familiar with.

"Do you remember when you went to Marcus after Grandma Piperi passed on?" Apollo reached for the bottle of soda.

"Yes." I handed him a cup, wondering where he was going with this. "Kind of hard to forget that day."

"Humph." He sniffed the top of the bottle, shrugged and then poured himself a small amount. "Well, then you should also realize that there is another oracle."

I glanced at Marcus. He arched a brow as he leaned against the counter. "What does this oracle have to do with this?" he asked.

I thought of Kari. "But didn't she pass on, too?" After a few strange looks, I explained. "I met her in the Underworld. She said she knew what was going to happen."

Apollo nodded. "She had a few visions before her... departure. Probably had something to do with your own untimely visit to the Underworld. See, the thing about oracles is that they... own their visions. What they see is not seen by others and I can only see what the oracle tells me." He lifted the plastic cup, took a tentative sip, and immediately made a face. Guess grape soda wasn't his thing.

"It is part of how it all works—why we need an oracle at all, instead of me just knowing the future," he continued, looking up at me. "Did she say anything to you while you were there?"

I shook my head. "Just that she knew she would meet me and... and that she knew how it ended. And knowing how it ends doesn't really tell me what to do."

Apollo grimaced. "Figures the dead oracle would know. And Hades is not about to let me go down and talk to her now, not after the thing with my sister. Prophecies are always changing. Nothing is set in stone."

"Artemis said that." Aiden sat beside Lea. "Has the prophecy changed?"

"Not exactly."

My patience was running thin. "So what's going on, Apollo? Artemis said there was still hope and she mentioned something about the prophecy. Can you just, I don't know, get to the point?"

"The new oracle has not had any visions, so the last is tied to the dead one. So all we have to work off of is what we know." His lips quirked into a half-smile. "Some of us believe that you will be able to stop Seth. The prophecy—"

"I know what the prophecy says—one to save and one to destroy. I get that, but what I don't get is why any of you would risk Seth going all Godzilla on you guys. Eliminating me does eliminate the problem." I ignored Aiden's dangerous look as I stood. "There's something more to this. You know something else."

"And you know the prophecy says there can only be one of you. There is no way around that." Apollo leaned back, letting his arms drop over the back of his chair. "Do you really think all of this was Lucian's idea? That he knew about you without anyone telling him? That he has gained as much support as he has based on his charm alone?"

I started pacing. "I wouldn't give Lucian that much credit."

"Good. Because he has had help, I am sure of it," Apollo said. "Which means stopping Seth from becoming the God Killer does not fix the overall problem. The god behind this will just find another way to push Olympus to the brink of all-out war, and if that happens, it will spill into the mortal realm. What you saw Poseidon do? That will be nothing in comparison to what can happen."

"That's just great." I was going to wear a path in the kitchen floor at the rate I was going. "Do you have an idea of who this god is?"

"There are many of us who like to cause discord and chaos for the fun of it."

"Hermes," Marcus said. All eyes turned to him. He raised his brows expectantly. "Hermes is known for creating mayhem and mischief— chaos." No one said anything. Marcus shook his head. "Didn't any of you pay attention in your Greek Legends class?"

"Getting Lucian to turn on the Council and the gods isn't mischief," Aiden said. "And why would Hermes want to do that? Isn't he putting himself at risk from Seth?"

"Not if Hermes controls Lucian." I stopped. A sick feeling crawled down my spine. "Lucian controls Seth… completely. He'd be safe."

"Hermes has always been Zeus' personal joke and punching bag." Apollo stood and moved around the table. At the bay window, he grew pensive. "And as of late, Hermes has been… missing. I was unaware of this, because I was here so much. You see, we all come and go, never staying away from Olympus for too long."

Marcus tensed. "Do you think it's possible that Hermes has been around us?"

He looked over his shoulder at us. Strands of blond hair fell forward, shielding half his face. "Like I said before, if the other god made sure we did not cross paths, it is possible. Keep in mind, it may not be Hermes. It could be any of us. Whoever it is will need to be stopped."

I stared at him, wondering how Apollo expected any of us to stop a god. Only Seth would be able to and he wasn't playing for our team right now.

"How can she stop him?" Lea asked, her voice hoarse. "How can she stop Seth? Isn't that the point of all of this?"

Apollo gave her a little smile. "That is the point. Alexandria would have to kill him once she Awakens."

CHAPTER 34

I COULDN'T HAVE HEARD HIM RIGHT. THERE WAS NO way. "What?"

Apollo turned back to the window. "You would have to kill him, Alexandria. As an Apollyon, you will be able to."

The idea of killing Seth horrified and sickened me. There was no way I could do that. I ran my hand over my face, feeling nauseous. "I can't do that."

"You can't?" Lea stared, her eyes glistening in the light. "He killed my sister, Alex! He killed those Council members."

"I know, but it's… it's not his fault. Lucian has warped his mind." And he'd hesitated before he took out the Council. I'd seen that. For a moment, the Seth I knew didn't want to do it, but afterward… he'd looked thrilled. "It wasn't his fault."

And it sounded like I was trying to convince myself.

Lea's lips thinned. "That doesn't make what he did okay."

"I know that, but…" But I couldn't kill Seth. I sat in the chair heavily, staring at the remains of Spider-man. "There has to be another way."

"I know a part of you cares for him," Apollo said quietly. "You were… built to feel that way. A part of him is you and vice versa, but it is the only way."

I met his eyes for a long second, and then Apollo looked away. A shadow passed over his face. A strange, almost-bad taste sprang up in the back of my mouth. "Is there another way, Apollo?"

"Does it matter?" Lea slammed her hands down on the table, causing me to jump. "He needs to die, Alex."

I flinched.

"Lea," Marcus said gently.

"No! I'm not going to shut up about this!" She shot to her feet, coming alive. "I know it doesn't seem fair, Alex. But Seth killed those people—*my sister*. And that wasn't fair."

My throat closed up. Lea had a point. There was no arguing that, but she hadn't seen what I'd seen... and she didn't know Seth. Then again, maybe I didn't even know him.

"And it sucks," Lea continued. Her hands balled into fists that shook. "I even thought Seth was hot, but that was up until he *incinerated* my sister. You like him. That's great. You're a part of him. Awesome. But he killed people, Alex."

"I understand that, Lea." I looked around the room, my gaze settling on Aiden. "Everyone keeps saying there's hope. Maybe we can save him. And Artemis mentioned something about power going both ways. Maybe there is something to that."

Pain flickered in his silver eyes, and then I remembered his words and my own realization. *Sometimes you have to know when to let hope go.*

She sucked in a sharp breath as she clearly struggled to rein her anger and sorrow back in. "You loved your mom, right? You loved her even after she became a daimon."

"Lea," Aiden cut in sharply.

"But you knew she needed to... needed to be stopped," she rushed on before Aiden could shut her up. "You loved her, but you did the right thing. How is this any different?"

I recoiled from the table. Her words were like a punch in the stomach, because they were true. How was this any different? I had done the right thing with my mom, so why was it so hard for me to understand why this needed to be done now?

"I think that's enough for today," Marcus interjected.

Lea stood her ground for a few more seconds, but then stormed out of the room. Part of me wanted to go after her and try to explain myself, but I had enough common sense to know that wouldn't be wise.

"She's in a dark place right now," Marcus said. "She hurts. Maybe later she'll understand that this is hard for you, also."

"It's not as hard as it is for her." I tucked my hair back. "I just can't… the idea of killing him makes me sick. There has to be another way."

Apollo glided toward me. "All of this… can wait. Today is your birthday, your Awakening."

"Yeah, well, I don't know what's going on with that." I stared at the runes on my palms. They glowed faintly. Nothing had changed about them. "I feel the same. Nothing's happened."

"When were you born?" Apollo asked.

"Uh, March the fourth."

He arched a brow. "What time, Alexandria? What was the time of your birth?"

I pursed my lips. "I don't know."

A dubious look crossed Apollo's face. "You don't know what time you were born?"

"No. Do people know that?"

"I was born at 6:15am," Aiden said, trying to hide his grin. "Deacon was born at 12:55pm. Our parents told us."

My eyes narrowed. "Well, no one told me… or I forgot."

"Marcus?" Apollo asked.

He shook his head. "I don't… recall."

"Well, you obviously have not hit your time of birth yet." Apollo pushed away from the window. "I think we have had enough serious talk for the day. It is, after all, your birthday. A time for celebration, not making plans for battle."

I shuddered.

"You will be fine." Apollo placed his hand on my shoulder and squeezed. That was the closest offer of comfort I'd probably ever get from Apollo, and that was fine with me. "You do not feel the bond from where we are, so he cannot connect with you. You will be fine."

I kept watching the clock. When had I been born? I had no clue. It was almost 8:30 in the evening, and not a damn thing had happened. Maybe I was doing something wrong?

"Stop it." Aiden grabbed my hand, pulling it away from my mouth. "Since when did you become a nail-biter?"

I shrugged. We were sitting on the couch in the small sunroom. Outside the window, it looked like a winter wonderland. Night had already fallen and moonlight reflected off the untouched snow that covered the deck and trees.

"Do you think I'm weak?" I asked.

"What?" He tugged me over so that I was in his lap. "Good gods, you're one of the strongest people I know."

I glanced at the closed door, but then figured *oh, what the hell*. Allowing myself to relax, I rested my cheek against his chest and pulled the rose out from under my shirt. "I don't feel very strong."

Aiden settled his arms around me. "Because of what everyone was talking about today?"

I traced my fingers over the edges of the rose. "Lea had a point, you know? I faced down my mom, but I can't… do that with Seth."

"Apollo was right." He placed his chin atop my head. "He's a part of you. In a way, it's different than what happened with your mom."

"It is different. My mom was a daimon and there was no coming back from that." I sighed, closing my eyes. I saw Seth's face as I begged him, the indecision in his eyes. "He's still in there, Aiden. There has to be another way. And I think Apollo knows, but he's not telling us."

"Then we'll talk to Apollo. He mentioned the oracle, and maybe something has changed." He shifted slightly, and then I felt his lips against my forehead. "But if there isn't another way…"

"Then I have to face it. I know. I just want to make sure before we decide he needs to be… killed."

Aiden placed one of his hands over mine. "Maybe we need to go see this new oracle. Who knows? She may be able to tell us something, visions or not."

"That is if we can get Apollo to tell us about her."

"We will."

I smiled up at Aiden. "You're amazing."

He grinned. "What makes you say that?"

"You're easily the most sup—*ow!*" I hissed as I jerked my hand free from his. "Something stung me."

He straightened a bit and grabbed my wrist. "Alex, you're bleeding."

Tiny pricks of blood covered the top of my left hand, but that wasn't what I was staring at. There was a blue glyph taking shape, forming something that looked like a music note.

My pulse pounded as I sat up quickly, scanning the room. A clock shaped like an owl showed that the time was 8:47pm. "It's happening."

Aiden said something, but another burst of hot, fiery pain stung just below that mark, and blood beaded on my skin. I pulled free from Aiden, my legs shaking as I stood. "Oh my gods…"

"Alex…" He came to his feet, eyes wide. "What can I do?"

"I don't know. I didn't—" I gasped as pain shot across my arm. Right in front of my eyes, more blood appeared. Just tiny drops, as if I was under a tattoo needle… "Oh gods, the marks—the marks are like tattoos." This hadn't happened with the other marks—the ones Seth had brought out early.

"*Gods.*" Aiden reached for me, but I backed away. He swallowed as my eyes met his. "Alex, it's going to be okay."

My heart was racing, double-quick. Pure terror flooded my stomach. The marks would be *everywhere* once complete, and it was coming so, so fast. Pain spread up my neck, dampening my skin. When it reached my face, I screamed and hit the floor. On my knees, I doubled over, my hands curling in the air around my cheeks.

"Oh… oh man, this is gonna blow." I struggled for air.

Aiden was beside me immediately, his hands reaching for me but not coming into contact. "Just… take a deep breath, Alex. Breathe with me."

My laugh came out strangled. "I'm… I'm not having a baby, Aiden. This is—" Sharp bites of pain swept down my back, and I screamed again. I placed my hands on the floor, trying to draw in a deep breath. "Okay… okay, I'm breathing."

"Good. You're doing really good." Aiden inched closer. "You know that, *agapi mou*. You're doing great."

As my back bowed, it didn't feel that way. I'd rather face down a hundred aether-starved daimons plus a legion of Instructors than this. Tears leaked from my eyes as the marking continued lower. My legs gave out, and with Aiden's help, I lay down on my stomach.

The door opened, and I heard Marcus. "What the—oh, my gods, is she okay?"

My face hurt too badly to stay like this, but the skin on my back felt raw. "Shit…"

"She's Awakening," Aiden said, voice tight.

"But the blood…" I heard Marcus move closer. "Why is she bleeding?"

I eased onto my side. "I'm being tattooed by a giant, mother fu—" Another strangled scream cut off my words as a different type of pain settled in, moving under my skin. It was like lightning racing through my veins, frying every nerve ending.

"This is… wow," Deacon said, and I pried my eyes open. There was a whole audience by the door.

"Get them out of here!" I screamed, jackknifing on the floor. "Gods, this sucks!"

"Whoa," I heard Deacon murmur. "This is like watching a chick give birth or something."

"Oh my gods, I'm going to kill him." I could feel the beads of blood breaking out under my jeans. "I'm going to punch him—"

"Everyone leave," Aiden ground out. "This isn't a godsdamn show."

"And I think he's like the father," Luke said.

Aiden rose to his feet. "Get. Out."

A few seconds later, the door closed. I thought we were alone until I heard Marcus speak. "She's my niece. I'm staying." I heard him come closer. "Is it… is it supposed to be like this?"

"I don't know." Aiden's voice sounded strained, near panicked. "Alex?"

"Okay," I breathed. "Just… just don't talk. No one—" It moved up my front, searing my skin. I jerked up, hands shaking.

Holy crap. I couldn't breathe. Pain was everything. I was going to kill Seth. Not once had he told me that the Awakening would feel like *this*—like the skin was being filleted from my bones.

My body buckled as another wave of pain rippled through me. I didn't remember hitting the floor or Aiden pulling me into his lap, but when I opened my eyes, he was there, above me. Skin somewhere, where I wasn't sure anymore, caught fire. Another mark was being tattooed. I couldn't hold the cry back, but when it leaked from my lips, it was nothing more than a whimper.

"It's okay. I'm here." Aiden smoothed the hair off my damp forehead. "It's almost over."

"It is?" I gasped as I stared up at him, squeezing his hand until I felt his bones rub. "How in the fuck do you know? Have you ever Awakened before? Is there something—" My own hoarse, weak scream interrupted my tirade. "Oh gods, I'm… I'm so sorry. I didn't mean to cuss at you. It just…"

"I know. It hurts." Aiden's gaze drifted over me. "It can't be much longer."

I squeezed my eyes shut as I curled toward Aiden. His soothing gestures helped ease some of the pain. I stiffened as blinding light flashed behind my eyes. A rushing filled my ears, and I could suddenly see the blue cord so strongly in my mind.

It was like a switch had been thrown.

Information rushed me all at once. Thousands of years of the Apollyon memories dumped into me just like Seth had warned they would. Like a digital download, I couldn't keep up with it. Most of it didn't make any sense. The words were in a different language—the one Aiden spoke so beautifully. The knowledge of how the Apollyon was born passed onto me, as did the nature of the elements and of the fifth and final one. Images flickered in and out—battles won and long since lost. I saw—I felt—akasha shooting through someone's veins for the first time, igniting and destroying. Saving—saving all those lives. And the gods—I saw them through the eyes of the past Apollyons. There was a relationship there, strained and full of mutual distrust, but there was… and then I saw her. I knew it was Solaris, felt it in my core.

I saw her turning on a beautiful boy, raising her hands as she whispered words—powerful words. Akasha flared from her, and I knew in an instant that she had turned on the First. Not to kill him, because there was infinite love in her eyes, but to subdue him, to stop him. I grasped at the information, but it moved on through the years until the First… *the First*.

The cord was snapping, rushing out through space and distance, seeking, always seeking. I couldn't stop it, didn't know how to. An amber-colored glow covered everything. In a burst of swirling lights, a hazy face came into focus. The natural arch of his golden eyebrows, the wicked tilt to his lips and slant of his cheekbones were all painfully familiar. I couldn't tell where he was. He shouldn't have been there. We were too far apart.

But at the end of the cord, I saw Seth and I wept.

I knew in an instant that the distance between us had meant nothing when it came to our bond. It may have diminished our ability to feel each other, but it couldn't prevent this. Not with the four marks, not when he had pulled on my own power. And I also knew Seth *had* planned this… just in case I fled.

A pulse of light went through my cord and I felt it—*felt him*—breaking through my shields, filling me, becoming a part of me. It took just a second—*a second* and I was surrounded by him. I *was* him. There was no me in here, there was no room. It was all about him, always had been.

I couldn't breathe anymore. He was there, under my skin, his heart beating next to mine. His thoughts were mixing with my own until all I could hear was him.

He opened his eyes. A light that had never been there before glowed from behind them.

Seth smiled.

Light crackled and flashed, and the world fell away.

I was shaking—*no*. I was being shaken. The pain receded slowly, leaving behind a raw stinging that covered every inch of my body. That, too, faded as my body was rocked back and forth. There were voices droning in the background, overshadowing the soothing words being whispered.

I inhaled deeply, breathing for what felt like the first time. There was so much in the air around me. The heavy scent of pine tainted the edges. I tasted spice and sea salt on the tip of my tongue.

"*Agapi mou*, open your eyes and talk to me."

My eyes fluttered open. Everything… everything looked different—sharper and magnified. Lights dazzled, and colors shimmered in amber. I focused on the man cradling me. Eyes the color of heated silver stared down at me. They widened, pupils dilating. Shock shot across his striking features.

"No." That one word sounded like it had been torn from the depths of Aiden's soul.

A popping sound filled the room. Footsteps encroached upon us. Shapes came into focus, one burning brighter than the other.

Apollo peered over Aiden's shoulder and swore. "Let her go, Aiden."

His arms tightened around me instead, holding me close to his chest. *To the end,* I thought… foolishly brave and loyal *to the end…*

"Let her go now." A door slammed shut somewhere behind the shining god. "She's connected with the First."

The First—my whole purpose for existing. Mine. My other half. He was here, waiting. Already inside me, seeing what I was seeing, whispering to me, promising me that he was coming. *Seth.* Mine.

And they all were going to die.

I smiled.

Dying sucks—and high school senior Ember McWilliams knows first-hand. After a fatal car accident, her gifted little sister brought her back. Now anything Ember touches dies. And that, well, really blows.

Ember operates on a no-touch policy with all living things—including boys. When Hayden Cromwell shows up, quoting Oscar Wilde and claiming her curse is a gift, she thinks he's a crazed cutie. But when he tells her he can help control it, she's more than interested. There's just one catch: Ember has to trust Hayden's adopted father, a man she's sure has sinister reasons for collecting children whose abilities even weird her out. However, she's willing to do anything to hold her sister's hand again. And hell, she'd also like to be able to kiss Hayden. Who wouldn't?

But when Ember learns the accident that turned her into a freak may not've been an accident at all, she's not sure who to trust. Someone wanted her dead, and the closer she gets to the truth, the closer she is to losing not only her heart, but her life.

For real this time.

Cursed

Jennifer L. Armentrout

Author of Half-Blood

978-0-9831572-7-4

MINDER

A GANZFIELD NOVEL BY

KATE KAYNAK

Just because
Ella can burn
someone to the
ground with her
mind doesn't
mean she
should…

But she wants to.

elemental

EMILY WHITE

978-1-937053-04-8

BETRAYED

A GUARDIAN LEGACY BOOK

Being one of
the Nephilim
isn't as easy
as it sounds.

EDNAH WALTERS

Life has been hell for seventeen-year-old Emma since she moved from sunny California to a remote Alaskan town. Rejected by her father and living with the guilt of causing her mother's death, she makes a desperate dash for freedom from her abusive stepfather. But when her car skids off the icy road, her escape only leads to further captivity in a world beyond her imagining.

Angela J. Townsend

Amarok

January 2013

Having poison running
through your veins and
a kiss that kills really
puts a dent in high school.

Kelly
Hashway

Touch of Death

PODs

A Novel

The end
of the world
is only the
beginning.

Michelle
Pickett

Coming in June 2013

A cruise ship.
A beautiful island.
Two sexy guys.

What could possibly go wrong?

In the Bermuda Triangle—a lot.

Triangles

Kimberly Ann Miller

Coming in June 2013

ACKNOWLEDGEMENTS

Short and sweet—Thank you to Kate Kaynak and the wonderful team at Spencer Hill Press: Marie Romero, Patricia Riley, Rich Storrs, and Rebecca Mancini. Another big thank you to Kevan Lyon, for being an awesome agent. Each time I write these, it gets harder and harder to make sure I'm getting everyone. So a big thank you to everyone who has supported the series and has wanted to take part in Alex's journey, and who has kept me sane during the process.

Photo by Vania Stoyanova

Jennifer L. Armentrout lives in West Virginia. All the rumors you've heard about her state aren't true. Well, mostly. When she's not hard at work writing, she spends her time reading, working out, watching zombie movies, and pretending to write. She shares her home with her husband, his K-9 partner named Diesel, and her hyper Jack Russell Loki. Her dreams of becoming an author started in algebra class, where she spent her time writing short stories... therefore explaining her dismal grades in math. Jennifer writes Adult and Young Adult Urban Fantasy and Romance.

Come find out more at: **www.jenniferarmentrout.com**